Feathertide

Beth Cartwright has taught English in Greece and travelled around South East Asia and South America, where she worked at an animal sanctuary. A love of language and the imaginary led her to study English Literature and Linguistics, and she now lives on the edge of the Peak District with her family and two cats.

Feathertide is her debut novel.

Feathertide

BETH CARTWRIGHT

First published by Del Rey in 2020

1 3 5 7 9 10 8 6 4 2

Del Rey
20 Vauxhall Bridge Road,
London SW1V 2SA

Del Rey is part of the Penguin Random House group of companies whose
addresses can be found at global.penguinrandomhouse.com.

Penguin
Random House
UK

www.penguin.co.uk

A CIP catalogue record for this book is available from the British Library.

Hardback ISBN 9781529100662
Trade Paperback ISBN 9781529100679

Typeset in 12/16.5 pt Dante MT Pro
by Integra Software Services Pvt. Ltd, Pondicherry

Printed and bound in Great Britain by Clays Ltd, Elcograf S.p.A.

Penguin Random House is committed to a sustainable future for
our business, our readers and our planet. This book is made
from Forest Stewardship Council® certified paper..

MIX
Paper from
responsible sources
FSC® C018179

For Grandma and Granddad, who never got the chance
to turn the pages of this book,
and
for Joe, my love for you has no full stop.

PROLOGUE

A midday sky at a midnight hour.
It was the Night of the Great Winter Star: crackling bonfires and chortling mirth, warmth in the cold and light in the dark. Jewelled colours somersaulted through the sky, momentarily mapping out new constellations in the darkness. The swish of a rocket and the swirl of a wheel. Frost shimmered on the rooftops and left long, glistening trails along the pavements. The world stood – watchful, whisperful, wonderful – counting down the minutes to the end of something frayed and worn at the edges, and to the start of something woven with promise and hope. The old unravelling into the new, when another year was safely tucked up into the warm folds of memory.

A luminous star-filled sky; wish-ready.

It was the night I was born.

That morning, a heavily pregnant Lemàn had been out buying fresh mackerel from the old weather-worn fisherman at the port. They greeted each other with a customary nod and a half-smile and nothing more; he knew what she needed. She waited as he quickly worked his glittering nets between his hands, untangling the fish and separating them from the clinging crustaceans, a bucket for each. Despite his swollen fingers and knotted knuckles, he still caught more fish than anyone else half his age. Experience had taught him well. A faded salt-stained cap tamed his buoyant grey curls and a clay pipe balanced at the side of his mouth as he rattled through his treasures, tossing the broken pieces back into the sea and whistling the old songs of long forgotten sailors.

It was the second batch Lemàn had sought that morning; the first devoured before she'd even arrived at her doorstep, and with a deep rumble in her belly she had headed straight back down the hill to the port, seeking to satisfy what she already knew to be an insatiable hunger.

Lemàn's craving for fish, morning, noon and night had grown stronger during the last eight months, and now it was all she could swallow without feeling empty and hollow inside. After about the sixth month, when her belly was as ripe as a summer fruit, her cravings grew so desperate that she no longer bothered to boil the fish into a soup or take the time to sprinkle them with herbs carefully chosen from the market. Instead she bit right into

2

their scales, tearing their skin apart with her teeth, picking at the splinters of tiny bones left behind in her mouth, her lips sleek and oil-smeared.

Although she had the face of a doll, there was nothing dainty about her. Her limbs were long and sinewy and her hands were made for strangling; it was therefore with great ease that she was able to sling another sack of mackerel over her shoulder, as though it was filled with nothing but feathers. About to climb back up the hill, she suddenly felt a strange twinge deep in her belly. Dismissing it as just another hunger pang, she quickly dropped the sack to the ground, where she unknotted the top and reached inside to scoop out a fish. At that moment, a sharp, stabbing sensation felled her like a woodman's axe. This time, the pain was lower than her belly, and unlike anything she had ever felt before. Of course, she knew she was carrying a child, but she'd not kept any dates. She just watched her stomach grow and evolve like the phases of the moon, a crescent slowly made whole, until its milky fullness was ready to spill. Then it was just a matter of time.

'She'll come when she's ready,' she'd tell anyone who asked. She knew I was going to be a girl, because she'd seen me in a dream. I was playing with washed-up shells on a long stretch of empty beach, collecting broken pieces of green glass, like pretend emeralds, the colour of the sea. The tide was still a long way out and the sand was dry golden powder like the remains of a city which had long ago turned to dust. Circling above me was a bird, solitary and blue and beautiful, but its shadow grew larger and larger and the world grew darker. Then with a rush of air it swooped, but she was too far away to pull me to safety. It was always at that moment that she woke up with a pounding heart.

Now I was ready.

Wincing in pain, Lemàn fell against the crumbling wall of the inn. Hunched and panting, she steadied herself until the pain suddenly subsided like a break in a thunderstorm and she straightened. Abandoning the fish on the ground like coins, she staggered back up the hill. The fisherman kicked the mackerels into the gutter for the beggar cats who roamed the streets, silent as floating feathers, and put the empty sack back in his boat. He didn't like to see anything go to waste. A swooping gull squawked in annoyance; the cats had got there first.

Finally, she fell through the doorway and crawled up the stairs, demented by pain as she collapsed on her bed.

'She's coming – she's here – it's happening!' Her cries were so loud that they shook the walls.

A clatter of heels and a jangle of jewels quickly followed, and a cluster of beautifully adorned women gathered around her bed as she fell sweating and panting against her pillow. One of them held a damp cloth to her forehead as she writhed on the sheets.

'Push!' they chorused like a joyful choir, holding hands prayer-like, lips pursed in wonder as they exchanged

excited glances and nervous giggles, their eyelashes fluttering like a release of summer butterflies.

Lemàn needed little encouragement and pushed and
pushed, but I was stubborn and refused to move. She was
strong and had the patience of a desert cactus. Only when
night came and the room was lit by the flicker of candles
did I begin to stir. My head appeared before the first stroke
of midnight, but my feet were slow to follow and it wasn't
until the sound of the chimes had died away that I had fully
emerged. It was impossible to say which day I had been
born but it is said that babies born on the Night of the
Great Winter Star suffer from a melancholy disposition and
will be forever followed by sadness. Nobody wanted that.

Slippery as a fish, I was quickly swallowed up in a huge
pile of blankets and placed on Lemàn's heaving chest. Like
a boat, bobbing rhythmically on the ocean, moored by an
unbreakable bond, I lay and blinked in my new world,
and eyes blinked back, as though I was a miracle. They
warbled and bubbled like a happy coop sprinkled with the
morning grain.

'What a good head of hair!' exclaimed one of the
women, her own, a whirl of candyfloss. 'It grows all the
way down her neck.'

'Such a beautiful orange colour, like a sunset,' marvelled
another.

'A flame to light a midnight room.'

'What's that?' one asked suddenly, clasping her hand to
her chest. The whores peered closer.

'Goodness, it looks like a tiny cluster of feathers.'

'Is it some kind of birthmark?'

Suddenly, a door slammed somewhere in the depths of the house and the sound echoed all the way up the stairs and along the corridor; the room hushed. The patter of the whores' excited footsteps had aroused suspicion from below.

Moments later the door flung open and everyone quickly parted as a woman glided swiftly through. Her cheekbones sliced through her skin, hard and sharp like the glinting blade of a knife. Her hair, pinched tight at her temples, whitening her skin, was swept high in a complicated conundrum of pins on the top of her head where it sat like a hive. Sorren, the mistress of the house, had arrived, and nobody dared to speak and nobody dared to breathe, as all eyes fell quickly to the floor. She fixed her stalactite stare on me, and Lemàn clutched me tighter against her chest.

The room wilted; her words carried the power to destroy us all.

She stepped closer. 'Our visitors must not know there is a child in this house, they would not like it, and neither would the authorities. Do not be careless,' she admonished.

'She could be taken from us ... or worse!' exclaimed one of the women.

The other whores tutted at the thought and furiously shook their heads. They were my guardians, each one promising to love and protect me as fiercely as though I was their own.

'Your worry should be for the business, not for the child,' she snarled. The whip of her words stung, and the woman who had spoken out realised too late her mistake and stifled a sob before shuffling back into the shadows.

Then her eyes, full of scorn, flashed from me to Lemàn and she took another step closer, bringing with her the waft of funeral lilies. Her eyes narrowed as they suddenly fell upon the tiny feather cluster growing from my shoulder. Her mouth twitched and for a brief moment she had let it reveal something, but what? Confusion, alarm, fear, regret and the brief flash of something else – recognition. Stiffening her shoulders, she stood with rigid authority while addressing the room. 'Our visitors do not like to think of us nurturing anyone's needs but their own. You must keep her well hidden, and quiet; there is room in the cellar. Do not let this become a distraction.' Her eyes fell back to Lemàn, holding me in her arms. 'Do you understand?'

Lemàn bowed her head and so too did the other women; like roses in a windswept garden, they nodded rhythmically in deference to the queen bee.

Then she turned and swished from the room. As her footsteps faded, the women let out a collective sigh of relief, and just like that their wish was granted – I could stay.

'What a quiet baby,' pondered one of the women suddenly, her face crumpled in confusion. 'Aren't babies supposed to cry when they're born? Do you think there's something's wrong with her?' Their previous amazement suddenly turned to growing alarm, and their smiles tipped to frowns.

But there was nothing wrong with me at all. What reason did I have to cry? I was staring at the most sparkling, adoring eyes, like a gallery of stars taken down from the sky, just for my delight and amusement. I couldn't have been more content. I captivated a whole room. Slowly the women drifted away, until it was just me and Lemàn left, and there, through a half-opened hatch in the roof, I caught my first glimpse of the outside world. A sky filled with explosive fire; a world of dazzling colour and magical light that danced over the town. A world of wishes, half whispered, half-understood, and rockets that reached for the moon.

For years loss had slowly rinsed her of all colour, but that night her cheeks had the rose-pink glow of a summer evening. Her hair – more silver than grey, lit by the luminous sky – fell softly against the pillow; the colour of wishes in a fountain. Tenderly, Lemàn stroked my head and nuzzled her face against mine. 'You're my little firecracker,' she said into the blaze of my hair, and with dancing fingertips she began to explore every inch of me. Suddenly she gasped in astonishment. Nothing could have prepared her for what she saw then. There weren't just a few little feathers on my shoulder; the skin behind my neck was covered in them, so small and pale that nobody else had seen them. Unfolding the layers of swaddling, she discovered they grew in wisps down the length of my back, so delicate and fine they were like the top of a dandelion. She laughed then, as though she should have expected them all along. Smiling in wonder, she ran the tips of her fingers up and down my spine. It tickled. Soft down covered the whole of my body in a golden light, fuzzy as a little peach. 'You remind me so much of him,' she whispered into my ear, before sinking back against the pillows, overcome by a feeling of completeness and fatigue.

Gathered above us, around the edge of the hatch, were several birds, their heads tilted in curiosity as they watched me lying there in Lemàn's arms. When she spotted them, a storm fell over her face and for the second time that night, she held me a little bit closer. 'I will not lose you to the sky,' she whispered, and with her last burst of energy she reached for the pole and hooked the end round the clasp, giving it a sharp, sudden pull. The window clattered shut, and, with a dark spread of wings, the birds flew away, vanishing into the night. I turned and grumbled in her arms. Then a single glossy feather floated through the air; it brushed against my cheek like a goodnight kiss, and fell onto the bed unnoticed.

She murmured my name then: Maréa, after the tide … never imagining that one day I would float away.

CHAPTER 1

The whorehouse was a crooked, crumbling monster of a thing. It stretched five-storeys to the sky, with a peaked roof the colour of shrivelled oranges. At the front, four well-worn steps led to the wide, panelled door that welcomed our many visitors. Breathless from the steep climb up the lane, they would pull on a long chain, and the clang of a bell would announce their arrival. Its cry was much louder than the chimes of the church in the town, tinkling like tiny goat bells across the fields. Muted by distance, I would listen for the faint call to worship; an invitation we were too far away to receive. Perhaps the sound of a bell offered comfort to some or served as a timely reminder to others that there were more holy pursuits. Round at the back, the door opened onto a yard where the firewood was kept in uneven stacks, and a square patch of long grass. Beyond it, a tangle of brambles and untamed thickets grew all the way to the lane, and then there was nothing but an endless stretch of green.

From a distance, the house looked like a fat candle which had been lit too many times, ready to collapse in on itself; its chimney an ever-burning wick. The windows were kept dark, like suspicious eyes squinting at the town below. It was perched so high on a hilltop that, on some days, particularly in the autumn months, its roof would completely disappear into dancing mist. Sometimes, it was so clogged with cloud that we would have to bring a chimney sweep from the town to clean the flue. Even then, its chimney pots were already dusted with snow; a prophecy of the winter to come.

It was a place of many windows and doors and draughty high-ceilinged corridors. In the summer, it was a sticky, boiling broth of oppressive heat. Swarms of flies buzzed through the cracks in the walls to plague the kitchen – windows had to be fastened shut because of the festering sewage, and the air was so humid that sweat would roll down our bodies and create pools where we stood.

Winters were always worse. We had to wrap ourselves in sheepskin rugs and stuff our walls with cow dung to try and prevent frostbite. One year, several winters ago, one of the older whores lost all of her toes and all but one of her fingers to the cold. We were careful after that.

Washing was impossible to dry. For days our sopping sheets hung like giant sails from hooks in the ceiling. As a baby, I would sit beneath them, splashing in a metal tub whilst Lemàn scrubbed my legs with carbolic soap and sang me songs I would always remember. Her voice was gentle, but her arms were strong. I loved the way her hair spilled over them and she'd let the ends dangle into the water and spread around me like a gossamer web spun on water. Her blue eyes deepened then. As time stretched away, taking her further from my father, she let her hair grow into a tangle, which was too much for any comb to conquer; it became as abandoned as the hope she'd once held. Often, I imagined I was in a boat sailing far away, but Lemàn never liked this game. She feared losing me, and the storm in her eyes made me drop anchor before we both capsized.

A set of stone steps took you beneath the kitchen to a place of secrecy. It was here, amongst the root vegetables and the swollen sacks of potatoes, that I was hidden like a precious jewel, a sparkle in the dark. Despite the damp wafting from the cool stone, it was warmed by the kitchen above. On the walls hung pictures of dancing princesses, little bears, glittering waterfalls and enchanted forests, an endless myriad of magical tales. Each one given to me by a different whore, painted on paper with powder, rouge, kohl and lipstick pulled from their many fragrant draw-string bags. My favourite thing of all was my bed. It was like a giant, wooden sleigh carved from a special tree that could grant wishes. Its sides were patterned with swirls of butterflies and knots of roses and a silken pink canopy fell in waves around the cushioned headboard. The bed had four golden wheels, and Lemàn told me that once upon a time it had belonged to Sleeping Beauty. For such a long time I believed that all of it was true, but the midnight hour was never far away and that's when the magic disappears.

Even though I loved my fairy-tale kingdom, it came with a set of golden rules. First of all, I wasn't allowed to leave my room alone, and secondly, I was never to go outside. But the first rule was impossible to follow and it was a rule I broke, and often. I did try to be obedient, but boredom and curiosity pulled me from the cellar like a powerful drawing ointment.

The stairs up from the cellar led into the kitchen and through there into the main corridor. At one end stood the front door, ominous and wide, and at the other end was the door to Sorren's counting house, which was the most menacing door of them all. Every fairy tale has a Carabosse and she was mine. Skulking against the walls, I would dart in and out of the shadows. They were my only playthings and I had fun chasing them; ever-careful not to let the giggles escape my mouth for fear that Sorren would fling open her door and find me there.

One corridor wound into another, taking me past forbidden doorways, forever closed, and I imagined that behind each one were banished creatures from the tales

Lemàn told me. When I could no longer hear the clanging of pans or the rattling of spoons, I would turn and hurry back to the familiar percussion of the kitchen; it was the place I loved most of all. It was never empty, someone was always in there, baking or washing or stitching, but whenever the whores saw me, they would try to shoo me back to the cellar with the bristles of the large sweeping brush they kept propped up in the corner.

Sometimes, when I was feeling especially brave, I would climb the staircases to the third and fourth floors where the visitors disappeared for hours behind closed doors. Kneeling down, I peered through keyholes, just large enough to reveal the shapes and movements within, mere shadows, but nothing more. I had learned where the stairs creaked and the doors groaned and I trod barefoot – sound-less – to avoid discovery. I listened to the walls chatter or perhaps it was the visitors behind them, sharing their stories. I tried to convince myself that I wasn't really breaking the rules, just bending them a little bit out of shape, but I knew if I was found, there would be trouble, especially if Sorren found out – well, I shuddered at the thought of what she would do to me and Lemàn. The monster wasn't hiding under my bed; it was waiting behind the closed door at the end of the corridor.

Most of the time, the whores were in their rooms with their visitors, but occasionally, Sorren would announce there was to be a party, leading to a flurry of excitement. Barrels of rum would be rolled up the hill or delivered on the back of a cart. The whores would wear their finest attire of lace and silk and fix their smiles of delight, stretching out their arms to welcome the visitors who arrived in their dozens.

On these nights the bedrooms would be abandoned and their doors flung wide open. Instead they would entertain their audience in the dimly lit salon of the second floor. Sound was muffled by the thick ancient walls of the whore-house, but, if I listened carefully, I could still hear the laughter drifting down the stairs and the voices buzzing from the pollenated garden above. Like an inquisitive rabbit, I tiptoed round the warren, with Sorren – the vicious, sly fox, ever-watchful – waiting to pounce and claim her prey. But no matter the risk, I could never resist temptation.

CHAPTER 2

In the cellar there was a little oblong-shaped window high up along the wall, and it was all I knew of the world. The light that tiptoed in was meagre and timid, and I was forbidden from opening it. It overlooked the gutter and the street beyond to the square patch of grass, where a pear tree grew, small and solitary. An emerald flourish of summer followed by an empty leafless winter; it became my marker of passing time.

Occasionally feet would hurry past in a blur, but, more often than not, I would sit for hours and watch the birds outside, fascinated by the fluff and puff of their bodies. I loved how they danced and hopped and played in the puddles after the spill of rain. If I listened without breathing, I could hear them ruffling their feathers with the flamboyancy of tiny stage performers, always aware of my gaze, yet surprisingly unmoved by it. I'd try and copy them until I grew dizzy and breathless, then I would quietly slide my chair under the window and stand on my tiptoes, until I was almost able to reach them. If I flattened my nose against the glass and tilted my head at a certain angle, I could see even further. I could see the birds sitting in the pear tree, decorating the lower branches – a giant leafy throne, transformed majestic gold by the deft stroke of autumn. Once again, forgetting Lemàn's rules, I would reach up and push the window open where I'd leave little scraps of food I'd salvaged from the kitchen. I envied their freedom, how easily they could just lift themselves from the ground and move on: rootless, untethered and wild. Sometimes, they seemed hesitant; waiting for me to follow as though, somehow, they knew I too had feathers hidden beneath my clothes. But, unable to join them, I sadly let the window click quietly closed.

Instead I drew them. Lemàn brought me a roll of paper and a tin of beautifully coloured pencils. Working quickly, but carefully, I soon had hundreds of sketches, so many that they had begun to replace the fairy-tale characters that had covered my wall. Where once there had been princesses and bears, now there were birds and feathers, and the green trees had been buried beneath an endless blue sky. It wasn't long before all the fairy tales had vanished, lying forgotten in a world I had left behind. My hidden kingdom had grown much too small, and I was becoming more and more curious about the world and my place in it. I knew there was real magic out there somewhere, and I longed to find it.

Some of my new sketches were of birds alone in the sky; others were of them huddled together in the pear tree. When I felt most lonely, I would draw myself sitting with them under the branches of the same tree. I once brought them into my room by drawing them all around me as I slept. In those pictures, I gave myself long flowing hair; another forbidden wish. Instead, my hair was shorn to my scalp, a protective measure against the visitors' desire. Should I be seen, they would hopefully dismiss me as nothing more than a curious boy. But in my pictures, my hair was always a burning sun, streaming across my pillow in great long, golden ribbons. I drew the birds snared in the strands, no longer able to fly away. Once I had run out of wall, I spread them across the floor like stepping stones, and hopped between them, laughing. Sometimes I fell asleep amongst them and dreamed of flying far away. Where would I go if I had wings to take me? I imagined myself soaring and gliding and swooping through the sky, barely skimming the earth before I would let the whoosh of air lift me once again. But I always woke up. Restless and frustrated, I would leave the cellar then in search of a sense of freedom, no matter how small.

Always, I was drawn to the small door at the end of the corridor. Past where all the jars of jam and the pots of honey were kept, to where Sorren spent her hours. The door stayed mostly shut, and, whether it was locked or not, I did not know, because I was never brave enough to turn the handle. Once, though, the door had been left ajar and a dim light was seeping out. Edging closer, I could see Sorren standing alone in the shadows. Wisps of her hair had loosened from their pins and fell softly against her neck. In that moment, she looked captivating, but I knew what was hidden beneath: a beautiful cake made of curdled milk. Pressed against her face, I thought she held a handkerchief, but when she lowered her hands, I could see she had in them a pretty cream petticoat, three pearlescent buttons sewn down the front, its edges finished with lace; it was small enough to fit a doll. Tenderly, she laid the petticoat on the desk and began to smooth out the creases with her fingertips. I could hear the quiet hum of a lullaby. Mesmerised by the image, I hadn't realised that I had been leaning too heavily against the door, slowly pushing it open inch by inch until it was too late, and I was quite visible in the widening gap. Gasping, I stepped back and the creak of a floorboard gave me away.

The spell was broken and, without looking up, Sorren quickly thrust the petticoat into the top drawer of the desk like a guilty secret, and slammed it shut. The objects on the desk rattled. Then she snapped up her head and, with the clench of her jaw, all trace of softness vanished. She glared, and her solemn eyes, swollen with sorrow, hardened against me; she had the look of a condemned woman. In a sudden explosion of rage, she flew across the room, hurtling towards me. I cowered and held my arm high above my head to shield me against the blow I was certain to feel, but instead the door slammed shut in my face and everything fell silent. Filled with relief, I turned and ran towards the warm smell of baking bread in the kitchen and the safety of my room below. I knew then that there were some secrets much bigger than me being kept in this house.

As I grew, so too did my feathers. They were now longer than the hair on my head, beautiful and silky and I loved them. Lemàn told me they were so special that no one outside the house was allowed to know I had them; otherwise they would want to steal me away. That made me flush with happiness, and back then I believed every word she said.

The feathers grew thickest down my back and plumes exploded from the knots of my shoulder blades like pauldrons and fluttered their way to the base of my spine where they became thinner and shorter. Tufts sprouted from my shoulders and spread across the tops of my arms almost to my elbows. Everywhere else, my skin was covered in a soft tawny sheen, like golden thistledown, light enough to be blown away in the breeze. It was only noticeable in certain light and sometimes even I would forget it was there. The whores marvelled at my feathers, and every time they saw me their eyes would widen in astonishment as though they were seeing them for the very first time.

My favourite whore was Marianne. She used to be a plumassier in La Ville Lumiere, preparing feathers for hats and bags and scarves. She would stroke and smooth my feathers, crumpled from restless sleep. I loved it when she lifted them in her accomplished hands and stretched them out, magically weaving and shaping them into something sleek and luminous. I would watch as she curled them under the steam of a boiling pot and cry in delight as they sprang joyfully from my fingers. She spoke in elongated vowels, telling me how my feathers would make women feel beautiful. How they would wear them in their hats or sew them into the front of their dresses in a cascade of colour. In those moments I felt truly special, and I dreamed that maybe one day I would be able to do what she did. Every so often, Lemàn would take a cloth soaked in vinegar and wipe it up and down the length of my quills. Yet another protective measure, this time against the cellar dust that dulled their shine.

The whores took it in turns to feed me, bathe me, play with me and love me as though I were their own. They brought their fairy-tale pictures to life by giving me gifts: a pair of glass slippers from the ball, the pea that kept a princess awake, a golden lock of hair, a pumpkin seed which could grow into a carriage, gingerbread and lollipops taken from a witch's house, a thorn from a rose which had the power to put me to sleep for one hundred years, and, painted in silver nail polish, a wand made from kindling for the fire. Twirling it, I went in search of mice that I could turn into horses to pull my carriage to the ball.

Marianne made me a bird marionette from her leftover feathers. It was shaped out of wood with long knitted legs and a head that wobbled. I loved it instantly. Dangling on four strings from a wooden cross, I took it everywhere with me like a much beloved pet.

Sorren gave me nothing but scornful glances from darkened doorways. Her lily scent clawed at the back of my throat and made my heart beat too fast. It meant she was somewhere close by, which made me want to hide. Upon finding me out of my room, she would never chastise me with her words, but her glare was that of a snow queen, and, by the time she had sent for Lemàn, I was already back in my room as though I had never been anywhere else.

All of them took pleasure from dressing me in silks and fine lace, painting my nails and attaching sparkling sequins to my feathers. They clipped large jewels onto my ears, thickened my eyelashes with mascara and dabbed perfume on my neck. My pout made pink and shiny. They held up mirrors for my eyes to admire my own reflection. My feathers and I were celebrated until the moment a visitor knocked on the door or worse; Sorren's footsteps came echoing down the corridor, each thud like a nail being hammered into my coffin. Then they frantically stripped me bare and scrubbed the make-up off my face until I was bright red and raw, before smuggling me away in the washing. I was a precious secret, after all, and one they had promised to keep since the day I'd been born.

Most of the time I fell asleep curled in the soft, warm bundles, but sometimes I would be quietly sobbing when Lemàn finally came to dig me out again. Carrying me down to the cellar, I would ask why I was a secret and had to be hidden away, but every time her answer was the same: it is because you are too beautiful to be shared with the world. On those nights, she shushed me into bed and spent a little longer tucking me in, telling me stories, her mouth full of memories and tales, part-truth, part-fiction. They were supposed to offer comfort, but her words came from a thorny place, of brambles and stinging nettles. It was as though she had dipped the tip of her tongue in a salt pot and then licked the wounds of my innocence.

She spoke of poisoned apples and talking mirrors; of wolves that gobbled grandmothers; of a woman with a head of hissing serpents; of giants and trolls and goblins hidden under bridges. Of rats so riddled with disease, they could destroy entire towns in less than a day. But the most terrifying tale of all was about a woman alone in a forest, who stole away children to stop herself feeling so lonely. Every year, children disappeared, snatched away without trace from their beds; shutters and bolts didn't keep them safe. The men of the village would take it in turns to patrol the streets at night, and giant, salivating dogs were kept on long chains to howl at the sign of any intruders, but the only howl came at dawn when another mother discovered the empty bed of her child. Not knowing what else to do, the villagers hunted the forest with their knives and guns, their lanterns lighting the dark, but the deeper they went, the thicker the trees grew and tangles of thorns ripped at their skin, making the cold heart of the forest impenetrable. They would return defeated and weary, collapsing into the arms of their weeping wives, their clothes soaked in blood, their wounds never healing and their eyes haunted by the guilt of surrender. No one knew how the woman came to be there, or for how long. She was hidden, just like you, she would say, making me promise to stay out of the forest and other dark places.

These stories stole away my sleep and I would tremble for hours in the dark burrow of my blankets. Lemàn would come and hush me into the warm folds of her skin until I fell asleep in tear-drenched dreams. One such night, I noticed the small tattoo of a bird, pulsing on her wrist. Curious, I asked her about it, and she just smiled sadly and turned her wrist over so I could no longer see it. Kissing me goodnight, she told me everything flies away eventually. She knew these stories weren't enough, but at least in these moments it was just the two of us, and I loved to feel the warm weight of her arm against my own and the comfort of her fingertips lost deep in my feathers, as though she was searching for something. The bird on her wrist connected us in a way I didn't yet understand. Somehow it gave her comfort too.

When I asked her where my feathers had come from, she laughed and told me they were a gift, but from whom, she wouldn't say. Whenever I asked her, she would become much too busy with something to give me an answer: a bubbling pot to stir, a sink to unclog, or an exaggerated yawn feigning sleepiness hours before the light had even begun to slip from the sky.

CHAPTER 3

On my seventh birthday, Lemàn came to my room holding a glass jar. It was so large that when she handed it to me, I had to take it from her with both hands. At first, I thought it was the jar I had found in her room, when, once again, boredom had drawn me out of my hiding place.

It had lain deep in a drawer, hidden under a pile of clothes, but, as it had rolled towards me with a heavy clunk, I'd gasped out loud in astonishment. Inside the jar, a strange silvery mist had swirled, glittering like starlight. It may have had a label a long time ago, for there was a sticky residue left behind on the glass, but it had long since peeled away, and whatever was inside had remained a mystery. I'd tried to unscrew the lid, but it was stuck tight and the effort had left me breathless. Admitting defeat, I'd put the jar back where I'd found it and crept from the room.

But this jar was different. It was clear, and at the bottom sat six pale shells, whorls of wonder. I stared at them through the glass.

'Every year on your birthday, you will choose something else to go inside this jar,' Lemàn said. 'When the jar is full you will have a decision to make.' She looked away quickly, pulling at an invisible thread of her dress, her eyes unable to meet my own. I saw something in them that I didn't understand then. Now I know it was fear.

'But where will I choose them from?' I asked. There was nothing in this house I wanted to hold onto, but her.

'Put these on,' she said, handing me a pair of boots and a long black cloak. 'I will show you.' The boots were heavy and ugly and far too big, but I didn't complain because moments later, unable to believe what was happening, I was leaving the whorehouse for the very first time.

Lemàn smuggled me out of the back door, hidden under the folds of her shawls. Where they thinned, I glimpsed black, sombre trees; the char of winter and the fields piled high with snow. It was as though someone had sprinkled a giant spoonful of sugar over everything and left it there to melt – waiting for the summer to pour out its warm brew. The ground underneath our feet was a slippery crackle and I clung to Lemàn's thick woollen stockings to keep myself from sliding to the ground. The squeak of her boots in the snow was loud in my ears.

The hill sloped steeply and I was grateful when it finally levelled out and we had reached the bottom. It was here on the edge of the town, hidden behind a woodpile, that she unveiled me like a magic act. Hooded and cloaked, and only after any stray feathers were adjusted and meticulously tucked away, did we walk into the marketplace, not side by side, but never more than a few footfalls apart. *Arm's reach,* she would hiss at me. It was a difficult task to keep me close, but not close enough to raise suspicion. If someone saw Lemàn with a child tugging on her arm, then questions would surely be asked. The whorehouse was no place for a child, beautiful or not. But if we were to stay too far apart then I could be lost or stolen. Hidden deep under my cloak I felt safe. The hood was tied so tightly underneath my chin that I could feel it cutting into my skin, but I could not let it slip from my head for fear of discovery.

My eyes opened wide at the sight of the babbling crowd; I had never seen so many people all at once. It was more exciting than the first time I had tasted caramel. More vivid, more wonderful, more everything. I had only ever seen a snapshot of the world before, through the oblong shape of my window: hurrying feet blurred by rain; a clogged gutter; a patch of grass; and, of course, my beloved pear tree. Now it felt as though the window had widened and opened up into a whole new world, instead of one of halves. Suddenly, it felt overwhelming, as though I had stuffed too much caramel into my mouth, too much to swallow all at once. I grew dizzy watching the groups of children dart between the stalls, playing a breathless game of chase, jousting each other with icicles they'd snapped off doorways. I was fascinated by two girls who were hopping up and down on squares of chalked numbers cleared of snow. The bobbles on the tops of their hats danced merrily as they played their game. Boys with their icicle swords came swerving towards us in a rush of excitement and Lemàn quickly ushered me away into an area crammed with stalls of fruit and vegetables, flowers and herbs.

The marketplace had a row of little huts, which looked as if they had been made out of gingerbread. A girl suddenly shot out of the crowds towards me and for one terrifying moment I feared she was the lonely woman from Lemàn's story. I breathed a sigh of relief as she ran straight past me and into the open arms of a smiling man. 'Papa! Papa!' she cried happily, snuggling her face into the warmth of his coat. He picked her up and spun her round and their laughter filled the marketplace. She would never be lonely as long as she had her papa, I thought. Putting her back on her feet he knelt down and pulled something from his pocket. It was a fabric doll with tumbling golden hair like curls of breakfast butter, but instead of legs it had a tail made of sequins, which dazzled against the snow. The little girl's eyes widened, and her mouth fell open in a gasp of delight as she squeezed it to her chest as if it was the most precious thing she had ever been given. Standing there, watching them, I felt a stab of envy in my quills, and I wished I had someone to welcome me like that; someone to spin me high into the snowflakes; someone to give me such a beautiful thing as a doll with a tail. It was the first time I really wanted a papa of my own, and that was the beginning of everything.

A lady was labelling chunks of cheese on wooden boards and another wobbled on a stool with a clutter of saucepans at her feet. We walked further into the square, crammed with traders and shoppers. An old man was sitting in front of what looked like a black bubbling cauldron, ladling something into tin cups without handles. Lemàn took one from his frosty fingers and I glimpsed shapes floating in the hot dark as she lifted it to her lips. I shuddered in horror and turned away, convinced he was serving dark magic potions filled with floating frogs' legs and bats' wings.

Lemàn walked and drank, holding the cup tightly, finding comfort in its warmth. She stopped to rummage through a pile of flannels and, remembering not to stay too close, I shuffled along to the next stall. Something made me stop; a smell I couldn't quite place. I scanned the stall, my eyes finding nothing but a jumble of hand-carved wooden toys and piles of linen.

'Lemàn, Lemàn,' I hissed, tugging at her coat, forgetting we were meant to stand apart.

'What?' She didn't hide the irritation in her voice, as she dropped her change into a knotted purse. Then she kicked at my feet to remind me to keep my distance.

I stepped away. 'What is that smell?'

She sniffed the air like a hunting dog. 'It's just cinnamon, now arm's reach remember.'

But it wasn't cinnamon I could smell; it was something else. I knew the woody sweet smell of cinnamon; Lemàn sprinkled it over the cooking pears whenever she baked. This smell wasn't sweet at all; it was all salt and brine and reminded me of supper.

I kicked at a little pile of fallen snow and trudged after Lemàn, who was scooping chestnuts into a brown paper bag, which she dropped at my feet as she moved on. I knelt to pick it up and felt inside; each one like a hot coal warming the ends of my fingers. I lifted one out, cracked half open from the heat and dug my thumb into the shell until I felt the release of soft sweet flesh. Digging a little more, I broke it open and crunched it in my mouth before throwing the shell to the ground. I had become distracted and deep in thought, and for one terrifying moment I couldn't see Lemàn anywhere. Then my eyes found her up ahead, dawdling at the last stall giving me the chance to catch up.

'Arm's reach. Arm's reach,' I repeated to myself, as I rushed towards her. I was trying my best. Just then something else caught my eye and my feathers prickled as I turned to look at a glittering silver display. I wrinkled my nose; the salty smell was so much stronger now. Lemàn was watching me out of the corner of her eye and saw me approach the stall of silver.

At first, I thought they were trays of shiny coins piled high, one on top of the other, but I soon realised they weren't coins at all; they were scales, hundreds and hundreds of tiny scales, all smooth and wet and glistening. The only scales I knew belonged to the dragons in Lemàn's stories, and I thought perhaps one had been hunted and its pelt brought here for sale. Then I noticed the eyes with their protruding blank stares and I gawped in horror and fascination. As I reached out my hand, I heard Lemàn's voice so close I could feel the warmth of her breath, and I stepped away.

'They're just fish,' she replied impatiently, 'brought here from the sea.'

To me, fish came in soft white chunks next to my potatoes at supper time. I hadn't seen fish with scales and eyes before.

'Can you take me to the sea?' I asked.

She shook her head, frustrated that I was not remembering to stay within arms' reach, but then something inside her seemed to soften and collapse like an undercooked cake. She looked down at me with a heavy sigh, and there was pity in her eyes.

'Ah, very well ... follow me.'

Quickly, she led me away from the huddle of huts down a wide sweeping path where there was no longer any trace of snow. We followed a long crumbling wall and with every step the salt smell grew stronger and stronger until it tingled on my tongue. I felt my feathers fluff in anticipation of what was waiting for me, and I had to pull my hood tighter still for fear they might unfurl like ferns from within.

Over the wall I could see the bustle of boats, all lined up like restless, tethered creatures waiting to be set free. I breathed in a lungful of the fresh tangy air, grateful to be able to rinse my body of the fetid stench of the whore-house. A gull screeched overhead and instinctively I ducked for fear it would swoop down and carry me off in its talons. Lemàn laughed, and came to a sudden stop.

'Here it is,' she said, closing her eyes and inhaling deeply. For a moment, she stood still, peaceful, lost in her own thoughts.

But when I looked out, I gasped and flew under Lemàn's skirt for fear we had reached the very end of the world – one more step and we'd fall right off.

'What is it?' I whispered.

She didn't answer straight away and seemed to have forgotten I was there. I tugged sharply on the hem of her skirt to remind her.

'It's the sea, of course. It's where all those fish came from.'

For so long, I had heard the whores and their visitors speak of the outside world and all of its wonders, but nothing could have prepared me for what I saw as I lifted the hem over my head and tentatively peered out. There were merchants down below, passing crates and boxes, loading and unloading boats with a clattering haste, and I could hear the splash of an anchor. Beyond them a grey-blue stillness gleamed far into the distance, much further than I had ever imagined possible. At first, I thought it was the deflated wrinkled bag of a giant balloon spread out before me, but as I peered closer, I watched in wonder as the wind conducted the waves. Being outside felt like a miracle.

In the distance, I saw a blemish on the horizon, slowly spreading like a bruise across the water. I realised it was an approaching boat with three large blue striped sails flapping triumphantly in a breeze of its own making. Even from so far away, it was much larger than any of the other boats that had already come to rest in the harbour; it must have been carrying a heavy load. As it neared, I saw its sides were painted in a swirl of large golden letters boxed in green. Lemàn hadn't noticed the dark shape on the water, but when I tugged on her tights to ask her what the letters said, she gasped, stepped back and we both nearly tumbled into the slush.

'Quick! Move!' she hissed, pulling me to my feet and dragging me back up the hill. She seemed to have forgotten her own rule about arm's reach, and it wasn't until we were safely home, with the door shut firmly behind us, that she finally let me go.

That night I rubbed at my arm where she had held me too tight, and wondered what had made her flee up the hill so fast that I could still hear her heart pounding hours later as she kissed me goodnight.

I thought the biggest danger was the lonely woman hiding in the forest, not something from the sea. It wasn't until years later that I learned what that boat carried, and then everything changed.

CHAPTER 4

After my first taste of freedom, Lemàn announced that it was too great a risk to go outside. It felt like I had been given a gift that I couldn't keep. I sulked and stamped my feet in sullen silence, refusing to give in, until finally a compromise was reached: I would be allowed to leave, but only once a year on my birthday. Still, I was disappointed – it wasn't enough – and so Lemàn decided that if she couldn't take me out into the world, then she would have to bring the world inside to me

A few weeks later, I met Professor Elms. He arrived carrying a small leather satchel. I remember thinking that the world must be a very small place if it could fit inside there, and be tucked so neatly under his arm. He was a peculiar-looking man, small and hunched at the shoulders, yet sprightly in his step. He wore a waistcoat embroidered with stars and his trousers were neatly pressed, yet he still managed to look crumpled. His face was a map of age, but his eyes glittered knowingly behind thick-lensed spectacles. It was the face of a kind man.

I watched him with growing curiosity as he methodically unpacked his bag, piling book after book upon the table. I had never seen so many books all at once, each one like a temple of worship and wonder. It was a city constructed of words and knowledge, and it reminded me that a whole world existed beyond the window.

'Lemàn says there are some cities where the fog is so thick it's just like pea soup. Is that where you're from?' I asked.

My question made him pause for a moment, then he shook his head with a light chuckle. 'I'm from a place much further away than that.'

'Much further?' I asked astonished.

'I come from a place without clocks ... it is a timeless place.'

'So how do people know what time it is there?'

He widened his eyes and told me that it wasn't just clocks that told the time and that time can be measured in lots of different ways: from the curve of the moon or the length of a shadow, the warmth of a teapot, the colour of a tomato, the bristles of a beard or from the soles of a pair of shoes. There, time was measured in every way, apart from by the ticking hands of a clock.

'These are really good,' he said, admiring my drawings, which covered the walls.

My eyes flickered over to the pictures and I nodded. 'I love birds,' I said. Then, feeling unusually bold, I added, 'It's because I am one.'

The professor smiled. 'Yes, Lemàn told me all about your feathers.'

'She did?' I was astonished. She never shared my secret with a stranger.

As though he could read my mind, he spoke again. 'I have known her for many years and she has healed my heart. In return I can keep a secret, especially yours.'

I relaxed. His eyes were shining, polished with kindness. 'She said they make me beautiful. Do you think feathers make a person beautiful?'

'I think they are a wonderful thing to have; don't you?'

I sighed. 'I suppose so, it's just … '

'Just what?' The professor watched me with a frown and waited.

'Lemàn says they are the reason I have to stay hidden down here. That if people see them then they will want to take me away and that makes me feel a bit … a bit sad, I suppose. Do you have any feathers?'

He laughed. 'Ah, no … nothing as interesting as that, I'm afraid. I'm just ordinary – skin and hair. In fact, I've never met anyone with feathers until you. You are special, and when you find something as unique as you are, why then you must treasure it.' The professor stopped and peered at me over his glasses. 'What are you doing up there?'

When he had arrived, I'd been standing on a chair pulled right up to the window. 'Just watching the birds,' I replied with a sigh, and I could hear the longing in my own voice. 'It's not fair that they get to fly away, yet I'm stuck down here all the time. Do you know anything about birds?'

'There might be a section on them in here somewhere,' he said, picking up a book and flicking between its pages.

'No,' I said, jumping down and landing with a soft thud on my scattered drawings. 'Tell me something *you* know about them, not something you can read from a book.'

The professor placed the book back on the table and thoughtfully rested his hand on the closed cover.

'Once I travelled deep into the heart of a forest filled with warm, luminous rain and there I found the smallest bird in the world. It was much smaller than my thumb.' He held it up in front of my face for inspection. 'About half the size!'

I peered closer and then held up my own for comparison.

'It can fly up or down, forwards or backwards and even in somersaults through the air. Its wings beat up to fifty times per second.'

I felt my eyes widen at the thought of it.

'And did you know that the heart of a bird beats much faster than ours?'

I wasn't sure what my heart was – bird or human or something in between. The knowledge startled me, and I felt a small shiver of panic. Did that mean I would live my life twice as fast? I tried to push the fear away, like a dessert plate after a feast.

Slowly, he filled my head with images of birds made from elaborate drawings and intricate diagrams. I brought even more of my own birds to life with my pencils, and this time they were more sophisticated, each one copied and carefully labelled from a textbook. I stuck them over the other drawings, which now looked ridiculous for being so primitive and childlike. The fairy tales were growing ever distant: a palimpsest of my childhood.

Professor Elms placed his hand over mine and the pencil dropped from my fingers, rolled across the table and fell to the floor. 'Do you know the best place to learn about birds?'

I thought for a moment. 'From books?'

Professor Elms shook his head. 'No. Try again.'

I shrugged.

He leaned forwards in his chair, then in barely more than a whisper he spoke. 'To really learn about birds, you need to go outside.' But we both knew that going outside was absolutely forbidden unless it was my birthday.

Professor Elms' words stirred up my curiosity. Over the months, I learned that his satchel didn't carry the world, only fleeting glimpses of it. The more he filled my mind with ideas and knowledge, the more of an insomniac I became; even lavender milk wasn't enough to quieten my mind. There was too much to think about, too much to imagine and explore. One night, unable to sleep, I lay awake thinking about the professor's words: *To really learn about birds, you need to go outside*, and each one felt like a bolt slowly loosening and sliding across a door. Finally, after many hours, sleep came in tumbling waves.

The next day, I woke early, so early the rest of the house was still sleeping. I reached for my cloak and crept from the cellar up the stairs and into the kitchen. I didn't dare use the front door, but the back door led to the lane away from the town, to the fields and the woods. The door was old and heavy and bolted twice, once at the top and again at the bottom. The key waited in the hole, ready for turning. It was only my obedience up until this moment that had kept the door locked. Nervously, I slid open the first one and then, balancing on a stool, I carefully slid back the top one and quietly jumped down. Holding my breath, I twisted the handle and the door creaked open. I paused and waited and listened, but the house slumbered on, and so I stepped outside and into the world. I had forgotten I would need shoes, but as soon as I felt the tickle of the grass between my toes, I couldn't resist and I knew I wouldn't go back for them. I propped the door open with a stone and dared myself to just go as far as the gate. I crept through the garden and once I'd reached the gate, I dared myself to go a little bit further – this time just to the bend in the lane; I would be able to see everything from there. It wasn't until I reached the bend that I saw the sky stretching away in the distance, all lit up in a smouldering orange molten glow. Fearing the world was on fire I fled back up the lane and would have woken the whole house with my screaming, if a hand hadn't suddenly clapped over my mouth to keep me quiet. At first, I struggled, then relaxed at the sound of a voice I recognised.

'Shhh,' said Professor Elms, as he slowly removed his hand, and pushed me back through the door.

'What are you doing here?' I gasped.

'I'm always out walking early. I like listening to the dawn chorus, it's when I get most of my thinking done.'

I was so relieved it wasn't Sorren, but I knew my small act of rebellion wouldn't go unpunished. 'Please don't tell!' I begged. It was one thing to creep from the cellar and wander the corridors, but actually going outside was no longer just bending the rules. It was snapping them in half and crushing them into tiny unfixable pieces.

Professor Elms shook his head, and patted me a little awkwardly on the shoulder. 'I feel responsible,' he said solemnly. I realised he looked even more worried than I did. 'After all,' he continued, 'it was me that put the notion of going outside into your head in the first place.'

'I won't do it again,' I promised, but as soon as the words left my lips, I tasted the lie.

Professor Elms remained silent for a few moments and I thought perhaps he was going to change his mind and tell Lemàn everything. 'Do you remember what I told you the first time we met?'

I paused. 'That you come from a place without clocks?'

Professor Elms laughed. 'Yes – I did tell you that, but what else?'

He always made me think. 'That the best place to learn about birds was by going outside.'

He waved away my answer. It wasn't the one he wanted. 'You're right, I did tell you both of those things, but I told you something else, something much more important.' He lowered his voice. 'Remember that I told you I can keep a secret.' His eyes glittered with mischief. 'So, let's make this a secret worth keeping.'

A few days later I was woken by a gentle tapping at my window, and to my surprise I found Professor Elms was outside, crouching on all fours. He told me to dress quickly, bring my cloak and meet him at the kitchen door. I smiled nervously as we both pressed our fingers to our lips. Sssh. I kept mine there to stifle the giggles I could feel rising in my chest. If they escaped, I wouldn't.

'We are going on a little outing to see the birds,' he said. 'They always wake up before the rest of the world.'

Five minutes later, Professor Elms was leading me out of the whorehouse, past all the apple barrels and the upturned wheelbarrow and the piles of wood to the lane that sloped away from the town. It was only once we had gone around the hedgerow that I dared to breathe again. As long as we went early and stayed in the back lanes, there was no one to see us, only the occasional rattle of a passing cart or a herd of slow-moving cows with their sad blinking eyes. A farmer would mistake us for father and daughter out for a walk, and I wanted a father so much that I liked to pretend it was true. Being seen with a whore from the whorehouse was another thing entirely and couldn't be explained away so easily. Whores were not meant to be mothers, and, if they were, then they certainly weren't expected to keep their children with them.

I cherished those early mornings when the birds were the only ones awake and their happy chatter brought the woods to life. I thought the sound came from the trees themselves, or maybe from the stolen children in Lemàn's stories, but the rustle in the leaves and the sudden flaring of wings revealed the true source, and I could breathe again.

I loved it most of all when the inquisitive rain rummaged through the ground, unearthing the damp smell of leaves. It filled the lane and the woods and clung to my skin all the way home. I could still smell it long after I had closed the door behind me. Sometimes, I mistook fallen leaves flattened in the lane for giant paw prints, and, rushing nearer, I was always disappointed to see it was just a footprint left by autumn. Later, under snow-filled skies, I would gather up fallen pine cones and keep them in a box under my bed. Whenever I sensed a change in the air I would reach inside and lift one out to examine its scales, and, like my feathers, they were always closed against the rain, long before it arrived.

During that first outing to see the birds, I found a fallen egg; it was a dull speckled thing but to me it was remarkable. I slipped it gently in my pocket and made a nest for it in a box of socks. Each night I made a wish in my bed that the egg would hatch and I'd dream that there was a bird flying around my room. In the morning the egg looked exactly the same, not a single crack had appeared. I tried to push away my disappointment; instead I thought what a shame it would be for something so perfect to break apart. In the end I picked it up and hid it under the bed in the box of pine cones.

After one particularly long hot walk we flopped down in a meadow under a tree, and I let the leaves sieve the sunlight onto my skin. Sitting cross-legged, blowing the floss off the top of a dandelion stalk, I noticed the birds glide silently between the trees, resting then taking flight then resting again. Lying back, I watched them lift themselves off the branches with an easy, gentle flap of their wings. A sudden feeling of enormous longing swelled inside me and I stood up. I could taste the fantasy of flight. Hastily brushing the grass from my cloak, I went to the nearest tree and felt around its trunk, but I was disappointed not to find a foothold; its nearest branches too high to reach. Pleased to see that Professor Elms had fallen asleep in the shade, with his hat covering his face, I wandered further into the wood. A little way in, I untied my cloak and let it drop to the ground. If I had feathers like a bird, then surely I could fly like one too? I had wondered about that often, but whenever I had asked Lemàn, she'd just laughed or changed the subject; I don't think she really knew the answer, and perhaps she thought that finding it would be too dangerous.

Finally, I found a tree I could climb, and began to pull myself up into its twisted tangle of branches, higher and higher until I could see the whorehouse perched on the hill in the distance. I steadied myself on the widest branch and tentatively stepped out a little bit further, feeling the shape of it underneath the curve of my feet. In the distance, there was a scattering of farmhouses, and then just the endless blue of sky and sea. Like a beautiful painting, nothing moved, and time stopped ticking. I knew that if you followed the lane back up towards the whorehouse, and continued a little further along, it would suddenly widen and drop down the other side towards the cacophonous chaos of the marketplace, and beyond it to the vast sweeping sea.

I wasn't sure what to do, being so high in a tree. Birds didn't just jump out of trees; they spread their wings and flew. I might have had feathers, but I didn't exactly have wings, just two feathery stumps sprouting from my shoulder blades. Still determined, I stretched out my arms and lifted them up and down until I found my balance and my rhythm. They might not carry me far, but surely, they would be enough to carry me somewhere. My feathers tingled, as though they were warning me of the danger, but I couldn't stop. I had to know if I had flight within me.

Professor Elms woke at the very moment I dared to step off the branch. I saw his eyes widen in alarm, but it was too late; my feet had already left the branch. No amount of furious flapping kept me in the sky for long, and I felt myself plummet to the ground. Professor Elms rushed towards me in open-mouthed terror, holding out his arms to try and catch me, but the force of my landing sent us both to the ground. Miraculously, I was unhurt. Not everything with feathers can fly, he warned, and we never mentioned it again.

Another secret kept.

CHAPTER 5

Inklings of winter crept closer on silent feet. First came the unmistakable crisp bite of autumn, when I would wake to find my window sparkled with frost. It left behind its strange handprints on the glass. Its icy breath decorated my window with its swirling patterns and coded messages, but I knew what they meant: my thirteenth birthday was coming. A special day brought to me soon after the first snowflake, when the world outside was half hidden under a ghostly lilac light.

This year I knew with absolute certainty what I wanted to buy; a piece of my own coral. Professor Elms had told me it was a self-healer, able to regenerate from the smallest fragment of itself. A miracle. Lemàn decorated the house with bowls of it, like other people might keep bowls of fruit or pots of flowers or fancy ornaments. She believed it could purify the house, but I doubted there was enough coral in the whole of the world's oceans to cleanse us of our visitors.

I chose my coral carefully, feeling the power of the sea. An ocean bloom eternalised. Walking along the bustling sea wall, away from the hollers and bellows of the herring-sellers and cockle merchants, we didn't stop until we reached the last bench. Here the only cries flew from the beaks of the hungry gulls circling above us, waiting for the return of the trawlers. My eyes never grew tired of watching the sparkling expanse of blue. I would wait for the boats to appear as though out of nowhere, like a mirage in the vast gleaming desert. I let my tongue taste the salt on the air; it filled me with excitement.

Lifting my coral to the light, I marvelled at the pinkish tinge of its rough ridges in my hand, shaped and sculptured by the sea, astonished by how this strange, twisted rock could rebuild itself and grow anew.

'It's too big to fit in my jar,' I said in sudden dismay. There was no room left for something so big, especially now my jar was over half full.

'Let me see. Perhaps we could break a piece off.'

I handed the coral to Lemàn and she examined it carefully, looking for a sign of weakness. She laughed. 'It's a tough old thing.'

Looking down, something in the harbour caught my eye. Then its shape became familiar. 'Look!' I cried.

'Hmm?' she replied, too distracted to lift her eyes.

This time I could make the letters into words and I read them aloud: 'The Boat of Floating Freaks and Oddities.'

Her eyes flew wide then, full of terror. In shock, she dropped the coral and it smashed into pieces at our feet. The shards scattered and flew, blowing out across the water. I bent down to pick up a fragment before she clutched at my hand and dragged me away, just as before, up the hill and into the swirls of people. This time, however, we were too late; the boat had already docked, and showed no sign of activity. Whatever it had been carrying had already been brought to shore.

In her panic, she seemed to have once again forgotten all about her own rule – *arm's reach, arm's reach* – and I felt her grip tighten. I tried to keep my hood in place, but the speed and jostle of people made it impossible, even with my free hand flattened hard against the top of my head. Just for a moment, I let go of Lemàn's hand to pull my hood tighter around my face, but when I reached out to take her hand again, I felt nothing but the snapping jaws of winter air and the whoosh of heavy coats. Swept up in a sudden blizzard of people, Lemàn was nowhere to be found. For a moment I was seized by panic; the only thing I knew how to do was hide. Looking around, I realised everything was familiar to me: the stalls; the shop windows; the crowds. I knew all of it. Excitement and uncertainty tugged me in different directions, but suddenly I wasn't afraid. I knew where I was, and, more importantly,

I knew the way home, but I wasn't ready to go there just yet. I wanted to explore.

Just then, two girls skipped past, with strings of liquorice dangling from their mouths, cheeks flushed from the cold. They seemed to be in a hurry to get somewhere, one buoyed along by the other. Everything about them bounced: their feet; their shoulders; even their perfect little curls. Curious to know where they were going with such urgent delight, I followed them through the crowded market towards the edge of the town where the trees began to grow into a forest, and I wondered if the lonely woman from Lemàn's story was watching me. Here the girls stopped abruptly in front of a large blue and white striped tent, where a crowd of people had begun to gather.

I heard a voice shout out, 'Sixpence for admission.'

A man in front of me jeered. 'It's these freaks that have got some admitting to do.' He laughed at his own joke and slapped his friend's back in mirth, coaxing a splutter of a laugh from his lungs.

The girls both pulled out coins from their pockets and clutched them tightly as they edged further into the growing crowd, all waiting to get inside. I desperately wanted to join them, but my pockets were empty. To the side, a group of boys were all nudging each other and whispering, then one of them gave a signal and another dropped to his knees and began to burrow under the tent flap like a fat rabbit. Instantly, a man saw what was happening and started to shout. The boys whistled their warning and ran, but it was too late for the fat rabbit, and the man marched over and hauled him to his feet. Somehow, he managed to wriggle free and panted after his friends. Seizing the opportunity that the distraction had brought, I sprinted round the back of the tent, and quickly lifted the flap and dived underneath, before anyone had time to notice me.

I don't know what I expected to find there, but if I thought I would escape the crowds, then I was wrong; it was crammed full of people, almost as many inside as there were waiting outside. A circle of seats was fast-filling with men, women and children, all bustling and jostling for a place; excited murmurs swirled through the air. It didn't take long for every seat to be filled, and still more people were pushing to get in. A sudden hush descended then, broken only by a nervous shuffling; eyes darted round the tent in search of whatever it was their sixpence had promised.

'Ladies and gentlemen, boys and girls ...' The voice came from a squat man, bulging and popping at every seam and buttonhole. His long tailcoat flapped with the flamboyance of a Lady Amherst's pheasant. 'Welcome to the show. The Boat of Floating Freaks and Oddities has been brought to shore just for your delight.' He twirled then to address the other side of the ring. 'You won't believe your eyes, but believe them you must.' Then he lowered his voice to a whisper and the shuffling stopped. 'What you will see here today will shock you ... it will astound you ... it might even frighten you.' His voice rose to a crescendo.

The two girls I had followed were giggling, and I watched them nudge each other nervously. The air was thick with intrigue.

'But I can promise you one thing: you will never forget it!'

Then, from the shadows, there was a scuffle as a cage was wheeled into the inner circle. The girls' giggling stopped, and they suddenly grew quiet, reaching for each other's hands. People muttered and bottoms lifted from seats in the hope of a better look at whatever had just arrived. Through the gaps between the petticoats, I could see there was something moving in the cage. I crawled forward on my hands and knees. It was crouched, animal-like and cowering, but this animal wore a waistcoat and a pair of checked trousers. The master unhooked the door and the audience gasped and then gaped in astonishment as the creature's eyes shone in terror, amber in the darkest cave. It sat motionless.

'Please welcome the Bear Boy!' cried the master in jubilation, yet there was no applause, only an air of uncertainty. He lifted a long cane and rattled it through the bars of the cage. The Bear Boy turned and snarled, revealing a set of vicious pointed teeth, which made the audience gasp again and cringe. The master prodded at the Bear Boy until it leaped through the door of its cage. Its feet were paws, with their unclipped, gnarled claws.

'Freak!' The word exploded into the air loud as gunpowder.

'What is it?' cried a voice at the front. 'It's hideous!'

There was a rumble in the audience. Many of the women gathered their children into their skirts and buried their faces into the arms of their husbands. I didn't turn away; I watched, stunned. Not at the Bear Boy, with his face and body covered in fur, but at the master and the audience for their cruel taunts. The master reached into his bag, and lifted what could have been the raw red heart of a deer, high above his head. 'Watch it devour this in a single bite! Look at the power of its jaws!' He threw the slimy object to the dirt and the Bear Boy growled and pounced. One woman turned her face, wincing in pain and retching uncontrollably into a handkerchief. It was too much for another, and she promptly fainted to the floor.

The Bear Boy suddenly rose, and his front legs revealed themselves to be arms, which had been bent under him in ursine pretence. He stood, now a boy. Taller and older than me, but not by much. The audience grew silent, not quite understanding what they were seeing, but I did. From his skin grew the fur of a bear and from mine grew the feathers of a bird. He was different, just like me. The Bear Boy ran around the ring to a hesitant ripple of applause. He slowed then to let the braver members of the audience reach out and touch his fur. Some flinched, others stroked it and nodded approvingly at its softness, others tugged at it, not believing it to be real. I wanted desperately to reach out and touch his fur, to make sure he was neither boy, nor bear, but a mixture of the two, something in between, something other. In that moment, I knew I wasn't the only one, but the quick relief this knowledge brought me was instantly forgotten as I realised how he suffered for his difference. With a sudden bow and a cheery wave, he skipped away, but as he did I thought I saw sadness shining in his eyes. These people had called him a freak, and, when they realised he was just a boy with fur, their disgust and fear had turned instead to disbelief and suspicion, then to amusement. Instinctively, I pulled my hood tighter; suddenly I wanted to shut out the world. The master began to announce the next act: Frogman; a man whose skin could almost stretch from one side of the tent to the other, and a woman so small she could pirouette in the palm of your hand, but I had seen enough of people being ridiculed and displayed for the amusement of others.

'I heard you've got a mermaid?' shouted an impatient man. 'I'll pay double to see that.'

A couple of voices rumbled their agreement. The circus master held up his hand and waited for quiet. 'You heard right, but first you must be patient. We are saving the best till last. No one eats the pudding before the main dish.'

The crowd wasn't listening and driven by the heckler, the whole tent erupted with the same chant: Mermaid! Mermaid! Mermaid!

In that moment, I understood at once why I had been hidden all this time. It wasn't because I was too beautiful for the world at all; it was because I was too ugly. I was deformed; I was a hideous creature and, just like the Bear Boy, I was a freak. What would they do to me if they discovered my feathers? Hoist me to the rafters and watch me fly? My eyes swept the full height of the tent and dropped back down again; it was a fall I wouldn't survive.

In a panic, I scrambled back towards the canopy, feeling the betrayal and the sting of tears in my eyes. As I wiped them away, I saw something moving in the shadows hidden from the audience by a second tent flap and a giant folding partition. On a table lay a woman who was being inched and squeezed into the large silver-blue tail of a fish. It had been stitched to a wide flesh-coloured strip of elastic, and attached seamlessly around her waist. She was clearly the star attraction, but she wasn't real, not like the Bear Boy. Once securely fastened, they lifted her from the table and hoisted her over the top of a large glass tank, then with a quiet splosh, they dropped her into the water. One of them reached up to spill the contents of an ink bottle into the gloom and the woman inside swished her tail and swam round in little circles swilling the ink until the water inside shone a luminous blue.

Strange patterns waltzed across the ground and leapt up the walls of the tent, before quivering back down again in nervous retreat. She perched on the edge of a giant nautilus shell, which must have been carved out of marble. Mesmerised, I watched as her hair tumbled and wrapped itself around her, glittering like golden tinsel in the water.

It shone with pearls, each one like a tiny iridescent moon. She reminded me of the doll I had seen on my first visit to the market, the one given to the little girl by her papa. A mermaid. Her bare flesh gleamed and shimmered, and I was held captive. It was then I felt her soft gaze fall upon me, and I stepped back until I could feel the canopy wall of the tent behind me, and I could go no further. This was a beautiful act, but it wasn't real. Slowly she raised a finger to her mouth and pressed it gently against her lips, and I swear I could hear the sound of the sea. It felt like I was drowning, there in the watery gloom where I could no longer separate myth from reality.

'Here's another one!' yelled a voice in disgust.

It was then that I noticed the heckler from the audience was scowling down at me as I sat on the ground. Other faces had begun to turn their attention my way and they all wore the same expression, one of revolt and pity. The liquorice-sucking girls stared wide-eyed with wrinkled noses, as though they could smell something unpleasant. Then they scurried away as though I might fly towards them and peck them both to death.

The man rolled his eyes in exasperation and turned away from me. Then he clapped his hands and rubbed them together as though in readiness to devour some delicious feast. 'Who cares about the rest of these freaks with fur or feathers! They just get stuck in your teeth, which is why you must first pluck a goose before you can eat it!' His words were followed by a loud cheer of agreement.

'We want the mermaid!' he cried, rousing the audience once again. 'Mermaid! Mermaid! Mermaid!'

I thought I saw the dark shadow of a giant feathered wing pass over me just as I felt a firm hand clasp around my wrist and pull me backwards out of the tent.

CHAPTER 6

The hand belonged to Lemàn; she had found me crouching under the tent and was hauling me to my feet.

'You must never do that again!' she threatened in a tone that I had never heard her use before, dragging me all the way back to the top of the hill in breathless anguish. 'You do not understand the cruelty of this world.'

'But I stayed away from the lonely woman in the forest.' I protested, biting back the tears.

'The danger is not in the forest,' she replied, shaking her head.

Visibly shocked and trembling, she led me to the cellar and quickly shut the door on my questions. This time, it was my heart that pounded relentlessly, not Lemàn's, but it wasn't with fear; it was with anger and something else that I couldn't name then, but later I learned it was the first pang of desire. The feelings that freedom could bring.

There was something about the girl in the water that I couldn't forget. For some reason, I wanted to touch her, but not in the same way I wanted to touch Bear Boy, to see if he was real or not; I already knew she wasn't what she was pretending to be. I had watched her being stitched into her disguise and seen the breathing tube lowered into the water after her. This was something else, something more urgent, and more incessant, and I couldn't possibly have known the trouble that desire would bring.

Lemàn had lied to me for all these years. She had hidden me because I was an ugly little secret, ugly enough to be mocked and ridiculed and paraded around inside a circus tent like the Bear Boy. More monster than princess. For a long time, I refused to come out of my room, and whenever I heard her footfalls on the stairs, I turned my body against the wall.

'I'm so sorry, my little firecracker,' she would whisper night after night into the unwelcoming dark.

Her words made my feathers bristle and we both suffered in the continuing silence. It was only once I heard the sound of her quiet retreat that I released my breath into a sob against my pillow. The midnight chimes had finally rung out and the spell was forever broken. The only person

I spoke to was Professor Elms, and even then my words to him were angry and few.

'Do you know how much Lemàn loves you?' he asked in earnest, as I sat on the floor, sorting through my pine cones.

'Lemàn is a liar.' My words bit, hard as bullets. 'They are all liars.'

Professor Elms looked shocked. 'They were trying to protect you.'

I shook my head. 'No, they weren't. They made me believe I was special and beautiful and—' I felt my voice break and fall apart.

'And you are all of those things.' He spoke softly. 'Unfortunately, the world is not always such a welcoming place.'

'You mean for someone like me? Someone with feathers.' I scrunched my face in disgust, and threw the pine cones back in the box with a clatter. It was then that I noticed the egg. In a fury, I grabbed it and crushed it in my hand. I had expected there to be a yellow puddle inside, but instead it was dry and empty. Fumbling the lid closed, I shoved it back under the bed.

'Some mothers are forced to sell their babies at birth … others have no choice but to give them away. Some are desperate for money, others desperate to—' Professor Elms looked startled, as though he had suddenly revealed too much.

'Others are desperate to what?' My voice was filled with angry insistence; it demanded an answer, but none came. 'Fine – don't tell me then … keep your secrets.'

There was a long pause, filled with nothing but the sound of dipping rain at the window.

Finally, he spoke. 'Others are desperate to escape the shame.'

'See, I knew it,' I snapped. 'You think I'm something to be ashamed of too?'

'Of course not!' Professor Elms looked wounded. He came closer and sat down on the bed, his chin sinking to his chest. 'Lemàn wanted to keep you with her, no matter what the risk was. Don't you see – it is her lies that have kept you safe all this time.'

'Safe?' I spat the word at him.

'The world doesn't always understand things that are different. It was the fear of others, and not the shame of you, that made Lemàn lie. Her whole life, since you arrived, has been spent protecting you.'

He left me alone after that, and I wondered about all the mothers who had given birth to babies they weren't allowed to keep. I wondered about Bear Boy's mother. How long had she been able to hold him or had she rejected him the moment she had seen the thick fur covering his body? Had she cried in anguish or in relief when they had come to take him away? Even the crushed egg had a mother who perhaps still wondered what had happened to it. Inside I ached. Although the world might see me as ugly, deep down I knew that when Lemàn said I was beautiful, she really meant it.

That night, before Lemàn arrived, someone else came to my room and it was the last person I expected. Although the footsteps were unmistakable, and the waft of lilies familiar, I couldn't believe it until I saw her standing in the doorway with her silent lips pressed tightly together, simply waiting. Her eyes offered no approval as they narrowed with intensity, making me pull the blankets over the tremble of my hands. What had brought her here? It was a game of patience and the next move was hers.

Finally, she broke the silence, but didn't move further into the room. I realised then that I didn't know her voice; it was strange to me. Sorren usually chose not to address me directly and I had heard so few of her words that I wouldn't have recognised who spoke them from behind a closed door. Even now, she spoke briefly and with unquestionable authority.

'You are being selfish,' she said, bluntly. It was said with such assertion that no one would have dared to argue. 'You do not think about the sacrifices Lemàn has made for you.' She paused for a moment, holding me in her glare. 'The sacrifices she continues to make.'

If I had been dog, I would have whimpered and cowered in a corner, but instead I just nodded, burning hot with shame. Then Sorren turned and disappeared and just like that it was all over. Later, when Lemàn crept down the cellar stairs, I was already half asleep, but when I woke again some hours later, she was in my bed and I was in her arms.

'I made a terrible mistake,' she murmured into my ear. 'Please forgive me for it.' Her voice shook like a storm-filled wood.

Reaching for her hand, I held it in my own, and pressed myself against her shoulder. I heard her inhale the scent of my feathers, and then she sighed as though she had been relieved of a great weight, one she could no longer carry without it breaking her back.

'You must promise that you will always tell me the truth,' I said.

She kissed my ear. 'I promise.'

Feeling safe again, I snuggled deeper into the shelter of her arm.

'To me you will always be beautiful, and I never lied about that, but people see things in lots of different ways and I can't change that. If I had a magic wand I would; then the whole world would see you just as I do.'

I nudged her in the side. 'Enough of the fairy tales,' I said, and we both quietly giggled.

'What happened to your marionette?' she asked, in alarm.

Dawn light had begun to filter into the room, and in the corner she had seen the broken heap of my marionette; its feathers torn from the wood and scattered all over the floor.

'I was angry,' I replied, flatly. It had been such a foolish thing to do, just like the egg. In my rage, I had destroyed what I loved most and, in doing so, the only person I had punished was myself.

'What a shame,' she said, reaching out and lifting it from the floor and onto the bed. As she did, its leg fell off followed by a fluttering feather. It was such a sorry sight that I couldn't bear to look at it.

'Don't worry; it can be fixed. See how beautiful it is under all those feathers, and how smooth? If we scrub away all that glue with warm water and then polish the wood with beeswax it will be a marionette again. Perhaps more of a giraffe than a bird, though,' she said, trying to find its lost leg, which was somewhere under the bed. Giving up, she dropped the marionette back to the floor and held me close. Her breathing grew steady and I knew sleep wasn't far away.

'There is still magic in the world you know,' she said, drowsily. 'Often, it is spun by the heart and felt so deeply that you never stop smiling. Sometimes it is so bright that it makes you believe in the impossible. My wish is that one day you will find it.'

I didn't sleep after that. Her words kept me thinking and hoping, and, lying there in my bed, I allowed myself one last wish: to find the magic she had spoken of.

Although I had forgiven her, my anger hadn't gone away completely; instead it had turned to my feathers. Once I had thought they made me feel beautiful and special, but now I saw them as the enemy. Whereas before they felt light and fluttery, now they hung like a thick, heavy coat worn in summer. I had once loved their shine and longed for the whores to play with them in wonder; now I shuddered at their glances and shunned their touch, as though I carried a disease. My feathers were an affliction that could never be cured, and I hated them.

One day, I was helping a whore soak her body in almond oil. Massaging it into her skin, soft and white as a boiled egg, I loved how my hands glided up and down her arms, how silky it felt beneath my fingertips. When I had finished, I secretly dropped the oil into my pocket and, later, in my room, I tried to rub it into my own skin, but the feathers stuck to my fingertips and then to each other until I was left with wet, sticky tangled clumps that looked like spewed fur balls. I remembered Lemàn's words about my broken puppet: *how beautiful it is under all those feathers, and how smooth* and how it could be *fixed*. Once more, I was reminded of my ugliness. In frustration, I threw the jar of oil against the wall; it smashed and out spilled a memory.

It was from one of my first visits to town. I was standing in the street by the open doorway of a shop. I could see white movement within, so much white that it looked like it was snowing inside, and I peered in disbelief at what I thought was a spectacular swirl of snowflakes. Searching through the blizzard, my eyes began to take in the scene within, and, to my horror, I saw a sitting man plunge a chicken headfirst into a bucket of boiling water. Lifting it out, he thwacked it across his grimy, grease-smeared knee and began to pluck out its feathers with furious speed, tossing flurried fistfuls of them into the air, creating the feather-storm I had seen from the street. I felt faint and had to steady myself against the wall. In a matter of minutes, all that was left was its pink, pimpled and puckered body, which he flung heartlessly on an ever-growing pile, only to begin all over again. It may not have been snow inside the shop that day, but it left me just as frozen.

The memory gave me an idea, and, grabbing a fistful of feathers from my left shoulder, I pulled as hard as I could. The pain made me scream out loud, but their roots held strong and deep. I released them and lifted one up by itself, holding it between my finger and thumb, I tugged, but still it held firm. I tugged again until finally it loosened and then fell into my palm. But I could hardly pull them out one by one, there were far too many for that.

Later that night, unable to sleep, I crept into the kitchen, and, taking a pair of scissors, blunt from cutting into too much fat, I chopped away at my feathers until I was left with nothing but ugly stubs, sharp as little daggers. Still, I didn't have the silky, smooth skin I desired. My stubble reminded me of the demons who came to the whorehouse not just to satisfy their needs, but also sometimes for a clean and polish, like a tea set brought out for a special occasion. The whores would lather up their faces and take the sharp edge of a blade to their neck, scraping them clean of both foam and bristle. Afterwards, their faces would look pale and smooth like boiled potatoes. Men reduced to boys with the flick of a wrist.

My frustration made me bold and reckless. I knew where the blades were kept and slid one from the drawer. I held the sharp, glinting edge against my upper arm and then without hesitation I sliced into my skin, too deep, right down to the bone. I didn't notice the blood immediately or feel any pain as I continued desperately to slice up and down my arm, pleased as I watched the remaining bits of feather flutter to the floor. Then, slowly realising what I had done, I dropped the razor blade with a clatter. What started as a slow trickle soon became a dark flood and I collapsed to the floor.

How much time passed, I do not know, but when I opened my eyes, I felt myself being rocked in Sorren's arms, revived by the smelling salts which she held in a pouch under my nose. I could see her hands were smeared with my blood and patches of red soaked into her skirt like great flowery blooms. Then it was Lemàn's face I saw in the doorway, crumpled in panic, her cheeks wet with tears. She rushed into the room and lifted me out of Sorren's embrace and began to bathe and bandage my wounds. My feathers, which I so desperately wanted to hide, were now all over the floor as though a fox had feasted in a hen house, only this time the fox wasn't to blame. Sorren said nothing, and when I looked round the room, she had gone. After that, I knew to leave my feathers well alone. Within weeks they had grown back again and had lost none of their shine, and no one would ever have known I had ever tried to cut them from my skin. It's only if you look very closely that you can see the silvery scars beneath, a permanent reminder of my mistake.

CHAPTER 7

As the years passed, my lessons with Professor Elms continued happily. He was encouraged by the curiosity of my mind and my inquisitive thoughts, and taught me so many things. Leaving my childhood behind brought a sad end to our secret walks in the fields and the wonder-filled woods, which were gradually replaced with the reading of articles, then books. Finally, he heaved great tomes up the hill so I could learn about things I might never get the chance to see: year-long battles; emperors who ruled the world from their palaces; nomadic tribes in their shelters of skin and bone, temples of worship and rivers of larva, deep oceans and distant stars. He tested my mind on solving impossible equations and different scientific theories, but my learning became stilted and slow, and, whenever I lost interest, my eyes would wander from the books to the oblong light of the window and yet another world I seemed to have left behind.

One day, Professor Elms was trying to teach me about algebra.

'It's the reunion of broken pieces,' he said, but my mind held no space for numbers and, sensing my distraction, he let the book fall shut with a thud. It woke me from my reverie. Then, reaching for one of my pencils, he began to draw.

'There is so much out there,' he whispered, as though whatever it was might hear us. 'Beyond the lane and the woods and even the ocean, and further than the eye can see, lie the Scatterings.'

'What are the Scatterings?' I looked up, suddenly wanting to know what lay beyond the shiver of blue.

'Islands … floating cities, lost at sea.'

'Floating cities,' I repeated his words. 'How far away are they?'

'Too far to count the number of days it will take you to reach them. They float in the many seas.'

'And where did they come from?' I sat crossed-legged on the edge of my seat, as though this would somehow bring them closer.

'Some are held together by seaweed and cartilage, their towns are protected by the ribcage of something much bigger than a whale; others tumble down ochre rocks, too steep and creviced to climb. There is one conjured from mist and another shaped only by the rain.' He paused then for a moment, as though he had forgotten something, or all of a sudden had lost his way in a place of tangled cobwebs. 'Many were once stars that burned so brightly, they fell from the night sky in an explosive burst of light, where they were cooled and hardened in the sea.'

He made these islands and floating cities sound so magical, and I couldn't imagine anything existing like that somewhere out at sea. It was just an endless blue, but I supposed the boats that arrived must have come from somewhere. Absentmindedly, he reached into his top pocket for a watch that had stopped ticking long ago. I wondered why he carried a watch at all, and thought it was perhaps because he had lived so long without one.

'Why do you check the time on it if it's broken?' I asked.

'I'm not checking the time – it's a reminder,' he replied, dropping it safely back into his pocket with a gentle pat; I could see its round shape bulge beneath the cloth.

'A reminder of what?'

He looked weary, as though his own mechanism suddenly needed winding again. 'Someone I once lost.'

I frowned. 'You can't just lose a person; it's not like a coin that falls out of your pocket or a button that comes loose from a coat.' His expression told me I was wrong, and I wondered then what he knew of love and loss. Like me, the world seemed to have rejected him. He smelled like a rainy day, or a dusty armchair that nobody sat in any more: musty and damp in the first moments, then the senses would grow accustomed to it, and it was only when a sudden draught rushed from under a door or through an open window that you would be reminded of just how abandoned he had become. I imagined that if you patted his jacket, great choking clouds of dust would float off into the air. But underneath all of that, I knew there was in fact so much there to be loved. It made me happy and relieved to think that someone, somewhere had loved him once. Love was the only topic that seemed to confuse him. The one topic for which he didn't have all the answers.

Glancing over I saw that he had been drawing something, and a place had begun to emerge on the paper. He brought it to life with the strokes of his pencil, telling me of long stretches of water and bridges that took you over them; of domes and spires high enough to pierce the moon; of narrow twisting streets and tall bell towers; of morning mists like returning ghosts and damp evenings; of water washed stone and sunlit squares. Buildings, like fresh loaves rising and shaping, baking in the slow warmth, and by mid-afternoon everything would be golden with sun-glazed roofs, too hot, even for the cats' paws to prowl upon. A place where the weather was dependent on the emotions of its residents rather than any atmospheric shift. There, the sky was not bound by the changing seasons. After the death of a child, dark clouds mourned the loss. It always rained longer and harder then. The sun gleamed like a medal during celebrations, and weddings were always shiny and warm and bright. A humid tension hung in the air just before a wife discovered a husband's betrayal, and when he got home, lightning would rip open the sky and a storm would rage long into the night, and sometimes into the next.

My mind was tangled. Barely able to breathe, I traced the images he had drawn with my finger, until there was a smudge of grey left on its tip. 'Is it one of the Scatterings?'

The professor nodded. 'They say there are mermaids living in its waters.'

'Mermaids? But that can't be true; there is no such thing.' All those years ago, in the gloaming, floating half-light of a circus tent, I had learned that mermaids don't really exist. 'They are just an illusion,' I said, as though he was a fool to suggest otherwise.

'An elusive truth, perhaps … but just because you have never seen one doesn't mean they don't exist. Believing in magic is the only way you'll ever find it. In this place, there are brightly painted doors where you would least expect to find them, slotted in between a drab shoemakers, and a cluttered apothecary. These are called the wishing doors; different colours grant different wishes.'

'Have you been there?' I asked, excitedly. 'Did you make a wish?'

Professor Elms quietened and, reaching into his pocket, he pulled out a large handkerchief, which he then dabbed at the sudden sadness in his eyes.

'Yes, I made a wish.'

I frowned. 'And did it come true?'

He smiled. 'In a way, I suppose it did. What I really wanted was to find the love I lost; instead I found a different love.' Absent-mindedly, he patted at his pocket watch. He did this often like a nervous habit, to check that it was still there.

'How does your watch remind you of loss?'

'It is set to the moment I first saw her, one minute before seven. It was a warm spring evening in the lively square of a faraway city.'

'But how can you be sure it was one minute before seven?' I asked.

'Because I can still hear the pretty chimes of the towering clock above us. I often fall to sleep with the sound of them in my ears.'

'But you lost her and it makes you so sad?'

'Sad?' he asked, in confusion. 'I'm not sad. I will never lose that moment. All I have to do is close my eyes and I can see the smile of delight on her face as she looked up at the clock face with its blue background speckled with stars. The hand of my broken watch always brings her back to me. Sometimes there is beauty in broken things.'

He closed his eyes and seemed to be breathing in her memory. I closed mine too and tried to imagine a beautiful girl and a glittering clock and the professor's face, much younger than the one I knew.

'They also talk of Sky-Worshippers, bird men who come from the mist.'

My eyes flew open and my mind was caught on the word *bird*. Bird men – people just like me, out in the world. 'I have to go there. Where is it? Tell me where it is.' I was clutching at his arm so fiercely that I made him wobble off his chair. Just then the air filled with the delicate scent of lemons and Lemàn appeared at the door dressed in her loose flowery robe.

'Professor Elms is telling me about a place of magic,' I said, loosening my grip.

Lemàn rolled her eyes playfully. 'And what place might that be?'

Turning my gaze towards the professor, we both waited for his answer; it seemed to take forever to come.

He looked at me and then back at Lemàn, and, like migrating swallows, the words flew gently from his lips: 'Ah, well – that is not so easy to answer. The city changes its name depending on what you will find there. Follow the accordion player to the night shops and there you will find your token, which will reveal everything.'

'A token?'

'Yes, they are small stones collected from the canals. I still have mine somewhere,' he said. I watched as he patted at his pockets and began fumbling on the inside of his jacket. A moment later he retrieved a flat silver stone upon which I noticed there was an inscription: *The City of Water*. 'This is the official name for those who have yet to be touched by its magic, and it is always the same, but a token always has two sides and if you flip it over you will find another story waiting for you.'

I watched as he turned it over in his narrow palm and held it out for me to see: *The City of Awakening* swirled its way around the edge.

'So, it's like a prediction?' I queried. 'And the inscription changes for every person?'

Professor Elms nodded. 'Yes, that is how I knew I would find love there, and that my heart would be woken. A heart never goes back to sleep after that.' Quickly he slipped the token back in his pocket. 'It is a place of difference.'

Lemàn's face lit up, then her smile faded. 'I lost mine.'

'Have you been there?' I asked, staring at her in disbelief.

She nodded. 'Yes, a very long time ago.'

'What's it like?'

'Hush, now my little firecracker, I have business with the professor,' she said, hastily returning from wherever her memory had pulled her. She smiled in his direction, and his face seemed suddenly content. Then she stared into the distance again, drifting in and out on a tide of memories. I waited until the waves washed her back to shore. Finally, she looked at me and uttered something quite unexpected, 'It's where I met your father.'

Then before I could utter another word, she was ushering the professor out of the door. They both disappeared up the stairs with their matching smiles and happy eyes. I had seen the whores blink strange liquid into their eyes on the nights of the great parties as though it was some kind of perfume. Seconds later their pupils would swell like a dark hypnotic spell. Now when I looked into Lemàn's eyes, they were already full without the pretence of a potion, like juicy dark berries of desire. I thought then that it wasn't just Lemàn who had mended the professor's heart, but that perhaps in some way he too had mended hers.

CHAPTER 8

Later that evening, I found Lemàn in the kitchen wringing out a bowl full of stockings over a bucket. Steam billowed around her from two giant cooking pots, which dampened her hair to her neck. There was moisture in the air and a light sheen to her skin. She looked like she had been walking on a desolate winter moor, a long way from home.

'You should be in your room,' she said, recognising my footsteps before I had even got through the door. She was grumbling, but she wasn't angry. 'You know that Sorren doesn't like you wandering the corridors by yourself.'

'But I'm not wandering the corridors by myself; I'm here in the kitchen with you,' I replied, settling onto a stool.

She shook her head at me, but I could see her eyes dance in amusement.

'Why does Sorren hate me so much?'

'Nonsense, she doesn't hate you.' I could hear her tutting from across the room.

'Then why is she so mean to me?'

Lemàn sighed. As I grew, she found my questions more difficult to answer; they often chased her from my room.

'Loss can make good people seem cruel, when really they're just sad.'

'Like the woman in the forest?'

'What woman?' She looked confused, forgetting her own story.

'The one you told me about, the one who was so lonely that she stole all those children.'

'Ah, yes – that's right.' She nodded, and smiled affectionately at my innocence.

'Is Sorren the reason I have feathers? Did she put a curse on me when I was born?'

Lemàn clicked her tongue. 'You and your fairy tales. If anything, it was you who put a curse on her; you make her remember things she'd rather forget. Besides, I already told you – they were a gift.'

I watched as she lifted another pair of stockings from the bowl, rolled them between her huge hands and twisted out the water.

'A gift from my father?'

Lemàn paused, but her face revealed nothing. She lifted the bucket and threw the soap suds out the back door. 'Yes,' she replied simply, bolting the door shut again.

'Tell me about him.'

The pots bubbled and hissed on the stove, and she moved between them, stirring the contents with a large wooden spoon. From the way she gripped the handle, I could tell that the mention of my father had deeply unsettled her.

'There really isn't much to tell,' she protested.

'But there must be!' My voice grew desperate, wanting to collect her memories.

'All right,' she sighed, reluctantly. 'I will tell you what I remember, but it isn't much.'

I watched and waited as she went back to pegging her stockings onto the clothes line which stretched the full length of the kitchen. Water dripped slowly from the toes onto the stone floor. I willed her to hurry up, impatient for the story to be told, but she seemed to be taking much longer than was necessary, pegging each one with deliberate precision. Perhaps she was trying to decide how or where to begin. When the last pair of stockings was finally secured, she still didn't come to the table; instead she crossed the room, reached high on the shelf in the alcove, and grabbed a bottle of rum and a glass. Uncorking it with a squeak, she sloshed the contents into the glass before sitting down opposite me, finally ready. Between great gulps, she unravelled her memory like a ball of wool, her words knitting together something soft and warm.

'I don't remember his name.' She paused and corrected herself. 'Actually, I don't remember it, because I never knew it. How can you remember something you were never told?' She laughed, but the sound of it was too shrill and brittle to be real.

'You never knew his name?' I wrinkled my face in disbelief, wondering how that was possible.

'There wasn't time. I met him at the market in a square filled with the flutter of birds. It was more of a glimpse than a meeting.' She stopped, closed her eyes for a moment, and when she opened them again, they glistened like distant stars. I shuffled restlessly on my stool, eager to hear more of the story. She smiled at the memory and the skin around her eyes crinkled softly. 'The birds were everywhere; on the rooftops, on the window ledges, circling the sky and strutting over the stone slabs on the ground. They seemed to come out of a strange silvery mist.' She gazed around the kitchen as though they were here now and she could still see them. I checked the beams just to make sure, but we were quite alone, apart from the scuttle of a mouse.

'Then what happened?' I suddenly realised how much colder and darker the room had become and I shivered. Lemàn pushed back her stool and it scraped against the floor. In the corner, the fire had fallen asleep, and, with a great iron poker, she provoked the flames until they snarled back to life.

I watched her from behind; the crooked slope of her back and the heave of her chest. Her once silken hair had become a bramble brush that she let grow wild and free, like an offering to a nesting bird. Cow-thick lashes still shaded her eyes, but she never really looked out to see what was in this world. I ached for her loss then, and, even though it wasn't my own, I felt it just the same. She was a hollow vessel with only the occasional rusty rattle of escaped memory. It was as though she had left herself behind, and someone had scooped out the flesh of her happiness. A fruit pecked empty by a bird; a gutted fish, a withered leaf on a winter path. I tried to imagine her as a young girl, but it was impossible; time had puffed her up like a pigeon and ruffled all her feathers. But it wasn't just time that had left its mark.

'That night,' she continued, 'quite by chance or fate or magic we found each other again. He came to the window of the Uccello Hotel where I was staying; it was as though he was floating in that same silver mist I had seen in the square.'

Her expression changed then, lit by happiness. Something had been unlocked inside her and her face was more animated than I had ever seen it before. Her thoughts were full and frothy, like a saucepan full of boiling milk about to spill over.

'I don't remember going downstairs to open the door, or him knocking to be let in, but somehow, moments later, he was right there with me in the room. It's as though he had flown right through the window.' She laughed at how absurd it all sounded and her eyes grew forest dark. 'The rest you can imagine.'

'What was he like?' I asked, not willing to let go of the story just yet.

She hesitated, smiling sadly at a memory untold. 'I remember him as though I saw him yesterday. You are very much like him, with the sunset in your feathers and the sky in your eyes – the same clear, infinite blue. I remember lying in the tender cradle of his arms. They were like warm wings covering me in a quilt of feathers, and there we nested through the night. When morning arrived, I awoke to find he was gone, not realising he had left a part of him behind.'

Wings! I couldn't imagine it.

The room flickered and grew silent apart from the slow steady drip, drip, drip of Lemàn's wet stockings creating puddles of water, which ran into the cracks in the floor. The only other sound was the sigh of the wind collapsing in the chimney. Even the mouse seemed to have fallen asleep.

Finally, I spoke. 'I want to find him.'

Lemàn sighed a deep and heavy sigh.

'I'm afraid that is all I can tell you. The story is short. I wish there was more.' She closed her eyes and tried to wipe a tear from the corner of her eye, but it fell too fast and splashed onto the table. It was then I caught sight of the bird tattoo pulsing on her wrist, and finally understood its meaning.

Lemàn seemed so far away then. For too long she had given all her colour to keeping the memory of my father alive, and now she sat like a lost ghost. Eventually, she reached out her hand and tenderly stroked the soft feathery down on my arms. 'I know you feel it,' she said.

'Feel what?'

'The connection to the birds outside.'

'Yes,' I admitted, thinking about all the hours I spent watching them and drawing them and how, whenever we passed the farm gate, I lingered a little longer when the hens were strutting around the yard. Deep within I had always known I was connected to birds, and now I was old enough to know the full story, it all made sense.

'The birds gathered on the roof the night you were born, watching and waiting for you to arrive. I tried to shut out the sound of their wings, but flight is within you, and I was mistaken to think I could stop it. I should never have even tried.' Her face flickered with regret for a moment, but then it was gone. 'I have something to show you,' she said, rising from the stool and disappearing from the room.

I reached across and dipped my finger into the large teardrop left on the table, and with it I traced the outline of a small feather. Moments later, she returned to the room and handed me a book I had never seen before; *The Art of Hot Air Ballooning*. 'Open it at the beginning – go on,' she urged.

I took it gently into my hands like a prayer book, and did as she requested. There between the pages lay a glossy copper-gold feather; an offering. 'It's all I've got left of him.' She sighed sadly. 'And, of course, I have you.' Then I felt her hand upon my back and my feathers rose, craving her touch.

Tentatively, I lifted the feather from the page and twirled it between my fingers. The vane was the length of my wrist to my elbow, longer and darker than any of the feathers that grew on my body, but the colour was similar, the smouldering flame of a late summer evening. I held it to my nose; caught on the barbs was the smell of cool mountain air, of rain-filled afternoons, and storm-swept nights, of drifting smoke and shivering treetops and something else I couldn't name, but if sadness had a smell then this would have been it. This feather held all the coordinates of loss. A precious offering, I didn't want to let it go, its silkiness soothing my fingertips.

'Was he really a bird?' I whispered, scarcely able to believe what I was asking.

'More that than anything else,' came her reply.

Lemàn was no longer a beautiful woman – her body was too misshapen and her face was too grief-etched – but in that moment I saw her eyes sparkle and shine, and her face transformed into something all-knowing and translucent, just like the night I was born. She collected up her memories like breadcrumbs leading her back to a place of happiness.

'I went back to the City of Water, but he had vanished. It was like he had never really existed, but was just a strange and delightful dream, and for a while I thought I was mad, but my growing belly convinced me otherwise. He belonged to the air and the sky and I knew searching cafés and courtyards would reveal nothing but disappointment. I even took ballooning lessons, so convinced was I that he had flown away and lived amongst the clouds.' She tapped the book by way of explanation. 'Me, my balloon and my basket heavy with fish to satisfy my constant craving. But I think it was you growing inside me who wanted the fish really. I flew so high I could have polished the stars, one by one, but none of them would have granted my wish.'

All these years she had been carrying a sorrow so large and looming that it created shadows all around her, yet I had known nothing of it. But then what good would my knowing have done? Maybe I was comfort enough, the piece of him she could still hold on to. The piece that brought her peace.

'Every time a gust of wind swept my balloon from the ground, my heart would lift with it and together we would soar, but I was foolish to think I could find him. The migration of a bird is long and far and constant. A simple balloon is no match for the wings of a bird; I could never have followed his path. I was a fool to think otherwise.'

'How long did you look?'

'I spent months searching the skies for your father, but each time I returned with nothing more than the smell of damp mist clinging to my hair. Still I flew, even when my belly had swollen with you inside. One day, an unexpected wind came and the weight of you sent me hurtling to the ground. I never returned after that; I had you to think of.'

'If it wasn't for me, do you think you would have stopped looking?' I suddenly felt overcome with guilt, as though I had become her anchor, weighting her to the ground. She could have continued her search, if she didn't have me to think about.

Sensing my guilt as only a mother can, Lemàn wrapped me in her arms again. 'If it wasn't for you, my little firecracker, I would never have even started.' Then she kissed the top of my head and I heard her sigh happily. Finally, she let go and, taking the feather, she replaced it lovingly between the pages of the book and then slapped it shut as though she should never have opened it at all.

'Come on, my little one. It's late, time to dream,' she said, rubbing at the aches in her back.

'Little one?' I said, and we both laughed, for I had grown much taller than her years ago. 'I have one last question.' She paused. 'What did your token say?'

She smiled. 'The City of Miracles, and for me it most certainly was.'

As we left the kitchen, too full of memories, I knew Lemàn wouldn't sleep that night; even the rum bottle wouldn't be enough to soothe her mind. The indelible print of my father and my past lay not just on her skin, but in her bones, her cells; it lay behind her eyes and flowed through her veins, it filled the whole of her heart and it was the beat within. I longed to know more, but she had finished their story, and the rest was for me to find.

Even though Lemàn still called me her little one, I knew it wouldn't be long before it was time for me to leave, but leaving would break her heart and I didn't know how to tell her. I was torn between head and heart, between girl and bird.

I confessed my decision, and with it my fear, to Professor Elms. It was our last secret.

'She is stronger than you think,' he reassured me, and when I looked into his face, it wasn't just her sadness I was worried about. I shook my head in doubt. 'Sometimes, being too close to something means you can no longer see it clearly.'

I had emptied my birthday jar, spreading the gifts over my bed, sorting through them one by one as Lemàn appeared in the doorway.

'Seventeen,' I said, letting the last one clatter back on the top. We both gazed at the jar. 'It's almost full.'

'Yes,' she replied, not meeting my eye. 'It is.' We both knew what that meant, but neither of us wanted to say the words.

'Maybe there's room for one more.' There was a tremble of hope in her voice.

'When you gave me this jar, you said that once it was full, I would have a decision to make.' I nestled it on my lap and pretended to study the contents, although I had seen them all so many times before. For so long I had been keeping an ocean inside, but now I wanted to sail away upon its waves.

Lemàn sighed deeply. 'Yes – I remember.'

'Well, I have decided.' There was a crack in my voice, a fissure of guilt that I couldn't hide. She seemed to have aged before my eyes and I had never really noticed before. Her jaw was slack and saggy, deep furrows burrowed into her cheeks and across her forehead and she held her back often as though it ached every time she moved. I gulped back the guilt, still unable to find the words I needed. She sat down and began clasping and unclasping her hands as though she wanted to say a prayer, but wasn't quite sure what to pray for. I spoke quickly before I changed my mind.

'For my next birthday I choose my freedom.' As soon as I uttered those words, I regretted them. I wanted to snatch them back, and swallow them up until they were all gone, but it was much too late for that.

Then there was nothing but a heavy silence just like the one all those years ago after my discovery inside the circus tent. When I finally dared to lift my eyes to her, she was sitting motionless, as though she had stopped working, like the hands of Professor Elms' pocket watch. I had fallen into a black hole, and a ladder weaved out of the Milky Way was the only way I could climb back out again.

Lemàn pulled me close. 'Well, that's something that definitely won't fit in a jar.' She tried to laugh, but it sounded more like a long-held sob. I felt the warm tickle of her breath against my neck and my feathers ruffled all the way down my back, damp from her tears. My own fell fast and I let them. We sat in the growing dark, wiping away each other's tears, until the last trace of light had tiptoed from the room.

'I thought I wanted to keep you here with me always, but I do not want you to live a life like mine,' she said solemnly.

'Is that why you told me the story about the woman in the forest and the stolen children, so that I would be too afraid to leave?'

She shuddered her final sob. 'All I ever wanted to do was to protect you, but I know I can't be there for ever. That story might not have been true, but there are many versions of it that are.'

I nodded, trying to understand something I had yet to discover.

'Risk can be beautiful. It is time for you to leave this place. The heart is a wanderer and you must follow it.' She gave a small half-smile, but her mouth was uneven and I knew her happiness would always be a crooked thing.

It was like opening the door of a cage to free a bird that had never been taught how to fly, and for a while I sat and wondered about my place in the world. Lemàn had only shown me a small glimpse of the past, no bigger than the view from my window, and to understand the rest, I needed to find my father. Only then would I discover where I had come from and where I really belonged, and for that I had to go back to the start of the story.

Later I asked Professor Elms how I could get to The City of Water.

'Ah, for that you will need a boat,' he replied, as though it was the simplest thing in the world.

CHAPTER 9

I knew the sea visitors from the shine on their boots. Instead of leaving mud piles at the door, they left salty trails that led to the distant, unfathomable shores of the Scatterings. They didn't pay with coins; they paid with barrels of rum, which I could hear clatter through the door and rumble down the corridor in readiness for a night of revelry.

Restless in my room I sat and waited. Upon hearing the unmistakable sound of a rolling barrel, I waited some more, just long enough for the visitor who had brought the barrel to satisfy his needs, and then, slipping on my cloak, I left my room in search of him.

I had timed it to perfection, as I knew I would, and found him standing by the door adjusting himself. His dark brown face was covered in a messy tangle of hair and dark tousled curls sprang from his head like a sea sponge. His shirt hung untucked and unbuttoned revealing sprouts of hair on his chest and down his large stomach, before disappearing beneath the top of his trousers. I could smell the salt on his skin and the faraway cities netted in his hair. Clutched in his hand was his jacket; the fourth looped stripe around the cuff told me that I had found a captain. Blushing, I looked away and shuffled back further into the shadows as he bent to retrieve his boots. Straightening up, his eyes found me and fell to the swell of my breasts, then to the curve of my hips, where they lingered a little too long and I felt myself blush again. My short hair was no longer disguise enough for his lascivious, dancing eyes; he seemed to be able to unpeel my layers no matter how tightly I pulled them around myself. I now had more to hide than just my feathers. I didn't want to be touched, not even by his eyes, but the intention in them was clear.

Then he laughed, shook his head and started pulling on his boots to leave. They hadn't stomped through endless muddy fields, instead they reflected everything around him. Even the large polished buttons of his jacket gleamed and I could see in them the corridor stretching away behind me. In that moment I took my opportunity and stepped out of the darkness.

'Do you have a boat?' My words were barely audible, nothing more than a nervous whisper, and he gave no acknowledgment of having heard me. I tried to repeat them, but my mouth was too dry and I had to lick my lips before I could loosen the words. I had never spoken to a stranger without permission, and I kept my hands in a hidden clasp behind my back so he couldn't see them tremble. Then I waited without daring to breathe.

He stopped and eyed me curiously. 'What if I do?' His voice came suddenly, as coarse as a brush, and as deep as a cave. I wasn't used to hearing such a sound, and it caused me to shudder.

'I wish to sail to one of the Scatterings. Does your boat go there?' Although my heart was pounding, I tried to keep the panic out of my voice; with a little tilt of my chin, I held his gaze in pretend defiance.

He looked mildly amused at my charade. 'There are hundreds of islands out there. Any one in particular?'

'The City of Water,' I said.

With another tug of his boot, he stood up and stamped his foot inside. 'I will be leaving for the east in three days, but it is a long way and it will cost you a purse bursting with coins.'

He saw my face fall, and I opened my mouth to speak, but I had nothing to offer him. He shook his head again as though I was nothing more than a foolish child who was wasting his time. I had nothing to barter with and he knew it as he opened the door to leave.

'Wait!' I dropped my arms to my sides and rushed forwards, and without thinking I seized his arm.

He turned and paused in the doorway, and I quickly withdrew my hand, more alarmed than him at my sudden outburst. His eyes narrowed suspiciously, but I had at last got his attention again.

I could hear the cogs whirring in his mind, and a flash of mischief appeared in his eyes. 'You could offer me another type of purse, I suppose, and I will fill it for you.' He grinned, revealing a golden tooth, so blindingly bright it was like staring at the sun. I gasped, for the meaning of his words was unmistakable.

Just then I heard a noise behind me and a sudden movement. Reflected in the shine of his top button, I caught a glimpse of Sorren, standing, arms folded in judgement. I felt the scorch of her eyes like a high desert sun.

'Three days,' he repeated. Then he was gone.

Without daring to turn around, I scurried back down to the cellar, but it was too late, Sorren had heard every word.

I thought she would tell Lemàn about my encounter with the captain, but nothing was mentioned. She was keeping my secret, but I didn't know why. Nausea burned in my throat at the thought of giving myself to a demon. Through keyholes, and at soirees, I had seen the whores perform their duties from beneath their ruffles of cloth and layers of fabric, without having to remove a stitch, but it was a risk I wasn't prepared to take. If Lemàn found out – I quickly cast the shameful thought from my mind. I would have to find another way, even if it meant scrubbing the deck, setting the sails, securing the ropes and pulleys or lifting and dropping the anchor. I could sit high on the mast and watch. I would love it up there, like a bird navigating us through the water until we arrived. I had learned enough from the professor's books and stories to be of some use on board a boat. Even if that wasn't enough for the captain I had met, then surely there were other captains and other boats that would agree to my offer. I would just have to find one.

On the eve of my departure, Lemàn helped me pack a small case. There wasn't much to fill it with, besides a few clothes, a sea sponge and a box of marzipan. Sitting on my bed, I watched as she meticulously folded my night-dress again and again until it was small enough to have been mistaken for a handkerchief lying on her lap. Suddenly she began to sob, and I lifted my nightdress to her eyes to wipe away the tears. Falling against her, she wrapped her arms tightly around me. She had always, until this moment, been my protector – my sea wall; my mother – but now my path led me away from her, and we both knew it.

'You can grow your hair,' she said softly, stroking my shorn head, as though that were reason enough to leave.

I remembered all the times I desperately wanted to have long hair. I would creep into the washroom and rummage through the baskets of clothes, pulling out the cleanest pair of stockings I could find. I'd fix them on to the top of my head, holding my nose against the sweaty smell of feet, and I'd let the legs swing down my back like two ponytails, smooth and long and perfect. Now, though, it didn't seem to matter.

Lemàn kissed me so tenderly on the cheek that I had to swallow back the fizz of emotion bubbling its way up my throat.

'I'm afraid,' I mumbled. The words left my mouth unexpectedly.

'What are you afraid of?' she whispered in my ear. I felt her hand lovingly stroke my cheek and I lifted my eyes before finally finding the words.

'I'm afraid of you not being there any more.' She held me then, longer than she had ever done before, and for the first time since I was a child, I fell asleep with the pulse of the blue bird vibrating in my ear.

The tender stroke of Marianne's hand upon my cheek roused me from a deep sleep; she had come to tell us it was time to go. For a moment, I wished I could have stayed there for a hundred years like Sleeping Beauty, but that spell had been broken long ago. I turned to see that Lemàn's eyes were already open and I wondered if she had slept at all.

'I wanted to give you a gift before you leave,' said Marianne, holding out a small object wrapped in pink tissue.

Drowsily, I reached across and took it from her, it felt light in my hand.

'Open it,' she encouraged.

Carefully peeling the tissue back, I found, hidden within its layers, a small oval-shaped hair brush. The intricate design of a peacock had been painted onto the wood; its cobalt-blue body filled the handle and its train fanned into the casing, filling it entirely. Dozens of sparkling eyes of lapis lazuli haloed in a shimmer of jade and dipped in gold stared back at me. I knew that her long, slender hand had made it.

'It's beautiful, thank you,' I murmured.

'The bristles are made of curlew feathers,' she added, smiling.

'But I don't have any hair to brush.'

'No, not now you don't, but soon you will.'

Kneeling in my nest of blankets, I shuffled towards her and flung myself in her arms.

'I just wish I could be there to help you brush it,' said Lemàn, and the three of us held each other for the little time we had left.

I wrapped the brush back in the tissue and placed it in my case on top of my nightdress, a damp reminder of an impossible goodbye. Outside I found twenty-nine whores sobbing into their handkerchiefs. Mourning without a death, a burial without a body. The professor seemed startled by their outpouring and pretended to busy himself straightening his cravat. Before I left, he handed me a red velvet pouch and told me to open it once I'd arrived. Thanking him, I dropped it in my bag.

'Goodbye, Mama.'

Lemàn clung to me like a wild vine and nuzzled into my feathers, her breath so warm and lemony. A familiar comfort that I already missed. 'It's time for you to go and find out who you really are. To find out all the answers I couldn't give you.'

I nodded against her neck.

'Promise me one thing,' she said, suddenly releasing me.

I nodded again, and held her gaze.

'When you find him, tell him I searched for him. Tell him I tried, and let him know that I'm so sorry we ran out of time.' Then she pulled me back towards her and held me for an endless moment.

Looking up, I caught a movement in the upper window of the house; it was Sorren. She hadn't gathered with the others to say goodbye, but she was there watching, palm flat against the glass, her expression unreadable.

Finally, Lemàn released me from her arms, and I was relieved to feel the heavy fabric of my cloak crush down the bulk of my feathers. Once upon a time, when I was a little girl lost to the world, I thought my cloak hid buried treasure, but now I saw this treasure as a curse that I wanted to lift. I thrust my hands in my pockets, which should have been empty, but instead, my fingers brushed against something soft and bulging. Pulling it out, I found it was a purse, heavy with the weight of coins. I gasped in astonishment at the unexpected gift and the enormity of what it meant. There was only one person who could have put it there, but when I looked back at the window she was gone.

The professor and Lemàn stood in the doorway reaching for each other's hands when there was nothing else to hold onto. At a distance, when I was sure they were all too small to be seen, I turned and looked back. All I had ever known was falling away, nothing more than dancing specks of light, shards lost in the wind, blurred by my tears.

CHAPTER 10

Through the fog, the harbour was alive with the chug and chatter of endless vessels. Small tug boats and returning night trawlers bobbed up and down next to the larger, more imposing ships, which stood like magnificent icebergs glistening in the sun. Crates were being thrown between boats and loaded onto carts. The horses, with their slow sulky plod, took them up the hill into town. The high-pitched cries of the gulls mingled with the hurried exchanges between the traders and the merchants. Fearing I was too late, I pushed my way through the impatient crowds with a jostle of elbows, in search of the captain. He was at the far end of the harbour, quickly unwinding a thick coil of rope through his calloused hands. The boat had begun to move.

'Wait!' I yelled, running towards him. 'You said you'd take me with you to The City of Water – don't you remember?'

The look on his face suggested he didn't, but then as I came to a halt, there was a sudden spark of recognition provoking the lustful grin I had seen three days before.

'I have this.' Without hesitation, I lifted out the purse of coins. 'I can pay for my passage, there is more than enough here … check if you don't believe me.' Breathless, I jangled the purse in front of him.

His eyes fell from me to the purse, then he snatched it from my hand, stretched it open, peered inside, and, satisfied, dropped it into his pocket. For one frightful moment, I thought I had lost both the money and my passage, but then to my relief, he reached out his hand. 'Welcome aboard,' he said.

My cabin was airless and cramped, lit only by a kerosene lamp, which swung from a beam, casting strange shadows, which limped across the floor like deranged, tormented creatures. There were two low-slung hammocks hanging from hooks on the walls, but the other was empty. This pleased me, for I could remove my cloak without the fear of questions.

Mostly, I stayed hidden in my cabin, listening to the voices and laughter and the scuttle of ravenous rats, which swilled through the boat. When the waves grew choppy, I could hear the occasional sound of retching from above.

I had a single tin bucket to be used for both washing and for waste, and would hurry onto the deck and fling my dirty water overboard before it stunk out the cabin. Despite this efficiency, the boat still reeked of sweat and damp and sewage. There was no standing headroom below deck, so I spent hours huddled in a ball of hibernation, waiting for the harsh winter months to pass in the dark, damp gut of the boat. Slowly, I emerged from this darkness and began spending more time on deck, breathing in the salty air, and staring in wonder at the vast expanse of sky. I was always sure to wear my cloak then, not just to shield me from the fresh breeze swept up from the waves, but to avoid finding myself on a different kind of boat: a boat of freaks and oddities.

I rarely saw the other passengers – there were not many of us on board – but I heard snatches of their curious conversations. Whispers of canals filled with wishes, shops that only opened at night and so many bridges that a person could easily lose their way, and even suffer from altitude sickness on cloudy days. One man was already bartering with another about the price of a boat; it seemed you couldn't move quickly through the city without one. In amongst all these stories, I kept hearing the same word repeated over and over again. It shone like a bright fruit on a dark tree, or the moon at midnight: mist. Islands of mist, boats of mist and jars of mist. Even though everyone whispered about it, I never heard enough to discover its importance.

There was one woman in particular who caught my eye, always accompanied by a man I presumed to be her husband from the way he held his arm around her waist. I noticed her because of the hat she wore. It was dark blue with a spray of indigo and amber feathers, twirling proudly from its velvet trim. In the sunlight it blazed and sparkled as though it was a firework and I couldn't tear my eyes away. She liked to watch the sea and would turn her face and squeal playfully each time the wind brought a splash of waves to greet her. Marianne had been right; the woman held onto that hat as though it was the most precious thing in the world, and for a moment it made us both feel beautiful.

Heaved across the endless silver blue, the distance between myself and all that I knew lengthened. I could no longer see any patch of the land we had left behind, and the rocky outcrops, which had given me comfort, had all been lost to the deep waves. We were in a watery wilderness with nothing to cling on to and nowhere to drop anchor; we were a tiny capsule at the mercy of the sea. On we floated, guided by the magnetic moon and the turning tide. We could have been lost and I wouldn't have known. I no longer knew if what lay behind was any further away than what lay ahead. My great sense of longing was now borne out of the need for arrival rather than departure. Answers were waiting for me across the water and whatever they were spurred me on. Physically,

I could go no faster than the boat allowed, but my mind had long ago raced ahead.

Every day was the same, and for a while I wondered if we were moving at all. I would climb to the top deck in the hope of seeing something new or something that had changed: a mackerel boat like the ones I'd left behind; the dark fin of a hunting whale, or the straggle of floating seaweed, but there was nothing out there. The sea was empty. Above all, I grew restless for some small sign of land, but no matter how much I squinted into the distance, all I could see was the endless dazzling blue of sea and sky, as indistinguishable as the passing hours.

At night everything turned black. Then, unexpectedly, something did change. I felt it hours before it arrived and I sensed the heaviness in the air. When I asked the captain if there was a storm coming, he thought the journey was making me mad, for when we both looked up at the sky it was sun-spilled and a spotless blue. But I grew uneasy and my feathers ruffled under my cloak, even though there was no wind to move them.

That night I slept fitfully, disturbed by the encroaching prowl of thunder, which nobody else could hear, but me. My feathers kept me awake, chattering and whispering in the dark. I was reminded of once upon a time, when I had been high in my childhood tree wondering if I would be lifted into the air, should I dare to step off the branch. My feathers answered me, but I didn't listen then, and now their warning was even clearer. Finally, in the early hours, I gave up completely on sleep and climbed to the upper deck to empty my bucket. The cool night air was a welcome tonic and I lay down on the salt-splashed deck, relieved that I could still see the stars in the restful sky. Perhaps I had been mistaken, I thought, getting to my feet. Then peering over the side of the boat, I saw that the waves had begun to stir. Troubled, I went back to bed.

It felt like I had only been asleep for a few moments when I was awoken by a loud clunk; the lantern was swinging wildly from its hook, sending a tribal dance of shadows spinning frantically round the cabin. Reaching for my cloak and staggering from my hammock I tried to climb the steps. I had only managed to get about halfway to the top when a sudden jolt knocked me against the wall and I tumbled to the floor, landing with a heavy thud. I could hear the chaos exploding from above. This time I crawled up the steps on my hands and knees and pushed open the door. As soon as I did, a vicious torrent whipped me across the deck, just as we plunged into the watery darkness. I managed to reach for the bottom of the mast and clung on as we flew upwards just long enough to fill our lungs with air before the dark water swallowed us up again. I heard the shout of the captain and searched for him through stinging eyes. He threw me a rope and, not letting it slip from my fingers, I secured myself to the mast, wrapping it three times round my waist and fastened it in a double knot, as he had taught me on the first night. The storm did its worst, raging without mercy. I scrunched my eyes closed, and held on tight. There was nothing else to do, but wait to see what survived.

By morning we were balanced again, mournful in the water. For a while I couldn't loosen my grip; my fingers were tight and stiff with pain. The boat, although broken and bruised and splintered in places, had survived. The sea and the sky shone clear and steady as the captain and the crew set about fixing the deck with hammer and nail. I helped to unfurl the sail, tattered and torn at its edges, like a broken wing, and together we did our best, until the sail caught the wind again.

I searched for the woman with the hat, and eventually I found her standing at the very end of the boat. This time though, she wore no hat, and her hair hung loose and flat. She was sobbing into the shoulder of her husband and I wondered if they were tears at having lost something so beautiful.

'Don't worry,' I heard him say, 'I will find you another.'

'I don't want another,' she protested; 'I want the one I lost.'

'Then I shall have to buy you a jar of mist instead.' He took her hand and pressed it to his lips.

She returned his gesture with a smile. 'I hope we're in time.'

I wondered then if this mysterious mist was some sort of magical remedy, a cure for disappointment. I reached under my cloak to where I knew my feathers grew long and smooth and shone the colour of sunlight through honey. I gave one a sharp tug, and felt it loosen into my hand. Soundlessly, I approached her and she looked up through her tears. I held out the feather and she stared at it in confusion.

'Take it ... it's for you,' I urged. There was surprise in her eyes, and then slowly she did as I asked. 'You can wear it in your next hat.'

'Thank you,' she said quietly, with a flicker of a smile. Gazing at it, her eyes were filled with admiration. 'But why are you giving it to me?'

'Because you reminded me that feathers are beautiful,' I replied.

I knew she might ask me where I had found it, so by the time she looked up I had hurried away to save myself from the lie I would have to tell.

Wind-raw and salt-parched, I closed my eyes and must have drifted off to sleep. When I opened them again, something was circling high above me. Blinking against the glare of the sun, the shadow seemed to grow bigger. Shielding my eyes, I could see a curve of silver, like a splinter of moon. For a moment, I thought the storm had shaken it from its hook in the sky and sliced it into tumbling pieces. But instead of falling, the shape soared and I realised then what it was.

'Captain!' I called excitedly. 'Look! Up there!'

The captain glanced upwards just as the gull screeched sharply and flew into the distance.

'We're not far from land now,' he yelled, his swollen belly juggling with relief and too much rum. Heaving the nets to one side, he started to work on the shattered prow. 'How did you hear that storm hours before it broke? You must have the instincts of a bird.'

I smiled at how right he was. Like my pine cones, I had always been sensitive to the weather. On my walks with Professor Elms l always knew when the rain was coming and how heavy it would fall. I didn't just look like a bird; I thought like one too.

Then came the mist, dancing around us on its tiptoes. It thinned and swirled then thinned again, weaving an ancient potion, shaking us loose and wrapping us up and sweeping us along as though we were the missing ingredient. Then came the drift of smoke and something familiar and sweet, like pine resin or jars of jam and summer honey like the ones stored outside Sorren's door. It was a relief from the constant smell of damp and sweat and salty fish, which had swilled around my lungs for far too long.

Floating closer, I began to make out the murmur of ghostly shapes, spied briefly through the vapours that reared up like sea monsters from the depths below. Hypnotic shapes, sirens of the deep, twisting and tempting us closer until arrival was no longer a choice but instead a compulsion. Whenever the mist magically lifted, like the lid of a secret trinket box, it revealed towers and domes and sloping roofs trembling beneath a delicate lavender-coloured sky. Ribbons of twilight tied themselves around the tallest towers, delivering the city like a wrapped gift, ready to open. A place of half-water and half-land swelling and shrinking, being cast like a spell, right before my eyes. It felt like we were drifting through the hushed conversations of lovers in the evening. Spires rose like masts, its domed roofs like sails caught on the wind. It was as though someone had packed the whole place – its people and belongings – on to the deck of a majestic ship, ready to set sail at a moment's notice. Should someone discover its secrets it stayed on the run.

I stared in open-mouthed wonder. What was this place? It was more exquisite, more bewitching, more enchanting than I could ever have imagined. My eyes weren't big enough to take it all in and I was afraid to blink in case it all vanished like a dream. I wanted desperately to brush my fingertips against its walls, for my feet to balance on its stone steps, as though touching it might somehow make it seem more real and long-lasting. Like a cake, you had to taste it to know how delicious it was.

Trust you to fall in love with a sinking city, Lemàn had said before I left.

I had laughed at her words then, but now with the city floating before me, I was no longer sure. Was it quivering in fear or excitement? Was I?

Finally, came a tiny jangle, like the sound of the bell above the sweet shop door in the marketplace. I always imagined what it would be like to sneak inside and explore its multi-coloured edible wishes. Drifting closer, the sound grew louder, like the clink of glass against glass, a thousand flutes toasting an evening's celebration. The captain steered us slowly into the sheltered waters of the lagoon, gliding towards the fast approaching walls of buildings with their crumbling balconies and shuttered windows. We slipped into the shade of a small canal and the captain tied the boat to a mooring pole, its restless spirit stilled.

Spellbound, we had finally arrived.

CHAPTER 11

This was where we parted. The captain and his small crew stomped away in search of a night of revelry and mayhem. There was no backward glance, my money had bought my passage and nothing more. The other passengers scattered like breadcrumbs until I was left quite alone, standing by the side of the canal in a fast-darkening city. I could follow them or find my own way. For a while I hid in a doorway, uncertain of what to do or which way to go. My body still seemed to sway from the endless days upon the floating vessel, and I waited for everything to steady. Finally, a distant clock chimed, summoning me from my musing, and, hood up, head down, I drifted into the city.

The smell was different here; it wasn't the cool, woody air, which reddened my cheeks and followed me home from the fields. Here the air carried something heavy and rich and warm: a dark infusion of intimacy; a lover's bedroom.

Heart aflutter, I meandered down streets that tunnelled and twisted into the depths of this magical place, grateful for the solitude I found there. I had left behind a muddy, muffled world, a place of grey and gloom, with damp corners and clogged chimney pots. Now I had stumbled into a city of sunset reds and pie-crust browns; of summer-baked apricots and dancing golden coins all reflected in the shimmering water. The brightness twirled and spun all around me like a lollipop. Buildings crumbled from both sides of the canals, and where one ended and another began, it was impossible to tell. Every stone seemed to cling to another, refusing to let go, out of fear or love, desperate for something. I let my eyes marvel and wonder at the doors that opened straight into the water. How strange, I thought – if there were no boats, what would the occupants do; just swim away? Bridges appeared out of nowhere; some were so small that I had barely set foot upon them before I had reached the other side; others were almost vertical, snatching at my breath as I climbed to their summits. Captivity had made me weak, but now as I walked and watched and listened, I could feel the energy pulse and release, flowing through my bones. I was stretching into life.

So far, I hadn't passed a single person; the streets were deserted. Beneath the dusky fast-falling shroud of twilight, everything seemed watchful. My bearings had been snatched away like a net of trawled fish, but I felt no fear now, only a nervous excitement.

It was time to find my father and to do that I had to go back to the beginning, I had to find the Uccello Hotel. I don't know what I expected to find after all this time, maybe nothing, but he had been there before and perhaps he would go there again. Maybe someone remembered him; a man with wings and burnished feathers would be impossible to forget. I had memorised its location from Lemàn's description and the professor's maze of maps.

I plunged back into the infinite alleys and strode across the squares, stopping only once near a wall of wisteria, to get my bearings before racing off again, using the water as my navigation point. My heart quickened with each step, until I crossed a bridge and headed down to where the canal ran at its widest. I knew that the market-place should be just up ahead, and was relieved to see the empty stalls still stained with streaks of fish oil and the dark canopies resting above them. By my reckoning, the hotel should have been some way back, behind the Church of One Hundred Souls, but somehow, I had missed it. Across the water, I could make out the warm lights and hear the welcoming laughter of people, yet there was no bridge to take me there. I had gone wrong somewhere, but where? There was no sign of the church and churches don't just pack up their pews and vanish into thin air.

Disappointed, I carried on. The water was never far away, occasionally spilling onto the flagstones in dancing, frothy pools, and, even when it couldn't be seen, I could still hear it murmuring against the stones. It had the steady breath of a dreamer. In my mind The City of Water was never silent.

The first person I saw was a man with a wizard's beard; he was polishing the handle of a vivid indigo-blue door, so bright it made me gasp in wonder. I was certain it was one of the wishing doors Professor Elms had spoken of, but I wasn't brave enough to ask the man despite his friendly face. I still wasn't used to questioning strangers.

Ahead of me, a street came into view. Some of the shops here still had their doors open, but the shopkeepers were slowly gathering themselves in for the evening like autumn fruit, and the bristles of darkness swept people away.

A woman with a face the colour of a saddle shouted as I waited to pass. She was rummaging in a basket filled with vibrant pomegranates, polishing them against the hem of her skirt, which was as filthy as the ground she sat upon. Without stopping, a man tossed a coin at her feet and she smiled a toothless grin and threw a fruit towards him. He caught it in the air; a playful, timeless ritual and much rehearsed. Smiling, I did the same, and the fruit felt smooth and warm in my hand.

'Uccello Hotel?' I asked hopefully.

She waved the way up ahead and I wasn't sure if she was being dismissive or helpful. 'Beware of temptation,' she rasped, gathering her shawls around her shoeless feet, as tiny as matchboxes.

Endlessly the alleyways wrapped around each other like thin, stretched hollow bones. The further in I walked, the more the silence grew, but I had to keep going. There was no sign of the Uccello Hotel and by now the night was throwing out its confetti of stars in celebration of the darkness. The alleyways wound even narrower, and in places the width between one building and another was so small, I grazed my shoulders trying to squeeze through. I felt more and more uncertain of where I was going. Then something up ahead made me stop and gasp and clutch at my cloak; it looked like a ghost. Suddenly it flapped towards me and I laughed in relief, realising it was just a bed sheet strung up between two iron balconies.

Occasionally I would see lights flare over doorways, but mostly it was sinister and murky. Every city had a darker side, and this one seemed to be no exception. A little way up, to my relief, I saw that both street and canal widened, allowing two or even three people to now walk side by side without bruising themselves. From here I could see that the water stretched into the open sea. In the lamplit doorway of an inn, women stood in huddled whispers. Here at least, the darkness was perfumed, warm and inviting. Perhaps, at last, I would find a place to stay.

Rushing forwards, I was aware of something resting on the water. It was a boat, large and looming and strangely familiar. As my eyes fell to the gold-leaf lettering, I felt my feathers ruffle and lift as their meaning became clear. My heart quickened, lurched and then stopped completely – in front of me was The Boat of Floating Freaks and Oddities, close enough to touch. What was it doing here? Had it followed me? But I shook the ridiculous idea from my head, like a rotten apple from a tree. It had been years since I had last seen the boat come to shore and pitch its giant circus tent at the edge of the forest. Whatever reason the boat had for being here, it wasn't anything to do with me, yet it still made me afraid. Stumbling back into the dark, I turned on my heel, and, with my cloak flapping behind me like a giant wing, I fled as fast as I could.

My legs finally gave way and I fell panting against a damp wall. Unable to straighten, I searched for a place to hide and staggered into the dark, shallow depths of an alcove. Each ragged, panicky breath caused another stab in my chest and each one made me grimace in pain. When my breathing finally slowed, I cast a furtive glance over my shoulder and slipped back into the endless, empty street. It wasn't long before I sensed I was being followed, but every time I turned around, all I saw were shadows vanishing into the darkness. I hurried my pace, hoping to lose my pursuer and when I paused to listen for footsteps, all was silent. Perhaps it had just been the echo of my own.

Just then, a man hurtled out of the gloom towards me. Startled, I cried out and nearly lost my balance before he quickly side-stepped out of my way, with a mutter of apology. Clutched to his chest there was a large jar, and inside danced a strange swirling mist. It was just like the one I had seen years ago in the jar in Lemàn's room, and I wondered what it was, but, before I could ask, he was gone. The pursuer or the pursued. A love lost or a love found.

Up ahead, the alleyway widened again, and I found myself back in the empty market square. I had gone around in circles and my search for the Uccello Hotel would have to wait. Exhausted I needed to find a place to sleep.

Across the watery darkness, a luminous street of shops welcomed me, but I couldn't reach them; they were too far away. Something scuttled then, a rat or a beggar, or worse. I whirled round just as a hand shot out like a serpent's tongue, empty and cupped, awaiting my pity. Impatient, it tore at my ankle and as I tried to shake it off, I stumbled backwards and lost my footing.

I remember falling, fast.

I remember an icy blast.

And after that, I remember nothing at all.

CHAPTER 12

Slowly opening my eyes, I half expected to find myself lying in my old bed, in my old room, in my old world, but everything seemed strange and unfamiliar. I was surrounded by low, crooked walls on all sides but one; this instead was made of glass, allowing the light to flood in. Through it I could see the city's roofs rising half-formed and still drowsy, the thick mist slow to lift like the veil of a shy bride. My whole body ached, but I couldn't remember why. A small scratching sound made me turn my head, and I came face to face with a peacock standing only inches from my face. It was peering at me with mild curiosity before all interest quickly dissipated and it strutted off through an open glass door, which I could see now led into a small courtyard. The peacock reminded me of Marianne's parting gift and the overwhelming memory of home made my throat constrict.

As I tried to sit up, my head pounded and it took several moments to blink in my strange new surroundings. The room seemed large compared to the dimensions of the sullen little cabin I had grown so accustomed to, and I quickly realised how full of dust it was, and how stacked with clutter. Towers of books rose precariously in piles, some of which had already collapsed and spilled across the floor like stepping stones. Scattered on the shelves were boxes of candles and pots bursting with flowers and jars of herbs tied in loose, powdery bundles. A straw hat lay upside down on a rickety chair in the far corner, so large I could have curled up and gone to sleep in its crown. The peacock was now outside preening himself in a pale puddle of sunlight. His tail feathers shone with the magnificence of a stained-glass window – no wonder he expected to be worshipped! Then the sudden and unexpected grunting sound of other unseen animals and the warm breath of straw drifted in on the breeze. It reminded me of the farms behind the whorehouse, and the surge of another memory was too much.

A sudden flicker of movement startled me, and, glancing up, I realised I was staring into a large mirror on a wooden swivel, and at a reflection that was as unfamiliar as everything else in the room. It was me, but it wasn't. The jumble of my feathers was in such a state, it looked as though I had been mauled by a cat, and left for dead. If I had had wings they would have been broken beyond repair. But what astonished me, more than anything else, was my hair. It fell in soft curls like a half-peeled orange around my ears and I hadn't even noticed. I had never known myself with hair before and it looked strange. It felt butter-soft and beautiful beneath my fingertips, and I suddenly thought of all the glittery hairpins spilled across Lemàn's dressing table and how lovely they would look now, fastened in my hair. Professor Elms had been right – there are many ways to measure time without a clock – and although I had lost count of the number of days we had been at sea, the length of my curls told me it must have been many.

All sound came from outside, but it was a deceptive quiet within, because all of a sudden I heard a loud scrape as though something heavy was being moved across the stone floor of an adjacent room, followed by a moment of silence.

'Rest!' bellowed a voice from somewhere in the depths of the house, but no one came.

I reached for the bed sheets and pulled them up around my chin as the heavy thud, thud, thud of footsteps pounded closer. Each one made the shelves shake and sent another book toppling to the floor; even the candles rattled fearfully in their boxes. For a moment, I was reminded of the giants in Lemàn's stories and I squeezed my eyes tightly shut. When I opened them again, I saw a bear of a woman standing in front of me. Hands on hips, she seemed to fill the room entirely.

'Where's the boat?' I mumbled. Something half-formed flashed in my mind, but I wasn't sure quite what it was.

'You must rest,' she repeated, kindly this time. Her eyes were lit with the mischief of a child and shone an astonishing blue, like hyacinth blooms gathered after the rain; her skin wrinkled dark like damp sand, and her hair was husky-thick. She could have been a century old or the age of a new mother; it was quite impossible to tell.

Overcome with dizzy fatigue, I sank back against the pillows. Satisfied that I was at last obeying her request, she tucked the sheet firmly around my shoulders with such affection, it made me ache.

'You remind me of my mother,' I whispered, my voice weak and hoarse.

'I hope that is a good thing.' As she smiled, her face shone with kindness.

'It is.' I smiled too, and closed my eyes.

Next time, it was the smell of sizzling tomatoes and herbs that roused me from my slumber; someone was cooking. Ravenous, I lifted myself from my pillow and instinctively reached for my cloak, but only my boots sat on the floor and next to them my bag. A quick rummage inside revealed what I already knew; my cloak must have been lost in the water. I pulled the edges of the bed sheet towards me and wrapped myself in its folds. Then, swinging my legs onto the floor, I followed the smell. It led me down a small sun-coloured corridor into an even smaller clutter of a kitchen. The woman was busy stoking the coals in a tiny stove. She greeted me without turning around.

'Feeling better?'

'Yes – much better – thank you.'

'You must be hungry,' she grunted.

Without waiting for a reply, she slid a plate of sardines in tomato sauce across the table. It was fish – my favourite – but how did she know? I took it as an invitation to sit down. I ate noisily using my fingers until there was nothing left but a watery red slurp of oil. Then she took a chunk of bread, ripped a piece off and handed it to me.

'Mop up the juice, it's the tastiest bit,' she encouraged, her eyes open wide and eager.

'Thank you,' I said shyly, doing as she instructed until I had polished the plate clean.

'What happened to me?' I asked, when I had finished.

'I found you in the water,' she replied by way of explanation.

I shuddered at the returning memory; of the boat and the hand in the dark and then of falling.

'So, you pulled me out of the canal?'

She nodded. 'You weren't in there long; not long enough for the cold to get into your bones, so I brought you here, stripped you down and wrapped you in every blanket I could find. I see you have forgotten to take one off.' She chuckled.

I suddenly felt aware of my feathers, mangled and damp beneath the flimsy sheet, and I felt exposed in the edges of this tiny space. Even though this stranger seemed to fill every room she was in, somehow my feathers felt even bigger.

'Did you find the cloak I was wearing?' I asked, wondering if she had perhaps pegged it up somewhere to dry.

She shook her head. 'Just your bag, which thankfully you dropped on the side before you fell in.'

I realised then that my cloak had been lost to the watery darkness and, sensing my unease, she spoke to reassure me. 'Believe me, I have pulled stranger than you from these waters. Ha – the sights I have seen!' She chuckled again, lifted her own plate's mountain of fish and tipped the whole lot straight into her mouth. In one gurgling gulp it was gone and a dribble of tomato and oil fell off her chin and back onto the plate. Quick as a cat, she slurped it up and then belched and pressed her hand hard against her chest as though to dislodge some stubborn bone.

'Right then – let's sort those feathers of yours out.'

Before I had time to protest, she flung the bed sheet into the corner and began tugging at my back with her large, rough hands. There was none of the tenderness of the whores here. She worked quickly, unknotting and smoothing the feathers as though they were the tangled nets of fishermen, until at last they lay flat against my skin.

'Ouch,' I yelped more than once, but each cry went ignored. She whistled while she worked, and, with each pull and tug, I clenched my teeth and winced against the pain, waiting for it to be over.

'They are in such a state,' she tutted to herself.

When she had finally finished, she pulled the bench closer to the stove, I wasn't sure she'd be able to squeeze herself into any chair, without having to pop back out again like a cork. She told me to sit with my back to the coals so as to dry my feathers back into shape.

'Thank you,' I murmured. 'For saving me.'

She nodded. 'You are not the first I have saved, and you won't be the last.'

'What time is it?' I asked, suddenly alarmed. I hadn't given up on my search for the Uccello Hotel and, after yesterday, I knew it wouldn't be an easy one.

'If you need to go to the market, you're too late. All you'll find there now are the ragged, rotten remains of vegetables and piles of stinking fish, no use to anybody but the hunger-scarred cats. Whatever it is you want to buy, I'm afraid it will have to wait until tomorrow.'

'I don't need to go to the market, and I don't need to buy anything. I'm looking for—' I hesitated. I wasn't sure if I could trust her with more. A life lived in a cellar had made me wary.

'You are a stranger in this city.' More statement than question.

I nodded.

Her calm eyes took me in then with their peculiar purple-blue stare. Hot under her gaze, I shifted around uncomfortably. She seemed to be contemplating something important, like I was a riddle that she would win a prize for solving. I remained silent, leaving her to her thoughts. My own eyes scanned the room, distracted at once by a tiny window, a crumbling thick square set deep into the wall, more like a delivery hatch. It was so low that anyone wanting to see in or out would have to crouch down or drop to their knees. I saw then what had really caught my attention, for a small bird had settled on the ledge outside. Tilting my head, I saw it glistening with the faint misty rain which it carried on its feathers. It peered inside and it fixed me with its single, dark inquisitive stare.

All of a sudden and quite unexpectedly she reached out across the table and grabbed my upper arm between her large thumb and finger and squeezed in a pincer-like movement. I cried out, but before I could twist away, she had already released me.

'Hmm,' she pondered for a moment. 'Follow me.'

Rubbing at my arm, red from her rough inspection, I followed her through the low-ceiling rooms. She seemed to have to stoop to pass through them until we arrived in the square courtyard, open to the sky, where she straightened with an audible creak. The peacock lifted its haughty head briefly, and then resumed pecking at his seed tray; he had already dismissed me once. She led me towards a small pen in the corner, and, lounging within it, were half a dozen scraggy-looking dogs.

'These are my most beloved possessions! My boys!' she exclaimed, lifting the latch and swinging open the gate. 'Like you, I pulled them from the canal. Someone had tied them up in a sack and slung them in the water to drown.' The sound of her voice roused the sleeping creatures and they began to lift their heads and sniff the air with their wet inquisitive noses. Two of them yawned and stretched out their long taut limbs before staggering to their feet, still groggy from their nap. The others followed until they were all clustered around her, nuzzling against her legs, as she tickled them one by one under their chins, smoothing back their ears and kissing their glistening noses with such adoration, you would think they were her children. She introduced them one by one: Vorias, Levantes, Notias, Zephyros, Afros and Vithos. This was the most knotted, matted pack of dogs I had ever seen, and I felt my nose scrunch in disgust as they slobbered and panted against her ears and mouth. She clearly relished their affection and did nothing to discourage them.

Sliding the lid off a wooden tub, she pulled out a large sack and emptied the contents onto the ground; half-gnawed bones, apple cores, hard-boiled eggs, chunks of slimy carrots and wilted cabbage leaves. The dogs bounded in delight, and sloshed their way through the rotting debris, while I hid my nose from the stench of decay that spread through the courtyard and drifted high beyond its walls.

'I used to bring in boats piled high with fruit from the Island of Verde, and fill my wheelbarrow with fresh cuts of meat from the farmers' market, but they turned their noses up at all of it, preferring this instead ... unbelievable!' She chuckled to herself. 'Now I wait under restaurant windows for them to throw out their leftovers, catching them in my nets and hauling them back home.'

It wasn't long until the ground had been licked clean. After filling their bellies, the dogs squeezed back through the gate and collapsed onto their straw bed from the effort of it all, apart from the littlest one, which splayed itself out across the warmth of my feet, its skin as soft and smooth as a mushroom. Looking down, I watched as it flickered its enviably long eyelashes at me, content at having found itself a new bed.

'That's Vithos. He was the runt of the litter, never really grew from being a puppy. You're lucky – he likes you. He doesn't trust people easily, and never so quickly.' Her mouth widened in sudden delight, as though a prayer had at last been answered. 'So – when can you start?'

I shuffled my feet and tried to flick him off, but despite his size, he was a heavy weight and refused to move. I heard him grumble. She laughed, and scooping him up, nestled him back with the others.

'Excuse me?' I asked in confusion. 'When can I start what?'

130

'The job. It comes with a bed, of course – the one you woke up in, which I think you found most agreeable considering how many hours you've been sleeping in it. I promise you it's a better offer than the guest houses you'll find round here with their flea-infested beds and extortionate prices. They make the young lovers weep!'

'What exactly is the job?' I had no idea what I was being offered, not that I was in a position to refuse.

'I need someone to take the dogs for a daily walk. At least an hour, longer in the rain, but times can be negotiated. I would do it myself, but I carry too much weight to go far now. I have the speed, just not the stamina.' She sighed wistfully. 'It's not that I am afraid to feel pain, my body is too old to feel anything else, but I just cannot keep up with them any more.'

I had no experience of dogs. I had seen them before on the farm, but I had never touched one before, never mind taken one for a walk. She must have seen the look of doubt in my face and raised her eyebrows.

'It's a good deal I'm offering, but if you'd rather pay for a bed, then I won't keep you here. You can wake up with your pockets empty and your legs bitten to incurable infection and I won't say I told you so.'

'Yes,' I exclaimed with a sudden shudder; my mind was made up. 'I'll take it. I'll take the job.' Besides, they looked peaceful and gentle enough, and what choice did I have if I wanted to stay? The coins left in my pocket might buy me a night or two, but not much more.

'Good,' she said, clapping her bear-like paws together. 'After all, you will be staying for quite some time.'

'How do you know that?' I asked, startled. I hadn't mentioned my plans to her and I had no idea how long it would take me to find my father, or even if he was here to be found.

'I know most things, most of the time. It's my gift; some may say my curse.'

'Who are you?' I asked in astonishment.

'My name is Sybel. Come back inside, and I will tell you the rest.'

CHAPTER 13

Slowly, she unfolded her story like a tablecloth, shaking out every last crumb.

I learned that she was a prophetess, able to speak the future truth and deliver messages to eager ears. She was also a woman of ancient alchemy, trained to mix secret remedies to heal both the body and the mind. With others, she shared only their benefits, but never their ingredients. Querents paid fistfuls of coins for a reading and they travelled from neighbouring Scatterings to hear their fate spoken from her lips, such was its certainty.

'They want to tax me,' she said, in a sudden flurry of angry words, glad to have someone to rant to.

'Who does?' I had heard the whores talk of taxes in the same fierce, outraged tones, but I didn't really understand what they meant.

'The city officials, such fools! They daren't, though,' she spoke in conspiratorial whispers. 'Most of them are my querents. It's all a ridiculous pretence, but it's a tiring act, and I have no patience for it. Sometimes, when people can't afford to pay, I accept a meal, or a jug of wine; once or twice it's been a nest of quail eggs or a peacock, who you have already met. One old woman handmade me a silk dress, the colour of forget-me-nots, far too small and delicate for my monstrous frame. I don't know what she saw, but it wasn't me.' She looked down at her body and shook her head in dismay. 'It just hangs, never worn, on a hook and I often look at it and imagine myself, one-day-beautiful, wearing it to the Teatro or walking over the Bridge of Longing, hand in hand with the lover I will never have.' Her wistful voice suddenly filled with frustration. 'How can you put a price on that? How can you tax gifts of kindness, gestures, hope? It's an absolute disgrace! A folly!' she exclaimed in a burst of emotion.

I remembered the whores being infuriated every time a man dressed in a dark suit, carrying a leather case, arrived and was led down the corridor to Sorren's room. It was the only time a man ever departed with more coins than he arrived.

I wanted to tell her that finding love could make her just as miserable as not finding it, but what did I really know of love, having lived my whole life in the shadow-swilled cellar of a whorehouse? It was the one place where love was definitely not welcome, whether it wiped its feet on the doormat or not.

The copper pot started to babble and spit on the stove, and she quickly lifted it up, soothing its contents into two large cups. Dark and steaming, it looked like melted treacle. I inhaled its warm, nutty smell.

'Drink,' she instructed.

As I did, my eyes widened; it tasted bitter at first, then thick with a sweet aftertaste. Blowing into the cup I watched the dark liquid dance in its brown ruffles, but before I had finished, Sybel stood up.

'The dogs need a run around the city,' she said, unhooking a long, thick rope from the wall and untangling its complicated loops and knots.

'Around the city?' My blood ran cold. I had been so used to hiding that the thought of leaving the house filled me with fear.

'Well, you can't very well just walk them around the courtyard.' She chortled, working with speed and deftness until she had shaken out all of the complications. I could see now that in her hand she held a rein, attached to which were six collars.

Although Sybel had seen my feathers and felt them in her hands, they still made me feel shameful, and, sensing my reluctance, she unhooked one of her gigantic patch-work coats from the back of the door and offered it to me. It was of pantomime proportions and drowned me immediately as I lifted it over my shoulders, covering me from head to toe. It carried a smell of damp and loss, and wearing it made me feel like a dull clown. Nonetheless its heaviness offered me the secrecy I craved and I didn't complain. Without my cloak, there was little choice.

She marched out into the yard with me and the rope trailed behind her; she flung it like a net over the dogs. After safely harnessing each one, she then passed the end of the rope to me.

'Don't worry, they know their way.'

The dogs, alert to their freedom, were not about to miss an opportunity, and yelping in delight they lunged forward through the iron gates without any hesitation.

'They haven't been out for a while, so they might be a bit ... excitable!' called Sybel, but it was too late; I was long gone.

Any hope of finding the Uccello Hotel quickly vanished in a whisk of paws and dust and the sound of panting dogs; all I could do was hold on tight. The street, although barely wide enough for the dogs to pass side by side, didn't slow them down. Their skin skimmed the walls and I was dragged behind at such speed that I stumbled into sun-splashed squares, before plunging back into the narrow shadows of dark and winding alleyways. I felt as if I was back on the boat suffering the storm. If I had hoped to savour the magic of the place, I was sadly mistaken for there was no time for reflection. They whirled me around the city, stopping only once at a marble fountain, just long enough to quench their thirst. Then we were off again.

They ran like prize-winning racing dogs, ears back, paws scarcely touching the ground. People veered off into doorways and alcoves, shrieking and shouting. A man walking a dog of his own raised his fists and shook them in the air, angry at nearly being toppled head first into the canal. A pair of black cats, in a quiet game of seduction, were quickly parted; the first scaled a wall and arched its back with a hiss, the other quivered into a crevice, its tail flicking behind in obvious annoyance. They led me out beyond the city to a long wide stretch of pavement running alongside the open water. In the distance, I could make out the rise and fall of land, smaller islands shimmering on the horizon. Up ahead, a series of steps rose steeply. In no mood for climbing, the dogs turned a corner with such speed and surprise that I scraped my elbow on the wall and almost fell to the ground. Tumbling back into the maze of streets, I felt the reins slacken and eventually they slowed to a gentle pace. I could finally breathe and my senses returned and things became familiar once more: the bakery on the corner, the window box filled with geraniums the colour of late afternoon, the door down the street with the muddy boots drying on the step, a sudden aching reminder of home. Then at last, Sybel's crumbling wisteria-covered wall and the iron gates, standing open to welcome us back.

Exhausted, I flopped onto the bed, glad not to have sustained any serious injuries, but just a few sore muscles.

My hair felt knotted between my fingers and no amount of tugging seemed to loosen them. Bending down, I opened my case; the contents spilled out in a jumble and I had to rummage around before I could find my hair brush. Just as I clasped the smooth handle, my eye glimpsed something lying on the floor; it was the red pouch Professor Elms had given me. Lifting it up, I already knew what was inside from its shape and weight and as I emptied it onto the bed, the professor's pocket watch slipped out like a tiny heart with no beat left inside. I held it in my hand for a moment, and then put it on top of the pouch and laid it down on the table right next to my pillow. The professor had given it to me, hoping that I would be able to set it to trigger a memory of my own one day. It was then that the enormity of leaving home settled upon me, and I felt a tear escape and roll down the side of my face into my hair.

As though she could hear my thoughts, Sybel's voice startled me from another room. 'Don't worry, you are right where you need to be.'

Yes, I thought, but I still miss everything that I left behind.

CHAPTER 14

After revealing my feathers to Sybel, or rather, after having discovered them for herself, she hadn't questioned them at all, and for that I was so grateful. They hadn't seemed strange to her and I was learning quickly that things in this city were different, and nothing here was hidden away. Being towed through the streets by half a dozen panting dogs didn't cause a stir, unless of course we got in someone's way. But I had grown up as a secret and it felt too soon for my feathers to be on display; I hadn't forgiven them for sprouting from my skin. I still heard the loud jeers and mockery of the circus tent, and, after all this time, they still couldn't be silenced.

Unable to convince me that there was no risk involved, Sybel found a long white strip of gauze and bandaged my feathers down until I could hardly breathe. Now I would be free to conceal my secret under thinner, much cooler, fabric. But it was my mind I needed to heal, and the flow of shame that I needed to staunch and suture. Always, at the last moment, I would still unhook Sybel's clown-like coat from its peg in the kitchen and slip it over my shoulders: a comfort I wasn't yet ready to cast off.

In the warm hush of the kitchen, where secrets were tempted out of their hiding place, I shared my story with Sybel. Lighting the darkness, I told her about Lemàn and the whorehouse and of Sorren who had been the one, in the end, to buy me my freedom. Friend or foe? I still didn't know the secrets she kept. Her story remained untold, but I knew one thing for sure; the petticoat I had seen in her hand that day didn't belong to any doll. I spoke fondly of Professor Elms and finally I told her what it was that had brought me here – the search for my father – but she had already sensed it, in that all-knowing way of hers. If anything, she seemed to have been expecting me.

'I do not really know who I am without him,' I said.

'Then you must find him and your answers.'

'But where is he? I asked.

'The Sky-Worshippers are difficult to find,' she admitted with a heavy sigh. 'They sometimes come to the city market, but no one knows when, not even me.'

'Do you know a place called the Uccello Hotel?' I asked. It was the only starting point I had.

She pondered for a while, then shook her head. 'I don't think I do … it doesn't sound familiar.'

The disappointment showed on my face, and she offered immediate solace just as Lemàn would have done.

'Perhaps it's changed its name. Names are interchangeable here, as you know. It could have become another fancy restaurant to please the visitors who have started to flood this city, even more than the water. What else do you know of him?' she persisted.

The risk of loss was greater if I didn't reveal what I knew, so after some hesitation I told her as much as I could. I told her of Lemàn's glimpse of him in a marketplace and I told her of migrating birds and of the cradle of warm wings. I didn't need to tell her my father was more bird than anything else, and, besides, I wasn't even sure if that was the truth. She could read between the lines, even if the space left between them was so small you needed a magnifying glass to see what was there. Sybel could read the letters before the words had even been written.

I grew silent for a while, wondering if I had revealed too much – Sybel was a stranger, yet she didn't feel like one. She felt as soft and safe as the mother I had left behind. But I was so used to being hidden away, unseen and unheard that I suddenly felt like an open wound exposed, despite the bandages I wore. I shrank back into myself and Sybel again sensed my fear and filled my pause with her own secrets. Her story became my tourniquet.

She explained that she hadn't always lived here; some years before, she had fled 'The Third Plague' of her city. It had devoured the people in their hundreds and those who had survived were left scarred and forever haunted by the horror they had seen. Houses lay deserted, filled with bones and dust. Rotting carcasses of dogs and cattle lined the roads and the air had the fetid stench of death that lingered, clawing at your throat. Everyone knew someone who had died. Few lived. Sybel lost her grandmother and her mother to the disease. She had lost her father years before, when he had left to fight in the forgotten war and never returned. Although her mother half expected him to walk back through the door one day and still kept his slippers warming by the fire, Sybel knew it wouldn't happen. She had seen it in a vision; his body cold and sprawled in a ditch, an empty socket where his eye used to be. Her mother had struck her across the face at hearing her describe what she had seen, but her grandmother nodded knowingly and soothed her sobs against her chest. She had seen it too; it was a gift they shared. Huge pits were dug just outside the city walls to collect the dead. With no one left to love, Sybel knew she must leave, and even though the city was under quarantine, one night she crept away.

'I left with few possessions,' she said. 'What I had, I carried in a drawstring bag upon my back. A favourite teapot the colour of summer, several bundles of my grandmother's healing herbs and my father's slippers, still warm from the fire.' She paused in memory. 'I don't know why I took them really; perhaps because they were the only thing left of his. In my pocket I had a wooden comb, and a small silver mirror. I cared about the way I looked back then. That was it; it wasn't much, but it was enough. I left most of my memories behind; they were too heavy for me to carry. I hid my heart in a place so deep that the thickets grew over it and I tried to forget I ever knew how to love. Then the dogs came and snuffled it out.'

She told me about the morning when a boat carrying spices from the east dropped its anchor in the harbour and she saw her chance of escape. When she was sure there was no one watching, she gathered up her shawls and her courage and crept on board. Like me, she sailed out of the harbour and for many days the sea became her home. By the time they discovered her, it was too late; there was no turning back. They threatened to leave her in the next port, so that evening she prepared a magnificent stew from what she could salvage from the storage barrels below deck. Then, unfastening one of the bundles of herbs, she sprinkled in her magic, and served the men their supper. The meal silenced them and they ate without chatter. Sybel watched with a satisfied smile on her face; she knew they wouldn't be dropping her anywhere after that. It was only upon seeing the silver domes of this city decorating the horizon that she felt compelled to step on land once more. By then, the choice was entirely her own.

'You see, it was something different that brought me here, and no matter how hard I searched for my father, I knew I would never find him.'

'So, what was it then? What did bring you here?' I grew curious listening to her story. Her words were spoken low and warm, like the fading embers of a sleepy fire.

'I've never really thought about it,' she said, sounding surprised by her own admission. 'I loved the light and the air, but sometimes we are drawn to something for no reason or without explanation. I still don't know, but this city is my home now and I'm glad I chose it. I would never go back.'

Not knowing of any Uccello Hotel, she had promised to enquire further. After her morning errands, she returned with bread and cheese and a jug of milk, but no answers. In the afternoon, a man came to drop off fresh bales of straw. As he unloaded them into the dog pen, she practically had him pinned against the wall while I hid round a door and watched him shake his head and scratch his whiskers in bewilderment.

'It's hopeless.' I said, dropping my head onto the table with a loud clunk. 'Maybe it's just a story after all.'

'Nothing is ever just a story,' she said, lifting my head up and cradling my chin in the pad of her hand. 'I sense you will find it, but not as it was when your mother and father met. There is much changed in this city, but a lot still remains the same.'

'Lemàn is a great storyteller,' I added.

'I'm sure she is. But you're not imagined, are you?
I smiled.

'I have several appointments tomorrow, one with the rat-catcher. No one knows the intricacies of this city better than him. If the Uccello Hotel is here, he will know where to find it and if it's not—' she paused '—then I have no doubt that he will be able to tell us what has become of it. His ancestors have lived here since before the record books began. I will ask him for you, but are you prepared for change?'

I nodded; prepared or not, I had to know.

All morning I paced the house, waiting for the rat-catcher to arrive. Every time there was a knock at the door, I leapt from my chair and peered into the corridor trying to catch Sybel's eye as she led each visitor into the kitchen, hissing through my teeth, 'Is that him?' Each time, she shook her head and waved me away with a warning glance, before shutting the door firmly behind them. All that remained was the warm waft of bread drifting down the corridor. Sybel's business was just as private as the business in the whorehouse. Revealing the soul is as intimate as revealing the body – maybe even more so – and I continued to live in a world of closed doors. I thought about resting my ear against the wood and listening, but I didn't care to know this man's future – I only wanted knowledge of my own – and so I stayed in my room and waited. Time passed slowly. I could taste every metallic tick, and feel every echoing tock. It felt as though I was doing penance for a crime I hadn't committed. I tried to console myself with the books on the shelf, but I kept reading the same line over and over again, and nothing was able to hold my attention for long.

I was getting nowhere. Unable to settle to even the simplest task, I shuffled around the room, picking up objects, but not really looking at any of them before placing them back on the shelf. The Uccello Hotel was my starting point and I didn't want it to be my end point too.

Finally, I heard Sybel's voice in the corridor saying her prolonged goodbyes and even before the latch fell, I was waiting for her in the kitchen.

'He's not coming, is he?'

She lifted a bubbling pot from the stove and began to crush a bunch of herbs inside, stirring it with a twisted root, before replacing it and waiting for it to boil again.

'He will be here at sundown,' she said. 'It won't be long now; you just need to wait a little bit longer.'

'Sundown!' Why hadn't she told me that before? I had wasted all day listening for the rap of knuckles upon the door. I heard the chime of the hour – it was already late – and I stood up.

'Where are you going?'

'To wait by the door.' If it was nearly time, I wanted to be ready to greet him.

'Why on earth would you want to wait there?' she exclaimed. 'He won't be coming inside.'

A while later, and still in the kitchen, I heard what could only be described as a faint rattle at the little window, and Sybel crossed the room in a single stride and pushed it open with a judder. Lowering herself to the ground, she shoved her face through, searching the darkening street for the rat-catcher, and I heard her voice call out, low and full of whispers, followed by the scuttle of footsteps advancing quickly towards her. She straightened with a groan and went to fetch the pot from the stove, poured the contents into a jar and sealed it with the lid before the heat could escape. Then she returned to the window. I could hear her voice, the words indistinct, and his raspy replies, which were all too quiet to understand. Finally, she handed him the jar and he snatched it with a slosh. Dropping a coin on the ledge I watched it spin, and before it had even landed, he was gone.

'Why didn't he come inside?' I asked, fearful of the answer she would give.

'A rat-catcher! Inside?' She laughed mirthlessly and began scrubbing vigorously at her hands and her arms all the way to her elbows. 'A man who catches rats is never far from disease. You should see his face – what's left of it!'

I shuddered – my imagination was another curse I carried. 'Does he know where the hotel is?' I asked, trying to push the pity from my voice.

She shook her head.

'But you said he knew every part of this city.' I couldn't say any more as my voice began to break with the weight of disappointment; a heap of snow on a trembling branch.

Suddenly Sybel rose from the table and handed me a coat. 'He may not know where the hotel is, but he gave me the name of a person who does.'

'Where are we going?' I asked, already fumbling over the buttons.

'To find him.'

CHAPTER 15

The sky was scarred with the encroaching night and the darkness would soon conquer the light, but for now we could still see enough of the way.

'Where are we going?' I repeated breathlessly, as we sped through the streets.

'It's not far,' she replied.

We continued deeper and deeper into the narrowing streets. Once again from across the water, I noticed a luminous huddle of shops. They were unmistakably the same ones I had seen the night I arrived. Their glow was so inviting when everything else was shuttered and somnolent. A ragged man with the happiest grin was sitting at the entrance of the street, playing his accordion for no one to hear but us.

'What is that place over there?' I asked.

Sybel didn't need to look; she knew what I meant, and answered without hesitation. 'Those are the Night Shops of Vesper Square.'

'Isn't it a little late for the shops to be open?' I asked, curiously.

'Perhaps it would be anywhere else, but not there. The merchants of these shops are nocturnal. Their ancestors were cave dwellers, and they much prefer the light of a candle than the sky.'

The Night Shops. I remembered what Professor Elms had told me about the tokens, and how on the reverse I would discover my fate in this city. My fascination nearly got me lost. Sybel was no longer next to me, but had gone on ahead and was already at the end of the street about to disappear around the next corner. I raced to catch her up, my feet slapping against the uneven flagstones. It wasn't long before we were standing at the foot of the giant clock tower. Its face was midnight blue and each Roman chapter was marked by a different design: a spinning wheel, a pair of lovers, a woman seated between two pillars, another taming a lion and an angel blowing a trumpet, a cloaked man with a lantern held aloft to light his way, a woman sitting upon a throne holding a sword in one hand and balancing scales in the other, an acrobat hanging upside down from a tree, a tower struck by lightning, a sun, a moon and a twinkling star.

Wheezing and panting, I tried to catch my breath. I may have been less than half her size and less than half her age, but I was no match for Sybel's speed. She pounded the streets like a bear, with the speed of a whippet.

'I told you I had the speed, but not the stamina, and these days my dogs need both.' She patted me hard on my back and I fell to my knees. It seemed I had neither. Apologising, she helped me up, and I managed to finally straighten my body.

'The rat-catcher is right: there is one person who will surely know about the Uccello Hotel,' she said, tilting back her head back and squinting into the distance. 'I can't believe I didn't think of him myself.'

'Who?' I asked, following her sky-fixed eyes.

'The Keeper of the Hours ... now follow me.'

The building of the clock tower was damp and dark. In the corner, an old staircase spiralled upwards into further gloom and we rattled our way to the top.

'Hello!' called Sybel, her echo disturbing the silence.

Suddenly a figure took shape like an apparition clad in darkness. Then a light flickered in front of me, and a man emerged holding a candle in one hand and a can with a long spout in the other. Sybel greeted him like an old friend and I realised he was the same man I had seen polishing the handle of the indigo-blue door.

'Have you come to watch me restore the hours?' he asked. 'I'm in a bit of a hurry, I'm afraid.'

'Restore the hours?' I questioned, forgetting my shyness of strangers for a moment.

His eyes fell upon me and I stepped back, blushing into the shadows.

'The city clock loses time, so somebody has to fix it,' explained Sybel.

'Yes, twice a day, once in the morning and then again in the evening. Turning and twisting and oiling.' He sighed wearily, holding up the can as proof of his endeavour. 'I have numerous jobs in this city, but most importantly I restore the hands and move them on, for they always fall behind. People need to know when time is lost.' I could see his dark, ancient eyes sag into the deep lines on his face and his beard wilted down to the button that held his robe together. He was like a Christmas log felled in the snow. There are more ways to measure time, I thought, but held my words in a net of timidity.

'We are looking for something.' said Sybel. 'And because you know this city better than most, we have come to ask for your help in finding it.'

The Keeper of the Hours shifted his weight from one foot to the other, as though standing still for too long made him uncomfortable. He didn't like to keep still. 'Ah, well, I can help you find lost time.' He seemed to heave the words out of his chest, as though speaking was a great effort.

'Why, where does the time go? I asked curiously.

The Keeper of the Hours considered my question. 'Time is neglected, forgotten, squandered, people fritter it away like careless gamblers. In a single moment everything can change and you can lose it all. People always want it back, but time is unredeemable.'

I frowned.

'We're not here about time,' said Sybel.

'Well, I must go to ring the bell, so, whatever it is, we will have to discuss it on the way,' he said, and with unexpected speed hurtled himself down the stairs. He strode across the square with his hand held around the candle and disappeared into another tower. I had seen it on my walks around the city, an unmistakable structure, tall enough to skewer the stars. Its bell was large and loud and shook the whole city when it rang, before it faded back into silence. A reminder of time lost.

Inside was a small square room and stone steps twisted up and out of sight. I could hear the Keeper of the Hours and his footfalls, but I could no longer see him. Every twenty steps or so there were sconces fixed to the wall, and he lit the candles at each turn. I knew he was lighting them for us as, from the look of the well-worn steps, he knew his way. I soon grew cold and tired and my neck ached from trying to see to the top. I lost count at one hundred and twenty-three steps. Finally, I heard what sounded like a heavy bolt being slid open and the scrape of a door and to my relief we had arrived. The Keeper of the Hours rested his candle on a ledge. Although evening had settled in, patterns of light still chased each other across the sky like wilful children protesting about being sent to bed too early.

It was a small square slab of a room, open to the sky on all sides. A roof steepled above and from it hung the largest bell I had ever seen. I had never been afraid of heights, and as I stared down at the city, I realised this was the highest I had ever been, higher than any of the trees I had climbed. Roofs rose up and then sloped back down again, impossible to know where one ended and another began. I was sure you could cross the city in half the time, just by jumping from one roof top to another. Shapes of buildings lurked like prehistoric beasts, glowing green and bronze in the fading light, and I was reminded of how much of the city I hadn't yet discovered. I was so amazed by where I was and by what I could see, that if someone had given me a telescope and told me that if I put my eye to the lens then I could see all the way home, I would have believed them.

'It's so high up here,' I marvelled, watching the Keeper of the Hours as he reached for the bell's thick coarse rope, twisting it three times round his hand. 'Is it so people can be closer to God?'

'Don't let all the churches here deceive you; this is not a God-fearing city,' he replied solemnly. He told me that many years ago the mayor decided that he wanted the moon for his daughter and so he built this tower to reach it. Soon after, he died, and the tower was never finished. Then a group of thieves sailed in and, noticing the unfinished tower, decided they would use it to spy on the wealthy merchant ships docking for the night. They were caught and thrown to their deaths. The tower was only finished when a king decided he needed somewhere to lock away his daughter, too tempted was she by the wrong sort of love, if there was such a thing. Now it was for stargazers or people wishing to have a view of the city from above and the endless stretch of sea. It was a navigation point to find your bearings in a coiled city.

I breathed in the cool night air. A few stars had already begun to appear as though they had been stitched into a dark-blue cloth. Night was almost upon us.

'There are over two billion stars out there somewhere,' said the Keeper of the Hours, noticing my amazement. 'Some of them are no longer there; even though we can still see them; it's the best magic act of all.'

My thoughts flew back to Professor Elms, and to Lemàn and my father; none of them around, but still very much there, even if I couldn't see them any more. I felt the now-familiar ache of longing in my chest, and tried to keep my sadness inside.

'Between each star lies miles and miles of empty space and between us and them even more.'

It was unfathomable, a beautiful skyscape, an after-dark performance, the star-studded event. It made perfect sense and I thought of Lemàn reaching them in her balloon and making them shine and sparkle.

'Cover your ears,' ordered the Keeper of the Hours. 'It is time to let everyone know that lost time has been restored once more.'

Then he tightened the rope around his hand, in a lasso of time, and the bell swung its heaviness until its chimes echoed around the room and spilled out into the sky. A flock of birds had been resting above us and the sound sent them spluttering into the distance. I reached out for them, but as I did, I felt a swoosh of air and Sybel pulled me back from the ledge.

'You are too close,' she warned, before returning swiftly to the safety of the steps.

The Keeper of the Hours dropped the rope and retrieved the candle. I watched the birds soar and slide and disappear. Loss can be felt so suddenly and in so many different ways.

'Do you know a place called the Uccello Hotel?' I asked.

'Yes.' The simplicity of the word startled me.

'Yes?' I repeated, hardly daring to believe his answer.

'Well, I knew of it.'

'What does that mean? Did it change its name?' I asked hopefully.

'It no longer exists; it was closed more than a decade ago. Where it once stood, there are now only houses.'

I felt a sinking feeling of despair; no wonder I couldn't find it.

'Can you tell us where it was?' asked Sybel.

'Can I see it from up here?' I asked, racing back over to the ledge, but in a dark city everything looked the same. The buildings were a slumbering herd of unfamiliar creatures.

'Perhaps you could write the address down here, or draw a little map for us,' said Sybel, pulling a piece of paper and a pen from her pocket and handing it to him. In his big looped handwriting, an address emerged.

'Here.' He handed me the piece of paper, which I folded and slipped into my pocket.

'Perhaps someone living there now remembers something from before,' Sybel said, before we were ushered back onto the steps. Spoken from a prophetess, her words offered some comfort at least. The Keeper of the Hours insisted we went first, and I heard a faint hiss every time he snuffed out the flicker of a candle behind us.

'Why do you want to find the Uccello Hotel?' he asked, as we eventually stepped back into the square.

'My father stayed there,' I replied simply, too tired to be swaddled in secrets any longer. 'I thought that perhaps someone from the hotel might remember him, or know where he is.' I had nowhere else to start.

He paused. 'And was your father from this city?'

I shook my head. 'I don't really know where he was from. I don't even know his name.'

The Keeper of the Hours frowned. 'So, what do you know about him?'

'Only that he was a Sky-Worshipper, who came out of a silver mist,' I said. I didn't want to reveal too much, but I wondered if he knew more.

Bending down his long frame, he looked at me, more in careful scrutiny than with a cold, hard stare, his candle held aloft illuminating my face. Wisdom glinted in his eyes. 'I can see now that you too are more air than earth. His eyes seemed to see what was hidden beneath my coat and I clutched at my buttons. He shook his head. 'Do you realise that the only person you are hiding from is your-self?' Then he straightened up with a creak, like a branch burdened with sheltering birds, before he stretched away into the night.

CHAPTER 16

L ittle by little, parts of the city became more familiar to me, and so too did its inhabitants. The dogs were quick and restless creatures and at first it seemed they were the ones taking me for a walk. Ducking under the wisteria, we left our yard on the Street of Lost and Found past the house with the geraniums and the doorstep with the muddy boots, following the smell of bread until we reached the corner bakery. The proprietor was a smiling man with a bristling moustache. Since his bread had risen long before the sun, he spent most of his morning leaning in his doorway, arms folded, watching the world pass by. Sometimes, he preferred to sit on a stool. The first time he saw me, he laughed heartily at the pantomime display of the dogs speeding by with me tumbling behind them.

I could still hear him laughing three streets later. After that he always raised his hand in cheery greeting, but I was still too nervous to engage in conversation, grateful not to have the time to stop.

I had begun to navigate my way through the city with surprising ease and enjoyment, so different from the world I had left behind. From my window in the whorehouse, I could only ever have imagined a moment as thrilling as this. Slowly, my shoulders dropped and my eyes lifted as the map of the city slowly grew in my mind. Where I grew up, distance was measured by the number of fields between one place and another, but here it was measured by the number of bridges. Sometimes I explored a different way, one I had never been before, knowing that it would eventually lead me back to the Street of Lost and Found. From the corner bakery, it was left to the apothecary or right to the marketplace where the barges were stacked with deliveries and sent on their way. Across from the market stalls, where the canal ran at its widest, lay the Night Shops of Vesper Square. Beyond that was the clock tower. I wondered if it was the same place that Professor Elms had fallen in love all those years ago; I smiled at the thought of it.

It wasn't long before I realised that if I pulled tightly on the rope at certain points, then I could steer the dogs in the direction of my choosing. Out of the hectic alleyways, we trundled along the Street of Shining Puddles, where the peddler of sugared almonds wheeled his creaking cart.

Visitors arrived early on the little water buses that chugged in from nearby islands. Their luggage was piled high on the damp flagstones, while they loitered with dainty white parasols held aloft to keep out the drizzle or the sun. The city had a fast-changing temperament. Forgetting a parasol was never a problem; they could often be found strung out above the streets like washing on a line, and visitors were encouraged to help themselves. At the end of the Street of Brewing Teapots there stood a large public park, known for its abundance of bluebells. A parade of flower sellers spent all day trying to tempt the visitors with their posy bundles and fragrant scoops; the scent drifted through the air and into the neighbouring streets. The park offered many secluded spots for secret lovers, but the dogs were just grateful to find the shade of an old leafy tree, and, with their noses nestled in their paws, they quickly fell asleep. I too must have dozed off, and when I awoke the dogs were gone.

A flood of fear drowned me, and my heart rattled the cage of my ribs. The dogs were nowhere to be seen, no trace – nothing. They had simply vanished. By now they could have been anywhere and I had no idea how long they had been missing. I crunched up and down the gravely path, glancing in all directions, rummaging in the privets as though by some miracle I would find them there and pull them out like rabbits from a magician's hat.

My distress must have been clearly visible, because as I let the privets spring back into place, a little old lady - dressed in black - reached out her arm to touch my hand.

She began muttering some words of consolation, which I didn't understand. I realised I was shaking and sank onto a bench, trying to figure out what to do. Sybel would be furious and grief-stricken if I didn't return with every last one of them unharmed. How foolish I had been to fall asleep. I tried to think rationally. The dogs were curious creatures by nature and greedy and had probably grown bored of the park and its limitations. Half a dozen bois-terous dogs galloping round the streets couldn't be too hard to find. With renewed hope, I walked the length of the canal, glancing fearfully every time I saw the unguarded steps leading down into the murky water; I worried they may have slipped in and drowned, but quickly shook such alarming thoughts from my mind. I cursed myself; it seemed I was losing things far more quickly than I was finding them in this city.

Just around the corner, I came upon the Bridge of Solace where I stopped. In the middle stood a gypsy woman clutching the handles of a wheelbarrow. Closer inspection revealed her hair was matted with mud and twigs and thistles. She chewed on her cheek noisily and hummed a tune I didn't recognise; it sounded like a nursery rhyme. She had no eyebrows; in their place was an arch of multi-coloured jewels. I was momentarily mesmerised. If the lonely woman from Lemàn's stories had been true then this is what I imagined her to look like all grown-up.

'What's your pleasure?' she wheezed, tilting the wheel-barrow up so I could inspect the clutter within: pots of herbs and trays of half-withered flowers, paper bags with muddy potatoes and tomatoes, lettuces, cucumbers and artichokes, all past their best. Jars of beetroot balls and shaved garlic and twisted grubby fingers of ginger as well as crusty baguettes tied with filthy string. Nothing appealed, but until she moved out of my way, I couldn't pass. I looked again, my eyes searching for something useful.

'Thyme,' I replied, reluctantly tossing a coin in her wheelbarrow. It missed and we watched as it sank below the water. For a moment her eyes narrowed in suspicion and she stopped her relentless chewing. I tossed another one, and this time it landed at her festering feet. She collapsed quickly like a deckchair to scoop it into her palm, and, after several minutes of rummaging, she pulled out a bundle of thyme and thrust it into my hand.

'Have you seen six dogs?' I asked, not sure her glassy eyes saw much of what was in this world.

She mumbled and pointed over her shoulder. Then with a cough-inducing chuckle, which created sudden spasms in her chest, she picked up her wheelbarrow and hobbled away.

I dashed in the direction of her pointing, down the Street of The Tired Hermits, until I came to a wide avenue lined with trees, but there was no sign of the dogs.

I stopped to ask the almond peddler if he had seen them, and he pointed down the long path ahead, towards some kind of great monument in the distance.

I didn't wait for him to say anything else. I leaped up and sped down the path. As I approached, I could see the statue of a man with a bronze lion sitting at his heels. Beneath them, there was a circular pond filled with fish and turtles and for a moment I didn't notice the missing dogs or rather I didn't realise the splayed dark shapes at the foot of the monument actually belonged to them. I thought they were part of the lasting tribute to some great historical figure. It was only when one of the dogs kicked its legs in the dust, that I realised I had at last found them. Such was my overwhelming sense of relief, that I closed my eyes and sank to my knees. Any passer-by must have thought I was worshipping this historic hero with such pride and admiration. A great tribute to the past, but in truth I had no idea who he was.

The dogs, catching my scent, scrambled to their feet and trotted unashamedly towards me, as though I had been the one to get lost, not them. It was late and I didn't have the energy left to scold them, so I quickly picked up the harness and knotted them in.

Leading us through the city, the darkness draped itself over the domes, skewered on the spires, blackening the bridges, tumbling across the tiled roofs and glooming the gates. Lanterns slowly burned on street corners, allowing me to navigate my way, deciphering the dusk. The Bridge of Longing, its name carved into the stone, appeared up ahead, its lights twinkling in welcome. As I approached, a strangely marvellous sight greeted me: along both sides of the bridge, dozens of little jars hung haphazardly from hooks. All of them were completely empty, their purpose a mystery. We continued a little further until the dogs came to a curious standstill and I could hear the sound of biting and crunching. Peering down, I could see the ground was scattered with chestnuts, probably fallen from the cart of a passing street vendor. The dogs were delighted, snuffling at this unexpected treat, and were in no mood to be hurried home, despite me tugging on their lead.

This part of the city was old and quiet, like a hidden manuscript with a story still to tell. Wearily, I leaned back against the railing and decided to give the dogs another five minutes to crunch their way through the chestnuts. It was then that a plaque on the wall opposite caught my eye. I was alert to the name written upon it, which seemed strangely familiar. I reached inside my pocket, fumbling for the address the Keeper of the Hours had given to me and stared in disbelief – the name on the paper matched the name on the plaque; the Street of the Pomegranate Dealer.

As I glanced upwards at the crumbling walls, scorched brown from the sun, I realised I was in a residential neighbourhood; standing in front of what must once have been the Uccello Hotel. Dragging the reluctant dogs behind me, we crossed the bridge and passed along a narrow street perfumed with the oleander trees that grew nearby. A sweet, distinct lament floated down from one of the rooms, growing louder with each footfall. Pausing, I tried to find where something so beautiful was coming from, and my eyes fell upon a half-open window; golden light slipped out like a secret lover.

A young couple hand in hand stopped, as I had done, enraptured by the sound. Nobody spoke; we just stood there, unable to move, simply listening to the voice that drifted around us, and my feathers danced. In the half light and shadows, I could see a silhouette moving against the wall of the room behind the window. Teasingly, it arched across the ceiling and flickered away again.

Moments passed, how many it was difficult to say, but I suddenly realised I was alone again. The young lovers had wandered away and the street stood empty. I looked again at what the Keeper of the Hours had written, and then back at the street plaque. There was no mistake; this was it, the street where Lemàn had met my father all those years ago. My heart quickened. I set off along the canal, without removing my gaze from the window and the singing that came from behind it. I was almost directly below now, with only a stretch of silent water and a twenty-foot scale between me and whoever was inside. Quite abruptly, the singing stopped and there was a rattle at the window, then a face appeared and two arms stretched out to reach for the shutters. A girl, maybe a little older than me, looked down and noticed me imme-diately. For a brief moment, she held my startled gaze. Her hair floated around her, spilling over the ledge like sunflowers. Like an inquisitive cat, her face was small and triangular, framed by the golden light of the room beyond. My feathers tingled with excitement, touched by something inexplicable. I had never experienced anything like it before. It wasn't the same sensation I had felt standing at the top of the tree or being on the boat in the storm; this was something quite different. This time it wasn't a warning; it was a wanting.

She hesitated, then smiled, before pulling the shutters towards her and latching them shut. I stood quite still, half expecting her to open them again and call down to me, but what would she say? And what would I say in return? Nothing happened, and the moment had gone. There was nothing left to do, but move on.

The next corner revealed the Church of One Hundred Souls, as I knew it would from Lemàn's revealed memories. It was a small, square box wrapped like a gift. Its walls slumped with the weight of regret and confession. Always open, no matter the hour, I felt compelled to enter.

After the afternoon's madness, I didn't trust the dogs to be left outside, so I led them up the steps and through the open door. Everyone was welcome here, I'd been told. Inside, the cool air hung heavy with incense. I blinked it all in, letting my eyes adjust slowly to the shadows. The church was empty and still dark apart from the tapered candles flickering in trays of sand to my left and to my right. Reaching into my pocket, I dropped one of my last coins into the collection box, and selected a candle from the box. Lighting it, with the prayers of others, I pushed it into the sand towards the back and closed my eyes. I had never really prayed before and was unsure of the rules, or if indeed there were any. I wondered if I needed to address my prayer like a letter. I wasn't sure if this was the same, so I whispered my thoughts into the solitude and they fluttered away like moths attracted to the bright flame of hope. I tiptoed across the uneven mosaic floor with the trail of dogs behind me, their claws skittered against the floor, the sound echoing high into the vaulted ceiling. Ornate pillars supported the lower walls and the altar was roped off, a sacred place not to be disturbed by the unblessed. I didn't venture any nearer.

About halfway up, I selected a pew and we settled ourselves along the left-hand side. In front of me there was a large wooden cross which rose into the gloom and above that, a tiny window allowed in a pinprick of a twilight sky. I knew it was an opening to release the souls, I had seen one before, drawn in a book. Kneeling, I prayed for the ones I loved. I prayed for Lemàn to sleep without waking to a pillow damp with tears and for Professor Elms to find love rather than to lose it. I prayed for Sybel's happiness and I prayed for the father I had not yet met. Thinking it prudent to count my blessings, I added thanks for my safe arrival in the city and for things I was still to discover. This was everything that mattered to me, and for now it was enough.

CHAPTER 17

'There you are,' cried Sybel, when we finally trundled through the gate, much later than expected. Clearly, she had been waiting in the courtyard, fretting over our late return. Even knowing where someone is doesn't stop you worrying.

The dogs were so tired they barely made it to their straw pen before collapsing into a snoring huddle, their splayed legs twitching in immediate sleep.

'I lost ... track of time,' I said, wiping the hair out of my eyes and handing her the bundle of thyme from the gypsy on the bridge.

'Ah, I see you met the gypsy woman,' she said, brushing the filth from the roots. 'I think she has brought you good fortune. Now wash your face and come to the kitchen; I have some exciting news.'

At the tap outside, I splashed my face with cold water and held a cloth to the back of my neck. I felt dizzy, with a kind of seasickness, which swept over me, and I had to steady myself against the cold wall for a moment, letting it pass. There had been too much chaos for one day.

'Are you unwell?' asked Sybel, as I entered the kitchen.

'I'm not sure,' I replied truthfully.

She held her palm flat against my forehead and then replaced it with her lips.

'Hmm,' she pondered. 'No fever. Probably just too much walking; it was unexpectedly warm today and despite your bandages you will insist on wearing that coat.'

'It hides me well,' I mumbled, but she didn't hear or if she did, she didn't question me further. I tried to focus, but exhaustion weighted me and even sipping tea was an effort I could barely manage.

'Is it too strong?' she asked, mistaking my weariness for distaste.

Before I had chance to protest, she was already lifting a jar of dried flowers off the shelf. Unscrewing the lid, she grabbed a fistful of crumbling leaves. 'This should revive you,' she said, crushing them into another pot of water and turning up the heat until a smoky peppermint smell chattered noisily into the kitchen.

'I was thinking about your father today.'

This surprised me.

'I know the hotel isn't there any more, but I sense you won't find your answers there anyway.'

'No,' I mumbled.

'I have another way.' Sybel poured the tea into a mug and handed it to me. 'Wait here,' she said, disappearing into the corridor.

The tea was light and refreshing and despite the steam rising off it, I drank it in quick, welcome gulps. She returned with a dusty yellow newspaper and began flicking through the pages, which were so old they almost crumbled in her fingers.

'What are you looking for?' I asked, bewildered.

'Here it is!' she exclaimed, swivelling the paper round so I could read it.

At first, I didn't see anything of significance, but when my eyes came to rest in the bottom corner of the page, they widened in surprise. It was a blurred image of a man with his arm wrapped around the shoulders of another man in mutual respect. Although it was difficult to make out, I could see one of the men had the features of a bird: feathery hair, a long, sharp nose and round, hooded eyes. His limbs were long and thin and his feet shoeless and splayed out like those of a great sea bird. I gasped. There was no mistake, he looked like me and even though the newspaper was black and white and yellow with age, I could tell his eyes were the same beautiful blue that Lemàn spoke of. Underneath the image, a caption read: '*Secretive bird tribe uncovered by Professor Bottelli, leading ornithologist at the University of The City of Water.'*

Tearing my eyes from the page, I looked up at Sybel. Her eyes glittered with excitement.

'Is that really him?' I whispered in disbelief, trying to smooth out the creases in the paper to make the image clearer. I squinted again at the page searching for a date, but it had worn away to nothing more than a dark smudge.

'Yes,' she whispered back, 'I'm certain of it. Your feathers triggered a memory and then when you mentioned Sky-Worshippers and a place of mist it reminded me of something I'd read a long time ago about a bird tribe on a floating island.'

My mind loosened as though someone had finally untangled a thousand knots, and let the threads run free. It was like the jagged edges of a puzzle had suddenly been made smooth and were beginning to slot together after all this time. The mist was dissolving, and the way ahead was a little clearer.

'I can't believe it,' I said, not lifting my eyes from the paper. 'And to have kept it all this time.'

'I never throw things away. If something had meaning for you once, then maybe it will again. I grew up with nothing, so now I keep everything. They are piled high in a tin cupboard on the roof, I've spent most of today rummaging through them; I almost gave up, there are so many. Besides, in each of these newspapers at the back, amongst the obituaries, there are messages from people offering their gratitude for my help and there are many I have helped. You must never underestimate the power of gratitude. On darker days, I read them one by one to remind myself of my worth. It's more potent than any tincture. It chases away the shadows.'

She answered my next question, before it had even left my lips.

'Tomorrow we will take the boat out to the university and see what else Professor Bottelli can tell us about your father.'

'Tomorrow?' My eyes widened.

'Yes, tomorrow. No point waiting any longer; I think you've waited long enough, don't you?'

That night, sleep brought fear. I was plagued by terrifying dreams, of sea creatures and darkness and drowning. I woke cold and damp and restless. I needed to empty the nightmares from my head, so I climbed the stone steps to the roof terrace. The night was fresh and sweet like taking the first bite of a succulent fruit. It was such a relief to escape from the tangle of sweaty sheets. When I first arrived, Sybel had taken me up here to show me the city. Not many places in the City of Murmurs had a garden, but all of them had a roof and many of these had terraces, where pots of plants and trays of flowers grew happily, being that little bit closer to the sun and the rain. Sybel spent hours up here, tending to her herbs, which perfumed the air, and blew all the way out to sea. I rubbed the leaves of rosemary and lavender between my fingers in a crackling whisper, and lifted them to my nose, inhaling their calming fragrance. At once it was a reminder of home, and of the warm lavender milk Lemàn used to make for me at bedtime. Loss made my heart ache more than ever and I was beginning to understand the powerful curse of memory.

The murmurs of the city crept in everywhere, but up here at this time it was cloister-quiet; no boats, no engines, no people, no birds – nothing moved, not even the flutter of a bat to disturb the silence. I was too far to hear the constant murmurs of the water, even the sea had paused. Distant lights flickered behind unknown windows across the city, but other than that everything was dark and deep and snug. This was what it felt like to peep inside the night. In a city such as this, the moon always shone low and clear and luminous. If I reached far enough, I felt certain my fingertips would slide against its cool marble exterior. Polished and precise like a majestic relic from a long-lost palace. The fleet of stars keeping watch over their black sea. I wondered then who there was in my new world to look after me or if I even needed looking after any more. I was glad to have met Sybel; she made me feel protected and I didn't regret telling her my secret, not for a single moment.

Most of the time, she preferred to sleep in the courtyard with her beloved dogs, but sometimes, on warmer nights, when the stars were visible and bright, she would climb all the way up to the roof to seek silence and solitude. I found the pile of blankets and cushions she kept tucked in a corner under a waterproof canopy and I dragged them out, arranging them into a cosy nest. I had never slept outside, but strangely I felt safer than I had ever felt before. In a few hours I was going to meet someone who knew my father; I could hardly believe I was one step closer. Until that moment, lying under the stars, I don't think I realised how much finding him had meant to me. Now, it was clear and bright and tangible. The ache I'd felt earlier hadn't left me, but was the ache for something lost or something found? It was impossible to tell.

Stroking my feathers, I finally found comfort in sleep. A little while later in the depths of my dreams, I felt a little bird softly land on my shoulder; it watched me as I slept. When I opened my eyes, I found a long feather nestled between two of the cushions. I didn't know how long it had been there or where it had come from, but it definitely wasn't one of mine.

CHAPTER 18

The city, which only a few hours ago had been deep in silent sleep, now pounded and pulsed with energy and heat. From the street below, two men were arguing about the price of fish and, beyond that, boats had begun to putter their way along the waterways, crates clattering between them. Hours ago, the world had seemed an endless reach away, so quiet and distant like there was nothing there at all, but now it felt as though I was sitting right on top of it. I had meant to escape to the roof for only a few moments to rinse my mind of lurid dreams, but instead I had fallen asleep there and for the first time awoken to the sun warming my face. I tidied away the blankets and went inside, where I found Sybel clattering pans around in a cupboard.

'How were the stars last night?' she asked, as I sat down still drowsy from sleep.

'Closer than I imagined.'

She laughed and handed me a slab of toast and I watched a fizz of butter quickly melt into its warmth.

'The boat's ready when you are. Eat up – you need this to warm you; it will be cold out there on the open water.'

The bread looked too thick to swallow and I pushed it away. 'I'm afraid,' I confessed.

Sybel ruffled my hair gently with her giant hand. 'It's to be expected, but do not fear what you do not know.'

'But I think I'm afraid of finding him.' I whispered. 'What if he doesn't want to meet me? He doesn't even know I exist. I think it's all a mistake.' I babbled the words out in a tumble of emotion.

She sighed and looked deep into my eyes. 'Turn your fear to courage and be brave. That's what I had to do when I left my city behind and you were brave enough to do the same. You are much stronger than you think. Discoveries, no matter what they are, can bring uncertainty because they can change everything. That's perhaps what you fear the most.' She pushed the toast back towards me and I lifted it from the plate and ate; each mouthful got easier to swallow.

Sybel's boat was tucked into an alcove a short walk from the house. I got in and sat down as she quickly released the rope. Picking up the oars from the bottom of the boat, she rested them on either side and then dipped the paddles into the water. 'Once we get out of the lagoon and into the sea, it shouldn't take too long.'

Pushing us away from the damp, stone steps we rocked out between the high narrow walls and joined what seemed to be the early morning rush hour. The sun had barely lifted itself from under its blue blanket, but the canals were already dappled with watery light and sprinkled with morning mist. The only other boats on the water were transporting goods to sell to restaurants, whose kitchen windows were open wide above the water, ready for the busy day ahead. Sales took place, while chefs washed and chopped vegetables. Negotiations were quick and brutal, as windows often slammed shut and the sellers waved their carrots and cabbages with fury in the air at any rejection. Vegetable leaves and rotting cores like clenched fists bobbed in furious abandonment, a welcome feast for the city's rats or Sybel's dogs, if she was quick enough. It was all such a theatrical performance. In their haste, the sellers didn't try to steer out of our way and we were knocked into walls and left rocking up and down in the wake of their annoyance. Sybel would calmly lift the oars out of the water, and, with a sigh, rest them across her lap until the mayhem passed; there was nothing else you could do, and then we'd be off again. This continued until we finally glided past the last golden building towards the lagoon. I realised I was sailing past the canal that led to the former site of the Uccello Hotel. Turning my head before it slipped out of sight, I caught a quick glimpse of a closed shutter.

Once in open water, Sybel rowed in fast, easy stokes. Her strength propelled us with startling speed, and the boat flew along, leaving other passing cargo behind. I gripped the sides so tightly my knuckles clenched and whitened. The air was heavy with salt.

'There it is!' she shouted, at last.

Squinting my eyes, I could see a distant shape growing larger and larger with each stroke of the oars. Sybel expertly guided us towards a wooden jetty and secured the boat to a post. She climbed up the steps and gave me her hand to follow. All the curls had been blown out of my hair and my lungs felt raw and weak as I crawled along the boat and onto the narrow ledge. I felt a rising nausea, unsure whether it was from nerves or the choppy water I was glad to leave behind. The university was the only building on the island; some of it had been rebuilt or modernised, but mostly it remained rundown and neglected like an old museum. It was set in large gardens with clusters of trees for shade. Walking up a long path, well-tended and clear of weeds, we found the main entrance and went inside. There was a large airy hallway with a desk where a woman was having an animated conversation with someone behind her. She nodded at us, by way of acknowledgement, but seemed in no hurry to greet us with any words. I stared around me at the dark polished floors and the vertiginous arched ceiling; I felt like I was inside the belly of a whale and wondered whether my father had stood in this very same spot. My stomach began to swirl with anticipation and I quickly searched for somewhere to sit down.

Across the room, I noticed Sybel had approached a young man, who was carrying several documents rolled under his arm, and was now deep in conversation with him. The man was shaking his head and shrugging his shoulders and when she finally returned, her face was filled with disappointment.

'What is it?' I asked. 'Isn't Professor Bottelli available? Should we have made an appointment?'

'No, it's not that,' she said.

'Then what?'

She hesitated. 'I'm afraid Professor Bottelli died last December.'

'Died ... but—' I understood the words, and yet at the same time I didn't. I had come here to find some answers, but now I could barely breathe through my disappointment.

'All is not lost,' she exclaimed. 'I am told that Professor Bottelli had an assistant, and his name is Leo Hawkins. Come on; his study is at the end of the corridor.'

Despite knocking loudly on the door we presumed belonged to Leo Hawkins, no one answered. After a respectable amount of waiting, Sybel turned the handle and the door clicked open. Finding the room unoccupied, our eyes met in sparkling mischief.

Once inside, it felt as if we had stepped into another time and place. My eyes flited around, not resting on any one object; there was just too much to take in. The room reminded me of the cabin of a boat, with its dark wooden panels, but thankfully there was no trace of the fetid stench I had left behind. Instead the smell of beeswax and pollen imbued the air, inviting us further. Instead of sitting quietly, I felt compelled to search the room, desperate for something of my father and I wasn't leaving without it. Maps and carvings and strange masks hung from the walls and there were glass cases full of stuffed birds, skulls and bones and jars of gigantic speckled eggs. Feathers sprang from vases where flowers should have been, and sketches lay scattered across the desk illuminated by a small table lamp. A library of books filled two floor-to-ceiling alcoves, and a glass door on the far wall opened out into one of the gardens; its light didn't quite reach all the corners of the room. Boxes were filled with brown paper files, each labelled with obscure scientific names that I couldn't even pronounce. Riffling through the third box, my eye was drawn to a name – The Ornis Tribe – and underneath it written in smaller letters was another name and this one made my heart stop: The Sky-Worshippers. Filled with anticipation, I grabbed the file, and emptied it onto and desk, watching as a handful of small photographs fluttered out like leaves.

I spread the photographs before me like a fortune teller, revealing the future. Each one showed a man, who I understood to be Professor Bottelli, standing with different members of the tribe. There were close-up shots of faces, legs, arms and feet; feathers taken from different angles and in different lights; one picture zoomed in on an eye, but unlike mine, this one was round, with a large black centre like a drop of ink soaked onto a piece of bright-blue paper. And then I saw the one from the newspaper, only this one was much clearer and larger. I could see the expression on the man's face; kind yet bewildered, patient yet awkward. Our similarity was unmistakable. His hair, like mine, was a lava flow, a marigold field, a blazing bonfire. His eyes – the blue sky above.

'It's him!' I cried. 'It's my father.'

Sybel crossed the room and took the photo from my hand. 'It looks like it was taken outside in the garden.' She flipped it over looking for a date, but the back was untouched.

'What do you think these are?' I asked perplexed, handing her loose pages scrawled with strange loops and symbols.

'It looks like it might be some sort of language spoken by the tribe,' she replied, after a moment of musing. 'Yes, look here it is.' She pointed at the word 'Orniglossa'. 'I think Professor Bottelli had been working on a code to translate it and these are his transcripts.'

'They have their own language?' The thought had never occurred to me, but of course it would explain why there had been no words exchanged between Lemàn and my father on that long-ago night.

'Well, Leo Hawkins clearly isn't here and I have querents arriving soon. We will come back tomorrow,' said Sybel.

Quickly and without permission, I furtively slipped the photo of my father into my pocket and made a pretence of slotting the bundle of papers back into the file. When I was sure she wasn't looking, I fumbled a few pages of the transcript under the shadows of my coat, with every intention of returning them.

'Let's go out the back door,' she said, eyeing me suspiciously. 'It will be quicker.'

The journey back across the water was cold. There was little warmth left in the day and I kept my chin tucked into the collar of my coat. My thoughts returned to Professor Elms and his pocket watch, and my brief hope suddenly turned to bitter loss. I hoped that this photograph wouldn't be the only thing to tell me of my father.

'It is a promising start,' said Sybel, heaving us across the wide stretch of water.

'Is it?' I grumbled. I had expected Professor Bottelli to be there to greet us with his stories.

'Yes. Besides at least now you have something to read.' She raised her eyebrows in a knowing way, inclined her head and laughed into the wind.

Turning my face, I blushed at her discovery, foolish to think I could have kept it from her. Unfulfilled, I stared into the water-filled distance and then to the sky above. My father was out there somewhere, I just had to find him.

We rowed back into the city from the lagoon, and as we drifted into the canal near the Street of Hooting Owls, I glimpsed one of the brightly painted doors. This one was the fiery red of a rising phoenix.

'Is that a wishing door?' I asked, pointing towards it as we glided past.

'Yes,' she replied, without looking up.

'Is it true that there are different colours for different wishes?'

'That's right,' she said. 'Not everyone believes in God, but they like an alternative.'

Once we had arrived back near the Street of Lost and Found, and the boat was safely stowed in its watery alcove, I told Sybel that I wanted to walk for a while. She didn't question it, but surprisingly popped a kiss on the side of my head, as only a mother would do. I felt a little burst of gratitude then; I may not have found all the answers I wanted, but I had found her and she had given me a place in this magical city. I returned her kiss with one of my own and she smiled, telling me not to be long. She sensed an unforgiving storm was on its way, and I too felt a change in the air, but it was still too distant to matter.

It was wonderful to be walking through the city without six boisterous dogs to think about. I could walk at my own pace and pause wherever I chose for whatever reason; to look in a shop window, or to eavesdrop on a conversation as I was so used to doing. The rain had arrived and begun to fall and bounce from the flagstones, but I didn't mind, I wanted to see how many wishing doors I could find. I had no idea how many there actually were, but an hour later, which is about how long it takes to cross the city from the ancient walls of the ghetto to the last boat stop beyond the park, I had counted seven. Like the bridges and the streets, each door had a little plaque and a different handle to identify the wish within: indigo-blue for peace and forgiveness; pear-green for health and healing; dandelion-yellow for happiness; pink for love; silver for wealth and success; turquoise for freedom; and back to the fiery red door I had seen from the boat for those wishing for change. Each handle was shaped differently too, carved out of wood into a long olive branch, or a round apple, a smiling sun, a dainty rosebud, a glittering star, an open wing, and an acorn.

Standing there, drenched and shivering, I wondered with much indecision whether or not to reach for the handle and open the door. I wanted desperately to peek inside, and so, tentatively, letting my fingers grasp the wooden acorn, I slowly turned it anti-clockwise. It was dim and damp inside, but as my eyes adjusted to the gloom, I could see it was a tiny chamber, more the size of a confession box than a room. Attached to string from the ceiling were lots of tiny acorns, and there were dishes and bowls on shelves filled with even more of them. I could hear the rush of the canal and saw it through a hole in the floor. A sudden grunt alarmed me and it was then that I noticed a hunched-up man, slumped on a ledge, snoring, unaware that he was being watched. Quietly, I shut the door on his dreaming. It seemed they also granted shelter from the rain for those who were too far from home. Running through the incessant downpour, I had an uneasy feeling that someone was following in my footsteps. By the time I reached home, I thought I must have imagined it. I may have found the wishing doors, but I still missed sleeping in my own bed made of wishes.

CHAPTER 19

The next day I woke hoping to visit the university again, but it was impossible. As predicted, last night's rain had become a storm, tearing through the city like a rampaging bull seeking vengeance. I wondered what had happened to shake the sky into such fury. There was no way to cross the lagoon in the storm, and my next visit would have to wait until the storm had retreated. I thought about taking Sybel's boat, but it was no match for the wild water, which rose like a serpent, lashing the harbour walls and drenching those foolish enough to be passing by. Even the lagoon boats, which usually chugged about resiliently in all sorts of turmoil remained trembling by their posts, battered by the water. Others were taken in and harnessed, until every alcove of the city was full of boats on top of boats. People dragged them from the water and pulled them to the safety of old potato factories for fear of the water crushing them to the depths of the canals.

We stayed hidden behind shutters and the dogs had to be brought whimpering inside. The already small house now sheltered us all and we spent most of our time in the kitchen, the dogs shaking like winter shrubs at our feet. They squealed with terror every time the wind slammed and rattled the shutters against the glass. Sharing a room with a pack of snoring beasts wasn't easy and sleep was intermittent at best. Every few hours Sybel would bravely climb the steps to the roof to scan the sky for any sign of relief. Finding none, she would quickly return, shaking her head to let me know the storm still hadn't passed. Surprisingly, querents still ventured through the storm seeking solace. 'Storm or no storm, people will come for a reading,' she said, every time there was a knock at the door.

I didn't complain as they brought with them much-needed supplies: baskets of fruit and bundles of bread sodden from the rain, which we had to toast back to life in front of the stove.

'Someone must be really upset to unleash this tempest upon us,' she said, scooping up the dogs and stroking them one by one, murmuring soothing lullabies into their ears. 'But we have survived worse. Let's just hope the sirens don't sound, then we'll have to climb to the roof and wait there for it to be over.'

Sybel told me that years ago the water had drowned the city. It swept into the buildings like an uninvited guest and occupied every room. Instead of going to the main square for coffee, people would go there to swim. Cafés floated and people had to sit on tables rather than chairs to keep their feet dry. The central gallery was destroyed and paintings were carried away down the canals, along with masses of fruit and vegetables and old, soggy bread. The water was a thief, taking whatever it wanted, rifling through shops and ransacking houses. She had to wear fisherman boots up to her thighs, but it wasn't long before the water filled them and she was wading through it up to her shoulders. People had no choice but to climb on their roofs, fearing the water would reach their beds and drown them while they slept. One hundred people died during the great flood and the Church of One Hundred Souls was named in honour of their memory.

As the storm tore up the city outside, we played cards inside; warming our hands round cups of bubbling hot chocolate. On the fourth night, Sybel appeared in the doorway with a more hopeful look on her face.

'It looks like the storm is finally tiring of itself. In the morning, our shutters will be open once again.'

She was right, of course. By first light, the air was clear and calm, clouds fluffed the sky like clotted cream. People who had kept their doors locked for days, nervously slid back their bolts and slowly emerged into the world. Thankfully no deaths had been reported. The dogs were thrilled to be having their daily walks again and snuffled suspiciously at the uprooted trees and broken branches which lay strewn across pathways. This time, instead of hurrying past the bakery with a quick smile and a wave, I stopped to buy bread. The proprietor seemed pleased that I had finally found time for a quick word and took the opportunity to swirl the gossip round my ears. I left with a loaf under my arm and news that the grocer and his mistress had been washed away after one of their secret moonlit meetings. Storms uproot more than just trees and it isn't just the worms that try to wriggle out of the dirt.

After our walk, I left the dogs with their usual feast in the courtyard and headed back outside. The water was still filled with slush and debris, twigs and leaves, splinters of boats too late to be saved and broken flowerpots bobbing on the surface. Across the canal, I noticed the Keeper of the Hours, distinctive because of his long white beard and the long robe he wore. In his hand he held a long stick with a net fastened at one end, and I watched as he swept it through the water. It reminded me of home, where the children tried to catch crabs at the port; the memory made my heart feel too heavy to carry. The Keeper of the Hours raised his hand by way of greeting and I waved back, noticing that the water ran pink.

'Storms keep me busy,' he called, pausing to rest.

'What are you doing with the net?' I called.

'Unclogging wishes.' He loosened a collection of dried rosebuds and a mash of sopping paper, which had congregated near the steps. The pink tint in the water was the colour of trapped wishes.

'Won't those wishes come true now?' I asked, watching as he finally pushed them along.

'They will if they find their way to the sea,' he replied.

'You should be called the Keeper of the City.' I laughed, remembering all the places I had seen him. 'What else do you do besides restore time, polish door handles and unclog wishes?'

'I rescue the occasional stranded cat,' he called over his shoulder as he disappeared in search of more wishes to save.

I was eager to get back to the university before Leo Hawkins had a chance to notice the missing documents, but the lagoon's temper still quietly seethed, and Sybel advised that we had to wait a few more frustrating days.

One evening, I found myself meandering down the Street of Lost Buttons, which brought me to the entrance of Vesper Square. It was the only place open since I wasn't brave enough to drink alone and the churches were all too dark and empty. It was still a little early for these shops and not all of them had lit their lanterns yet. Even the accordion player was still asleep in a doorway. Stepping onto the cobbled courtyard felt like stepping into a fairy tale. The shops were narrow and crooked with pointed roofs like the hat of a witch. In the middle sat a gurgling fountain, which could just as easily have been a cauldron.

The shop doors were held open by stone weights in the shape of animals: an owl, a fox and a duck. It was a welcoming gesture, but I preferred to peer through the bow windows at the wonders within. There were snow globes and wind chimes that I could hear tinkling from behind the glass, even though there wasn't a breeze to stir them; a shop full of ticking clocks, and another filled with jugs and amphoras and copper cups. Across the cobbles, the windows revealed an odd assortment: flowery slabs of soap and incense; painted eggs and thimbles; sponges brought up from the bottom of the deepest oceans; velvet cushioned boxes filled with the sound of crunching snow or buzzing bees; teapots that played the song of a bird once you lifted their lids; brikia and thuribles hanging from long chains. The last shop seemed to float in the middle of a little canal, and could only be reached by crossing a small white bridge. As I stood wondering what curiosities it sold, I noticed a curtain blind shudder slowly open as though it was being manually wound. On the window ledge there were toppling jars just like the ones I had seen hanging from the Bridge of Longing. A flash of a face I thought I recognised appeared, quickly followed by a hand beckoning me inside.

The sound of the accordion player filled the air and looking over my shoulder, I could see a few more people had begun to tumble into the square. A boy, too young to be awake, was cloppeting around on a stick horse, creating an endless chatter between his feet and the cobbles. Stepping onto the bridge without fear, I made my way towards the door, lifted the latch and stepped inside. The shop was part library and part garden and I wasn't sure if its owner was a bookbinder or a botanist or something else entirely. I made my way through piles of paper waiting to be bound and plunged into a tangle of green. It felt like I was walking in a park or breathing in a forest. I wasn't sure what was for sale or whether there was anything to buy, but peeling back a large leaf I finally saw a counter. Behind it, sitting on a stool, was the Keeper of the Hours. He was watering a pot of overgrown ferns.

'Good evening,' he said. 'I am always a little late to open, because as you know I have so many things to do. I hope you haven't been waiting long.'

I shook my head. I hadn't been waiting at all.

'Very good. So you are here for your telling?'

'My what?' I frowned at him, not sure what he meant.

'Your token. What else would bring you here?'

'You sell them here?' I asked excitedly.

'No, no, they are not for sale; they are offerings from the bottom of the canals.' He stepped to one side to reveal the wall of shelves behind him. Lined with so many jars, I was reminded of the confectioner's shop at home. My eyes flited between them, finding not sweets but many different objects; dried rosebuds, tiny apples, paper stars, wooden yellow suns, wing feathers, olive branches and acorns. A few minutes later I realised they were all like the handles on the wishing doors, and the one I had opened had been filled with acorns. This shop was some kind of storage place for wishes.

'Pick a jar, then reach inside to find your telling token. It should feel like a smooth stone.' He spoke in a weary voice as though he had been doing the same thing for many years.

I scanned the jars once more until my eyes came to rest on a jar of feathers.

'That one,' I said, pointing to the top shelf. The Keeper of the Hours was so tall, he lifted it off with ease, unscrewed the lid, shook it up and offered it to me. I plunged my hand deep into the feathers; they felt warm and comforting. Swirling my fingers amongst them, I felt dozens of flat stones. Finally, I chose one, I lifted it out and held it in my palm. I squinted to see the inscription, but the light was too dim. The Keeper of the Hours kindly held a candle above my head so I could make out the letters more clearly: *The City of Murmurs*.

'What does it mean?' I asked, holding it out for him to see.

He was quiet, but seemed to be pondering an answer. 'Perhaps it simply means that you will never forget what you find here; it will always call to you.'

Before I left the strange shop, I noticed all the empty jars again in the window and called back into the hidden green depths, 'What are all these jars for?'

I wasn't sure if he could hear me through all the thick foliage, but then came a muffle of words, 'To collect the mist, of course.'

Rushing home, I was more restless than ever to get to the university and to find Leo Hawkins.

CHAPTER 20

'We have been invited to attend a masquerade ball,' said Sybel, busy spooning breakfast into the dogs' bowls. I could hear the scrape of metal as she ground the last dregs out of a large tin. 'It will distract you until the lagoon is safe to cross.'

A masquerade ball. I laughed. The idea brought with it a rush of childhood memories when I believed I could grow a carriage out of a pumpkin seed and would spend hours following the faint scuttles of mice hoping to transform them into horses. It sounded like a fairy tale. 'But why would I be invited?' I asked.

'Because I am and you will be my guest,' she said simply. 'It is all rather tedious for me now, but for you it will be a novelty and quite exciting, I imagine. I wouldn't want you to miss it.'

I nodded as she leaned in closer. 'The first time is always the best. We must, of course, wear our disguises. That's half the fun.' She clapped her hands in delight at the thought of it. 'It's difficult for a woman of my proportions to hide who I am behind a mask and a cloak, and therefore rather pointless, but I still wear them; it's the rule you see.' She lifted the reins from the hook and handed them to me. 'Take the dogs out and I will meet you at the mask shop in one hour; I have some errands to run first.'

Walking around the city, my head was filled with the thoughts of the ball. Everyone there would be hiding themselves, just like me and for one night I wouldn't be any different. I smiled, excited by the thought of it. After our usual jaunt in the park, I left the dogs at home and headed towards the mask shop, eager to find my disguise. It was while I was crossing the Bridge of Solace that I got the strange feeling of being watched again. I didn't know where it had come from, but it unnerved me and I pulled up the collar of my giant coat and quickened my pace. After some distance I slowed down again, stopping to buy a slice of olive bread, but when I stepped back onto the street, the feeling of uneasiness had returned. Instinct compelled me to pull my hood tighter around my face and lower my head to the ground. Now I was more concerned with being followed than getting to the mask shop, and, in my panic, I had become lost, winding deeper away from the crowds and further into the empty streets. Behind me I could hear hastening footsteps, echoing close to my own. Then a voice called out, the words were indistinct, but somehow, I knew they were meant for me. Suddenly, I felt a hand on my arm, and I span round to find the face of a man I didn't recognise. I wasn't sure what I saw in his eyes. Anger? Surprise? Curiosity?

'You have something I need,' he said, breathless from his chase.

His words gave me flight and without waiting to find out what it was he wanted, I shrugged myself free, dropped the bread at my feet, and ran faster than I had ever run before; swooping round corners, soaring over bridges and squares, slipping through passageways, trying to lose my pursuer. To escape, I flew. Breathing hard, I needed to find a place to stop before I collapsed. Thankfully in the middle of the next street I spotted a brightly painted yellow door; it popped up like a wish.

Moving closer, I held my hand against the beat of my heart until I could feel it steady itself once more, then with a deep exhale, I turned the sun-carved handle of the door and quickly disappeared inside. It took a moment for my eyes to adjust to the small dark interior, but when they did, I saw there were lots of tiny paper suns dangling from string and bowls filled of crinkled copper-coloured balls. Lifting one into my hand, I sat down on the little wooden ledge. Just like in the other wishing room, I could see the canal through a hole in the ground, ready to catch my wish. My chest ached, my legs shook, and I felt a twinge deep in my ribs. I closed my eyes, rolling the little paper sun between my palms, a soothing back and forth movement, waiting for my nerves to recover. I wasn't quite sure how the wishing rooms worked, but I remembered watching the Keeper of the Hours unclog paper from the canal and knew they needed to find their way to the sea, and so I dropped my paper sun into the water. Yellow for happiness, I thought, as I finally pushed open the door and tentatively checked for any sign of my pursuer. All was quiet, and, satisfied that I had lost him, I stepped back onto the street. Using the bell tower as a navigation point, I wound my way back through the city to the Street of Inkpots, where Sybel told me I would find the mask shop. When I arrived, she was already there waiting.

'You look like you've been running!' she exclaimed, taking in my dishevelled appearance, but I just nodded, not mentioning the strangeness of my afternoon. 'Sometimes whatever it is you are running from is the very thing you should be running to.'

Who was the man who had been following me? I tried to convince myself that he must have mistaken me for somebody else, but he had been so insistent, so sure it was me he wanted to talk to. I couldn't for one moment think what it was he needed from me, unless he had somehow seen my feathers. The idea made me gasp in alarm, and I began to imagine he had been sent from the Boat of Floating Freaks and Oddities? What exactly was it waiting for, moored on the edge of the city? I tried to push the dark thoughts from my mind, but I knew they would linger.

Above the door of the mask shop swung a little wooden sign, and written upon it in an elaborate flourish of green was the word *carnevale*. Its dark windows were split into many tiny squares and were so grime-filled and grease-smeared that your eye wasn't permitted to see what lay hidden within. The building had a weariness about it, like it had hobbled away to sulk in a back street. It reminded me of a hunched troll sitting at the foot of a bridge. Sybel leaned her weight against the door and pushed it open. A bell sounded and even that seemed reluctant. I was not prepared for the sight that awaited me then: row upon row of masks, all colours, sizes and shapes. I stared in open-mouthed wonder. It was the kind of place where I imagined a secret handshake or a surreptitious wink might permit you secret entry into a forbidden society. My eyes travelled up and down and along the shelves, but, before I had chance to look properly at one, my eye was already being distracted by another. Encouraged by Sybel, I drew closer and marvelled at each unique and intricate design. There was a whole shelf filled with animal faces, a fox and a horse and a rabbit with long straight ears; cats and mice and frightful bears. Each one seemed to tell its own story; varied and endless and alarmingly real, I thought they might actually come to life before my eyes.

'They are all so beautiful,' I whispered. They all seemed to be watching me and, in amongst the many masks, there hung rail after rail of cloaks, filling the shop with their swish of secrets whenever you brushed past them.

'Do you see any you like?' There was something in her tone that hurried me, but when I looked again, the choice was an impossible one.

I liked them all. I touched my fingertips to the smooth faces, tracing the swirls and stars on the surfaces. Some had the flamboyance of stage feathers, encrusted with jewels, some the simplicity of silver squares or blocks of colour. Musical notes danced across the cheeks of others and golden bells sang from tassels when I shook them. Carefully, I lifted one from its hook; it was made of simple black velvet with two oval holes cut out for the eyes. It had no strings or ribbons to hold it in place and I wondered how it would fix to a face.

Suddenly the owner appeared from the back room. His hair was a puff of misty grey like the head of a dandelion, or the snort of a cow in a winter field. Wisps so thin that I could see the mottled scalp beneath. His arms were covered in splashes of paint right up to his elbows and a streak fell across the bridge of his nose. I recognised him instantly. He had been for a reading the day I was waiting for the rat-catcher. He had arrived so early that Sybel had found him on the doorstep and had brought him in with the milk.

'Hello again,' he said, remembering me. 'I see you like The Morretta mask.' He hadn't yet noticed Sybel who was trying to hide herself, rather unsuccessfully, behind a cloak stand.

I looked down at the mask in my hand. 'I don't know which one to choose,' I admitted.

'Well, that one's a good one if you are planning a night of seduction.' He took the mask and held it against his face. 'Watch.' Then he let go, but the mask didn't fall; it stayed on his face.

'How are you doing that?' I asked, thinking it was a magic trick.

He dropped it back in his hand. 'There's a button here, see.' He held the mask out for inspection and I could indeed see the little knot of a button sewn onto the inside. 'You just bite it between your teeth and keep it there so it doesn't fall off.'

'But how can you speak with that in your mouth?'

'Ah, well, you can't; that's why it makes the wearer more enigmatic and so full of secrets. The talking must be done only with the eyes. It gives the wearer the chance to decide who she wants to talk to and in doing so, she must reveal herself, but only at the moment of her choosing. It's how many great love affairs have started – and ended,' he added quickly.

I replaced the mask on its hook and shook my head; it didn't feel quite right.

'What is it like at the ball? I asked, moving along the shelves, trying to imagine people wearing their costumes.

'It is the one night of the year when the Keeper of the Hours does not restore time and lets the minutes slip away, and anything you do slips away with it. It gives people a chance to lose themselves in celebrations held all over the city.'

But what if you are already lost, I thought to myself.

'You should know that the masks tend to choose you rather than the other way around.'

'Really?' If he was to be believed then everything here seemed to be filled with magic.

He nodded enthusiastically and his hair wobbled, and I thought it might blow away. 'But first you must think about what it is you love most in the world, and it will find you or a version of it will. Our disguise is often our desire.'

A sudden noise drew our attention. Sybel had got herself tangled in the cloaks and sent the whole stand crashing to the floor. She sprang fluster-full from the mayhem. The owner tutted and squinted into the gloomy corner to see who was responsible for causing such a commotion in his quiet little shop. His eyes suddenly opened wide with recognition and glee. 'Sybel, is that you?' He couldn't disguise the delight in his voice and quickly wiped the paint off his hands with his apron before rushing to assist her. She scooped up an armful of cloaks and began hanging them back on the stand.

'Don't worry about that,' he said, taking them from her and patting them in a crumpled heap on a nearby table.

Sybel began shuffling through the cloaks until she selected one and thrust it towards me. 'Here, I found you this.'

It felt smooth and heavy in my hands; a dark velvet fabric, with a purple satin lining. I pulled it over my coat and around my shoulders and twirled, delighted by the swish of the hem against the floor. No one would see my feathers under this. It felt like home.

'Perfect. Now for the mask,' urged Sybel impatiently.

'Choices cannot be rushed,' said the owner, thrilled to have Sybel captive in his shop. He was clearly going to make the most of this unexpected opportunity. Sybel rolled her eyes, realising her plan for a quick escape had just been thwarted by my indecision.

'Perhaps you would have time for a quick reading while we wait?' His voice took on the tone of a small child seeking permission for something that had already been forbidden.

Sybel sighed in defeat and pulled out the pouch from her pocket in which she kept her fortune stones. Such was her reputation, people would sometimes stop her in the street and ask for a glimpse of their future on a bridge, by a fountain, even on the steps of a church, but no one dared ask once they were inside. The warning in her eyes told me to hurry up and I returned to the difficult task of choosing a disguise. I picked up a porcelain mask of vibrant colours and scalloped edges. I held it against my face and stared at my reflection in the mirror, but quickly pulled it off; it felt too hot and cloying against my skin. Replacing it, I reached for another. This one had a bird-like beak and as I fitted it over my face, I shuddered at the mirror. I was reminded of the plague doctors from Professor Elms' books, and half expected to inhale the drifting scent of laudanum.

Moving further along the wall, I dismissed the half masks, which didn't allow for much secrecy, and the heavy-looking joker masks complete with collars and gold trims, which looked heavy and gaudy. It wasn't until I had almost reached the end of the wall and the shop itself, that I noticed a mask high on a shelf. It seemed to whisper to me and standing on my tiptoes I managed to push it forward from its hook until it dropped, like a wish, into my hand. It was smooth and cool to touch like water. Iridescent scales glittered above and below the left eye hole and two silver fish swam between them. Across the right cheek flew a flock of tiny birds painted in a bright cerulean blue against a white backdrop. Golden ribbons fluttered, one from each side ready to tie it in place.

'This one,' I said with absolute certainty, lifting it up to the dim light near the counter. Relieved that a decision had at last been made, Sybel scooped up the stones and dropped them back in the pouch with a clatter.

'The mermaid mask; how unusual,' said the owner, as I handed it to him, together with the cloak.

'The mermaid mask?' I looked again; I hadn't realised.

'Ah, yes – mermaids inhabit our waters, but you will be lucky to find one.' Then he furrowed his brow in a knot of distain, and corrected himself with a grumble, 'Or should I say unlucky. Cursed creatures,' he muttered, as he wrapped my purchases quickly and carefully in brown paper. The mask lay protected within the folds of the cloak. Once finished, he tied it loosely with a piece of string and then, dangling it from his finger, he offered me the package. 'Enjoy your ball.'

'What did he mean about mermaids?' I asked, as we left the shop.

'I wasn't listening,' she replied.

'About them being cursed?'

Sybel could see I wasn't about to give up until she gave me an answer.

'Haven't you heard about the siren's call? It lures you in and then abandons you on the rocks. Beware of the mermaid whose heart is made of nothing but water, for it will quickly flow away.'

CHAPTER 21

Dusk bowed over the city, a prelude to the night of carousing and merriment that lay ahead. As always in these thought-filled hours, my mind would take me home to the familiar damp smell of the cellar, which I never thought I would miss until I was no longer there. I missed Lemàn most of all. That last day, as she stood and watched me leave, I was filled with an unfathomable sadness. Not for me, but for her. At least when my father had gone away, he had left a part of himself behind. Now I had taken it away and left nothing in its place. A jagged thought that kept on cutting.

Sometimes, it would take all my strength not to rush to the edge of the lagoon and pace the flagstones until the next boat arrived bound west, but the need to find my father was stronger than my need to return. Sybel offered comfort by way of jasmine tea, which we'd sip long after the midnight chimes of the city had died away. We talked and laughed and shared our stories in the warmth of the now-familiar yellow kitchen, but eventually I would return to my room alone, where the sadness would rattle around my bones. They always seemed hollower then. So much had begun to fade: the warm smell of the whorehouse kitchen, the sound of a brush sweeping across the stone floor, the taste of baked pears in a pie, my bed made of wishes and the soft touch of Lemàn's fingertips lost in my feathers. Her voice was now so far away that even memory couldn't bring it back. I missed my home. Sleep became a distant stranger, who spoke in a language I didn't understand. I longed for the past, but needed my future.

'Are you ready?' Sybel asked, appearing in the doorway. 'We need to leave soon.' She was dressed in dark velvet and high stomping boots and her hair was crumpled about her head like tangled lovers' sheets.

I unfolded the cloak, lifted it over my shoulders and secured it at my neck with its small silver clasp. It was even heavier than Sybel's massive coat, and I seemed to move more slowly round the room with it on. Moments later, Sybel appeared again wearing a mask of pentacles and wands.'

'Where is your mask?' she asked in alarm.

I pointed to the bed, where it lay still packaged.

'Well, put it on,' she urged. 'It's bad luck to leave the house without it covering your face. Tonight, as soon as you step onto the streets you are no longer the same person. You are a mystery, an enigma, unknowable for one bewitching night. I have met some of my best lovers at carnivals.' She laughed. 'Although it seems like decades ago now.'

I lifted the mask to my face, and tied the silky ribbons around my head, adjusting it so I could breathe. My reflection in the mirror seemed strange, half bird, half fish, like I couldn't decide between a life of air or water. We hurried through the streets, which were crowded with people, all wanting to experience their unspoken desires. Sybel's size made our path easy and she pushed us through. Finally, we arrived in the main square where a long queue of people lined the steps leading up to a large domed building opposite the clock tower. To my surprise Sybel didn't slow her pace and instead of joining the back of the queue, she ignored it completely and continued across the flagstones, and into the Street of Thickening Plots, far quieter and murkier than all we had left behind. We were now entering the depths of the city.

'Be careful,' she warned. 'Eye contact here will cost you more coins than you carry in your pocket.'

On either side of the street, instead of tables and chairs inviting you to sit and while away the evening, the invitation was for something else entirely. The buildings were badly neglected; some no longer had doors, just open spaces where they should have been.

'Isn't the ball back there?' I asked, hoping we had taken a wrong turn.

'A ball, yes, but not our ball.'

Finally, Sybel stopped abruptly by some steps leading down to the canal. Moments later, out of the darkness, sailed a crescent-shaped boat. The driver steered over to us and Sybel took two tickets out of an envelope, and handed them to him. After a cursory glance, he nodded and she stepped on board, encouraging me to follow.

'We have to go the rest of the way by boat.'

Soon, we were travelling down canals I had never seen before, where the water seemed to ooze and stutter rather than flow. The streets here had no names, or if they did, they had worn away long ago until no trace of them remained. I thought I had uncovered all the secrets of this city, especially after my daily dog walks, but it seemed I was mistaken. Still, I knew nothing, only whispers. At one point the spaces between the walls were so narrow, they were barely the width of the boat and I feared we would have to swim our way through or be trapped here forever. I needn't have worried, with Sybel's strength and the oarsman's skill we didn't stop for long and the boat screeched its way through like a burning witch.

The sounds of the city had dropped away, leaving an eerie quiet. The buildings here were forlorn and abandoned, and instead of windows there were dark gaping mouths, their shutters broken or gone. Steps worn to rubble and roofs destroyed by storms. The stench was foul and festering, and I was grateful for the mask covering my nose. Occasionally I saw a dead rat, floating bloated-belly up, poisoned by the rotting debris that gathered in the alcoves. In the distance, I was horrified to see what I thought was the head of a small child mottled white in the water, but as we drew closer, I was relieved to discover it was just the half-chewed core of a cabbage. The light and shadow played tricks on the mind, a grotesque magic act; the lure of the lurid; sorcery at its worst. Even the birds didn't nest here, they had long since flown away, such was the sense of decay in the stagnant water. I began to wonder if the oarsman had taken a wrong turn – it felt as if I was being delivered to the gates of Hades – but then Sybel suddenly pointed up ahead.

'Look – we're almost there.'

Staring into the gloom, I struggled to see anywhere worthy of hosting a grand ball, but then my eye glimpsed a flickering light, then another and another until it looked like hundreds of demons' eyes were upon us. High on the upper floor of a crumbling ancient building, I counted eight large windows and realised now that the light came from the candles flickering within. The walls seemed to rise out of the canal like some dark, mythical creature. Once upon a time, I imagined this place would have been truly magnificent with its wide marble steps guarded by two winged lions, its facade warmed to apricot in the sun.

Its many imposing rooms filled with dignitaries from far and wide. But that would have been centuries ago. Now the gangrene walls were covered with slime and algae, an infection waiting to spread. A disease harboured in every crevice. The steps too, had lost their gleam, now dark and sunken like cracked slabs in a graveyard.

'Be careful getting out,' warned Sybel, as I stepped onto their slippery surface. I steadied myself against her arm as the boat silently pulled away and out of sight.

Most of the ground floor was submerged under the water and we had to walk across makeshift planks of wood on stilts, which rose out of the water like chicken legs. I hitched up my cloak to stop the bottom from getting damp. As we approached the grand staircase the sound of water began to fall away and so too did the darkness. At the top, we were greeted by the sight of a huge carving in the wall: a golden cherub on a winged chariot, holding the reins of two rearing horses. Next to this was an open archway in the shape of an hourglass and the most bewildering sight I had ever seen: the room was full of people, all of whom were still and silent as though they had been paused in time. Sybel fumbled in her cloak and drew out a large brass clock winder. I watched curiously as she slotted it into the wheel of the chariot, which had the face of a clock, and as she began to twist it widdershins, I was amazed to hear the welcoming sound of laughter and merriment, and of glasses clinking together in warm celebration. Through the hourglass, the room had suddenly

breathed back into life and time continued, but what time
was this, and what magic was I now a part of? It reminded
me of the night I had arrived. As we crossed the threshold
into the room, my heart burst with wonder and
anticipation.

'Where are we?' I asked, each step I took urgent with
excitement.

'The Palace of Sirens,' she replied.

The room was fluttering with disguise. It was starlit and
moon polished, and, looking up, it was impossible to tell
if the room opened straight into the night or whether
there was a glass ceiling to protect us from the rain, should
it fall. Hundreds of dancing candles exaggerated all movement, as smoke from rolled-up cigarettes and curling pipes
drifted into the unfathomable dark. I was convinced then
that I would feel the rain if it fell. Above us hung many
wooden clocks, too many to count, each one floating on
its invisible string. Their pendulums were no longer
swinging, their faces still, no shudder of movement, no
pulse of time, the hum of all mechanisms had stopped
just before midnight. A cuckoo was frozen on its perch
with its beak open; its message silenced.

All time suspended.

Painted on the floor in blue and glinting gold was a
giant clock face. The designs were hidden under the movement of hundreds of quick-moving feet, but I glimpsed
a spinning wheel, and a pair of lovers, and I realised it
was a replica of the one that stood in the square. Passing

by tables I noticed vases full of broken clock pieces. A reminder of timewreck.

In one corner a string quartet played on. The candles responded with their strange, hypnotic dance. Finally reaching the bar, I stared back into the room; there must have been hundreds of people here. They were all dressed in the same dark cloaks, their faces hidden behind an array of spectacular masks. An enticing, yet mysterious anonymity. I wondered if any of the faces were familiar beneath these masks: the happy baker; the gypsy woman; the Keeper of the Hours; the mask-maker himself or even my pursuer. I shuddered at the thought of him hiding somewhere in the shadows. Tonight, people's true selves no longer existed. Even the rat-catcher could be part of this world without fear and judgement. For tonight we could all be whoever we wanted to be, an angel or a demon or something in between. I felt like a part of this city, part of a secret society, tucked away in the unreachable corners of long ago. Ancient, guarded mysteries revealed here in this room. The bartender handed me a flute of something sparkling and sweet; a strawberry fizzed at the bottom, and I reached inside and lifted it out and popped it into my mouth. Melting instantly on my tongue, I swallowed the sweet gritty mush; it was the most delicious thing I had ever tasted.

'To disguise!' exclaimed Sybel, raising her glass.

I had drunk too quickly and my glass was empty apart from a little green stalk at the bottom. Feeling dizzy, I collapsed onto an old sofa and regarded the continuing celebration. Glasses rose up out of the crowds and people toasted their freedom. A woman with midnight hair and the mask of a cat had made her own dance floor in the corner and was swaying seductively; her discarded cloak floated to the floor and her short dress twisted around her hips. Both men and women looked up from their conversations, words hovered, while the whole room stared, strangely enthralled. She smiled, eyes closed, lost in the moment, and I wondered what it would feel like to captivate a room like that. I hadn't done it since the night I was born.

In front of me, a man was entertaining a group of purring women. Their cloaks had been pushed back over their pale bare shoulders, revealing heaving breasts that rose and fell beneath their bodices. Shrieking in delight, they flung their hair-tousled heads back, elongating the white flesh of their necks like swans. He wore the mask of a hundred hearts, but I could see the mischievous twinkle in his eyes as they intensified their pursuit. The room was like a kiln, and I had grown uncomfortably hot watching everything take shape before me, impervious to time. Beads of perspiration had begun to irritate the skin above my mouth, and I dabbed at them with the edge of my cloak just as Sybel appeared with another two drinks.

'What is this place?' I asked, mesmerised.

'A place of desire. It exists only because we all came here and only for one night. A shared illusion. Nothing more, nothing less. We have stepped outside time. Enjoy it while you can.'

I frowned. 'So, none of this is real?'

'For us it is. But morning will arrive sooner than you think, and drag us all home.'

'I don't understand.' Perhaps it was the drink, but nothing seemed to make sense any more.

'We crossed into a different world tonight, the world of water. This building is sinking; the lower floors are already completely submerged. That's why they call it the Palace of Sirens. It belongs more to them than to us.'

'It belongs to mermaids?' I asked, in a barely audible whisper.

'Yes. It's a secret place and soon it will be lost.'

Sybel disappeared again into the middle of an ever-increasing throng of people, laughing her heart into the air. Tonight, people's mistakes were not their own. Everything was fantasy and nothing was forbidden. Regret didn't receive an invitation to this party and blame didn't follow you home.

I heard a whisper in my ear; 'Don't be afraid of the boat,' it said.

I whirled round to see who had spoken, but through the jostle of warm swaying bodies it was impossible to know where it had come from. Perhaps the message hadn't been meant for me or perhaps I had imagined it. Then I heard the voice again – 'The mist is coming' – but still I couldn't tell who it belonged to, man or woman, for no lips moved.

It was in that moment that my eyes found her. It was the girl from the window, and this time she was standing quite alone in the arch of a doorway. It was her hair that revealed her to me; the unmistakable brightness of August sunflowers illuminating the darkness. She was barefoot and her feet looked strange and unlike any I had ever seen before. Even from across the room I could see that each toe was webbed to the next. Just like me she was different, something else, something other. We were the same. Then she moved, like golden sunlight glinting between the dark cloaked trees. Then Lemàn's voice returned; *Beware of the woman in the forest*, she said.

Dizzy, I tried to push through the crowds and my hand fell upon a man's back. He mistook my touch for desire and grabbed at my waist, but I pushed him away. When I looked again, she had vanished. Desperately, my eyes darted around the room, like minnows searching between the rocks for refuge. Gathering my cloak so as not to trip, I hurried towards the doorway. Peering into the corridor, I saw nothing, but then I heard a swish and to the left I caught sight of the end of her dark cloak and the bonfire spark of her hair disappearing around a corner. Compelled, I followed her into the shadows. The light had all but gone as I felt my way along the damp and musty walls, the sweetness of the strawberry replaced by the taste of the ocean's salt on my tongue as I plunged deep into the unfamiliar darkness.

CHAPTER 22

Finally, I saw a light quivering from an open doorway and I could hear the unmistakable sound of her singing. This room was gloomy, lit only by a single squat candle resting on the table. Shelves rose from floor to ceiling, and a pair of ladders leaned against the books displayed there. This was a library, or rather the relic of one. A small staircase led up to a cluster of armchairs positioned in front of a giant, stone portico. It was from here that she sat, watching me like a curious cat.

'I saw you outside my window.' She spoke in whispers, her smile never leaving her face.

'Yes,' was all I managed as I drew closer. With each step, my feathers seemed to grow larger and tingle in anticipation of what was to come.

'Sit,' she said, gesturing towards a chair.

Slowly, I moved up the stairs, each one groaning with age.

On the table in front of her lay a book simply entitled *The Sea*.

'I miss it so much,' she said, gesturing towards the book. Then with a sigh deeper than desire, she turned to gaze out across the lagoon. Her curls waltzed gently in the breeze. She wore a cloak but no mask covered her face, and I wondered about the rule. Her expression was as still as water, but her eyes shone emerald like a sun-filled forest. Behind them was a story I wanted to hear. It was the first time I realised that being flawed could be so beautiful, and for that reason I found myself drawn to her.

Up close I could now see her toes were webbed together by a semi-translucent, violet skin, too wide and awkward to fit inside any shoe. Even the large, heavy boots worn by the men down at the boat factory wouldn't do. She was more real than the mermaid I had seen years ago inside the circus tent, but mermaids were no longer just a myth. She was hiding nothing, happy to display her difference. She was brave, and everything I wanted to be. Lifting my eyes back to her face, I realised she had caught me staring, and I quickly looked away with my cheeks aflame.

'They help me to swim,' she replied. 'I never like to be far from water.' Then she hesitated, contemplating something. 'Do your feathers help you to fly?'

My cloak must have loosened as I sped after her along the corridors, and shyly I pulled it tighter, even though now it was too late to stay hidden. Shaking my head, I felt shame shoot up my spine like a surge of mercury. My cheeks burned.

She frowned, perhaps in disappointment. 'Why are you hiding them?'

'I'm not,' I lied, folding my arms protectively across my chest. My words left my mouth too quickly to be believed. 'I'm the same as everyone else here tonight.'

She moved closer then and I could smell oysters and clams and shells and the salt taste of the sea washed over everything. 'Your disguise is not just for tonight, though; is it?' Her mouth was large and a delicate pink and she smiled wider, revealing small pointed white teeth. Her wide eyes swam in front of me now more like glittering green fish. I was no longer inside the make-believe world of a circus tent, with its trickery and spectacle. Here and now, everything could be believed, yet it felt just as dream-like.

'You remind me of the sea,' I murmured. 'Is that where you're from?'

'And you remind me of the sky,' she replied, not answering my question. 'A beautiful, sunset sky.' I felt her fingers in my hair and shuddered as she gently lifted my mask and pressed her lips against mine without warning or hesitation.

Our survival centres on the mouth: breathing, eating, kissing. When she kissed me, I felt possibilities all at once.

Joy and passion, anguish and despair. The ebb and flow of yes and no; keep going, stop, discover, run and hide. Gridlock, landlock, padlock, wedlock, but there is no greater snare than heartlock. I learned early that whores give their bodies to strangers without thought, but mouths must never meet if the heart is to be protected. It is the only way in.

'What is your name?' she asked, pulling away. A curl of her hair brushed against the skin of my arm and this time it was a shiver that shot up my spine.

'Maréa,' I whispered. 'It means the tide.'

'Maréa.' Slowly she said my name back to me, letting the 'ray' sound in its middle soften and dissolve like sugar on her tongue.

'What is yours?'

'You are a Sky-Worshipper,' she said, once again offering no answer to my question.

'Am I?'

She smiled. 'You are filled with light and air and the sound of birds. I heard it on your lips and felt it in your hair.'

'What do you know of Sky-Worshippers?' I asked, barely above a whisper and yet still my breath made the candle flame flicker.

She leaned in close again. 'I know they move to a different rhythm, like me. Their voice is carried far through the air, so far it can even reach the depths of the sea. I hear the messages they share; simple yet secretive, just like the sound of water.'

'Do you understand them?'

My question seemed to break a spell and she stepped back.

'I must go,' she said quickly.

'Go? Do you mean back to the party?' I asked hopefully, but somehow I knew that wasn't what she meant at all.

'No.' She laughed. 'I didn't come for the party.'

'But you can't go yet; the first boat isn't arriving until sunrise,' I protested. The dark sky with its luminous edge like the glint of a sharp blade meant several more hours of the illusion still remained.

She laughed again, a deep throaty gurgle and climbed onto the high ledge.

'I didn't need a boat to leave this place,' she said.

'Please!' I reached out my hand to try and pull her back.

'Don't be afraid of what makes you different. Lose your disguise!' she said, unclasping her cloak and letting it fall into the folds of darkness.

I edged forward – 'Wait ... what's your name?' – but it was too late as I felt the soft curls of her hair slip through my fingertips and then nothing – nothing but the salt carried on the breeze.

The canal was a long way down, and the darkness revealed nothing. I rushed to get the candle and held it over the water, but there was nothing there, and nothing moved. All was quiet and empty and still. Apart from my heart fluttering free, uncaged by her kiss, already lost with nowhere to go.

Returning to the party, I felt a mixture of peculiar emotions, relieved only when the first boat of the morning drifted towards the steps. I had made my excuses to go outside for some air, unbelievable considering the stench that clawed its way along the canal like a mangled half-dead creature. Nevertheless, I had to escape the walls of the palace and search the water for any sign that not everything tonight had been an illusion. I was beginning to think that the strawberries had been laced with something rich and potent, such was the strangeness of my encounter. Of course, there was nothing in the water. The ledge had been on the other side of the building, looking out to the lagoon and beyond that to the sea, but the canals were all interwoven, one running into another, and I hoped that their secrets would connect and that she would be carried this way. I sat down on the last stone step, the hem of my cloak sopping beneath the froth of the water. I was no longer mindful of how quickly it soaked into my boots.

What had just happened? The truth was too absurd to trust. She had kissed me, that bit at least was real, wasn't it? I rubbed my lips together, but nothing of her remained. My eye drew quickly back to the water; there was nothing to see but darkness, fathoms and fathoms deep. I was suddenly startled by the creak of a boat lit by the tiny flame of a lantern on a hook. Sybel with her ability to sense everything appeared just as the first boat moored.

'If you sit so close to the water, a mermaid might just pull you in.' She smiled in amusement.

But it was too late; one already had and my thoughts dropped like pennies in a fountain, each one weighted with a wish.

CHAPTER 23

Waiting. All I ever seemed to do was wait. First, waiting to leave the cage of my room, then waiting to arrive in the City of Murmurs, then waiting to discover more about my father, and now waiting to catch another glimpse of the girl with hair the colour of sunflowers.

There was something about her that stayed in my mind. She was different, like me, yet unlike me she didn't hide her difference. I remembered her feet, and how strange they looked, yet she seemed proud to have them, like they were a blessing. The webbing looked too thick for any knife to slice through, and yet I somehow knew that she would never even have picked one up to try. I marvelled at her openness, and her bravery made me curious. Did I admire her or was it something else, something more? My growing fascination left me bewildered. The only visitors I had seen in the whorehouse were men; I never questioned it then, but now I wondered if what I felt was forbidden, and if feelings can ever really be forbidden.

I hadn't touched the transcripts since I had stolen them from Leo Hawkins' desk, and now, with newfound determination, I swept them up and took them to the solitude of the roof. I wanted to make sense of the words for myself, but as I looked at them, it was just a mysterious pattern of unconnected symbols and lines and colours tangled across the paper, and it all blurred into one.

From up here, I could see the roof tops of the City of Murmurs tumbling far into the distance like a gigantic unsolvable puzzle; their amber tiles varnished by the sun. Through the gaps and cracks between the walls of the houses, the blue haze of the sea flickered and a boat drifted away from the city. The sight of the boat meant that the lagoon waters had stilled, and so, bundling the papers under my arm, I raced downstairs to tell Sybel. My excitement quickly faded as I saw the door to the kitchen was closed and its latch dropped telling me she had a visiting querent. If I wanted to go to the university today, then I would have to go by myself.

Frustration overtook fear, and an hour later, I was knocking upon the door to Leo Hawkins' study. From within a voice called for me to enter, and, for the second time, I opened the door. The dark, damp day filtered very little light into the room despite the double glass doors being flung wide open into the garden. A lamp lit his workspace, and, spread out beneath it, were pages and pages of documents and files. Flexing his wrist, he looked up, his face a mixture of exhaustion and surprise.

'It's you,' he exclaimed, peering at me over his spectacles.

At first, his recognition confused me, but, as I stepped closer, I realised I recognised him too. He had been my pursuer.

In my panic I backed into a table, toppling an egg from its stand. I watched in horror as it rolled towards the edge and then fell to the floor shattering into hundreds of tiny pieces. I gasped at my clumsiness and bent down to try and gather them up. Leo Hawkins kneeled beside me and gently placed his hand on top of mine.

'I'm so sorry,' I stammered.

'Perhaps I should add damaging property to your list of crimes.'

I flushed red; he somehow knew that I had taken the manuscripts. Catching my eye, he smiled reassuringly, and swept my carelessness into a dustpan before discarding it in the bin. 'It's only one of hers. I was going to have it for my breakfast.'

At that moment, a plump chicken, the colour of summer freckles, appeared in a doorway across the room, which led into the gardens. It watched us with great curiosity and then flapped noisily onto the desk, where it settled clucking as content as a parlour cat.

'I didn't steal anything,' I said firmly. 'I just borrowed some documents, which I was planning to return, but then the storm came and it wasn't safe.'

'I'm more interested to know why you wanted them in the first place,' he said.

'Is that why you were following me?'

He nodded. 'I saw you leave my study and soon after I realised that some of my documents were missing. I never meant to scare you, but you move too quick for me and I never got the chance to explain.'

'But how did you recognise me?'

He reached out and lifted the edge of the oversized coat. His touch made me flinch, and I quickly stepped back snatching the fabric out of his hand. 'Sometimes, the thing you wear to hide yourself is the thing that makes you easier to find.'

He was right; the coat was much too big for me and too distinctive with its patches of purple and green – more bedspread than garment.

'I want to find this man, and I thought the documents might help me,' I said, pulling the crumpled photograph of my father from one of its pockets. 'He is a member of the Ornis Tribe. Do you know them?'

As he examined it carefully, I found myself studying him. I liked the open curiosity of his face and his gentle thought-filled eyes, dark as coffee beans and just as exhilarating.

'I'm afraid this was taken before I arrived and I don't know the man in it,' he said, handing me back the photograph. 'Professor Bottelli often spoke about the people who lived as birds, but sadly he is no longer here to ask. He said they live on an island that floats far out to the east of the lagoon. A place of trees and mist and water. Legend says it moves like a migrating bird, never staying in the same place for long. It has no fixed co-ordinates.'

'Have you ever been there?' I asked, my mind full of imaginings.

He shook his head. 'No, I wish I had, but I'm afraid it's an impossible wish. It doesn't appear on any map. Professor Bottelli believed it floated suspended in the air and not on water at all, hidden between swirls of mist and cloud and only accessible by wings.'

'But there must be a way to find him,' I demanded. 'If Professor Bottelli brought him here, then surely we can do the same.'

Leo sat back down at his desk. 'They visit the city from time to time, but the island is ever-shifting and there is no predictable pattern to when it will arrive. Some years they visit twice, then there might be no sign of them for years. It depends on the mist and the tide and the pull of the moon.' He stretched back in his chair, his body long and lithe, and I couldn't help but blush, before averting my gaze. 'I have some more of his findings here, if you would like to see them,' he asked, sifting through a pile of papers behind him.

229

I nodded and settled onto a little armchair. Listening to Leo read my father's words to me felt strange, mysterious, illusionary. I listened as his world slowly emerged from the pages on the desk, unravelled and untangled in this quiet little room on an island in the middle of a lagoon so far away from everything. This was the closest and the furthest I had ever been to what I wanted. I longed for Lemàn to hear these words too as they flew around the room, finally released from years of captivity. Leo told me all about the language they spoke with its varied whistles and warbles, some ear-piercingly loud, others soft little chirrups. Sounds loud enough to be heard over the rush of a waterfall, through the torrents of rain, carried high above the icy tips of the mountains and dropped into the deepest cave. The language of the birds bloomed in full colour.

I learned the tribe wasn't migratory, preferring instead to remain on their island, following its movements, strengthened by its mists. Its members had excellent vision and hearing, and could sense a change in the weather hours before it arrived. I thought back to the storm on the boat, and how I had been able to sense it before anyone else. I smiled at how much it was all making sense. I did have the instincts of a bird, and for the first time I saw it as a gift. According to the notes, their wings made a fast, clicking sound when rubbed together, usually in happiness, and their feathers bloomed and fluffed in fear or excite-ment, or desire. Feelings I was beginning to recognise.

The members of the tribe had soft down growing from their skin and what Professor Bottelli described as thick plumage across their backs and down their arms. The males grew a ring of dark-purple feathers around their necks upon maturity whereas it was the presence of a dark-red tail feather that signified female adolescence. I remembered mine well.

Waking one morning I found myself surrounded by a pile of moulted feathers. I thought I was being punished for the time I tried to cut them all off in the kitchen. When Lemàn had lifted my nightdress for closer inspection she laughed, realising that it was just my old feathers making way for the new ones. She fetched a mirror and held it up for me to see. At the bottom of my back, where my feathers grew the shortest, I saw the beginning of a tail feather, the vivid colour of vermillion. It looked like a fresh bruise or a trickle of blood against my skin, a wound that wouldn't heal. But now I understood its true meaning.

'The man you are interested in was one of the leaders of the Ornis Tribe. His name is Eddero.'

It was the first time I had heard his name, and I rolled it over and over in my mind like a lucky penny. It was as though I had been given a key to open a door I had yet to find.

'It says here that he loved the rain and would spend hours sitting under trees, letting it bounce off his head.'

I smiled at how similar we sounded.

'And look, I found these.' Leo placed a couple of sketches in front of me, so precise they looked real. The first was of a foot, large and splayed like a giant sea-bird. The second was of a face, but more specifically a nose, drawn from several different angles. Straight on, it was definitely a nose like any other, but from the side it curved as though it had once decided it might have preferred to be a beak. The last picture was an old withered hand; its fingers long and twisted with thick nails like talons. Writing, which I believed to have been Bottelli's, accompanied each drawing, detailing the size and colour and texture. The last sketch was a feather, intricately drawn and I ran my fingertips along it as though I could somehow bring it to life.

A question bubbled. I didn't want to ask it, but I needed to know. 'Does it say anywhere in the files that – he had any children?'

Leo looked up and his eyes softened. He recognised at once my apprehension.

'No,' he said quietly. 'There is no mention of children.'

I wasn't sure if that brought relief or torment.

'All we can do is wait for the mist.'

'The mist?' I had heard people mention the mist so many times, but never once had I imagined it was connected to my father.

Leo lowered his eyes and began to read from Professor Bottelli's papers: '"The swirling mist is seen as a remedy to cure many ailments, and most notably, heartache. From the bell tower rejected lovers watch for the mist to arrive and when it does, they race to their boats and sail out to collect it in their jars. However, this is not advised. It is better to wait until it is brought ashore by the members of the Ornis Tribe themselves. They bring it from the heart of the island, where the mist is pure and unfiltered and so much stronger. That is how you will know the Ornis Tribe, conjured out of mist and air, is on its way; always the silver mist precedes it.'"

The silver mist. Something clicked into place, and then the wheel turned on a memory. I remembered the unopened jar hidden in Lemàn's room, and the man I had seen on the night of my arrival, clutching the jar of swirling mist to his chest as though his life depended on it.

'I've seen it!' I crossed the room and perched on the end of the desk. 'On the night that I arrived, I saw a man with a jar of mist like you just described. He held it as tight as treasure.'

'Are you sure?'

I nodded excitedly. 'Yes.' There was no doubt in my mind.

'If this is true then the island won't be far behind.'

I felt my heart lighten.

'I'm still trying to work on this transcript,' he said, pointing at another document. 'I can't quite make sense of it, but there is something that keeps the tribe coming back to this city.'

'Really?' I asked, desperate to know what it was.

Leo seemed as keen as me to discover more and solve the mystery. 'Perhaps we can work on it together since you have the other sections?'

He was staring right into my eyes and I felt myself smile and blush again as his hand fell lightly against mine. At that moment my feathers fluffed themselves out in response to his gaze. No one had ever looked at me like that before, but now his expression had changed, and his eyes widened in surprise. To my horror I realised my feathers had swollen so much they'd forced their way from beneath my bandages. I had felt them stir a little, but had no idea they had sprung to life with such ferocious determination. Gasping, I dropped the bundle of transcripts and they fluttered to the floor. Quickly, I flicked up the collar on my coat to try and hide them, but it was too late and instinctively I ran into the shadows like an injured bird.

'It's okay.' His voice carried across the room, but still I couldn't move. 'I will be right here whenever you are ready to come out.'

I couldn't tell what he was thinking and so I waited, trying to work out my own thoughts. Shame nailed my feet to the floor. I could hear the loud ticking of a pendulum clock, which I hadn't heard until that moment, but of course it had always been there. Torn between the idea of moving back into the room and the humiliation which kept me crouching in the dark, I did nothing. The ticking seemed to grow ever louder and more insistent. I counted the movement of time, much slower than the beat of my own heart, its one beat to every two of mine. Moments passed and so too did my fear. Silently, I got to my feet.

'Did you see them?' I finally whispered.

'Yes,' he replied. After a pause he spoke again, 'But why do you hide them?'

I gave no answer, but in my head I knew why. For some reason it mattered what Leo thought, and I didn't want to give him a reason to find me ugly. I could hear him busy at his desk, the rummage of papers, the scratch of a pencil, the slide of a chair. I couldn't stay hidden in the corner forever, so I quietly stepped into the light. He looked up briefly and smiled before lowering his gaze to protect my modesty. I noticed the dropped transcripts had been tidied into a neat pile on the desk.

'Be careful, you can get lost in the dust and gloom of this room. A few footsteps into the corner and you'll disappear into another century.'

I had no choice then, but to trust him. 'They are my secret,' I confessed.

'What a beautiful secret to have,' he replied calmly, looking me directly in the eye. 'My secret is that my best friend is a hen.'

I laughed, and then we were laughing together. I was grateful he didn't look down at my feathers, although I was sure they were now safely tucked away out of sight.

Something passed between us then; an unspoken moment that meant we were no longer strangers. We had connected. 'I have one question though, and I think I already know the answer.'

I frowned, still not ready to reveal myself. 'What is it?'

'Why is it so important that you find the man in the photograph?'

I was relieved he wasn't asking about my feathers, but then I felt my pulse quicken and I wrapped my arms around myself in a protective hug.

'If I know why, it might help.' His words were warm and filled with sincerity. 'But I understand if that's another secret you want to keep to yourself.'

His words made me remember those spoken by the Keeper of the Hours: that the only person I was hiding from here was me. Leo was the one person who understood birds, and perhaps he would understand me if given the chance. Suddenly, I wanted to share what mattered most and for it to matter to him too.

'Because he is my father,' I replied. 'Finding him will help me to find myself.'

Leo nodded slowly; his eyes so full of thought. 'Then I will try my best to work all this out for you.'

'Is that what you thought I'd say?' I was curious to know how much he understood without being told.

Leo raised his eyebrows. 'That's exactly what I thought you'd say.'

'How did you know?'

'Because you look just like him. It's remarkable – unmistakable, in fact.'

Smiling, I crossed the room, still hesitant, but less nervous than before and peered once again at the strange letters. I let my finger trace the haphazard swirls and shapes on the page, whose meanings would soon be revealed, bringing me one step closer to finding him.

'What can we do now?' I asked, like a child impatient for more.

'I think all we can do now is wait for the silver mist to arrive.'

As we said goodbye, we agreed to meet again to share our findings and the idea pleased me. The light in his eyes made me feel something strange, something I couldn't describe. Fear – perhaps nerves or excitement? A feather-ruffled in reply, but I ignored it, unable to understand its meaning.

CHAPTER 24

Back in the city I tried to loosen all the thoughts in my mind, but they jangled loudly like a chain of keys waiting to turn a lock; there were too many doors and I wasn't sure which one to open. Knowing my father's name brought him that little bit closer to me, and I repeated it over and over again until I reached the Bridge of Longing. At first, I didn't notice that some of the jars were no longer empty, but by the time I had crossed to the other side, I saw that over half of them had been filled with mist. I reached down and lifted one gently from its hook to peer at the swirling contents. The island is on its way, I thought, anticipating what would happen when it finally arrived.

Finally standing back on the Street of Lost and Found, I could see that the shutter was down on the kitchen window, which meant that Sybel was still with a querent. Not in the mood to sit alone, I walked past the courtyard. Even though my head was filled with my father and with what Leo had told me, memories of the masquerade ball still hung heavy and bright like a net of oranges. I didn't know why, but I couldn't shake the girl with the sunflower hair from my mind and the thought of not seeing her again made my feet fall flat against the paving stones. Maybe just one glimpse would be enough to satisfy me; besides she had mentioned the language of the Sky-Worshippers and perhaps she could help me to understand it. I tried to convince myself that this was my only reason for seeing her again, but I had a niggling feeling of doubt.

I found Sybel's boat where she had stowed it in the alcove, unhooked the rope, and climbed inside. Nervously, I lowered the oar into the water and began to row just as I had seen her do many times before. The boat would bring me right beneath her window. The City of Murmurs by water seemed like a different place, slower, calmer, more hushed, and I found I preferred it. I tried to remember the way Sybel had steered us through the city towards the lagoon, where I would find her building.

Some of the waterways were dark and gloomy, the walls of the buildings towering above and too narrow for my boat to pass between, and then I would have to steer quickly in a different direction. Whenever I travelled underneath a bridge, I caught a fleeting and tantalising look at the other half of the City of Murmurs with its markets and churches and knots of people, only untied in the larger squares. The canal wasn't empty, but it was much less tangled than the streets around it. Occasionally, crescent-shaped boats would pass by, and I could hear the excited whispers of their wide-eyed occupants – some with their arms wrapped lovingly round each other, heads nestled against shoulders, smiling happily at the romance of it all. How many people came here to start their lives together? How many came here to fix them? The boatmen rowed methodically, unresponsive, just nodding occasionally whenever they passed one another. Worn down by repetition. Weighted by water.

Some windows were level with my eyes and I could hear the clatter of pots and pans from the restaurant kitchens within. Through another, I could see a pair of lovers stretched out naked on a bed, sleeping away the afternoon. A woman hanging out her washing between windows, carelessly dropped a sock into the water and shouted angrily at the canal, shaking her head in exasperation as she watched it float away.

Soft light drifted through the clouds like the splayed claws of a sleepy cat, and it was late afternoon when I reached her building. I recognised the bridge first and then her window with its blue shutters. I raised the oar and let the boat steady itself in the water. At this time of day, the sun fell against her wall, bathing it in warm translucent glow. I wasn't sure what I was hoping to achieve just by sitting there, perhaps nothing, but the knowledge that I was close. I didn't even know if she was inside or even if she was still in the city. Then it occurred to me that she might not live there at all. My heart sank with disappointment at the thought, but with nothing else to do, and nowhere else to go, I sat and watched and waited.

All we have is time.

If she was inside, what would she be doing, I wondered? I imagined her bathing in scented oils, her hair flooding around her like golden dancing anemones. Afterwards, she would slip into a silk robe, and sit at her table drinking tea and pomegranates, always pomegranates. I prayed for her to come to the window, but nothing stirred. Suddenly overcome with a feeling of loneliness I drifted away from the darkness of this waterway and re-joined the sunlit world.

There were still several hours of the day left and I decided to spend them learning my father's language. After dropping the boat back in the safety of its alcove I trundled to a little park I knew well from my walks with the dogs. Really it was more a patch of embroidered green, than a park, but the grass almost reached the water, giving long-stretching views across the lagoon. I hoped the great expanse of air would help to free my mind.

Settling onto the bank with my toes dipped into the cool, dappled water, I shook the satchel free of papers and began to spread them out in front of me. Scanning my eyes from one to the next, I realised I didn't know where to begin and I felt disappointment weigh heavily upon me. To me the pages were filled with a jumble of meaningless squiggles and lines and circles and numbers, and I had no understanding of what each one meant. Diagrams with stacks of horizontal lines confused me even more, and the spectrum of colours made my head hurt. Professor Bottelli had added phonetic descriptions under each one, but the notable excitement in the wild flourish of his handwriting made them almost impossible to decipher. I flopped back onto the grass in a little sulk of temporary defeat.

'It is the language of emotion,' said a voice I recognised instantly. I sat up quickly and saw that the girl from the masked ball was standing next to me, tilting her head to read the transcripts. 'Did you know there are six voices of the birds?'

I shook my head.

'Song, companionship, aggression, begging, fear and loss.' She reeled them off without hesitation. Then she looked right at me and smiled.

I couldn't keep my eyes from her; it was almost unbearable having her so close again and I felt awash with nerves. Inadvertently, I pushed my hair behind my ear then hugged my knees. Her dress was floaty, its fabric as thin as vapour, and the colour of the sea. Little straps slipped from her shoulders onto the tops of her arms where she left them to tickle her skin. She was barefoot, as I knew she would be. Her hair was wet – dripping wet – and soaked into the back of her dress, but she didn't seem to mind or even to notice. If she told me she had just been for a swim in the lagoon, I would have believed her.

'You and that coat,' she tutted playfully, kneeling down beside me on the grass. 'Aren't you hot?'

I shrugged; rather that than being revealed.

'I wanted to ask you to help me the night of the ball.' I said, unclasping my knees and shuffling through the papers. 'None of it makes much sense to me, and you seemed to … well, you seemed to understand—'

I'm not sure she heard me or if she was even listening, but she lifted a loose sheet from the pile. Her little nose was scrunched in deep concentration as she carefully scanned the paper, her eyes absorbing every word and shape. Still I couldn't avert my gaze. I was waiting for her to turn her head and look at me. Even though I had wanted to see her again, everything about her being here right next to me, put me on edge.

'This one is a song with its long syllables,' she announced, interrupting my thoughts so suddenly, it made me jump. She passed the paper to me as though it should all make perfect sense.

I frowned as she selected another page.

'Ah, this is something quite different. Look at the short bursts repeated over and over again.'

'What does it mean?' I asked, leaning close enough to catch the scent of the sea in her hair. I felt like I was riding on a beautiful carousel; brightly lit and brilliantly painted.

Going around and around and around with such giddy momentum that I feared the moment it would stop, not sure that I would ever find my feet again.

'It is a warning,' she said, biting her fleshy lip. 'And look at the brightness of the colour and the width of the lines.' She held it up for me to see, and I nodded. 'It was spoken in swift, loud utterances.'

For the rest of the afternoon, in the lengthening of our shadows, she helped me to unravel the mystery of Orniglossa with its fluctuations of joyful warbles interspersed with rattles of anger. She taught me the difference between the crush of syllables within a song and the two-note phrases used to deliver a multitude of messages. She read each one with such fluency that the sounds bounced off her tongue and sailed into the sky. Each one was answered by the flute-like notes of the tree-top birds.

'Now you try,' she encouraged.

At first, I was afraid to imitate the sounds she seemed to be able to recreate so easily, but she nodded at me in anticipation. I pursed my lips to form the first syllable and stuttered through each sound, clumsy and pause-filled, wincing with each attempt. My face felt as tight as a fist.

'Let your jaw loose,' she said, cupping my chin in her hand and shaking it gently, until I let it slacken.

She smiled, but there was no mockery in it, and when she repeated the sounds, she did so slowly enough for me to follow them. I tried again and this time it came much easier than before.

'Did you know that in Orniglossa there is no distinction between arm and wing?' she said.

I shook my head. Maybe we all have flight within us – in one way or another. I watched as she gathered her hair together and wrung it out before dropping it down her back like a heavy rope.

'I can braid it for you if you like,' I said, unable to resist the chance to touch her.

She smiled. 'Yes, I would like that very much.'

Shuffling over I tentatively scooped up her hair. Thrilled to have it in my hands, I began separating the sections between my fingers. It felt thick and smooth and my feathers danced as I lifted and folded it over and over again. Softly, she began to hum. I had watched the whores coiffure each other's hair into magnificent swirls and loops of gold and sometimes when I had been especially good and the day was quiet, they would let me sweep a comb through their curls and place pins wherever I fancied.

'You can practise while you braid,' she said, like any good teacher.

And as she continued to hum, I was clicking my tongue against the roof of my mouth in pretend annoyance and burbling my companion call as though I had known how to do it all along. Not finding me to be a suitable mate, a bird suddenly shook itself free from the tree, and flew away. I collapsed onto the grass in closed-eyed laughter.

'It is late,' she said. 'It's time to go.' Her words were like dark clouds full of rain threatening to wash away the happiness of the afternoon.

When I scrambled to my feet, I could see she was already standing at some distance away on the path.

'But I don't even know your name,' I said, fumbling with the piles of paper that still lay strewn all over the grass. Frantically, I tried to thrust them back inside the satchel with such urgency that I felt the buckle snap and break.

'My name is Elver,' she called.

'Wait!' I cried, cursing the broken satchel under my breath, but by the time I had the strap over my shoulder, the path was empty, and she was nowhere to be seen.

All the way home, I let my tongue revel in the new-found discovery of the bird language, and by the time I reached the house, its taste had become wonderfully familiar.

CHAPTER 25

After returning from another hurried walk with the dogs, I was surprised to find that Leo was waiting for me in the courtyard. I had not expected to see him so soon and his unannounced arrival brought with it a sense of alarm. He crossed the flagstones, and, instinctively, I tried to tuck my curls behind my ears. Of course, they refused to obey my command, and instead they sprang back out again in a fiery display of defiance.

'What is it? What's wrong?' I asked in panic.

He must have been running for at least part of the way as it took him several moments to compose himself before he could utter a single word. Until he spoke, neither of us were calm.

'I've got … something to show you,' he said finally. 'Come on.' Grabbing my hand, he pulled me out of the courtyard and into the street.

'If you are taking me to see the jars on the Bridge of Longing then you're too late; I've already seen them filled with mist.'

'We're not going there.' He smiled, enjoying the little guessing game.

'Then where?'

'You'll see soon enough,' was all he revealed, but he was smiling as he said it and I felt myself steady beside him.

He led me through the streets towards the market, where our pace was slowed by the sluggish tide of the crowd. On the corner, the familiar smell of bread was hard to resist, but before I had time to slow down and locate its source, I felt myself being pushed through a gap between two stalls and along a dark, winding passageway.

'Is it far?' I asked, suddenly shivering against the cold, and drawing my coat tighter around me.

'Just a little further,' came his reply.

After crossing a bridge, we were finally welcomed back into the warm sunlight. I breathed it in, glad to feel it on my face once again. Further along the canal path, a murky grime had gathered in macabre frothy bouquets at the edges of the water, like someone had swilled out the phlegm of a sanatorium, and I turned my face to focus on something less repugnant. This part of the city was slow and still and in all the time we had been walking, not a single boat had disturbed the water. The path curved round one long stretch of building, its windows were small squares like squinting eyes, blinded by age or the sun that fell mercilessly into them. Then through the air floated the quiet, but unmistakable sound of birdsong.

'Can you hear that?' I asked, stopping in wonder to listen. 'There are birds here.' I looked into the empty sky, then lowered my eyes to the rooftops, but there wasn't a winged creature in sight.

'You won't find them up there; they are shut inside,' replied Leo, gesturing towards one of the windows.

'Inside? Why?' I asked, horrified at the thought.

'People lock them in fancy cages, and dangle them from hooks in the ceiling. They are brought here in boats from places where there is eternal heat and forests filled with rain. They only bring the birds with the brightest of feathers: yellows and reds and blues, some are even the colour of rainbows.'

I knew of such birds from my lessons with Professor Elms, but the thought of them being locked in cages sent a chill through my bones.

'They are like sparkling musical jewels,' he added.

I listened again. The melody was crisp and plaintive, and I stepped back, scanning the multitude of windows to determine where it was coming from, but it was impossible to tell. I wasn't even sure if the sound I heard came from a solitary bird or was a chorus of many.

Bending down, I peered through one of the sunken windows, but there were iron bars fixed to the frame and a thick gauze curtain hiding whatever was behind it. The next window kept its secrets too, only this time behind a rusty decorative grille. These precious jewels, it seemed, needed protecting.

'Come on,' urged Leo, setting off again along the path.

I didn't move. I heard only birdsong.

'Maréa!' The sound of my name startled me, and this time I ran to catch up.

The birdsong had stirred a memory for Leo. 'It was a nightingale.'

'What was?' I asked.

'That bird you heard singing. It is a well-known tradition here for widows to keep nightingales for company; they do not have the pretty feathers of other birds, but their song is more beautiful.'

'How do you know so much? I asked in disbelief. I hadn't been able to see inside any of the windows and I was quite sure he hadn't been able to either. 'You couldn't even see it.' I challenged.

'I don't need to.' He smiled. Then he revealed a story.

He spoke about his love of birds, which had been encouraged by his grandfather, who would take him for long walks in the Northern woods.

'I got my first pair of binoculars when I was five, and by six I could name twenty bird songs from the first note alone,' he announced proudly. 'At night I slept with the binoculars under my pillow, but when I woke, I'd always find them clutched in my hand as though I had reached for them in my dream.' He laughed at the memory.

'Growing up I spent most of my time in a cellar.' I said the words before I had even decided I was going to.

Leo looked shocked. 'You sound like one of those nightingales kept in a cage.'

'I was, I suppose, but there were no locks; it was only my fear that kept me there.' I began to describe my life before arriving in the City of Murmurs. How I would have the birds for company, envious of their freedom. I told him about the gutter that ran the length of the window, and how the birds would gather there to wash themselves. How I spent hours watching them, wondering when it would be my turn to fly away.

'I had a professor,' I said. 'He taught me that birds have hollow bones, and for some reason, it made me feel sad.'

'They need hollow bones to fly. If you stay empty, you stay light.'

'I know.' I sighed. 'But it still makes me sad, like something is missing.'

'Sometimes you have to lose a part of yourself to be free.' He paused, wanting to say something, but not quite sure how. 'Birds are truly fascinating. Maybe that's why I like you so much.' Then, abashed, he looked away.

I felt myself blush at his admission, unsure of what to say next.

'I mean because you are part bird,' he added hastily, trying to cover up his embarrassment.

The laughter came unexpectedly, and I covered my mouth with my hand. It was true, but it sounded ridiculous said out loud, and Leo laughed too, glad that the awkwardness was over.

'Why do you hide your feathers under that coat?' he asked, more out of curiosity than judgement.

'I—' I faltered and hesitated for a moment. 'I suppose I have grown so used to hiding them, that I don't know how to do anything else.'

We walked over more bridges and past the park, deserted except for a pair of cooing pigeons, circling each other on the grass. We were both quietened by memory.

Too lost in thought, I hadn't noticed where we were, but now the water seemed louder and, as I looked around, it felt familiar. As the street opened, I suddenly realised where he had led me. My first instinct, as always, was to run and hide, but I didn't; instead I took a sharp intake of breath and seized Leo's shoulder.

'Why did you bring me here?' I hissed, my eyes were open wide in fear.

Just in front of me, rocking on the edge of the water was the last thing I expected to see; The Boat of Floating Freaks and Oddities. Leo was quiet for a moment, trying to make sense of my reaction.

'What's wrong?'

'That boat is the circus boat,' I said, releasing the fistful of his coat I had been clutching in my hand.

Leo shook the creases from his sleeve. 'Yes, and that boat is the key to finding Eddero.' Then he pulled me towards the boat before I could say another word. 'I think your father comes to collect something from it, and we need to find out what it is.'

I could hear the sound of sloshing water against the hull, and if I reached out, I would be close enough to run my hand along the wood. I imagined how rough its edges would feel and how its peeling paint would cut into my fingers, sharp and spiteful enough to draw blood. I still feared this vessel, no matter how worn or tired it had become.

'We need to go on board.'

'But—' My protest quickly fell silent.

I had spent a lifetime being protected from its tall fluttering sails and its creaking planks, that waltzing on board now would be utter madness. I hesitated. Maybe years ago, I would have been easily bought and sold, but now I had grown up and I made my own choices and I would never choose to be a part of that circus or any other circus. Larger than my fear was my longing and more than anything I wanted to find my father. If Leo was right, and this boat was the key to finding him, then I had to know. I lifted up my collar as high as I could and this time, instead of following Leo, I marched on ahead of him.

In front of me I saw a ragged slip of a man and I recognised him at once. The night I had arrived, I had seen him scurrying through the streets, clutching a jar of mist.

'What have you got on that boat?' I spoke hastily, in need of answers. He hadn't noticed us until I spoke and my urgency startled him, and for a moment he seemed suspicious.

'Very little. It's the end of the season. If it's a show you want, you'll have to wait a few more months.'

'Is there anyone left on board?' I asked, more desperately than I had intended.

'Anyone with feathers, perhaps?' added Leo tentatively.

The man smiled in recognition. 'You must mean the Sky-Worshipper.'

'Yes,' I said, edging closer. 'That's him.'

'I couldn't tell you his name; he doesn't speak.'

'Can you take us to him?' My voice grew softer, I needed his help.

He seemed to ignore the question and instead walked across the deck stopping only when he reached a small door. He pushed his weight against the wood, but it had swollen shut with the salty damp. He tried again and this time the door groaned open, and he beckoned for us to follow him.

The boat was enormous and motionless and the bright light of the sky was so suddenly extinguished as we went inside that I gasped out loud. It felt strange to be on board the boat that had brought me so much fear, but it wasn't fear I felt any more, just anticipation. The answers had been here all that time and I had been dragged away from them. The darkness was filled with hazy dust and I could see it through occasional cracks in the wood where pinpricks of light were welcomed through. I kept losing sight of the man, and had to rely on the sound of his footfalls but even they became dancing echoes around the wood. I pressed my hand to the vast creaking side of the hull as we were led along a sort of passageway. Each step brought with it the growing stench of rotting fish as though we were entering a sunken graveyard. My eyes finally adjusted to the surrounding gloom.

'Down here,' called the man from somewhere up ahead. He was motioning towards a rickety ladder.

It was an endless climb and the ladder shook with every movement. The air was damp and cold, and I felt my skin tingle with a sticky residue. Finally, we landed with a thud into the depths of the boat where the cloying sweet scent of resin hung in the air; it tasted of almonds or marzipan. If I had any chance of finding the ladder to climb back out again, I would have to grope my way along the walls. Our arrival had made something stir somewhere, and although my eyes refused to reveal what it was, I knew there was something in the shadows.

'Are you all right?' I was relieved to hear the sound of Leo's voice.

'Yes ... you?'

Something in the darkness glittered, hundreds of tiny specks of light danced around us. The air was silver. I heard a shuffle then, and the strike of a match and suddenly the space flickered into view. The man who had led us here was holding a lantern and was pointing towards something deep within the room. Neither of us could see what it was because the room was filled with a swirling mist, and my feathers responded with their familiar quiver.

'He's over there,' the man said, holding the lantern aloft. Its sweeping light picked up a shape slumped against the far wall. 'Just through the mist.'

I waited. Leo waited. Then I moved further into the room.

He was lying on the floor on a bed of dank moss and straw, with his crumpled wings wrapped protectively around his body, holding himself because there was no one else who could. At first, I thought he was dead, and my breath caught in my throat, but as I kneeled down on the floor in front of him, I saw the slow rise and fall of his chest, and I could hear his long raspy breaths. I knew at once it wasn't my father; his hair wasn't the same burning orange; it was much lighter like the hard-boiled yolk of an egg. Still we had a connection and it was strange to feel recognition for something I had never seen before. Unable to hold back, I tentatively reached out my hand to his wing, letting my fingertips brush against its long feathers. They were so soft, and warm as a nest, but then

I felt them loosen under my touch and flutter to the floor.
I withdrew my hand in shock. I had been so gentle.

'There's something wrong with him,' I called over my
shoulder.

The man and Leo approached and the light from the
lantern made the Sky-Worshipper groan and squeeze his
eyes tightly shut. He lifted his wing over his face as a shield
against the intrusion.

'He needs to rest, that's all.'

'Why are you keeping him down here?' I demanded,
and the man seemed flustered, lifting his cap and wiping
sweat from his brow.

'I am not *keeping* him anywhere,' he replied defensively.
'He is not locked in a cage and there are no bolts on the
doors! It is his choice to be here, to perform in this
circus.'

'Why?' asked Leo.

The man puffed out his cheeks and shrugged. 'All I know
is they send a different one each time, and they keep
sending them. I think they are searching for someone, but
they always return alone.'

The Sky-Worshipper shuddered under the crease of his
wing.

'He is ill,' I challenged at once.

'And that is what keeps him down here – he needs the
mist – I've been collecting it every few days until the others
come to take him back.'

'The others?' queried Leo.

'Yes, the others – just like him. They shouldn't be too much longer, now the mist is getting nearer.'

'How long?' I asked, rising to my feet and brushing the straw from my trousers.

The man began furiously scratching his head in thought, sending the lantern swinging its light around the room.

'The mist is still over half a day's sail from here, so experience tells me to expect them in a little under two weeks. Any longer and—' He didn't finish his sentence, but the unspoken words hung in the air, tight as a noose.

I was sure that at any given moment the Sky-Worshipper would be ready to slip from this world. 'I need a few more minutes with him.'

I could hear the man shuffle his feet with impatience and his sigh carried all the way across the room, but I didn't care. My attention returned instead to the Sky-Worshipper lying on the floor, and I reached my fingers to his face; his skin was cold and brittle beneath them, so cold it made me gasp. Grabbing handfuls of straw, I began packing them around his thin, frail body, in an attempt to keep him warm. A blanket was strewn in the corner so I shook it out and covered him with it, tucking it round his face. Then I lay down beside him and took his hand in mine. It looked just like the sketch I had seen amongst Professor Bottelli's notes. I held it between my palms, reviving it as though it were a frozen creature I had just brought in from the snow. Remembering the sounds Elver had taught me, I slowly released the guttural call of comfort. Until that moment, his eyes had seemed glued together, but my voice soothed them like chamomile and he began to blink them open. When his eyes finally found me, I saw there was still life left in them, burning like stoked coals. He was a fighter. I lay there until I felt Leo's hand on my shoulder, telling me it was time to go.

We left the boat and walked back along the canal. The bird I had heard before was silent.

'He looked like he was dying,' I said, choking on my words.

'The others will be here soon. They will know what to do.'

I nodded.

I could feel Leo watching me warily. He was trying to find the words to make me feel better, but the image of the Sky-Worshipper, lying there, cold and featherless, was hard to shake. How delicate birds are, I thought, and how easily they can be broken.

'Can you believe that soon you will finally meet your father? All that waiting will be over.'

I smiled and shook my head at the enormity of what was happening, like something was hatching after years of incubation. 'It doesn't seem real. None of it does.'

'Well, it is,' he reassured me with a nudge of my arm, and I nudged him back.

The boat stop was up ahead and we slowed our pace. Leo had moved imperceptibly closer to me, but my senses were heightened and I could feel his breath warm against my cheek. He was going to kiss me, I felt certain and shaken by the idea. My second kiss in this city. Did I want him to? I didn't know. I was confused by the moment and before I could decide, the moment was gone as the gypsy woman and her cart squeaked past.

I stepped back, startled by the interruption of this unexpected intimacy. Setting down her moveable stall, she smiled her toothless grin at us and began rummaging in amongst all her parcels and pots. Leo and I smiled shyly at each other, perhaps in relief at her sudden distraction. She pulled out a bunch of half-crumpled roses and, mistaking us for lovers, tossed them at our feet before picking up her broken cart and squeaking away towards the Bridge of Storms.

Nothing had actually happened, but something was different; something between us had shifted. She had broken a spell and I couldn't decide if I wanted to blame her or offer her my gratitude. It was as though I had been woken suddenly, and when I opened my eyes, I was no longer in the place in which I had fallen asleep. Like reaching beneath a wave for a shell that wasn't quite where you thought it had been.

Leo's boat arrived and at last we parted.

CHAPTER 26

I told myself there was no other way home, but of course it wasn't true; there were countless other streets I could have taken, and most of them would have got me there in half the time, but once I had crossed the Bridge of Longing, there was no going back. Secretly, the heart navigated you to where it needed you to be. To my astonishment and complete delight, the shutters had been pushed wide open in invitation, and she was right there in the window as though she had been expecting me all along. Her hair tumbled around her as it always did, spilling like golden coins over the ledge.

With a thudding heart, I watched Elver. Then somehow she seemed to know I was there, standing in the dark street, where the sun didn't reach, and the algae grew wet and slippery. In my sudden haste to reach her, I lost my footing and fell with a heavy splash into the water.

The water was icy and bit into my bones. I opened my eyes to find something to hold onto, like a desperate cat clawing its way out, but it was too dark and murky and I didn't have enough air left in my lungs. I lunged to the side with open-mouthed gasps, but felt myself sinking. I tried to kick to the surface, gasping again and spluttering, before returning to the darkness. Then out of nowhere came wisps, like tiny feathers tickling my and arms, then they were suddenly long and strong, tangling themselves around my body like reeds. Something had hold of me and it wasn't letting go, but I still couldn't breathe. Then to my relief, whatever it was began to lift me up to the surface towards the shimmer of light.

She hauled me over to the stone steps, where I coughed up the muddy water from my lungs. Once recovered, I was suddenly shy, barely able to look at her. I wanted to see her – it's what I'd been waiting for; a flaming desire, heart ablaze like a midsummer sun – but not like this, not half-drowned like a drenched canal rat. My hair slapped across my face like treacle. Her eyes searched mine, far reaching and with her arms wrapped around me she led me up the steps and into her room.

Inside, she removed my clothes. Beneath them she found my bandages, and paused for a moment before unwrapping them, layer by layer. I tried not to flinch, but the jeers and shouts of the circus tent were never far away. She paused again, wondering if perhaps she had hurt me. My skin was too cold to resist the dry warmth of a blanket, so I nodded for her to continue. She had glimpsed my feathers before but it was only a quick peek, and now they were visible in their entirety. There was nowhere left to hide. She didn't gasp, and her eyes didn't fly open in horror or surprise, but I thought I saw the corners of her mouth lift into a tiny smile of pleasure. At least that's what I hoped it was. I imagined her own body was just as strange and secretive as mine, and it chased the shyness away. She tilted her head and gently turned my body until she could see the length of my back; it was the place where my feathers grew the longest and the thickest. I could feel her gaze linger on them and I shuffled awkwardly wanting her to fill the silence.

After a while, she lifted a blanket from the bed and wrapped it around my shoulders before crossing the room to the kitchen. It was then I noticed how yellow everything was: the walls, the light, the flowers spilling from a jar on the table, the cups – dainty enough to be given to a doll, the cloth covering the table and her hair, always her hair, the streaming yellow light of the sun. I watched as she slowly stirred a teapot. Inside this room, there was a quiet stillness as though we were far away from every-thing. There wasn't even the ticking of a clock to remind me that time was passing, and for a moment I was suspended weightless; timeless; fearless. Here all the clocks had stopped and it would be our time for ever – just us.

It was simply furnished: a bed, low to the floor; a table and two chairs and a woven mat in the middle of the room, perfect for a cat, but there was little else. It felt too temporary, as though no one really lived there at all. I was suddenly overcome with unknown fear. The yellow room ceased to be bright and happy and instead became sickly and faded like a letter whose words had been destroyed by time. I was glad to be distracted by the lights of a passing boat, which swept the walls and trickled back onto the floor, illuminating a large jar of shells; it was just like the one I had at home. I stood up in my hunch of a blanket and lifted one out, holding it against my ear. A rush of memory; swept away by the reminder of a different life. I felt her hand on my arm and she handed me a cup filled with tea and I could smell the sugar. Gratefully, I held it warm in my hands before tilting it to taste its sweetness.

'I'm glad you came,' she said.

'I've been before.' Our words tiptoe around the room.

Professor Elms, despite all his lessons, had not prepared me for this. He had taught me about losing a heart, not discovering one.

'Yes, I know,' she said, and the way she smiled made my feathers quiver, like arrows ready to shoot at their target.

She nodded towards the long bandage that now lay unravelled at my feet, like the peel of some strange white fruit. 'You do not need to wear that. You must find a way to heal your own wounds,' she said quietly.

Before I could take another sip, she lifted the cup from my hand and placed it on the table. The blanket slipped from my shoulders as she gently pushed me onto the bed. No one had seen me naked before, except the whores when they washed and scrubbed me in the kitchen, but I was just a small child then; they knew nothing of my body now. Although my feathers ruffled and sang, her touch on my back made me flinch. She didn't withdraw her hand, but her fingertips seemed to hesitate and lighten, and I found myself wanting more. I guided her hand with my own and when I let go, it was lost deep inside my feathers as she stroked each one in turn.

She stepped out of her clothes and kissed me. Soft and warm and long and deep. I responded with a kiss of my own and watched her body move next to mine, her breasts like two anchored boats, rising and falling as she breathed.

'Does it hurt?' I asked, running the pads of my fingers along the skin of her legs. I hadn't expected it to be so sharp. It felt impenetrable, like beautiful nacreous armour.

She mumbled and shook her head, and when at last I lifted my fingers it was my own skin that stung, as though I had a hundred tiny paper cuts. Where scales once grew, there were now raised calloused whorls, the scars of what she used to be. Her foot felt wet against my leg, but when I reached down to check, I realised that it was just cold. I was curious about her difference and in amongst all of it I saw beauty and wondered if I would ever learn to feel that way about myself.

Her mouth met mine again. It curved wide like the smile of an oyster shell, so soft and fleshy inside. We moved together until she was familiar to me; soon I knew where she dipped and rose, and dipped again to meet the rising tide, where ammonites gathered in swirls. I couldn't get lost; I tried, but I surfaced and she met me once again with her mouth. Nothing here was forbidden. My feathers pulsed and frothed, and it felt as though they were stretching and doubling in size, no longer shrunken and flat from the canal water. Wordlessly, I collapsed, tangled in her limbs, where we lay on the bed like driftwood, shaped by an invisible sea, my fingers quickly lost in her hair, her own lost in my feathers. I felt no shame, and, for the first time since I was a child, my feathers gave me pleasure, and it was all because of her.

'We understand each other because we both belong to different worlds,' she murmured sleepily.

She slept then and I watched how she twisted like a coral reef. Her spine, the impression left by an eel gliding along the seabed. Her feet long and wide with their trans-lucent webbing between each toe. I was too fascinated to sleep and stared out of the half-open shutter to the sky above. It was black and empty, and I thought how wrong she was; I didn't belong to a different world, I belonged right there. In that night, in that room, we'd both revealed our hidden past. In sleep she drifted away from me and I reached for her hair as though I could pull her back. It was warm to the touch, and, lifting my fingers to my face, I smelled a mixture of salt, starlight and thyme, a comfort which finally brought sleep after so many days of longing.

A single shaft of early morning light shone through the window. From somewhere below, I could hear the slow movements of the boats. Reaching for Elver, I was startled to find the bed was empty; I hadn't felt her leave my side. Last night I had slept beside an ocean, but when I woke, the tide was out and I had been washed ashore. As I surfaced, I realised it wasn't just the bed that was empty, so too was the room. Tangled in my hair, I felt a starfish; a gift, an offering, an apology perhaps for not being there. Caught between my fingers were a few golden strands of her hair. I must have held on too tight, but still it hadn't been enough, and now she was gone. On the table, I found an abandoned cup of tea, half drunk and still warm to the touch. I felt strangely bereft.

Had she sat and watched me sleep? When had she left and why? When will she return? But my questions remained unanswered, for there was nobody there to hear them. I waited, with the sound of Sybel's warning ringing loud in my mind: *Beware of the mermaid whose heart is made of nothing but water, for it will quickly flow away.* In that moment I felt bewildered and lost. I had fallen asleep so safe in a beautiful tangle of knots from which I thought there was no escape, but in the darkness, she had quietly loosened the ties and released me just in time for morning. Did that always happen after a night of such pleasure?

My coat was still a sodden puddle on the floor, but I threw my arms into the sleeves anyway and hunched its heavy coldness over my shoulders. Bundling the bandages into my pocket, I quickly left the room as empty as I had found it.

CHAPTER 27

A few days later there was still no sign of Elver and no mention of the night we had shared. I filled my time trying to learn more of my father's language, but it proved too difficult without Elver's words of encouragement. To release my thoughts, I walked the dogs, pounding my frustration into the flagstones. Sometimes I would walk them twice, once in the morning and then again later in the afternoon during the golden hour when the light polished the city and everything was bathed in a warm glistening light like a drizzle of syrup. I would stretch myself under a lemon tree not far from the water's edge, wait for him near the ship to which he would return, and watch the water sparkle in the sunlight.

I brought *The Sea* with me and read it sprawled on a blanket while the dogs scratched the flies from their bellies, and collapsed in snoring bundles on the grass. The night of the ball, I had slipped the book into the inside pocket of my cloak, and every time I picked it up, I was convinced it held her scent and the memories of the other night surged. I studied the pictures: the sea, at its cruellest and then its most peaceful, full of emotion and quick to turn like a scorned lover. Its hidden depths were revealed page after page and famous quotes and poems filled the rest. In the last section, I read about the mermaids that in-habited the darker, deeper waters of the city. Here they were described as beautiful monsters with hearts of cruelty. Until I arrived, I thought a mermaid was just a beautiful girl stitched into a sequined tail, but now I knew the truth. Like me, she was neither one thing nor another, caught somewhere in between – a lost soul – and I felt even more drawn to her.

The City of Murmurs was a place of wonder and my feathers would not gain much attention here, yet still I held back. When I had first seen the boat, I had confessed my fear to Sybel. That boat is nothing more than a wreck, she had told me. We only have fascination for what we have never seen before and here in this city we have seen it all. Besides, the wait is always worth more than the reveal. But I've been on board and I've seen their exhibits, I had whispered, in tiny trembling syllables. You may well have done, she had replied, but you'll never see its circus performing on this shore. Sybel fumed at the thought, and I knew that if they tried to pitch their tent anywhere near this city, she would tear it from the ground herself and fling it far into the sea.

Leo and Elver had both made me less fearful of who I really was, but my feathers were *my* wonder and I wasn't brave enough to share them with the rest of the world just yet. Childhood fears of being displayed in a large glass cabinet or whipped to perform in a circus while some master greedily collected coins in his upturned cap still plagued me. I was not a spectator sport, nor a performer, and I had been taught to hide.

Leo often found me lying on the grass in a small park. I chose this spot because it was close to the boat and we were ever-watchful, both anticipating the arrival of my father. Sometimes we sat in companionable silence; other times we spoke about our future plans. How one day I would open a shop selling hats and scarves made of beautiful feathers and he told me his dream of travelling to faraway forests to discover unnamed birds, but there was hesitancy when he spoke, as though he was no longer sure if that's what he wanted after all. Neither of us spoke about the kiss we almost had, but unspoken things are not necessarily so easily forgotten.

I watched as he lay next to me, hands behind his head, idly chewing on a piece of grass, which made the muscles in his jaw flex through the dark beginnings of a beard. I could see dark coils of hair through the thin cloth of his shirt. He shifted onto his side and tilted his face towards mine and the light revealed flecks of green in his eyes. I had never noticed them before. He smiled and I smiled back, before pretending to return to my book. I always seemed to find myself caught between two things and my heart was no different.

'Who was your first?' he asked unexpectedly.

'My first what?' I asked confused.

'The first person you ever fell in love with?' He nudged my leg playfully.

I laughed nervously, not sure I had an answer to give.

'I loved a married woman once,' Leo confessed.

'Really?' That surprised me, and I lowered my book, resting it in my lap, curious to hear more.

'She taught me to play the piano in her house by the sea. It had floor-to-ceiling windows, but there was no one to see us.'

'Apart from her husband?'

He shrugged and told me how her husband took long business trips, and neither of them really knew what he did. Leo's mother had wanted to find something to distract him from his obsession with birds and decided to pay for music lessons instead.

'It didn't work, of course,' he said. 'I just developed another interest.'

'How did it end?'

'I had learned all I needed to.'

'Did that include the piano or not?' I teased.

'I learned to play the piano – very badly. Whenever I hear music, I still think of her sitting in that house by the sea.'

'So, you miss her then?'

He paused. 'In some ways I do, but I was too young and she was too old. We fell though the gap in between.'

'Did your mother ever find out?'

'No; at least I hope not,' he exclaimed, laughing. 'I don't think she'd be very pleased to find out what her money was actually buying. I heard she left her husband and a few months later the house by the sea was sold.'

'She just left?'

'We both did,' he replied wistfully. 'My mother still receives cards on special occasions, my name is always written in them. Her handwriting is more familiar to me than anyone else's.'

My memory returned me then to all those years before where I was on my knees in a circus tent. It was there amongst the freaks and oddities that I felt my first pang of desire for something that wasn't even real. It was so long ago, but still I could feel it.

The city bell chimed out the lateness of the hour and I knew the dogs would be ready for their supper. 'Do you think it's possible—' I hesitated, choosing my words carefully '—for people to have animal features, besides feathers?'

'What do you mean?' he mumbled, drowsy from the sun.

'I don't know.' I paused, trying to give the impression that I was thinking of something completely random. 'Like scales or feet with their toes webbed together perhaps.'

'So, some kind of fish?'

'More like a mermaid without her tail.' I tried to sound nonchalant.

He paused. 'This is the City of Water ... anything and everything is possible here.'

CHAPTER 28

Staring across the water the next morning, I was disappointed to discover that the mist didn't seem to be swirling any closer. Even when I climbed to the very top of the bell tower to measure its distance, it still seemed to be suspended an endless way away. Like a net of glittering silver stars hauled from the sky.

As I looked down into the square, something caught my eye. I didn't know what this was – there wasn't a familiar sight there and no one had called out my name – but I sensed something. Searching the cluster of crowds, I could see nothing of importance and was about to climb down when, all of a sudden, I saw her. She was stepping out of a small white building a little way from the main steps. The unexpectedness of finding her there made me freeze completely, but even from so high I was certain it was her. By the time I had come to my senses, she had been swept away again into the crowd.

Quickly, I fled down the steps and plunged into the thrum of bodies trying my best to reach her, but the City of Murmurs had a swift tide, offering you something, then quickly snatching it back again and giving you something else in its place. If you didn't reach out and quickly grab what you wanted, it would be gone. I searched the nearby shops and down the alleys, circling the flower market, but I was too late. She had simply vanished. I should have known then that she was never meant to stay.

Back on the street there was nothing left to do but retrace her steps back to the white building; I wondered what had brought her there. Climbing the steps, I found a brass plaque, polished to shine like the badge of a general. Engraved upon it, was a name: Doctor Marino. I vowed to visit him, perhaps he could tell me where to find her.

The next morning, I was back at the doctor's door. This time I pushed it open and found myself in a dark, pokey chamber which held the pungent odour of a rabbit hutch; the floor looked like it could have done with a good sweep. My brain started to whir faster than the wings of a tiny bird, as I tried to work out what medical emergency could have brought me here. Just then a door opened and a man called me in before disappearing back inside. To my horror I realised that any complaint would necessitate a thorough examination and thus the inevitable discovery of my feathers. Panic-stricken, I managed to shuffle myself through the door, all the time wondering what I was going to say.

Up close, I could see he was still young, but had silver streaks running through his black curly hair. His eyes were dark and clear and lit with kindness. Then he smiled at me like an old friend and for a moment I faltered, convinced we must have met somewhere before, although I'm sure I would have remembered him. A face like his was not easy to forget.

'Sit down.' He gestured to a chair. 'Haven't you brought the dogs?' he asked, peering over my shoulder, looking for something that clearly wasn't there.

'The dogs?' I queried.

'Yes, Sybel's dogs. I see you walking them most days around the city. I presumed that's the reason for your visit.'

I stared back, surprised that he already knew who I was. 'Feet,' I muttered, finally sitting down. I had decided on my feet because they were feather-free and the only items I would have to remove for inspection would be my boots.

'Okay,' he replied slowly, sounding a little confused. 'Is that why you are here? Because of the dogs' feet or because of *your* feet?'

'Mine.' I was starting to lose patience with him and his strange interest in Sybel's dogs.

I began unlacing my boots and wiggled my toes. Tentatively, he rose from his desk and came around to examine me. His proximity suddenly made me feel nervous and I wondered what was causing his hesitancy. I stared at my toes in sudden embarrassment; my feet may have been feather-free but they were certainly not pretty! He knelt before me, and I could see the top of his head, full of thick dark curls.

Lifting one of my feet in his hand, he stroked it gently between his fingers, then placed it back on the floor and picked up the other one, cupping it in the warmth of his palm. He examined them closely.

'I can't find anything wrong with your feet,' he said.

'But sometimes it's painful,' I flinched in an attempt to convince him of my lie.

'It's probably just the heat. Do you always wear those boots when you're walking the dogs?'

I nodded.

'Well, I suggest that you wear something else, something that lets the air in. Your feet can't breathe in those heavy things. Imagine being kept in a cramped dark space all day long; how would you feel?'

Trapped, I thought, but kept the answer to myself.

As he straightened up and walked back to his chair, I noticed the large shell displayed on his desk.

'Do you collect them?' I asked, pointing at it.

He followed my gaze and then smiled. His hand reached out and he lifted it from its stand.

'Oh no, I'm not a collector. That's just a gift from a friend.' He tried to sound dismissive, but something caught in his throat. He gestured for me to take it from him and tentatively I held it in my hand.

'A friend?' I probed. It seemed I was not the only one for whom Elver left gifts.

He nodded, but I could see him frowning, wondering the reason for my question. I mumbled my apologies and clumsily handed the shell back to him.

'So how do you know the dogs I walk belong to Sybel?' I asked, hoping to change the subject.

'Because they are my patients.' he replied, with a playful smile.

I suddenly realised my mistake. 'You're a veterinary surgeon?'

He nodded. 'I don't normally write prescriptions for people,' he said, handing me a note with his signature scrawled along the bottom, 'but for you I will make an exception.'

I felt a shudder in the tips of my feathers and my eyes widened in mortification. I gave a quick nod of thanks and then I turned and swiftly walked away before I could make an even bigger fool of myself.

'Don't worry,' he called good-naturedly, 'I'm sure the balm I've suggested will help, and if it doesn't, I can always recommend a very good shoe shop.'

CHAPTER 29

A niggling thought kept me company all the way
home, like a stone lodged in my boot that I
couldn't shake loose. There was something between
Elver and Doctor Marino. Was it just that she sought
some treatment from him or was it something more?
It was feasible that she would need his help, perhaps oil
for her skin, but it was the way he had gazed at the
shell on his desk, so full of longing, that made my throat
tighten.

Sybel narrowed her eyes at me as we ate supper. 'You
are distracted,' she said.

'Can you give me a reading?' I asked, stirring the tea,
not sure I was ready to confess my feelings about Elver
to anyone else. I half-laughed then, as I realised Sybel

would have already sensed them, no matter how much I wanted to keep them hidden.

She looked up and watched me suspiciously. 'If this is about Leo Hawkins then I don't need the cards to tell me what he feels and neither do you.'

'It's not about him,' I replied, but I could feel my face flush the colour of cherries.

'Very well. What shall the focus be?'

'The focus?' I asked. I had never had a reading before, and wasn't sure what she meant.

'You need to have a focus, something to anchor the meaning to. Call it a theme if you prefer: love, wealth, health or—'

'Love,' I interrupted at once.

'Very well – the heaviest anchor of them all.' She opened a big cupboard, and after some rummaging she produced a pale-pink candle and a box of matches. Lighting it, she set it down in an oyster bowl in the middle of the table.

'So, you want the Oracle cards?'

I nodded, not sure what I wanted, or what she meant.

'I must warn you that I will tell you what I see. There is no disguise. If I see shadows, you will know. I will not hide the truth from you, I never do. Before it even leaves my lips, you will know it.' She waited a moment for me to ponder her words. 'Are you sure you are ready for that?'

I nodded again, this time with much less certainty. All her talk of anchors and shadows made me suddenly afraid of what might be waiting to swallow me. She pulled the deck from her top pocket, and began to shuffle them with speed and skill. Then she handed them to me.

'Shuffle,' she instructed, and so I began. 'Think of nothing at first, let everything float free from your mind, then slowly focus on what you most desire. Fate will do the rest.'

Emptying my mind was more difficult than I imagined, and I tried to focus on the candle in front of me.

'Cut the deck into three and pick a pile. Take your time to choose the right one.'

I studied each pile carefully, until I felt particularly drawn to one pile over the others. Then I picked it up and handed it back to her. She dealt them in the shape of a star, flipping them over, one by one until they had all been revealed; her face was still unreadable.

'So, this point here is your past,' she said, tapping the bottom card. 'It shows me you were loved very much. I can see lots of people around you, most likely female and a dark crowd of men much further away, kept at a distance. There is also one important man here – not your father – although he loved you like one.'

I recognised him instantly. 'Professor Elms.'

'Yes, possibly a professor, as this card represents learning and wisdom. Don't worry about him; he is happy and has found new love from old.'

'Really?' I was astounded. Had his lost love returned? It seemed unlikely. Then I remembered the way he had held Lemàn's hand the day I walked away and how she had let him. I wondered if in finding each other they would eventually find a way out of the whorehouse.

'Is it with Lemàn?'

She laughed. 'The Oracles do not give you specific names; they are more abstract than that. They offer only associations by which you should recognise the subjects. In this case it showed you the idea of learning. I can tell you one more thing: it was your departure that created this connection.'

Had my leaving really brought them together? I felt a warm rush of hope, and it gave me much comfort to know that my leaving had united them and neither of them was alone in the world.

'The second point here is connected to your present. It shows confusion and restlessness, which swirls around you, and you cannot see clearly. The third point is your immediate future, where you will face a decision. Do not make it foolishly. You will find yourself with many choices, but you will lose them all if you are not careful. After that, decisions will be made for you.' There was threat in her tone.

I frowned; it didn't make much sense.

'Which brings me to the final point – the distant future.'

'What can you see there?' I asked impatiently. This is what I really wanted to know. I leaned closer as though it would somehow help me to understand the cards in front of me, but no matter how close I got, they were nothing more than jumbled images, just as indecipherable as the Orniglossa transcripts.

Sybel hesitated, just for a moment, but long enough for me to see that the shadows she had warned me about had appeared. I might not have been able to read the cards, but I could read her face.

'Tell me,' I demanded. 'You said you always tell the truth.'

Sybel sighed. 'The cards are showing something very bright, almost blinding, like a yellow storm. Then there is nothing but darkness and water, so much water everywhere.'

'Do you mean I will drown?' I asked, alarmed, for I had never learned to swim.

'Not in water, and not in the way you are imagining, but sadness will anchor you to this place.'

'What sadness?'

'One of your own making.'

I frowned. Why would I choose sadness? It didn't make any sense.

'There will be an endless wait, and an unexpected arrival, which will bring you much happiness. In the end there will be both unity and separation, but you will eventually find your way.'

'So, I will be happy!' I exclaimed, but I had tasted doubt and it simmered away in my stomach.

'I told you not very long ago that you should be running in a different direction.' Then she whipped away the cards and hastily shoved them back into the pack before I could ask her any more questions, but one escaped, slipping to the floor and I quickly retrieved it. She snatched it from my fingers, but its image had already been revealed to me in the future spread; a yellow sun, half swallowed by the sea. Its meaning was clear to both of us, and it compelled me to confess.

'I have met someone else like me,' I said.

'I know,' she replied, after a long pause – of course she did. She knew secrets before they had been told.

The room had darkened long ago, but I hadn't noticed time slip through the cracks in the floor. The Oracle candle still flickered.

'She was once a mermaid. Her skin is dry and calloused where her scales used to be, and her feet are webbed together so tightly that no knife could ever cut them free.'

For a long time, Sybel didn't speak, and then eventually she uttered a single word. 'Elver.'

'What?' I exclaimed in surprise. 'But—?'

'I told you I have pulled stranger than you from these waters.'

Then she began her story. Some years ago, she had been returning from a client's house over on the east side of the city. It was a wild and stormy night and she was a fool to be out on the streets, but her client had just lost someone and needed the comfort only Sybel could bring. The wind was so strong it tossed her into the air like a flower head and splattered her back down again; not an easy thing to do, given her size. The sea raged, foaming and spitting in defiance. Its waves rose higher and higher in a furious deluge. Boats were the innocent victims, snapped in two and carried out of the lagoon like abandoned coffins. The sea and the wind were in some kind of battle and everything else was just in the way. Many lives were lost that night and the city suffered.

Sybel had managed to find shelter in a doorway, where she stayed until first light. By then, the storm had exhausted itself, but the city was broken. Roofs had been torn off the buildings and windows shattered, hundred-year old trees fell in one night and park benches only good for fire wood. It was hard to imagine such a peaceful place torn apart in one night, but the anguish in her voice was real.

It wasn't until the light crept back into the sky that she was finally able to walk back along the waterfront, and there she noticed a green mound slumped over the steps near the boatyard. At first, she thought it was a tangle of nets or a pile of potato sacking blown through the factory door, or a huge clump of slippery seaweed ripped up from the depths of the water, but as she drew closer her senses heightened. Whatever it was, it was moving. Her thoughts then turned to an injured dog, but as she rushed closer, she could see it was something else entirely; something quite extraordinary.

'What? Was it really a mermaid?' I asked, as she paused her story. What Sybel was saying was too impossible to believe, yet I already knew it to be true. I had slept beside it.

She continued her story. She told me that where her legs should have been; she had the tail of a fish, with beautiful iridescent scales that glittered like coins you could never spend. Sybel explained how she had carefully scooped her up and ran back to the house where she wrapped her in blankets and made her fish broth, stirred with healing herbs. She was barely conscious and her tail had been torn beyond repair and it was starting to rot. Sybel scrunched up her nose then as though the smell still lingered in the room, but when I sniffed the air, it was just the rose wax of burning candles that I could smell. She told me the side of her head had been bashed and left bruised and her ribs were undoubtedly all broken. She told me how she cried out in pain as she slept, but by the third day she was able to swallow the broth she had brewed up from fish bones. The fear of infection sent her in search of a doctor.

'I didn't know if I was dealing with a girl or a fish.' She laughed. 'In the end, I decided a veterinary surgeon would be less likely to report what I had to show him. The next day I brought someone I knew I could trust, and swore him to secrecy.'

'Doctor Marino?'

'Yes.' She didn't seem surprised that I knew his name.

She told me how he would come every day not only to administer medicines, but to sit and hold her hand. After ten days, she was sitting up in bed and a few days after that, she was able to feed herself from a spoon. Whenever he came, Sybel could remember how her face would light up and she could hear them laughing behind the closed door. Although she grew stronger, her tail was shrivelled and wizened and had been so badly damaged that it would take months to heal, if it healed at all. She bathed it daily in buckets of salt water brought back from the Reef, but even that didn't help. A month later Sybel gave her a choice: lie in bed and wait for something that may never happen or walk.'

'So, you changed her? You gave her legs?'

'At first she was uncertain of what she wanted but one night, Doctor Marino stayed longer than usual and when I saw him leave in the morning, so full of happiness; I knew she had made her choice and I had a new pair of shoes waiting – not that she could wear them, in the end.'

'But how did you do that?' I asked, amazed by everything she was telling me.

'Before I came to the City of Murmurs, my grandmother had taught me her secrets. I thought it was her magic that turned a slow dull worm into a bright, fluttering creature. I believed that she had the power to turn the leaves from green to gold and that her heart was a magnet for the rain. Of course, as I left my childhood behind, I learned the truth, but there was still one thing that nature couldn't explain: the ancient Art of Meta. I used to watch, mesmerised, as she mixed earth, air, fire and water in little pewter pots, burning them over fires, deep in the heart of the great forest until we could both see shapes emerge in the smoke. It is there that I learned how to transform one element into another, creating new possibilities.'

'So, she chose to walk because of him?' I couldn't keep the bitterness from my voice.

'I'm not sure that was her reason, but perhaps it played its part. It is best if we leave the story there and she tells you the rest.'

Knowing she had stayed in this house made me restless. Everything I touched – a glass, a door handle, a pillow, a spoon – all made me wonder if she had touched it too. Her fingerprints next to mine – connected – one on top of the other.

'You know a mermaid is a slippery creature and her heart is like a slick stone. She takes what she wants and washes the rest away. Please be careful.' Her voice rose then in anguish, and she quickly stood to clear away the teacups. Her story had been told and she was tired, but I still had one more question left to ask.

'Can you change me?'

'Change you?' she blurted, alarmed at the suggestion. 'You don't need changing – you are perfectly well.'

She was right; I didn't have a tail of infected scales, but I had something just as painful. 'I want you to take my feathers away.' I plucked at the back of my neck. 'I cut them off once, a long time ago, but they just grew back,' I added, angrily.

Sybel gave a heavy sigh, and considered me for a long time as though she was trying to find the best words to avoid the disappointment that would follow.

'I will not take them away,' she said resolutely.

I pouted my lips in annoyance and I was that child again, being dragged away from the circus tent.

'You need to offer something bigger than your difference. Then your feathers won't matter because people will notice you for something else.'

I grumbled, unconvinced.

'It happened to me. That's why I have that beautiful dress hanging in the wardrobe, still unworn. If people saw me as I truly am, then they would know I could never wear a dress like that.'

I slumped back against the wall and felt the horrid things crumple against the stone. I crossed my arms and hunched my shoulders in a childish sulky bundle.

'When I first arrived in this city, I was ridiculed in whispered tongues, people snorted at my hideousness, my scars of disease, my wild hair and my swollen limbs, until they realised that I spoke with words of truth and sometimes comfort.'

By now the candle had burned itself to little more than a stump and had almost exhausted itself completely. Sybel stood poised with the snuffer in her hand. In front of its tiny light, she shone like a guardian angel and I half hoped that she was going to reconsider and give me her blessing.

She spoke softly. 'A change must come first from love, not hate. Besides, you haven't yet discovered who you are, and your feathers are an essential part of that.' She stroked my arm, as though somehow that would make me forgive her rejection.

Afterwards, in my room, my thoughts returned to Elver and to Doctor Marino. I remembered how Lemàn spoke of jealousy every time she watched the birds in the sky, blaming them for taking my father away. It filled all of her stories; queens who despised their beautiful stepdaughters so much that they wished them dead. And the woman alone in the forest, jealous of the friendship she never had. As a child, I thought she was evil, but now I understood her. Jealousy can make a good person do wicked things.

Love and desire. Which is more powerful? Which is more destructive? Love is time-worn desire. A pebble shaped and polished, forever changed by a river's flow. Desire is the storm and the wreckage it leaves behind. Love is the life raft, the rope, the drop of an anchor. It is the thing that secures us all. That night fierce dreams roared in my mind, chasing me all the way into morning.

CHAPTER 30

Sybel had promised me that the wait for my father was nearly over and a union would soon come from the mist. Still, I was restless. From my daily lookout at the top of the bell tower, the air seemed to have taken on a different taste and texture, sugar sweet and so full of shimmery wisps that I would carry them home in my hair. Up here in the sky, all thoughts were of my father, and how I would feel upon seeing him for the first time.

I remembered Lemàn then; her emotions were always large and looming, and never far away. I could tell when she was thinking of my father, which was often. She had carried the sadness of his loss with her for so long and, although I bandaged the wound, his memory still seeped out. I wished I could share my excitement about meeting him with her, but she was too far away from here. This meeting, I would have to make alone.

I wondered whether you could desire two people at once. When I'd asked Professor Elms, he'd told me the story of a Pacific Island tribe whose members were all born with two hearts, one beating on the left of their chest, the other on the right. If one heart got broken, it wouldn't matter, as they could manage perfectly well with the one that remained. I remember asking him what happened if the other one got broken too, and he'd simply replied that people shouldn't make the same mistake twice. He'd told me that all hearts in humans, mammals and birds have different chambers, two at the top and two resting underneath, and that one of these chambers in Lemàn's heart was just for me, protected by a cage of ribs. He told me that the heart was enclosed in a protective sac and the wall of the heart had three layers. I told him it sounded like a fortress and he laughed, and said it was exactly that. It's not meant to be easy to get into someone's heart he had said, and sometimes we open up one of those chambers and let someone in and then it's too late. Some people lock the chamber and the key is lost, sometimes for years, sometimes for ever. The drawbridge is lifted over a moat of tears, never to be lowered again. Talk of loss always drew our eyes to his top pocket and thoughts of the memory contained within. I knew what he meant and I knew Lemàn had a locked chamber for which she too would never find the key. From this conversation, I remembered one more thing: fish were different. Their heart didn't have four chambers; it only had two.

Does that mean they love less?

Does it mean they love at all?

The following days dragged like sopping rags. Bloated heavy and sodden and soaked with misery. I wanted to bundle them up and throw them all away.

Every time I walked past the Boat of Floating Freaks and Oddities, I did so more with excitement than trepidation, and I laughed, thinking of Lemàn's panic-stricken face seeing me so close to what she had mistaken for our enemy. Always I hesitated then; it seemed eerily forgotten and I wondered about the Sky-Worshipper sleeping within. Both Leo and I had been carefully watching for any sign of life, but there was never any flicker of movement. I thought about climbing on board and one time I even got halfway to the top of the plank, before turning around and rushing back to the street, making the wood judder beneath my feet. My fear of getting lost in the dark disorientating depths was too great, and I feared I might never find my way back out again.

Hours passed as I carefully worded and reworded all the questions that I wanted to ask my father when he finally arrived. As soon as I'd written one down, I'd reject it with a quick dissatisfied scribble. Soon there were dozens of scrunched up balls of paper chrysanthemums strewn across the floor like a high wind had swept in and de-headed the flower beds. *Do you remember Lemàn? Did you love her? Did you know she was pregnant? Do you know who I am?* Question after question after question. And then the most difficult question of all and the one I most feared: *Do you want to know?* From present to past and back again. I knew it was impossible to translate them word for word, but at least I didn't need to preoccupy myself with any syntax, for Orniglossa was not assembled into a fixed pattern; just like its speakers, it flew free, its meaning unbound by any definite structure. Elver had shown me how to capture the semantics in my tone and pitch and babble of loss and longing and everything in between. It would have to be enough, and so, finally satisfied, I folded the paper and put it in my pocket, hoping my curiosity wouldn't scare him away. I left the house and caught the boat to the university island where I would always find Leo waiting.

Chugging across the water, I could see the mist was tantalisingly close. From the edge of the city, a few people were clambering into a small boat with the rattle and roll of empty jars at their feet. Each one eager to mend what was broken. It wouldn't be long, I thought excitedly, noticing that nearly all the jars on the Bridge of Longing were now full.

The sun speckled the water and I decided to enjoy its warmth a little longer by walking through the gardens to reach Leo's study. He didn't notice my arrival and I stood and watched him awhile from the open doorway. I found myself remembering the almost kiss. I liked him. I liked his quiet sensitivity and the way his hair fell over his glasses. Sometimes, when he brushed it away, he'd forget about them and they'd topple unexpectedly from his face, and that would make me laugh out loud. He was intelligent and sensitive and he understood me perhaps even better than I understood myself, but something was missing. In the end my mind always closed the door and went in search of another one; one that wasn't quite so easy to open.

He had removed one of the mounted birds from its glass dome and was cleaning its feathers with a damp paintbrush. He lifted them one at a time, stroking the soft bristles down the length of each one. Then he smoothed each one back again, with a tenderness that made me ache. It was painstaking work and I could see how much it mattered to him. I felt an itch somewhere on my back in amongst all of my feathers, but I couldn't quite reach it or maybe it was an ache for him to touch me with the same warm affection. What a waste! That bird felt nothing. I stepped into the room and a creak gave me away.

'The mist is getting closer,' I said.

He lifted his head and smiled. 'Yes, I saw it this morning. I think it will reach us by the end of the week and the island too.'

'I have thought of some questions I'd like to ask, but I'm not sure if I've translated them correctly and I wondered if you could have a look.' I pulled out a crumpled piece of paper from my pocket.

'This is impressive,' he said slowly, raising his eyebrows. 'You are quite the expert. I haven't got very far with it at all, I'm afraid.' He handed me back the paper, and I tucked it proudly back inside my pocket, without mentioning who the real expert was.

I stayed a while longer and we chatted about his research. He made me laugh with stories of his grandfather and he drew me nearer with his tales of distant jungles and mountains. He knew more about birds than Professor Elms, and whatever question I had he had an answer for it. He led me over to a glass cabinet where three baby owls peered back at me with their glassy stare, captured in time. He explained how their feathers were soft but barbed to muffle all sound. He swung open the door and encouraged me to reach inside and touch one. It felt tiny and fragile as though the touch of my finger would be enough to crush it to pieces. As we went from cabinet to cabinet, I listened to Leo explain the different types of birds. The birds whose feathers were 104 degrees warmer than air to keep them insulated and how the nightjar could trap insects with the small, bristly feathers it grew round its mouth. There were birds who lived in the heart of the desert, whose wings soaked up water so their chicks could sip from them. Feathers could also sense the changes in the air, the impending rain or the threat of a storm, he said. Birds I had never seen before sat watchful with their emerald heads and sapphire tails like waterfalls. There were bundles of Marabou feathers and duck down, and ostrich and Macaw feathers blooming out of various earthenware pots dotted about the room. Above me a flock of white doves hung, motionless, from the ceiling. I noticed Leo try to stifle a yawn and I knew he still had work to do, and I didn't want to keep him from it any longer.

'It's late,' I said, finally. 'I should be going.'

He nodded his agreement. 'I like our chats,' he said, walking me to the door, where I breathed in his alpine smell, like a warm forest alive with discovery. His eyes met mine and lingered for just a little too long. I realised that for a moment I had wanted him to kiss me and I wanted to kiss him back, but it was just another almost-kiss and that's all there ever seemed to be between us. Being with Leo felt comfortable and steady, but I wanted the danger of the collapse and fall. Evening was unfolding like a newly discovered love letter, and, as I walked across the gardens, I felt the familiar ruffle of my feathers in the air, and even though I now knew what it meant, I still wouldn't listen.

CHAPTER 31

Despite the lateness of the hour, my mind was too enlivened to contemplate sleep. Back in the city, the thrum of wings was still in my ears, loud enough to keep me awake. Standing outside Elver's window, I could see the shutters had been pushed halfway open to a pause, and a little light shone out from within. Forgetting about everything else, I bolted up the stairs – my head suddenly clear and focused – I knocked loudly on the door. Pressing my ear against the wood, I tried to hear movement from within; the shuffle of feet or the stir of a teapot. I knocked again and was just about to leave, when I heard the turn of a key and the door swung open.

'Where have you been?' My words sounded harsher than I had meant them to.

She answered my question with a kiss, long and deep and wanting, and my mind was at once quiet, as she pulled me into the room. There was no almost kiss here.

This time when I woke, I was relieved to find her still there, her eyes closed and her breathing soft like shallow breaking waves. Now it was my turn to watch her. Her hair spread over the pillow like spilled marmalade. Content, I drifted back to sleep and when I woke again, she was standing in the kitchen.

'I'm glad you're still here,' I said sleepily. 'Last time I woke up, you had disappeared.'

There was a question in there, but it remained un- answered. She looked at me so intently I felt like something rare and valuable and worth studying.

'Will you disappear again?' I asked, crossing to sit down at the table.

'I thought you understood that I have to disappear some- times, and one day I won't be able to come back.' She made it sound as though it was my fault.

'Disappear where?' I tried not to sound accusatory and softened my tone, trying to coax more from her.

She laughed, and it sounded like a gurgle of water. 'Home, of course!'

'Sybel told me about the night she found you,' I said, inviting her to tell me the story.

She poured some tea into two chipped cups, but still no words left her lips.

'Do you remember?' I added cautiously.

'Yes – I remember,' she replied, handing one of the cups to me.

'Then tell me.' I kept my voice low and gentle, as though I was trying to tempt a wild woodland creature to feed from my hand. 'I'd like to hear the story.'

Slowly she slid into a chair and, for a minute or so of silence, her eyes flickered between me and the cup. Restless in decision, she stood back up and crossed the room, where she leaned against the window, gazing down at the water below. When she spoke, her eyes were elsewhere, and nothing in the room seemed to matter.

'It wasn't long ago when it happened.' She paused and for a moment I thought she had changed her mind about telling me, but then it fell out in a wave of emotion. 'That night I had been swimming close to the city. I liked to do that. I liked the way the lights twinkled in the dark. The sea can be so deep and black, a place where nothing shines. I would watch and wonder and wait to see how long each one would last. Sometimes, I'd trace my fingertips through the air joining them up to make different shapes.' She laughed at the memory and then her face darkened. 'But that night I was too careless.'

'The night of the storm?'

She nodded. 'I knew it was coming. I should have swum far out to sea where the depths are quiet and still, but I didn't listen. I thought I had time.' She paused. 'What did Sybel tell you?'

As she spoke, I had the cup raised to my lips, blowing away the heat of the tea which I was yet to taste. I rested it back on its saucer. 'She told me about the storm, and about rescuing you from the canal. About how she took you home and nursed your broken—' I hesitated. The word was too wondrous to utter.

'My broken tail?'

I nodded, and finally took a sip of my tea, wanting her to continue. It was her story to tell.

'I don't remember much about my recovery, but I remember that the pain was eased only by Sybel's ointments and herbs. I was so cold, and it even hurt to breathe.'

'And then?'

'And then?' She threw my question back at me.

I wanted to hear the next part, the part about Doctor Marino and what he meant to her – what he still meant, but of course I couldn't find the words to formulate such difficult questions. 'Well, what I mean is that you're still here and you don't have a tail, unless you're hiding it well.'

'I am not the one hiding anything, and you know that very well after the last time we met.'

She reached across the table and steadied my hand. 'You should cast off that old shabby coat; you are much too beautiful to hide.'

I felt suddenly shy and busied myself swirling the dregs of tea left behind in my cup.

'With Sybel's help, we changed everything.'

'Though the ancient Art of Meta?'

'Yes. I didn't believe her at first, but after weeks of mixing and burning and rubbing ointment into the cracks of my broken tail, they were finally ready to ask for the blessing of the sea. I was to be thrown in as a fish and hauled back out as a girl.'

'They?' I queried.

'Yes. We had the help of a doctor,' she replied simply.

'Why did you choose to become land-bound?'

'Why did you?' she asked.

Her question confused me. 'I didn't have a choice.'

'Remember what I told you about Orniglossa? There is no distinction between the word for arm and wing?'

'Well, for me there is,' I protested. 'I can't fly, or even flutter for that matter. A long time ago, I fell from a tree, and my feathers did nothing to stop me. As for wings ... well, I can only imagine what they would feel like.' I spread my arms as though to prove my point. 'How can I miss what I have never had?'

She leaned back. 'You will find your way; I am sure of that. It is within you ... all you have to do is follow your instincts.'

'And you – do you miss having your tail?'

She considered my question and all of its implications. 'I longed to be able to wear pretty shoes, even though it didn't quite work out the way I had hoped it would.' She laughed, staring down at her large, flat feet, too awkward to fit inside any shoe. 'Whenever the sea calls me, I must answer.' The conversation had turned cold, like a folding wave.

'Don't go,' I said, offering her my childish solution.

She saw the anguish in my face and came closer, wrapping her arms around me. 'I belong to the sea, and I carry it with me everywhere I go. It is within me, just as the sky is within you; I cannot truly love anything else, no matter how hard I try.'

I chose to ignore the honest warning in her words, and instead fell into the happiness of the here and now. After that we barely left the room; most of what we needed was right there. A time capsule; a secret grotto; a deep well full of wishes. At sunrise, Elver would lazily lower a basket out of the window, with a few coins in the bottom to ensure our request was met. Then we would fall back to sleep in one another's arms, waiting for the floating bakery to pass. When we woke again it would be mid-morning, we'd lift the basket back up to discover croissants and bagels still warm from the sun. In the evening, she would dive from the window and swim down the canal, returning a short time later with fish for supper. As we ate, she helped me translate the questions I wanted to ask my father, scratching out my mistakes and rewriting over them. I was pleased to see I had made very few, and that my studying had paid off.

I got to know her body and through it, her mind. The heart was somewhat trickier. Its rhythm harder to decipher, but I heard it every time I rested my head in the crook of her arm. Its beat as regular as the hands of a clock, but when I listened closer, I thought I could hear the distant murmur of water. She was right; it was never far away.

I loved to watch her at night, her skin even more like armour glinting in the moonlight. Her arms braceleted with tiny silver grains of salt, traceable beneath my fingertips. A restless sleeper. A dreamer. Sometimes, she spread her arms wide as though she was trying to catch a wave, other times her arms lay flat against her streamlined body, carried on the current far out to sea. It was always calling for her return and I would reach out to claw her back.

Finally, we left the room and entered a city gift-wrapped in silver mist, which tingled against our skin. It was warm enough to sit outside with our coats buttoned up and we ate sweet bread from the bakery, which flaked all over our fingers as we broke it off in pieces. I fed the crumbs to the expectant birds. Anyone passing would think we were old friends, maybe even lovers, comfortable with each other, familiar and happy.

She stopped outside a jewellery shop to admire a beautiful necklace of emerald glass beads. Before I could protest, she had thrust the bag of mussels into my hand and disappeared inside. Moments later she returned and handed me a little brown box tied neatly with a pink ribbon.

'Now you will have a reminder of me,' she said.

But why would I need a reminder if she was standing right there next to me? Pleased with my gift, I loosened the ribbon and slid off the lid. Lying on a plump velvet cushion was the necklace I had seen in the window. I held it up to the sun, and watched as the light passed right through it. The beads glinted like translucent wicked eyes, and tittered together as I rolled them across my palm. I had seen men in cafés hold similar, swishing them through the air with a rhythmic click to pass the time or perhaps to pass their worries away. She took it from me and fastened it round my neck where it caught on my feathers. Another warning I did not heed, and I smiled to hide my doubt. It was then I noticed her own necklace. At the end of a thin silver chain, a tiny starfish floating in the dipped pool where her collarbones met. Was this, too, worn as a reminder?

We continued into the backstreets, until we came to the end of the lagoon wall, where we caught a boat to the Reef. The journey across the water was breezy and brief; Elver had insisted we stand near the edge so she could see and smell the sea. We huddled together as the flames of our hair tangled and flared around us and I sank deeper into the warmth of my coat. As we arrived and the boat stilled, the heat returned.

'I will swim back,' said Elver, climbing from the boat.

I laughed at how absurd she sounded, and not for one moment did I think she was being serious. That was always my mistake.

CHAPTER 32

As soon as I stepped off the boat, the Reef felt like another world and completely different from the City of Murmurs. With its long wide avenues, and large open squares, it had the potential to be a majestic seaside place. Somewhere for the wealthy to come and spend their money, but unlike the beautifully preserved birds in their glass domes, the Reef was a neglected and tired place. It seemed to sigh wearily at our arrival. The air wasn't yet warm enough or impressive enough to entice visitors to flock here, but the residents came in the summer months to wiggle the sand between their toes and escape the confines of the dark huddle of buildings. I had never seen so much sky, as we ran, breathless and dishevelled, all the way to the sea.

'Isn't it beautiful?' she said, closing her eyes and inhaling deeply. 'It's always beautiful where the land ends and the other world begins.' She reached for my hand and I felt her fingers clasping mine, but they didn't slot together easily. The translucent skin that webbed each of her toes also webbed her fingers. Still I tried to hold on.

Looking out, the sea seemed gentle now, a peaceful grey-blue infinity; deceptive, for I knew the damage it could do. How many fishermen never returned? I remember seeing a woman collapse once by the harbour after being told of her husband's death. Lemàn rushed me past, but not before I saw her clutch at her shawls and try to rip her heart from her chest, such was her desire to join him.

'It's a dangerous beauty though,' I said.

Elver smiled at me. 'Isn't all beauty dangerous?' Then she began to pull off her clothes and throw them to the sand.

'What are you doing? There are people.' I said, looking round frantically only to discover that actually the beach was empty.

'Come on,' she encouraged, shaking off her dress. 'Let's swim.' She grabbed my arm, but I pulled back with such unexpected force that she fell against me.

'I can't,' I said, feeling foolish at having to admit the truth. 'I don't know how.'

Elver stopped and stared at me in astonishment.

'You don't know how to swim?' she said slowly. Her mouth fell open, and she blinked at the strangeness of my words, trying to make sense of them. For her, being able to swim was instinctive; nobody had to teach her not to drown.

I shook my head. Professor Elms knew too much of the sea to risk taking me there. He knew what would happen if an unexpected current swept me away. I learned then that death wasn't the worst thing; it's what was left behind.

She thought for a moment and then slowly began to undress me.

'I can show you,' she whispered, reaching out to unbutton my coat.

'I can't,' I said feebly, half turning away. 'My feathers.'

She ignored my protests and grabbed my hand leading me closer to the water. Furtively, I glanced up and down the sand to make sure there was no one to see, but it was still completely deserted. 'I can't,' I repeated, but my words were the half-formed things of winter light, and as she shushed me, I could no longer resist.

Closing my eyes, I felt my body lighten as my clothes fell to the sand in a crumpled pile. 'Please – not my bandages,' I said, and I felt her hand slip away in silent agreement. Desire can drive you to do unimaginable things and hand in hand we walked slowly into the frothy waves. At first the cold made me shudder and I cringed and turned my body away, but Elver encouraged me further and I waded out until I felt the sand gently shelve away beneath my feet. At that moment she dove under the surface and I could see her shadow, the iridescent gleam of her beneath the water. The seabed was just out of reach and I kept having to push myself up with my foot to keep my face out of the water, but I was reassured by the soft tickle of her hair against my legs. I grew dizzy, laughing and whirling round, trying to chase the shape of her as she darted between my legs, hair trailing like a shoal of playful fish. She had nudged against me and I stumbled, drifting too far from the shelf, and this time when I tried to push into the sand, there was nowhere for my foot to rest. I kicked wildly in a scramble to find the seabed, which was all of a sudden lost. I began to panic, gulping down great salty mouthfuls, and spluttering them back out again. The world was a watery blur and I splashed hopelessly as my sodden feathers weighed me down, heavy as a millstone.

Then she was there with her arms and legs wrapped around me, keeping us both afloat. Blinking away the water, I began to breathe again in little hiccupy swallows. I felt her hand smooth back my hair and wipe my eyes. The water was pushing us together and we moved steady and strong, to the rhythm of the sea. I imagined this was what drowning felt like; a hopeless struggle. Peace and stillness, then finally calm surrender and a strange sense of bliss.

'Don't let me go,' I whispered, and I felt her limbs clasp tighter around mine in reply.

Then she kissed my mouth, silencing the world. After a while I began to shiver and Elver swam us back to the shallows.

Wave-washed, we quickly dressed. I smuggled myself back into my clothes and hastily fastened my coat before anyone could see, but my feathers were hard to dry and I could feel the water seeping through its fabric.

'Why did you leave it all behind – the sea, I mean?' I asked, as we strolled along the pier.

She hesitated; maybe it was because she wasn't sure of her answer or maybe it was that she didn't want to share it with me.

'There was someone,' she said at last, but of course I already knew that. And I felt my heart lurch.

'Someone you loved?' I struggled to say, but she gave no reply and I stayed silent, regretting my words.

We walked as far as we could until the rumble and rattle of the slats ended and there was just a deep drop into the ocean. Standing there, we watched the sea fill with twilight. I liked the way the last of the day's light softened her face. I wanted now to last forever. It seemed something about the sea, encouraged confession.

'I was happy for a while,' she began unexpectedly, her thoughts returning to my earlier question, 'but the sea called me back; it always does. At first, I heard it in my dreams and then it was everywhere. The waves in the lagoon are constant messengers, sent to call me home.'

'And do you listen?' I asked fearfully.

'It is impossible not to.'

'Do you still see—?' The name, Doctor Marino, nearly spilled from my mouth, but I managed to swallow it back, just in time. 'Do you still see that someone you mentioned?'

She reached for her necklace, lifted the starfish and twirled it absent-mindedly between her fingertips. 'Sometimes, but not really.' She dropped the starfish and it sank back into its shallow pool.

'Will you return to the sea one day?' I whispered, half hoping the sound of the waves and the wind would carry my words far away so she wouldn't hear them. It was the answer I feared the most.

She turned to face me then. 'I will have no choice. When I have gone, do not look for me,' she replied, reaching for my hand. It seemed that just as my father's island was drifting closer, she was drifting further away.

We stood, silhouetted in intimacy at the end of the pier, under a darkening sky, close to everything that mattered. The horizon hinged two worlds together. It looked like the open spine of a book, its pages yet unwritten. The sea was a giant inkpot waiting to colour the quill's nib so our story could begin. It didn't matter that I had been warned against falling for someone with a heart of water, and even though she had been the one to warn me, I refused to listen.

Unexpectedly, she let go of my hand and then, without warning, she dived into the sea. For a moment, I wasn't sure what had happened, other than she had vanished under the water, but then I saw her head in the distance. I shouted her name, but she didn't turn and then she was gone again. I shouted again, this time in panic. Not too far away, I noticed a rocky outcrop and feared she may bang her head or get caught on their jagged edges. I ran back onto the sand and raced up the beach into the grassy dunes, where I saw an old man walking his dog. As I approached, he stopped and stared at me in alarm.

'My ... my ... she's ... the sea,' I tried to explain, but the words wouldn't come. He looked shocked and confused as I clung to him wildly, before letting go and stumbling off in the direction of the rocks. He called after me, but I climbed higher and higher, scraping my knee and my elbow and, as I dropped down the other side, I banged my cheek and knew there was a gash as something warm and thick began to trickle down my face.

'Elver!' Elver!' My cries went unanswered.

Running, staggering and falling into the water, the mocking waves pushed me back, guardians of the sea, and they wouldn't let me reach her. Exhausted and crying, I sprawled on the sand, half-drowned. I remembered her words as we arrived. Could she really be swimming back to the city? Composing myself, I leant down and tried to wash the blood off my face. It stung and burned, but I continued until the water ran clear. Shoeless and limping, people stared at me, some in shock, most in pity, drenched and battered. I heard Elver's words again and again in my mind: *When I have gone, do not look for me.* I was too distressed to see the mist dancing, twinkling and sparkling through the air. It had at last arrived, but what should have been a wonder-filled, mesmerising moment was instead filled with disillusionment and disappointment.

Even if I had looked up to see the mist then, my heart felt much too heavy to leap, and I trudged home through a skitter of stones.

Sybel winced when I returned with my face streaked with sweat, tears and the remains of dried blood. With a bowl of warm water and a cloth, she lifted my chin and began wiping my face, giving me a poultice to hold to my grazes. No questions were asked and I was grateful for that.

A shuffle and a whimper came from the corner of the room, and I moved closer to determine what could be making such a sound. Proximity revealed a cardboard box that had been filled with straw and blankets, and tucked in the middle of the bundle was Zephyros, the oldest and mangiest of all the dogs she kept. His eyes were swollen shut and his chest rose and fell in ragged little breaths. I was reminded of the Sky-Worshipper.

'What's wrong with him?' I asked, bending down to pat the top of his head. It was warm, too warm, and I withdrew my hand quickly as his whimpering grew louder. I was afraid I had hurt him.

Sybel shook her head wearily. 'He's too old for this world,' she replied simply.

'What can we do?'

'I have done all I can for now.' With great effort, she got to her feet and crossed the kitchen. She lay down beside him on the cold stone floor and rested her head on a blanket next to Zephyros's head. Her hair stuck to his cheek, fixed there by a thin trickle of drool, which fell continuously from his twitching mouth. I went to fetch another blanket and when I returned, her eyes were closed, but I knew she wasn't asleep because I could hear her humming the familiar sound of a lullaby. I covered her against the cold, and left the room, hoping that Zephyros would survive the night.

CHAPTER 33

'Wake up, wake up!' Leo was standing over my bed, tugging at the bed sheet. My first thought was for Zephyros.

'What is—?' It hurt to move my mouth, and my last word was lost in a groan.

'Where have you been? Come on, it's time.'

Disorientated, I sat up with a whimper; everything seemed to ache. 'Is he dead?' I asked groggily, trying to make sense of what had brought Leo rushing into my room with such urgency and insistence that he was now shaking my arm and making the pain worse.

He stopped abruptly and confusion spread across his face. 'Dead? Of course not; I've just seen him very much alive in the square.'

'Who?' I frowned.

'Your father.'

'My father? Are you sure?' I was fully awake and sitting up.

Leo nodded, excited to finish. 'I've just seen them take the Sky-Worshipper from the boat.'

'Then we're too late?' I cried. The boat had been our only connection to finding my father and now it was gone.

Leo shook his head and gave me a knowing look. 'I followed them. They have a little stall in the square and I know exactly where it is.'

I tried to smile, but smiling hurt even more than talking did, and I winced.

Only then did Leo seem to take in my bruises, and he stepped back. 'What happened to you?' His voice grew quiet with concern as he continued to stare.

Slowly, I shuffled towards the mirror, and away from his scrutiny. The gash on my face had begun to heal, and its edges were dry and crusted. I felt the weight of Leo's eyes still upon me. 'I'm fine.' I said, in a tone that ended the conversation before it had even begun.

Leo left the room and I dressed as quickly as my bruises would allow. Being with Elver blurred everything else away. How could she just vanish so easily? The story was true: mermaids were cursed creatures; they lured you in and left you to drown. Walking into the kitchen I was relieved to find that Zephyros was still alive. Sybel was on her hands and knees, trying to spoon an oily mixture into his mouth. His eyes were no longer open at all, and she had to prize his jaw open with her fingers to get the medicine down his throat; he had no strength left to do it himself. I felt an overwhelming surge of grief as she tickled him tenderly on his belly and he wheezed, trying to show his appreciation. I could hear the rattle of his lungs from across the room, but already he wore his blanket like a shroud.

'Leo told me your father has arrived,' she said.

I nodded, unhooking my coat from behind the door.

'How is he?' I asked, returning my gaze to Zephyros.

She smiled sadly. 'While there is a beating heart, there is still hope.'

I rushed forwards, flinging my arms around her; she was too wide for my hands to meet, but I felt her immediate warmth as I sunk against her. 'What's that for?' she asked, surprised by my unexpected affection.

I shrugged. 'I wanted to make you feel better.'

Leo was waiting for me on the steps, half hidden in the swirling mist. Up close, I could see its intricate pattern. Glittering its silver dance. As we walked, it felt damp on our skin like a sprinkle of tiny kisses.

'They're in the square behind the Church of One Hundred Souls,' he replied. 'Selling jars of mist to heal the broken-hearted.'

Of course, I thought to myself with a smile; the church Lemàn had spoken of, and I knew exactly where to find it.

It was the birds I noticed first. Hundreds of them. Scattered across the ground like giant breadcrumbs, sitting high on the roof tops, nestled in alcoves and on window ledges. It was just as Lemàn had described it to me. There was a warm humming sound of contentment, which vibrated across the square. For a brief moment I thought they must have been trapped by a giant net hanging from the buildings, but when I looked up, the square was open to the sky and the birds were free to come and go as they pleased. A solitary feather floated through the air from a pigeon grooming itself from above. It wasn't just pigeons, which strutted and preened; it seemed as though all the birds of the city had gathered in this one place and I knew exactly why. He was here.

Carefully, we waded through them to cross to the other side. The birds shuffled around slowly, unwilling to move out of the way and we struggled not to tread on them. One misplaced step would leave a crush of broken bones and flattened feathers.

'There!' exclaimed Leo, pointing up ahead.

We were standing in front of three wooden stalls hammered together with nails. The tables were lined with jars, row after row of them, stacked one on top of another, snuggled together side by side, various sizes and shapes, but all with the same magical mist frothing and swirling and twinkling inside. A small queue had formed and people were making their purchases, quickly and silently, furtively dropping their chosen jars into coat pockets or open bags or even under their hats before turning away, hoping they hadn't been spotted. Heartbreak sometimes required discretion. What mesmerised me more, though, were the two men at the stall. Both were tall and thin and fidgety, and all of them were covered, unashamedly, in a display of large feathers. There was no mistaking them and, unlike mine, they were long and thick and proud. Whereas I grew tufts on my shoulder blades, and nothing more, they had two magnificent gleaming wings, that lay folded over their backs like a warm cape. Looking closer, I was disappointed to see that none of these men had the pale-blue eyes of my father.

'I don't think he's here,' I said, scanning the square in disappointment. 'Are you sure you saw him?'

Leo tentatively approached the stall, and tried to make himself understood. The strange clipped words flew off his tongue, and the men stepped back, suddenly startled, not sure what to make of this stranger communicating in their obscure and secretive language. His babbles went unanswered; perhaps they were not understood. They turned to one another and I could hear the *crk crk* of their deeply animated conversation. I recognised the tone of curiosity.

Then something caught my eye. A man was filling a bowl with water from an old tap in the wall. He wasn't far away and I could see his outline from where I stood and the brightness of his feathers rage against the dull fabric of his clothes – ragged and ill-fitting, patched in places to hold them together. He sprang up and limbered awkwardly towards us. He moved as though his legs were not his own, all stiff with high exaggerated steps, as though he wasn't used to using them. I could see he was as thin as a reed with knots at his knees and elbows, which if untied would send him collapsing in a heap to the ground.

As he approached, I noticed his eyes; so blue, and so bright they shone like the surface of Neptune. They reminded me of the birds' eggs I saw as a child; delicate, fragile and so easily crushed. Then I remembered Lemàn's tattoo, the bird on her wrist, the same unforgettable blue; an exact match.

I knew with absolute certainty that standing right in front of me, conjured out of the wondrous mist, was my father. I had imagined him for so long, that, now he was here, I didn't know what to do. A moment passed, then another and another, and all we could do was watch each other, not yet ready for anything else. I reached out for Leo to keep me steady.

'It's him,' I whispered, placing my trembling hand on his.

'Yes,' he whispered back. 'It is.'

I could feel the unstoppable swell of tears, and everything I had been waiting for and wishing for was finally about to unfold. Time stopped then. I was too overwhelmed to breathe another word, and I felt myself lean against Leo's shoulder to stop myself from dropping to the ground. My whole body fluttered, inside and out, and I felt Leo's strong hand clasp around mine to still my shivers.

Through the blur of my tears, I watched as my father pursed his lips in thought, trying to make sense of the two strangers standing in front of him. We had never met before, yet I could tell I was somehow familiar to him. I had his eyes and his wild flaming hair. Our mouths were different; whereas his was small and thin, I had the wide, tilting lips of Lemàn. Instinctively, I lowered my collar and felt the jostle of my wakening feathers spring free. In sudden understanding, his mouth opened in shock and the bowl clattered to the ground, where the water spilled across our feet in a silent blessing. Neither of us moved for what felt like hours, and the water trickled away in tiny unbroken rivers. In that one instant, he knew what I knew, and we saw ourselves reflected back at each other.

CHAPTER 34

Not once did he avert his gaze from my face, as though he couldn't believe what was standing right in front of him; one blink to chase it all away. There was no kissing, no holding hands, no wild embrace. We were connected without touch. He stared at me in disbelief and I stared back. Then he reached out his long sinewy hand and gently touched the gash on my face.

'Shall we go somewhere to talk?' suggested Leo. 'The lilac gardens perhaps?'

I nodded, suddenly unable to find the words in any language. Leo stepped forward and began to translate. All the time my nervous excitement bloomed faster than a drop of ink onto blotting paper. As we walked, the sunlight lit his feathers and they shone and flamed against the warmth like gleaming treasure. We reached a quiet stretch of lawn by the fountain, where we finally sat down.

'My name is Maréa,' I said, starting with the easiest thing I could think of. I patted my chest and repeated my name. Then I pointed at him, 'Eddero,' I said.

He blinked, and I wasn't sure if he understood what I was telling him.

I tried to speak Orniglossa. 'Why did you leave?' I must have muddled the sounds because he still gave no sign of understanding. I turned to Leo for help, but he nudged me and nodded towards my father.

His eyes had begun to glisten with sadness. He looked down at his hands, in sorrow or regret or shame for all the missed years. Then he did something astonishing and completely unexpected – he spoke.

'I knew,' he said quietly. His words cracked open like fragile shells, and his voice sounded like it hadn't been used in years. Shocked, I looked at Leo, who sat in open-mouthed amazement.

'What did you know?' he asked, his voice soft and coaxing.

'You. I knew you were out there somewhere,' he replied, looking directly at me.

'But that's impossible – how could you have known?' My words burst from my lips. 'My mother left the city before she even knew herself.'

'I sensed it all this time. Each day I could hear the movement of your feathers. Once they grew silent and I feared you were lost for ever, but then the sound returned, stronger and clearer, and I never gave up hope again.'

He was getting used to his voice now, and each word sounded like the patter of a raindrop on a thick shiny leaf. He looked guilty as he spoke, but I reached out my hand and rested it on his knee, so thin and bony that I was afraid it might snap. For some reason it made me feel sad. His feathers lay one on top of the other, folded away neatly like the washing.

'I had to leave with the island,' he explained. 'I looked for her, but I couldn't find her. I tried so very hard, but it was too late—' His shoulders slumped and his whole body seemed to sink into some untold weariness, a heavy grief he had carried for so long.

Would things have been so different if he had found her? Would the slow swell of her stomach have been enough to clip his wings? I couldn't possibly know the answers, but I imagined them, allowing myself a glimpse of a different life. They were opposites in every way; one so large and safe, the other small and light; one with a voice so strong and clear it could blow away the clouds, the other so high and shrill it could pierce the sun in an explosion of warmth; one still and solid, the other ever-shifting and floating, near and far, earth and air. But both of them were mine.

That afternoon in the gardens, by a laughing fountain, two strangers slowly became father and daughter. A life-time of separation couldn't be resolved in the passing of just a few hours, but everything has to have a beginning and this was ours. It was the beginning of us. The first stitch to close a wound. Never again seamless, but at least the repair had begun. He told me his story, only occasionally stumbling over his words, and then I learned the answers to the questions I had been holding onto for such a very long time.

When he had left Lemàn, he had planned to return to the hotel the following night, not realising she had left that morning. Finding her room empty, he tried to ask the proprietor where she was, but he hadn't learned to speak and no matter how hard he tried, he couldn't make himself understood. The mist swirled and had begun to thin, ready to whisk the island away. He had no choice then but to leave with the decision to learn her language and the language of those who could help him find us both.

'Staying was impossible.' He shook his head hopelessly, regretting what had happened all those years ago. He explained how the Ornis Tribe needed the mist to give them strength. Without it, life would be limited and staying away from the island would be a death sentence. He had almost been too late.

The arrival of rain forced us to seek shelter under the nearby trees. Standing next to the lilac bushes filled with the rustle of tiny starlings, I watched my father. He remained standing in the grass with his wings spread wide, and his mouth open to the rain. He trilled happily, letting it bounce off his feathers for the whole world to see. You live as a bird, you become one, I realised. Enthralled, I wanted to be a part of it. Ducking my head beneath the canopy of leaves, I ran to his side and tilted my head to the sky. Somewhere a fire was burning and I could taste the smoke and ash in the air. Sensing I was there next to him, he lifted his wings and wrapped them around me in a warm embrace. A dark comfort. We laughed then, and returned to the trees where he shook the rain from his wings. I noticed how hunched his shoulders appeared, their blades knotted together making him look awkward and uncomfortable perched on the high stone wall.

He continued his story, and, with Leo's help, the mysteries between us slowly unravelled. I sat listening and stroking my feathery hair, thinking of our similarities. Our thin bones, almost weightless, our hair aflame, our ability to hear things from so very far away, to sense the arrival of something long before it appeared, and most of all, our eyes. Bright and alert, blue and sparkling like sunlight dancing on water. It was clear he loved Lemàn as much as she loved him, but they belonged in two different worlds, two different elements, and Lemàn was not the woman he remembered her to be.

It seemed he had remained faithful like the sun – warm and strong and burning with hope – whereas Lemàn had not. She had bedded hundreds of men, and no matter the reason, she had not remained true. Sometimes, her heart was as luminous and full as a harvest moon, but then it was sliced with the whirring blade of time into a translucent, mercurial crescent; a sliver of a thing. It knew nothing of love then.

'Where is she?' He finally sought the answer he had wanted from the very beginning.

I hesitated, not sure how much to tell him. 'She lives a long way from here. Her room is at the top of a crumbling house, hidden in the clouds so close to the sky.' I watched his face, but he was gazing into the distance as though he was trying to imagine it all. Leo nodded at me to continue. 'She told me about you. She still has your feather pressed between the pages of a book – I saw it before I left. She tried to find you too.' I reached out and placed my hand gently on his arm.

'Did she?' He seemed surprised, and blinked sadly at finally hearing the truth so many years too late. 'I suppose we both got lost along the way.'

After that we sat in silence, wondering about what could have been.

His question broke the silence. 'Is she happy?'

I nodded and smiled at her memory. The way she laughed and the way she hummed as she fixed pins in her hair; the way she danced and twirled around my room, her smell like summer-soaked lemons about to burst from the branch; the way she wrapped her arms around me telling me stories; the way she made me feel beautiful before I discovered the ugliness of the world outside, and the way she protected me from it for as long as she could, but then loved me enough to let me go. And it was true, she was happy – most of the time – but there were always moments when the memories gathered and fell fast, dampening her pillow even in her sleep.

I imagined a love like his didn't see size or shape, blind to change in all its forms, but Lemàn hadn't taken well to growing older. Her body sagged from overuse and her hair had been stripped of its colour like a winter sky. Wrinkles burrowed deep into her skin, like hibernating creatures and her eye lids drooped heavily, hooded as though she had seen enough of the world. Lemàn was worn out, but if Sybel was right, and she always was, then Lemàn had found love again. I didn't mention any of this to my father. Some things are best left unspoken.

After that, we left talk of Lemàn behind, and instead our conversation turned to us. Until a few hours ago, he had no idea I even existed, but then the recognition was instant and mutual. He still stumbled over his words as though he had just woken from a deep sleep, and when he got lost or wasn't sure of something he would slip back into his own language for safety. His intonation rose and fell quickly like steep mountain slopes, with its plosives and fricatives and its absence of any discernible vowel sounds. Sometimes, I caught the meaning, but he was much too fast and I got left behind.

'I would like to see you again tomorrow,' he said, with the curious tilt of his head that he did a lot.

'I would like that too,' I replied. As he came closer and rubbed his cheek against mine, I could smell long buried roots finally unearthed. Then with a noisy clacking of his shoulder blades he disappeared down the street.

I smiled, stowing deep the memory of the day. Walking back through the park with Leo, our hands brushed together and then I felt the warmth of his fingers as he clasped mine; I was too distracted to pull away. When we parted at the boat stop, he kissed me gently on the lips, and I was too exhilarated to understand its meaning and the promise it held; my mind was elsewhere. Thoughts turned to my father and I wondered where he was at this hour.

Strangely, the house was still awake when I arrived, and I could hear voices, low and hushed, stirring from the kitchen. I hurried to the door and inside I saw Sybel slumped at the table. I couldn't see her eyes or the expression they held, for she had her head bent as though in sombre prayer. Something was wrong. Instead of being clasped together, her hands were clenched in two fists of angry despair.

Movement coaxed my eye across the room, and there, kneeling by Zephyros's box, was Doctor Marino. It took me a moment to work out what was happening, and then with dark realisation, I suddenly understood the horrible anguish in the room.

'No!' I cried in alarm, not knowing whether to rush first to Sybel or to Zephyros; instead, I did neither. I was rooted.

Sybel didn't lift her head; she didn't move at all. Soundless, I couldn't tell if she was crying. It was as though she had nothing left to give, not even her tears. A fallen husk. When I sank to the bench, she didn't shuffle along to make room, but I squashed against her and wrapped my arm across her back. She was still soft and warm and breathing like bread just taken from the oven – not like a husk at all. I joined her in silent tears; each one a pilgrim of grief. Doctor Marino stood up to leave; there was nothing more to be done.

'It's time for me to go,' he said gently, lifting his bag from the chair.

Sybel closed her eyes, and held her chin tucked against her neck. Doctor Marino advanced towards the door, but as he past he paused for a moment and lay a hand gently on her back, just above mine. His touch, or perhaps the unexpectedness of it, made her lip quiver and her huge shoulders shuddered like a heavy rambling carriage along a rutted road. Although she didn't raise her head, she nodded, almost imperceptibly, and her gratitude was clearly understood. Words would come later, but for now it was all she had. Finally, she found the strength to lift her head, and her frightened eyes stared back at me, as though lost in the gloom of a deep, dark well.

CHAPTER 35

The next morning, Sybel was gone and Zephyros's box lay empty. The blankets were unnaturally cold as I carefully folded them away in a cupboard. They still smelled of him: straw and earth and leaves. I knew she had gone to request a blessing from the church; she had spoken of it over the last few days. I wasn't sure she believed in God, but she believed in ritual. Even the dogs seemed sad as I went outside to harness them for their walk. They snuffled forlornly round their pen trying to pick up the scent of their absent friend, but not finding it, they twitched their muzzles in the air, trying to find a trace of their friend carried on the wind. Wishing I could explain it to them, I slung the collars round their necks and checked them more carefully than before, Sybel couldn't take another loss. It was clear that the harness was now too big and one of the collars dangled from it, limp and empty, trailing on the ground like an injured limb. The sight of it brought tears to my eyes, and I blinked them away. I pushed open the gate and went to meet Leo's boat.

'What do you think of my father?' I asked, as we approached the square.

'Fascinating,' he replied without hesitation. 'The way he moves, the way he speaks ... I can't believe he actually learned to talk. The way he watches everything all the time. It's amazing – he really is just like a bird!'

'And what do you think he thinks about me?' My voice grew quieter, less certain.

'Well, it must have been a shock for him yesterday, but the way he looked at you, so inquisitive and eager and wanting to know more ... finding you has made him very happy.'

I nodded. 'Thank you – for helping me.'

He smiled and the pleasure was captured on his face.

I glanced sidelong at him as we walked. His dark hair and knowing eyes always deep in unspoken thought and a mouth that was always poised to ask a question, but rarely did, for he already had more answers than most. My eyes travelled from his face down to his hands – strong and smooth – and I had an overwhelming desire to hold one in my own, but I didn't, and instead I looked away.

It was then I saw her; she was crossing the Bridge of Illusion, too far away to hear me call her name. She was wearing a blue dress, which floated around her like water and her hair, as always, hung long and loose. At one point I thought I'd lost her, but she had just knelt down to tickle a cat under its chin. Under her arm she held a package, small and rectangular in shape, wrapped in brown paper and tied with string.

Time ticked on and the bell chimed across the square. She straightened and for a moment or two she seemed uncertain which way to go or perhaps she was looking for someone. Then I saw him. Standing at the foot of the bridge, waiting for her, was Doctor Marino. She hurried then and they embraced before she handed him the package. Elver looked happy, her head lifted upwards, laughing at something he was saying. I tried to tell myself that it was just the same as when me and Leo spent time together, only it wasn't the same at all. We had never lain together in the dark or fallen asleep wrapped in each other's arms; everything between us was almost, just a possibility. Past decisions hadn't been made with him in mind. Nothing had been sacrificed. They walked away from the Bridge of Illusion, until they were lost in the crowds. I felt my stomach tighten in a knot of anger and frustration. How easily the innocent woman in a fairy tale could be cursed by the wicked witch of jealousy.

'Come on!' shouted Leo, more impatient than annoyed.

'Sorry, I thought I saw someone I knew,' I replied.

My father was relieved to see me and I could hear the now familiar happy clacking of his shoulder blades. He joined us to walk the dogs, and we set off taking the longer route, leaving the sights and the sounds of the people far behind. We ambled along the eastern side of the park, until we found a patch of grass warmed by the sun and sat down near an abundance of flowers. My father, preferring to stand, rested his back against the trunk of a shady tree, its leaves a-quiver with birds. Several fluttered down and landed on the path, but the dogs lifted their noses and barked them back into the air. The park was a peaceful place and where else would a bird go in a city? I wondered how he had learned to speak and knew there was more of the story.

He told me that the day after Lemàn had left the City of Murmurs, he too had to return to his island, but he made a promise not to give up his search. He waited patiently and a little over a year later, the mist swept the island back to the city and this time, as well as selling jars of mist, he went in search of a boat. When he saw the Boat of Floating Freaks and Oddities, he had the answer, but the boat was already sailing out to distant shores, its outline soon became nothing more than a small dot on the horizon. As always, he was too late.

During one visit, Professor Bottelli had approached him at the stall, fascinated to learn more about the tribe. Reluctant at first, he soon realised the value of the encounter and saw it as an opportunity. In exchange for giving Professor Bottelli a rare glimpse of life inside the Ornis Tribe, he would be taught the language of the woman he was trying to find. The agreement was made.

The next time the island returned, he was fortunate enough to find the boat ready and waiting, and by then he had learned enough of the language to strike a deal. He wanted to be the one to find her, but he was too old even then, and he knew he wouldn't survive long without the mist in his bones. After much persuasion it was decided that one of the younger members of the Ornis Tribe would join the circus show, on the condition that he was permitted to search each place for Lemàn.

'This member of our tribe is known as the risk-taker,' said my father. 'Before it leaves, we stock the boat with jars of mist for release below deck.'

'But what if the mist runs out?' I asked.

'All risk-takers are fighters; that's why they are chosen. Each time, we select a different risk-taker, but always someone who is young and strong. Someone who will survive.'

'And this time? Is the risk-taker okay?'

'He is weak, but he should recover soon with the fresh mist we've brought.'

'Why would they do that for you?' asked Leo, astonished at the bravery.

'It is a way for them to prove their worth. They are honoured after that.'

'Like a rite of passage?'

My father nodded.

'And what if the boat arrived and the island wasn't there?' I queried.

'The birds are our messengers. We always know how to find each other and we can sometimes steer the island to a way of our choosing, if the mist is willing. It is always the mist that must choose the way.'

'It sounds like an enormous risk,' said Leo.

'Yes.' He looked up into the leaves, once again seeking the solace of birds. 'But the bigger risk was never finding you.'

If only I had known all those years ago, when I had lifted the flap of the circus tent to uncover a world of spectacle and curiosity just how close I had been to solving the mystery. The shape of the wing I had seen pass over my head hadn't been imagined and it wasn't just a shadow. Lemàn had spent years dragging me away from the one thing that could have brought us the happy ending we so desperately wanted. A sacrifice made without realising what was being lost. The thought struck me then with such heart-breaking clarity that I struggled to control my tears and before I could stop them, they came rolling down my cheeks. I was crying for every missed opportunity, for every lost chance, and for knowing now how close we had been. If only Lemàn had known what was waiting for her inside that circus tent. It would have brought my father back to her years ago, and I would have known him as a child and he would have been able to love me for a little bit longer. There is such cruelty in fear; yet all this time, she thought she was keeping me safe.

At first, he seemed startled and afraid of my tears, but then I felt his warmth fold over me and he rocked me under the protection of his giant feathers. I couldn't bear to tell him how we'd run from the boat and the happiness it could have brought us all, so I kept my thoughts to myself.

Slowly, we walked back along the lagoon, where my father sank to his knees and drank from the water in great gargling gulps. Like Elver, he seemed more content here, as though he could stretch out and reach all the way to the sky. His feathers sponged by the rain-damp clouds. He was reluctant to leave the open space and go back into the closed streets of the city, like it was a snare and he withdrew into himself, and the awkwardness of his gait returned.

As we circled back to the market, the dogs started to pull and tug wildly on their harness. They had caught the familiar scent of home.

'Eddero, when do you leave?' Leo's question brought a sudden sharp stab of despair, and I realised I hadn't been thinking about his departure.

'In two days.'

'Two days?' I exclaimed. 'But that gives us no time. Can you stay – just a little bit longer?'

He shook his head, and I could see how torn he was.

'Just one more day or even just a few hours,' I pleaded.

'He must leave with the mist,' Leo reminded me gently. He sounded just as disappointed as I did. 'There are only five days at most when the island floats close enough to the city; after that it disappears back into its swirls of mist and cloud. If he doesn't go then he will be trapped here.'

Tenderly, he wrapped his long feathery arms around me and we both clung on to each other, and even though we were holding on, this was really us beginning to let go. When we finally broke away, I realised Leo held the dogs at a distance, giving us some space until we were ready to move apart.

The sun hung low in the sky taking a soothing dip in the water, and the hours took on a different shine, each one as bright and precious as a gem stone.

'We must go to the old market now before it closes,' said my father gravely. 'There is something I must do.'

CHAPTER 36

Even before we turned the corner, I knew what was there to greet us because I could hear them. A cacophony. Loud and shrill and deafening. A fluttering of wings. My father stopped. It was the heart-breaking sound of caged birds. The street was enclosed under a long arch, more tunnel than street, and the only light came from the other end. It pulsed with a hundred tiny desperate heartbeats. He began tweeting wildly and gesticulating, his shoulders jerked everywhere in anguish, their clacking sound grew more furious and insistent, like a multitude of cicadas in the long grass.

Along one side of the wall hung cage after cage, crammed with birds. Other cages balanced precariously one on top of another, ready to crash to the ground. Birds flittered from one side to the other, clinging to the wire mesh that separated them from their freedom. Wings bashed and broken, hanging limp in their futile attempts to escape. Some had barely any feathers left, plucked from boredom or distress, plumage left in tatters and shreds at the bottom of cages, as though they wanted to unpick themselves from their misery. Their suffering was clear and painful. Some of the birds sat silent and still. All hope was lost.

'Birds should fill the sky, not cages,' he said, and I knew he had something on his mind, his eyes illuminated by an idea.

The burly bird merchants were deeply embroiled in conversation with their backs turned from our mission. They hadn't noticed us with their birds – yet. Carefully, my father crept into the tunnel and unhooked the catch on the first cage; the bird watched him in that curious way birds have. It didn't move, not understanding it was on the edge of freedom. Then he softly warbled and cooed and the bird immediately hopped down from its perch and onto the door, which swung wide, taking the bird with it. It was large and dark and its forgotten wings lay close against its body, like crumpled black silk. Cautiously it stretched itself out and then without warning it launched itself from the door towards the open archway and out to forgotten freedom. A swooshing sound made the merchants turn in surprise just as the escapee flew high over their heads. Cries of alarm carried through the street just as they realised what was happening, but he was already halfway through the tunnel, opening cage after cage after cage.

'Come on!' Leo hurried off back into the market, believing I was right behind him. Instead I was right behind my father helping him to open as many cages as we could, before the merchants could stop us. The more we opened, the more birds filled the tunnel and flew in the direction of the light. The merchants were cowering in the entrance, arms held aloft to protect them from swooping talons that came from all directions, blinded by a storm of feathers. I heard their cries and yells as we worked quickly, until all the doors were open and all of the birds were finally free. Those too weak to fly hopped away. Then we ran through the tunnel and out the other side into the sunlight. You couldn't tell where we began and the birds ended, but as soon as the sky appeared above us, the birds lifted themselves, no longer weighted nor caged, no longer held captive in the dark airless tunnel. People in the streets turned to watch, as though the release of so many birds was some sort of celebration or local ceremony, and children pointed and laughed as they watched them soar in a chatter of freedom. An old lady dressed in black saw it as an omen of doom, and crossed herself three times in prayer before hurrying past, not daring to look back.

Leo, who had been watching the spectacle from a safe distance, found us flushed and exhilarated, collapsed on some stone steps around the corner.

'That was madness.' He looked serious, but there was laughter in his voice.

'There was no convincing him otherwise,' I said. 'I suppose he wants to protect his own; it's not in his nature to abandon them.' I knew just what kind of heart he had after that.

'I think we need to get as far away from here as possible, before those merchants come looking for us,' warned Leo. 'We've just lost them their livelihood, and they will not be pleased.'

'Well, they shouldn't live off the suffering of others,' I said, getting to my feet with sudden defensive defiance.

As my father rose, he gave a sudden squawk of pain and reached for a railing to steady himself. It was then I noticed his feet: cut and bruised and bleeding into the stone.

'We need to get him to a doctor,' I said alarmed. The cuts ran too deep.

He shook his head stubbornly. 'I need to get back to the stall.'

'Help me with him,' I said, trying to support him on one side.

Leo lifted him from the other. His arms wrapped over our shoulders, warm and thick with giant fiery feathers. I could feel the flapping of his heart, much quicker than my own, as we hobbled together through the city. My father suddenly grew alert to something we couldn't yet sense, but as we crossed to the stall with the jars of mist, we could hear the shrill squabbling sounds of alarm thickening the air.

'What's happening?' I asked Leo, hoping he had been able to translate something from the chaos.

'I'm not sure.'

Forgetting his pain, my father flew across the square, where slumped against the stone wall was the risk-taker. I recognised him at once from the Boat of Floating Freaks and Oddities. His eyes, like those of a newborn bird, were swollen shut; they looked like copper coins bulging from purple pouches. I thought he was dead, but then he gulped the air. His tongue, like a dying fish in the tiny dark puddle of his mouth. Strewn all around him on the ground lay his feathers; he had lost them all, leaving his skin puckered and bare.

My father was on his knees; his own feathers had lifted and sharpened like long slicing blades and I felt my own prickle in fear. His fast, profuse octaves pierced the air and they all crowded round, in a frantic flutter and a noisy stir, not knowing quite what to do. There was a mad flurry of feathers then, as they began unscrewing the lids off the jars and shaking the mist over him in the hope of revival. They smoothed it over his limbs and tilted his head back to pour it into his mouth, but he was limp and unresponsive and his eyes stayed shut.

'We need to get the mist into his bones, into his blood,' said my father, moving swiftly to support his head. 'He is dying.' He looked at me pleadingly, as though I held the answer.

'Could Sybel help?' suggested Leo.

Sybel was too lost in mourning, and we needed something fast – a specialist, a surgeon. 'Come with me,' I said. 'And bring all of the mist you have left.'

This time, I had a genuine reason to appear at Doctor Marino's door. My father was old, but determined and, despite his bleeding feet, he summoned the strength to stumble through the city, carrying the risk-taker across his shoulders. Doctor Marino was at the top of his steps rummaging around in his pocket for his keys. I darted across the square and almost collided with him as he turned to leave.

'Please!' I said breathlessly. 'Please – wait.' I swallowed a huge lungful of air and by the time I had recovered enough to speak, Leo was already by my side explaining it all.

Seconds later we were all inside and awaiting the verdict. It didn't come right away; Doctor Marino was examining him in a side room and I could hear the movement of implements, and the clatter of metal, but my view was obscured by a half-shut door. My father was the only one permitted to enter and was explaining what needed to be done. He emerged looking drawn and broken like a wreckage recovered from the depths of the ocean. Taking several jars of mist, he retreated back into the room, leaving behind him a bloody trail of jointed footprints, more bird than human. Just before the door, the prints turned into one long smear as though he could no longer lift his feet and had to shuffle and drag himself along. All we could do then was wait.

Doctor Marino came out first, solemn in face. 'He needs to rest. I'm afraid we won't know anything until morning.'

In the room behind him, I could hear my father's soothing voice, light as a flute.

Doctor Marino noticed the bloody smears across the floor and realised that there was another emergency he needed to deal with; his eyes sought it out. He settled my father into a chair and lifted up his feet, wincing as though he could feel his pain. Leo paced behind us.

'They're infected,' he announced. 'Eddero, where are your shoes?' Then he shook his head for asking such a foolish question.

Doctor Marino opened a glass cabinet and began rifling through an assortment of bottles and tubes, grasping around in the half-dark clutter of the trays, until he found what he was looking for. He unscrewed the cap and began to dab it on the wounds, which bubbled and crusted like thick lava. My father screeched in a repetition of parched syllables, but I soothed his head and without any resistance, he quietened against my arm. Across his overlapping wings, I could see the heavy indentation left behind from the weight he had just carried.

'In the absence of shoes, I think it's best that I bandage your feet to offer some comfort; they are too swollen for anything else.'

He reached in his drawer and began to unravel a long strip of gauze which he then wrapped round both of Eddero's feet securing them with a metal pin. Tightly bound, he rose clumsily to his feet. He looked like he had got his legs stuck in two old Coburg loaves. He stared down with a look of bewilderment.

'Do these feathers not seem strange to you?' I felt suddenly compelled to ask.

He raised his eyebrows in a pretence of ridicule. 'As a veterinary surgeon, I am quite used to dealing with feathers!'

'Yes, but aren't you more used to dealing with them on animals rather than on people?' Before he had time to answer, I continued my lawyer-like appraisal. 'Then again, perhaps you are used to dealing with things that are neither quite one thing nor another.'

'I'm not sure what you mean, but my priority is always the recovery of my patients.' His words stung, not that he had meant them to, and he spoke in that usual measured way of his. I lowered my eyes. It was then I noticed the velum-bound book still sitting on top of the brown paper, the twine twisting off the edge of his desk like a strand of Rapunzel's hair. It was the package I had seen Elver carrying earlier. Without thinking, I lifted it up and immediately inhaled the scent of the sea and had to force myself not to press it against my nose. The picture of the front was of the teatro I had seen in the nearby square. Inside its pages were filled with songs.

'I love opera.' he said, laughing, half embarrassed by my discovery. 'If you haven't been, then I recommend you go. I would have been an opera singer, but my father was a doctor and my grandfather and his father before him. I sort of followed the family tradition; there really was no other choice for me. The book is a present – a reminder of what might have been.'

'A present?'

'Yes. Today's my birthday.'

'A present from who?' I had a habit of asking him questions to which I already knew the answers.

'A friend,' he replied, but there was a wariness in his voice.

'The same friend who gave you that shell?' Any more and I would reveal what connected us, perhaps I already had.

Doctor Marino watched me, and I could see he had questions, but he didn't know what they were or quite how to ask them. He was trying to make sense of some-thing just out of his reach and I hoped his thoughts wouldn't turn to words. Leo was helping my father to his feet and I crossed the room to open the door for them.

'Thank you,' I said, pausing for a moment. 'And happy birthday.'

'She was never mine to lose and she isn't yours either,' he said gently, before I pulled the door shut.

Outside, I saw the Keeper of the Hours striding across the dusky square, his back as long and straight as the minute hand. The tick-tock of his footsteps hurried towards the clock tower. Slowly we made our way back to the market stall, and to the last few remaining jars of mist, which were mostly scattered and smashed on the ground. By the wall, I found one still untouched, alive with the dancing mist, and I slipped it into my pocket.

As we said goodbye, my father told me there was something he wanted to ask, but it would wait until tomorrow. Parting, I heard the chimes of the clock ring across the rooftops, a reminder of time lost and time restored.

CHAPTER 37

Sybel's grief was private and Zephyros's cremation was conducted quietly and without invitation. She left the other dogs in the kitchen, muzzle deep and content in their gigantic bowls of rice pudding, oblivious to the despair contained within the apple box she carried outside to her boat. She returned hours later, subdued, but composed. Despite the warmth, she pulled the bench across the floor until it was angled towards the stove. There she stretched out her slipperless feet and wriggled her toes in front of the grate

She had been holding Zephyros for so long that now her arms didn't know what to do, and her hands flopped in her lap like two dead fish. Loss had reduced her in some way, and whether or not it was expected, loss was still loss, and the end result was always the same.

'I brought you this,' I said, handing her a jar of mist. 'It's to mend a heart that's broken. You can smoke it in your pipe, or empty it into your pillowcase and sleep with it there all night. It will make you feel happy again.' But she just stared at it blankly and pushed it to the back of the shelf, behind all the other jars.

'Thank you, but the worst is over now,' she murmured, reaching up and lifting the harness from its hook.

'Is it?' I asked.

'Yes.' She nodded. 'There is nothing worse than waiting for something to happen. I will grow around my grief, but it will change the shape of me and the way I look at the world. It will always be the cold, hard stone at the centre of everything.'

Then overcome by a sudden burst of practicality, she took a knife and began unpicking the sixth collar, loosening it from the harness, until there were only a few frayed ends left behind. She burned them away with the end of the poker. Afterwards, she dabbed at her eyes with an old, tatty handkerchief and that was the last I saw of her sorrow.

The mist had already begun to thin and lift, leaving behind delicate, narrow tendrils like forgotten balloon strings at the end of a party. It meant only one thing: the island – and my father – would soon be leaving. We had been to Doctor Marino's surgery, where the risk-taker had recovered enough to be sitting up and was sipping water. My father explained that they would be leaving the following day and the risk-taker must be ready. Doctor Marino began to protest, but he held up his hand, and it was clear that there was no negotiation to be had.

We walked down to the park and for the first time we were alone. Leo had been delayed at the university and for now it was just us. The mist was no longer low enough to dampen our skin, but had not lifted enough to rouse the drowsy sun. We stopped under a cluster of little trees, and as we sat down a bird suddenly swooped out of the sky and landed with a tiny rustle in the canopy of leaves high above our heads. My father and the bird began a duet of silvery whistles and friendly chortles. Listening, I wished I could understand what they were saying, but Orniglossa had proven itself too much of a puzzle for me to solve completely.

'Are you sure you have to leave tomorrow?' I asked, trying to keep the panic out of my voice. It was the closest I could come to asking him to stay. I knew the city was too narrow for him to open his wings and stretch out his feathers, and without the mist he wouldn't survive. Staying was not a choice; it was impossible.

He stopped, tall and still, like a sailing boat waiting for the wind to set him free. 'About that,' he said.

For a moment I thought perhaps he was going to change his mind and I could feel my heart burst with the wish of it. 'There is something I need to ask you.'

'Yes?' I encouraged, but he had grown hesitant or perhaps he couldn't find the right words. 'What is it?'

Distracted for a moment, I watched a worshipping bee lose itself in the gentle embrace of a yellow flower, every small detail magnified in anticipation of his question.

'Will you come with me?'

Of all the things he could have said, I hadn't been expected it to be that.

'Where?' I blurted, but the question was a foolish one; we both knew what he meant.

'Home,' he chirruped, and the word glittered between us like gold.

All of a sudden, I didn't know what to say. I looked back at the bee, but it had disappeared.

'Are you ashamed of your feathers?' His question was an unexpected gust of wind stirring the treetops.

'No, of course not,' I replied, but my words were too rushed, too insistent to carry the note of truth.

'Then why do you hide them?' He stepped closer, his eyes searching beneath my collar.

'I—' I didn't want to lie, but the truth felt like a betrayal. I couldn't confess how much I hated them; how they had brought me so much misery and how only a few weeks ago, I had begged Sybel to rid me of them forever. My rejection of them meant a rejection of him. I shuddered. 'I'm just used to keeping them hidden, that's all,' I said, finally settling on a sort of truth.

He took another step closer, reaching his hand beneath my collar, feeling for my feathers with a tenderness that made them rush to greet his touch. 'If you come with me, you can learn to use your wings on the Island of Mist.'

'But I don't have wings,' I said, and, for the first time, I felt disappointed not to have grown all of my contour feathers – disappointed that I wasn't more like him. Wherever I went it seemed I didn't quite belong, neither one thing or another. I had felt this difference for too long, following me like a dark shadow.

'Don't worry. Didn't you see? The risk-taker didn't have any feathers left on his wings yesterday, but they will be restored again.'

'The mist,' I breathed, realising the full power of its magic.

He came closer and I felt his wings fall around me. It was as dark as a nest as they closed together and their immediate warmth brushed against my skin. I closed my eyes and breathed him in, and as I did, it felt as though my feet had left the ground. Opening my eyes, I was astonished to be high above the world, but not the world I knew. Instead of the park, I saw stretches of shimmering green fields. The spires and domes of the city had disappeared, and in their place rose purple tipped mountains and dark sloping forests. There was water there too, but instead of narrow ribbons there were wide blankets of blue. The air was filled with melody; a bright silvery song that floated high above the rush of a distant waterfall. The air quivered and everything sparkled and I knew that this was the Island of Mist. Somehow, I had glimpsed it within his feathers. Just as I wanted more, I felt his wings open, lift and fold away behind his back and the spell was broken. I was disappointed to see that I was exactly where I had been just a few moments ago, and my feet had never left the ground.

'Give me your answer tomorrow,' he said, suddenly tilting his head to the sky. 'Ah – rain will be here again before nightfall.'

I sensed it too.

Across the park a group of boatmen, just finished for the day, seated themselves on crates around an upturned barrel scattered with playing cards and the day's earnings. They held their heads low in a hushed, studious mumble, inspecting what they had been dealt. Usually, I adjusted my collar at the sight of strangers, making sure it was lifted high against my neck, but this time as we passed them, I left it folded down and a spray of tiny feathers escaped. The boatmen looked up, but their eyes didn't linger long and soon they were back shuffling and dealing their cards, preoccupied by their own pursuit of triumph. I smiled to myself. Until that moment, fear had kept me hidden, and now little by little that fear was slowly fluttering away.

'My brave girl,' he said, his eyes half-closed in satisfaction, and my smile widened with pride.

We ambled along the canal and past the Church of One Hundred Souls. I wondered if he remembered this place wasn't far from where their hotel had once been, tucked away like a secret love letter in its dark envelope of walls. In the square beneath the tower, we said goodbye and I realised that the next time we parted it could be for the last time. I left him then, carrying the weight of indecision and continued through the city, distracted by thought. There was an open-windowed warmth to the evening and as I passed the houses, I could hear the secrets half-told from their hidden rooms: raised voices, a child's laughter, someone at prayer, one silent, but lit by a flickering candle. From another, the haunting sound of a cello played, then stopped, followed by a tiny splatter of applause. An audience of no more than one, but an appreciative one at least. I felt like an intruder, arriving at a party without an invitation in my hand.

I quickened my pace until the song of a bird made me pause, unusual in this enclosed part of the city, where there was an absence of both trees or sky. Allowing myself a diversion, I soon discovered that the sound was coming from the interior shadows of a back-alley house. There in the frame of the window, hanging from a hook was a small cage with a domed roof, and within it sat a bird. Had I not heard it sing just moments ago, I would have thought it had been stuffed like the ones at the university, for it was completely still. Then it began again, and its plaintive high treble vibrated out into the street. A mirror twinkled from a chain tricking the poor creature into believing it had a friend. A cruel trick. This window had no bars and, without thinking, I reached up and lifted the catch, releasing the door. The bird stared at me with its glassy eye and then jerked its head, suddenly noticing the open door. Warily it hopped down from its perch and fluttered to rest, with a tiny wobble, on the edge of freedom. After a moment's hesitation, it lifted itself into the air and was gone, like the flame of an extinguished candle. As I turned to leave, I heard the quiet rattle of a door coming from the depths of the house, and the slow shuffle of feet. Then a chestnut face appeared at the open window beneath the cage; it was that of an old lady, her grey eyes blinking in disbelief. She stood black-shawled and hunched as though everything ached, and in her gnarled, mottled hand she held the core of a half-eaten apple. Her mouth still chewed the last bite.

'Have you seen my bird?' she asked, in raspy syllables.

'No,' I lied, swallowing a stone of guilt. I stared innocently at the open cage.

Her mouth drooped and she sank against the window in audible exhaustion; too old and broken to be stirred into any action. Her eyes shone with sorrow, but she was too tired to cry. Setting one soul free had trapped another and whereas moments before I had felt like an intruder, now I had become a thief. The bird had flown away and left her companionless. She stayed at the window, and I watched as she rested the apple core on the sill as though it might somehow be enough to tempt the bird back. Guilty, I left her then, mourning at her window, and I couldn't imagine her ever latching it shut again. If I returned the next day or the next or the one after that I was convinced that I would find her there, waiting still. Perhaps it will return I thought, hopefully, just as a bird swooped and danced high above me in the evening sky, but we both knew that she would never see it again.

Forgive me, I thought without releasing the words; I had released enough.

The street was silent.

By the time I got home I had to shake the rain from my hair. The old lady and her bird had brought back a memory, and although she didn't look like Lemàn or Professor Elms or Sorren, or Sybel, she reminded me of them all: touched by the same hollow, empty loneliness, each suffering a different kind of loss, so crushing and tangible, it could be felt in the hearts of others. All of them waiting endlessly for something that had long gone, and for something that would never return.

I didn't tell Sybel about the decision I had to make and whether she sensed it or not she didn't mention anything.

Appearing in the doorway, she looked at me in startled alarm. 'I can see your feathers,' she said.

'I know.' I beamed.

'Ah!' She laughed with sudden understanding.

Sitting in the kitchen, she stroked the damp tangles out of my hair, as though I was a gutter cat in need of rescue.

As I kissed her goodnight, she paused in the candlelight. 'I'm so glad you are here. You are a blessing, especially now.'

My heart fell. An already difficult decision had just become an impossible one to make.

CHAPTER 38

The following morning, I left the house full of worry and turmoil. I still hadn't made my decision. It was too early for either Leo or my father and so I wandered the familiar city for a while until the warm, inviting smell of the bakeries tempted the dreamers from their beds, and the streets began to stir. This was the one place where I didn't have to hide; a place of friends and lovers and dreams and wonder, where wishes were granted. There were people who mattered here, and I would miss them if I left them behind.

Leo was waiting for me at the boat stop, and we walked together to the market in amiable chatter.

'Did you know our hearts have four chambers, each one like a separate room?' I babbled, trying to push the decision I had to make far from my mind.

Leo shook his head. 'No, I didn't know that. It sounds more like a guest house.' He laughed, continuing his jest. 'Do they have to check in their details at the lobby? Perhaps a concierge could relieve you of any baggage.' He nudged my arm playfully, and I rolled my eyes, laughing, glad to have my mind briefly distracted by something else.

The Island of Mist was my father's home, but could it ever be mine? I had found a place of belonging in the City of Murmurs, and I knew I wouldn't find it anywhere else. You could still be close to someone and love them just the same even when they weren't by your side. One of my heart's chambers would always be his – his and Lemàn's – the only place where they could fit together. Possibilities and loss again, but a place full of memory can never be completely empty. Memories cast into a grate can spark a fire to keep you warm.

Leo's face suddenly filled with concern. 'Your collar isn't up; I hadn't noticed.' He reached out to adjust it himself, and I brushed his hand away.

'It's fine as it is.' I gave a small smile of satisfaction.

He paused in disbelief, wondering for a moment if he had misheard me.

'I've decided to wear it like this from now on.'

'Really?' A look of pleasant surprise slowly spread across his face. 'I hadn't expected you to ever—'

'Yes, I know, but it's time, little by little.' I smiled. 'It's who I am.'

'Yes – it is.' agreed Leo.

'My father asked me to go with him when he returns to the island,' I confessed.

Leo's face twisted in anguish. A question formed on his lips, but stayed there, like a fledging afraid of the fall. We just continued to walk in thought-filled silence. Every so often, he looked like he was going to say something, but then, at the very last moment had changed his mind. It wasn't until we almost reached my father, that his question finally tumbled out.

'What have you decided to do?'

There was a pause of contemplation.

'I really don't know,' I admitted, and as I said it, I could feel my heart begin to tear in half.

We met him at the stall and continued down towards the public gardens, away from the suffocating streets and back alleys that led you around in circles. His hands twitched more than usual and he kept glancing frequently up towards the white furrows of the ploughed sky. In the distance, the sun had cracked itself open on the edge of a watery blue bowl and its light poured out, streaming in a thousand different directions.

'How is the risk-taker this morning?' Leo asked.

'Much better. We will help him when the time comes.'

'And your feet?' I asked, staring down at the bandages still wrapped around them. I thought about my own bandage then, wound back in the drawer, no longer needed.

'Getting better.' He smiled then, and I heard the tired, gentle clack of his restless wings, so ready for flight.

The sun had burned away the clouds, and now there were just tiny wisps trailing like unreachable kite strings. Leo took us into a building at the edge of the park, where we found ourselves in a jungle of exotic plants enclosed behind iron and latticed glass windows. It was like stepping into a giant warm green bath with the smell of an over-ripe larder. My father immediately disappeared behind a giant bush and I caught a glimpse of him as he swooped between the huge palms and then another glimpse of him as he fluttered between the endless vines. High above us, the leaves hung like enormous shiny umbrellas against the rain that would never fall.

'What is this place?' I asked in wonder. I no longer felt that I was in the City of Murmurs. It reminded me of Professor Elms and his tales of places on the edge of the world, where a bird the size of a bee hummed and cats bigger than people roamed wild and free. I half expected one to leap through the thick foliage and eat us for breakfast.

'It's a tepidarium,' said Leo. 'Flowers are nurtured here, until they are taken and planted in the public gardens dotted around the city. Sometimes they are delivered in golden carriages to the doors of palaces. They adorn the rooms of visiting dignitaries, or flourish in ballrooms.' Leo waltzed between the flowers and held out his arm for me to join him, but I just shook my head and laughed at his silly pretence. He shrugged and smiled. 'Just before the art exhibition, boats arrive and begin unloading their exotic specimens, which are cared for here until it is time for them to decorate the pavilion.'

I thought about all the fanciful things brought across the water on boats, and wondered if perhaps feathers were amongst them. I would need a plentiful supply if I was ever going to open a shop of my own. The birds here were brown and grey and sometimes splashed with white, but none of them had the flamboyant colours I had seen caught between the pages of the books I had read. The black blue hue of a raven, or the bird whose name I had forgotten, but whose feathers were the colour of spun gold. I loved the kingfisher most of all, and the way it wore its iridescent turquoise cloak pulled high over the sunburst of its belly. Water to quench the flames. How beautiful feathers could be!

'But they don't really belong here, do they?' I said, suddenly realising how beauty can have a price. I looked around sadly at all the plants.

'No, I don't suppose they do. Some are kept here for months, only grown to brighten a single night, others thrive until the first frost. Look at this one!' Leo rushed forward and lifted up the giant waxy leaf of a sprawling plant. Beneath its leaves, its bright red bulbs were ready to burst open like a sunset.

'It's amazing,' I said, searching for more blooms beneath the canopy.

'Yes,' agreed Leo, but when I looked up, he wasn't looking at the flowers any more; he was looking directly at me.

Quickly, I dropped the heavy leaves. 'We need to find my father,' I said, and set off with some urgency in the direction of the bamboo garden.

For a moment, I thought the whistling figure I could see at the end of the path was him, but it was just the gardener, methodically polishing the leaves until they shone like enormous emeralds. My arrival disturbed a sparrow, which fluttered from the foliage and out through the open door. By now, I had circled the building and was beginning to wonder if he had left, when I heard his familiar flute-like notes floating through the vivid green and the place seemed to come alive. After all, what is a garden without the song of a bird?

When I parted the leaves, I found Leo was already there, waiting at the foot of a tree. At the very top, on a long branch, perched my father.

'We need to get him out of here,' I hissed, glancing over my shoulder to make sure the gardener couldn't see us, but the leaves had sprung back into place and we could have been in the middle of a rainforest, so far from any city.

'Let's go back outside,' suggested Leo.

He had seemed lost, breathing it all in, until he heard Leo speak. Then he opened his eyes with a startled expression, as though he had quite forgotten where he was.

'Come on,' I encouraged, waving him down. I was sure the trees here were not for climbing or sitting in, and I listened nervously for the heavy plodding return of the gardener's boots along the path.

Back outside, we walked across the gardens, where the sunlight fell in diagonal slants through the trees. Still too warm, I suggested that we sought shade for a moment in the pillared building at the end of the path. Stepping inside, we quickly left the light and the heat behind. It was a welcome relief for me, but my father and Leo found the air shudder-inducing and insisted we return to the outside world.

'Just give me a minute,' I said, as Leo hovered in the entrance. 'I'll come out and find you.'

Leo nodded and hurried back into the sunshine. Although I now wore my coat with its collar downturned and its buttons unfastened, my refusal to remove it completely had left me feeling sweaty and uncomfortable. I was not quite as brave as my father thought, but I was getting braver.

Like warm sugar, morning stirred into afternoon and afternoon slowly dissolved into evening. We circled the outskirts of the city, avoiding all the enclosed spaces so my father could see the sky. I would have continued to walk in endless circles, if it meant he would stay one more hour. But every time I heard the loud chime of the clock, I was jolted back to reality, each one bringing me a little bit closer to his departure. The City of Murmurs didn't let you forget time.

Nobody paid him much attention and any glances which swept his way were ones of mild curiosity rather than sneers of disgust. It seemed that Sybel was right; the City of Murmurs had seen it all before. I learned quickly that this city had little interest in its inhabitants. It noticed only itself, and spent all day admiring its reflection in the mirrored water. At night it was the moon that worshipped its tiled roofs, and the birds which adorned its crooked arches in numerous feathery bouquets.

He stopped and rubbed at his bandaged feet, and although he didn't complain, I could see the pain in his eyes. We stopped to buy fish and a bottle of wine and water from a street vendor. Sitting on a wall, we ate in silence, muted by the impossibility of my decision. I gulped down the wine until my head began to spin and the world around me became hazy and blurred. I saw my reflection in the water – pale and ghost-like. My lips were stained the colour of the wine, and I rubbed at them with my sleeve. The whites of my eyes were pink and my pupils large as a hunting owl. Leo was checking the bandages on my father's feet as he scattered crumbs for the birds watching us from a nearby tree.

My father pushed his water towards me. 'Drink,' he said, softly.

'Thank you.' I lifted the bowl to my lips and drank it right down to the bottom in thirsty gulps. I wished I could drink away all the water in the world, so he couldn't sail away on his boat and Elver would no longer hear the haunting murmurs of the waves. Then I felt a hand rest on top of mine. It belonged to my father.

'Have you thought about what I said?'

His eyes were full of hope and longing, and I didn't know what to say. It was all I had thought about, and wherever my thoughts wandered, they always returned to this moment. I looked away to see the birds flutter up from the branches of the tree and disappear into the milky indigo sky. If I left, I would miss too much: the city, Sybel, Leo, Elver, the dogs, the comfort of knowing that there was always a docked boat to return me on a whim, back to Lemàn and Professor Elms. Although I had feathers, I didn't have wings. Even if they grew in the swirls of mist would it be enough or would I feel like the plants in the tepidarium, lost in a place I didn't really belong? I might survive, but was that enough?

I felt him squeeze my hand and then it fell from mine as gently as a feather drifting onto a lawn. 'There wasn't enough time,' I whispered.

'There never is,' he replied wearily, understanding then that I had given him my answer.

I felt as though I should offer him an explanation, but I didn't have one to give. I couldn't really explain it to myself.

'Will you come back soon?' My eyes watched his face trying to seek out the answer before it came and I saw the brief hesitation, just for a moment, but it was unmistakably there.

'I hope so.'

He seemed so much smaller and hollower than when he had arrived a few days ago. I noticed his feathers had dulled and thinned in places; some were so sparse I could see his protruding bones beneath. I understood all I needed to then.

He babbled something in his own language, something he did whenever the answers got too difficult.

'He's just not sure if he can make the journey. It's a long way and his bones feel heavier than before, but he will try,' said Leo.

'I thought you didn't understand!' I said to Leo.

He smiled. 'I understand enough.'

'Yes, try,' I said, turning back towards my father. For a brief moment I almost changed my mind, but instead I said nothing and we continued along the edge of the canal.

On the eastern edges of the city we came to the garden of remembrance. He had managed well on his bandages, but I could tell he was growing tired of his feet and he would stop to rest more frequently. Sometimes he'd sit on a bench, other times he would learn against the wall of a building or simply just stand still and wait for the pain to pass. We would wait too, until he was ready to carry on again. Although his wings were weary, they were restless and ready for one more flight.

He was a skilful navigator, always guided by instinct and the birds that circled above, towing him through the world by an invisible thread. The park trees loomed high above a large expanse of grass and the darkening water. No light reflected there. In the distance I could hear the sound of the great bell ringing out its mournful cry, the only thing left in the air, but there was no reply. Somehow I thought that if I walked the length and width of the city, in a tangle of footsteps, I could tie a knot in time, but there was no escape, and in that stillness there was nothing to do but wait. We found a bench and sat down.

'I once heard that a bird's heart beats much faster than a human one. Is it true?'

He nodded and lifted my hand to his chest so I could feel the swift pulse of his heart against my palm; it vibrated through my veins like music. I wanted to close my hand around it and keep it safe in the dark like a hidden creature, but he brought my hand back down again to rest in his.

'But doesn't it mean I will live my life twice as fast? That my life will be shorter?'

He smiled so wide that his eyes closed. 'It doesn't mean that at all,' he replied. 'Look at me; I have lived a long life, too long perhaps.'

I flung my arms around him and prayed for time to stop. After a while, Leo stood up and walked to the edge of the lagoon wall, where he picked up a pebble and skimmed it across the black water, watching it until it disappeared. He had to do something and that was all there was.

A thousand thoughts deep.

I began to tremble, not from the cold – it was a surprisingly warm evening – but from letting go of something I wanted so desperately to hold onto. I felt my father's dry feathery hand close back around my own and I grasped it like a handkerchief trying to quell the threat of tears. It wasn't possible and I fell against his chest and cried against the rapid little pulse of his heart, and now as I listened more carefully, it was more of a flutter than a beat.

'A heart that beats so fast, loves so much,' he said, and I wondered if that was an even bigger fear to carry.

Stroking my hair, he smoothed his twisted fingers down the length of my feathers, nuzzling his face against them as though I was the baby that he never got to hold. We stayed like that until the shape of a boat emerged out of the water. Finally, he released me and mumbled something in my ear, but I couldn't make sense of anything any more.

'What is it?' I asked, wiping away my tears. 'What did you say?'

'He said it's time,' replied Leo.

'But it can't be … it's too soon!' I protested, fresh tears pouring down my face. Now that I wanted time to stop, it seemed to spin ever faster, like a poisonous spider. I wanted the precious hours I had spent with my father to begin all over again. There hadn't been enough time to love him.

Slowly, he ruffled to his feet and still holding my hand, he led me over to the steps where the boat waited. It reminded me of the ancient myth of the Underworld.

The boatman arriving to carry the souls across the water to an afterlife of eternal bliss or eternal torment, but what of those left behind? Then he seemed to float through my fingertips and onto the boat where his three friends already stood, silently waiting for him. My hopelessness suddenly turned to delight, as he reached out his hand. I was just about to step closer to grab hold of it and pull him back to land, when I realised my mistake. He hadn't changed his mind as I had thought; he was simply reaching back to push the boat away from the wall into the water. Already he seemed so far away, and my throat tightened with the realisation that this was the last time I would ever see him. Our hello came too late; our goodbye came too soon. Looking up, I noticed a crack in the sky, a stark white light in the inky darkness telling us morning wasn't far away. I felt bone sad and I wished the sadness would pass right through me, but instead it burrowed deep.

I remained motionless, hoping he might come back. I stayed until there was nothing left, only the distant outline of the boat and then flying out of it and into the sky, four shapes emerged, soaring, wild and free. Three held onto one and I knew it wasn't the risk-taker being helped home; it was my father. The shapes split to become four distinct birds, each one a small silhouette against the sky, and the world seemed to withdraw and shrink beneath them. All possibility lost. All hope fading with the light.

In the water I noticed a single floating feather. A thousand sunsets deep, and, unmistakeably, his. Bending down,

I cupped it in my hand and lifted it out; it felt as soft as a fingertip. As I held it, my hand looked as though it had caught fire. I slipped the feather inside my coat and the dripping flames burned a hole in my pocket. A memory smouldered. Then I shook with the loss of him.

Leo pulled me close and I let him comfort me there on the lagoon wall. I leaned onto his chest and this time listened to the sound his heart made; its beat, heavy and strong against my own, so still and silent from loss.

'Don't cry,' he murmured against my ear and then unexpectedly his mouth was lost in my hair as he kissed me on the top of my head. Leaning my face back I looked up at him, my sight blurred by tears and wine and he kissed me again, this time right where I wanted him to, on my lips. I hesitated, but only for a moment, before kissing him back. Uncertain and gentle at first, but then fierce and wanting more. I'm not sure whether it was the wine or the loss of my father or the need to just hold onto someone who wanted to hold me back, but the kisses grew deeper until I became lost in them, forgetting everything else, even the need to hide my feathers. Then came the rain, almost as unexpected as the kisses, warm, sudden and intense. Half-stumbling, half-crying, we ran, holding hands into the park to find shelter under the trees. The heavy rain pounded the canopy of leaves above us, an auditorium of applause. Leo brushed the droplets from his hair with the flat palm of his hand, and then without warning, he pulled me towards him. Our faces flushed from running.

'I'm sorry,' I said, taking a step back.

He frowned. 'For what?'

'For this.'

'Don't you want to?' He still held my arms, his voice thick with longing.

'Yes ... no ... yes ... I'm confused.'

I looked at his face, still dripping with rain. His kind eyes waiting patiently for my answer, his face flushed now with desire.

'I'm not sure what I want,' I admitted, stumbling further away, just as he caught my arm and pushed me against the tree. His breathing was warm and heavy in my ear. His body hard against mine. His lips touched my neck and then I couldn't distinguish between the rain dropping onto my skin and his kisses, which came now without hesitation.

I thought of my father, far away in the sky.

I thought of Lemàn in another corner of the world.

I thought of Elver and her past: a territory I could not claim.

Then, I thought of nothing, but Leo's hands in my hair, his mouth on my mouth, his bare skin against mine and there was nothing I could do to stop it. My body was responding as though I had no control and we fell to the ground and lay together in the long damp grass. I had no idea if anyone saw us; it was such an early hour or a late one depending on your perspective, that I doubted even one of the city's drunkards would have found us there.

Sometime later a sound made me stir. Along the path in the distance, I could see the park keeper trundling along with his cart, stopping occasionally to pick up leaves and broken twigs. I grabbed my clothes and my fingers fumbled over my buttons, trying to cover my shame. Yet again desire had made me reveal too much. Leo groaned as I pushed him off my boot and yanked it back onto my foot.

'What time is it?'

'Still early,' I said.

'Where are you going?' He sat up, stretching out his arms to pull me back towards him.

'I need to go.' I threw his trousers at him. 'You better get dressed, the park keeper's here.'

Suddenly, the sound of the city bell echoed over the rooftops. The Keeper of the Hours had restored time once again; a warning of what was lost and how in a moment everything can change.

'Wait!' he cried, his face was so full of expectation.

'I can't … I'm sorry … this was – I just have to go.' Then I left, running out of the park towards the sound of the bell, thinking that if I could reach it, then I could somehow stop time, rewind the clock and reverse the night. I needed to restore more than time. I could hear Leo calling me, but his voice came from far away and I didn't look back until the only sound was the one made by my feet on the path. When I had put enough distance between us, I stopped, collapsed against a wall and sobbed. I hadn't realised the city had slowly woken up and when I finally lifted my head, I saw the market traders were arranging their stalls around me and the smell of bread was wafting out of the open door of the bakery. I felt no hunger, just a longing for the night that would never return, and the gnawing guilt of my betrayal. Then I just felt numb.

Once inside, I went straight to the mirror. My face was blotchy, damp and cold and there were dark circles looped under my eyes. Sybel appeared in the corridor and watched me suspiciously.

'That was a long goodbye,' she said.

'Yes, it was a long night,' I muttered, refusing to meet her eye. Leo's smell still clung to me like a gossip bubbling with secrets to share. Even my words tasted of him. Already I knew she knew everything; it was her way.

'It will be hard for a while. Loss is never easy.'

With those words, I collapsed into her arms. Tenderly, she began smoothing down the frizz of my hair, still damp from a night of humid rain.

'Elver came to see you.'

'Elver … was here?' My voice broke like a wave as I said her name.

'She left – you came too late.'

CHAPTER 39

To help Sybel and to distract myself from the night before, I offered to take Zephyros's urn to be engraved. It was early when I opened the door, and I was surprised to find Leo standing there, his hand poised ready to seek entry.

'Morning,' he said, stepping back to allow me out.

'Morning,' I replied, brushing past him, hoping it was Sybel he had come to see.

'I wanted to make sure you were okay after ... last night.'

'It was hard to say goodbye,' I replied, being deliberately obtuse. I tried to relax, but the taste of last night was still on my tongue.

Sensing that I wasn't yet ready to discuss what had happened between us, he quickly changed the subject. 'What's that you're hiding under your arm?'

'I'm not hiding anything,' I said defensively. 'It's Zephyros's urn that's all, I'm taking it to be engraved.'

'To the Island of Memories?

I nodded. Our exchanges had become awkward stutters.

'I've been meaning to go there myself … I haven't been to tend Professor Bottelli's grave for a while. Would you mind if I accompanied you?'

Intimacy had made us strangers and I couldn't meet his eye. I shrugged and gave no sign of protest.

When the boat arrived, it had few passengers. A woman, dressed head to toe in black, was hunched at the far end, tucked away in the corner, her head turned away from the world. We sat down at some distance and I realised she was crying gentle sobs into a huge white handkerchief held to her face. On her lap lay a bunch of flowers, red tulips pursed ready to speak, their roots still attached like gnarled fingers and at her feet, I noticed a bucket filled with gardening tools. It was impossible to know her age, but the large dark liver spots covering her hands suggested she had lived many years under the sun. The watery light slashed its golden swords across the wooden planks of the boat as we sailed north, across the lagoon.

Sitting there on the boat, we said very little. Exchanges about the weather and the water were all we managed before falling silent again. Thankfully the journey was so quick I could have rowed there myself. The boat glided towards a small walled island and came to rest in front of a chapel. Behind the wall, tall green cypress trees loomed like guardians, stretching into the low mist, which hung like a fisherman's net ready to catch the escaping ghosts.

We walked past the cloisters of the old monastery and under a red-brick archway. Inside, the air seemed damper somehow, more sorrowful and sombre. Row after row of gravestones spread into the distance, some sunken and forgotten, their inscriptions long since worn away; so old, there was no longer anyone left to visit them. Others were neat and clean, like well-made beds in the morning.

Crunching down gravel pathways lined with trees and occasional crumbling statues adorned with crosses, we finally came to a towering wall of tiny tombs. Each one like a little drawer of grief opened with the turn of a key, but never really locked. The walls were so high that rolling ladders were kept at each end so people could climb up to reach the highest ones and pay their respects. Hinged to each drawer were pots for flowers and the flagstones below were always wet where mourners had just watered them. Watering cans hung from hooks for everyone to use. Sadly, some pots were just a tangle of weeds or worse, completely empty and broken. An elderly man pushed the ladder past and positioned it a little further along the wall. I watched him climb to the top; he seemed disappointed when he got there, as though he was expecting the ladders to take him all the way to heaven. Slowly, he began to replace the flowers, dropping the old ones into a bag on the ground below. We hurried past and I could hear him quietly talking to a ghost.

In the square it felt more like a park than a cemetery with its well-tended grass and its cluster of trees, but death was clearly marked by little wooden crosses, which rose out of the green. The brightness of the flowers lay like blankets, trying to cover the darkness of loss beneath. We wandered between the graves, careful to stay on the path; a few people were kneeling on the soil, but there was an emptiness here.

'I need to find the engraver,' I said, looking towards a cluster of buildings towards the back of the cemetery, hoping that I might find him in one of them.

'Professor Bottelli's grave is up there,' replied Leo, pointing to the right. 'I'm going to search for a feather to lay on his stone. I think he'd appreciate the sentiment.'

I continued on the path, fascinated by the different inscriptions and trinkets left on the graves. The saddest of all was a pair of worn ballet shoes tied loosely around the top of a headstone, so small they could only have belonged to a child. I noticed the old woman from the boat. She was sitting alone in front of a gravestone in a heap of emotional exhaustion like wilted basil; her shoes damp with soil and the hem of her skirt heavy with mud. As I went past, she stumbled to her feet and her sadness followed me, even though she went in the opposite direction.

I found the engraver huddled in a small stone hut, shaped like a chimney pot. His head dipped low in concentration, quietly working on his latest inscription under the light of a desk lamp. I left the urn and, with it, Sybel's request, which was written in her large looped letters. Clearly not one to be distracted, he nodded without so much as an upwards glance, and I hastened back into the fresh air.

Back on the path, I could hear music and I followed the sound until I saw a woman in a long red coat, belted at the waist. She was sitting on a stool in front of a gravestone and at her feet stood a cello, which she was playing beautifully, oblivious to everything else around her. She held her head at an angle and I could see her eyes were closed, lost in some memory. Her loss was a fragile as a winter leaf left after a storm.

I wondered who was she playing for.

Closing my eyes, I listened to the infinite ache of the music and thought of Lemàn and my father, both now so far away, but who was further? When I opened my eyes, something seemed strange, as though the world had shifted out of place. It wasn't until a few moments later that I realised what it was. There in the distance stood Elver, and next to her was Leo. Quickly, I rose to my feet and marched towards them. I could no longer distinguish between the sound of my feet pounding on the gravel and the sound of my heart raging in my chest. My sudden arrival ended whatever conversation they had been having and they both looked up expectantly. My anger hadn't yet turned itself into words and I just stood there, trying to compose myself. My heart was like a caged lion, which had just caught sight of a lone antelope, and was ready to satisfy its hunger.

'Where have you been? I have been looking for you.' I didn't know if it was the words she spoke or the way in which she spoke them with such nonchalance, that finally made me pull the bolt across the cage door. I was certain that if she had never found me again it wouldn't have bothered her in the least.

'Where have *I* been?' I roared.

She hadn't been expecting my fury and her eyes widened in surprise. Then she looked uneasily at Leo, as though he could explain it all, but he simply returned her look with one of bewilderment. I took a step closer.

'You left me at The Reef. Why?' My words pounced without warning and then collapsed in mid-air.

'I told you—'

'Told me what? You never tell me anything! You just disappear whenever you choose without any thought for me. I had to say goodbye to my father. You'd rather spend time with that doctor!' My anger intensified; it chewed every syllable.

'Doctor Marino? He's just—'

Then my feathers flared and I was unable to contain my anger for a moment longer. I didn't give her the chance to say any more as my torrent of words washed all hers away. 'I'm always waiting for you to return, not knowing if you ever will.' Words flew from my mouth in a jumbled, meaningless babble, each one as harsh as a scouring pad. My mind sped up, then jammed again.

'I told you my time here is temporary – I was always honest with you. How could you think otherwise?'

Against my own violent ramblings, her voice was patient and measured, and it infuriated me even more. Reaching for her necklace, I yanked it violently from my neck. It snapped in half and the beads fired through the air and clattered to the ground, before rolling away into the grass like spent bullets. At first, Leo couldn't comprehend what he was witnessing, but then as understanding slowly flooded his face, I saw his eyes darken. It was my betrayal that had brought us here. I was torn between anger and guilt, with no words left to say to either of them.

Elver seized the opportunity to speak. 'It seems you weren't waiting alone.' Her eyes flicked to Leo, and before she could return them to me, I had struck her cheek with the flat of my hand, so hard it had made my fingers burn.

I don't know which of us was more surprised, but the cry I heard came from my own mouth. At first my words had been great sparks of triumph, like embers leaping from a fire, only to fall and leave scorch marks on the ground. That's when she moved, fast as a comet, hurtling and aflame; her hair was a furnace stoked by the wind and I needed to smother the flames. I chased the light of her hair, but she disappeared round corners before I even knew they were there, and lost me amongst the gravestones. I thought I'd found her hiding under a tree, but when I lifted the branches, I realised it was just a pile of windswept leaves and discarded flowers. Back at the entrance, I saw a boat leaving halfway across the lagoon, but I knew she wouldn't be on it and instead I searched the water for her shadow, her shape, a single strand of her hair, a ripple left behind.

'Elver!' I screamed her name into the wind-licked water. This was not the ending I wanted. But even if she suddenly appeared again, what was left to say?

Then I felt a hand on my shoulder. It was Leo, his face wretched and torn in confusion.

'You should have told me.' He shook his head at how foolish he had been and it was then I understood who the real fool was.

I wanted to confess it all, but the words cowered in my mouth and slowly crept back down my throat in surrender, fermenting in the pit of my stomach preserved in guilt for later – flammable and explosive.

'The next boat will be here soon.' His voice was cold.

When it arrived, we climbed on board. I noticed the woman with the cello standing behind us and the old lady with the gardening tools, and as we sat there on different sides of the boat, united by loss, I understood their pain completely and felt my own, greater still.

384

This time the journey across the water seemed endless and I felt like I was in purgatory all the way. I still hadn't let go of my anger, but it no longer raged inside me, rather it sat grumbling by my side. Deep down I knew the gifts Elver had given Doctor Marino were just gifts of friendship and nothing more. Perhaps in a way, I hoped there had been more, then at least I would understand why her heart refused to want me.

In a last fit of temper, I kicked at a little clump of soil, and caught Leo's foot. He didn't move, his head was turned, staring back over his shoulder at the way we had come. Sitting there right beside me, he had never been so far away. We didn't speak until the boat came to stop at the edge of the city. I waited for him at the bottom of the steps, a crush of passengers between us. I stepped out of the way as the cellist heaved her instrument up the steps and over the bridge. Then the street was empty apart from a couple far in the distance.

'I made a mistake,' I said. 'And I'm sorry.'

Leo didn't respond; instead he looked out silently across the water. To my relief, he didn't ask me what or who the mistake was, and I was no longer sure of the answer I'd give. Then, just like that, he walked away.

I thought about how much bigger the world had become since leaving the whorehouse. I thought about being with Elver in her hourless room, and how I had wanted to snatch those hours back again, but now, watching Leo leave, I wasn't so sure. She had warned me, and I should have known better than to fall for the song of a siren. No one knows anyone else's heart, and sometimes they don't even know their own. My thoughts turned to Leo and to the park and the smell of pine needles and the tangle of brambles caught in my hair, and I heard the sound of his laughter all the way home.

When I returned, I found Sybel in the kitchen; she was shelling peas into a colander on her lap. Pausing, she looked up. 'Did Elver find you? She came here again, so I told her where you were.'

I nodded dismally and sank into a chair. 'What's wrong?' she asked. Sensing trouble, she abandoned the colander and the half-shelled peas on the side and came to sit beside me.

'I don't know what I feel any more.'

'About your father or about Elver?' she asked slowly.

'About Leo,' I replied.

'Ah!' For the first time, the answer I gave wasn't the one she had been expecting.

'I doubt he will forgive me.'

'And that's how you lose everything. Doubt is the end of love,' she said, wrapping me in the comfort of her arms. Sybel's heart was huge and filled with forgiveness, but it wasn't her forgiveness I needed.

CHAPTER 40

Turmoil and guilt bolted the door to the outside world and I stayed hidden in the protective darkness of my room. Lying there in bed, I thought about the truths I should have told Leo and regret lodged itself deep within my throat; I turned over trying to loosen it. Elver had always been truthful with me, but I hadn't listened and my anger was displaced; I knew that now. I needed to unravel for a while. Eventually, though, I would have to face the demons that chased me into the darkness in the first place.

After that, whenever a knock came at the door, I would rush to answer it, ready to face what I had done. Each time I was greeted by a querent in search of answers, or the old man with his bales of straw, or the milk cart rolling past, or some other delivery of wax or wood, but never one of forgiveness.

Finally, Sybel persuaded me that I needed to stretch the knots out of my joints and shake the sadness from my bones. Convinced that a lungful of fresh lagoon air was the cure, she threw the harness over the dogs, looped the end over my wrist and pushed me out the door each morning in search of redemption. Crossing the Bridge of Longing took me near Elver's apartment, but the place looked empty, as though no one had ever lived there.

I spent longer and longer walking the dogs, ambling though a city that had become so familiar yet so strange all at once. My feelings for her had undoubtedly changed, but still I missed her. Places we used to pass together had lost their shine, dulled by her absence, and nothing felt the same. The bakery, the Church of One Hundred Souls, the marketplace, the clock tower, even the warehouses with the sound of heavy hammers, now sounded tinny and far away, like it was all make-believe. Circling the city in the soft patter of rain filled my mind with loss. My thoughts may have begun with Elver, but always, by the time I reached home, it was Leo who occupied the corners of my mind, and there in the middle of everything, burning bright like a votive flame, shone my father.

Desire is the sea. Love is the rock, solid, strong and defiant. Desire rushes to embrace you, and shower you with affection, wrapping itself around you and filling every crevice. But it is a disguise. With every touch desire reduces you, gouging out your surface, eroding your senses until you crumble; slowly sinking out of sight. We reshaped each other as lovers often do and then watched each other wash away, until there was nothing left, but sediment. Desire has no boundaries, but it is love that sets them straight. Desire is ruinous; love is the ruin left behind.

Memory-wrecked.

One sulky evening, Sybel called me into the kitchen, and told me to sit. She poured herself a gin, downed it in one wince-filled gulp, and poured herself another before any words had been spoken. I knew I was about to hear something I wouldn't like.

'I have a confession.'

'Go to church,' I suggested light-heartedly, trying to delay the inevitable.

'Not every confession is a sin.' She got up and paced the room, then sat back down and held her head in her hands. I had never seen her nervous before.

Silently, I waited, unsure of what else to do. Then she reached across the table and took both my hands firmly in hers.

'I have seen Elver,' she said solemnly.

That got my attention. 'What? When?'

'She needed my help.'

'Help with what?' I asked. Now it was my turn to be nervous.

Sybel sighed, pausing to choose her words carefully. 'With her return,' she said eventually.

I tried to whip my hands away from hers, but she sensed my movement before I had time to make it, and quickly tightened her grip around my wrist.

'Her mind was fixed. I'm sorry; there was no persuading her otherwise.'

'When will she leave?' was all I could ask.

'A few nights from now, when the moon is at its roundest. There will be time for you to say goodbye.' She hesitated. 'If you want there to be.'

I got to my feet and left without saying another word. Later, lying on my bed, I could hear the sound of her breathing in the corridor outside, like the low, heavy pant of a running bear. She didn't knock or try to come in; instead I heard her utter the words, 'She was always leaving, no matter what you did', into the keyhole, but they weren't enough to unlock the door.

In the middle of the night, I crept into the kitchen in search of a remedy to help me sleep. The shelves were better stocked than any apothecary I had seen. Each one was filled with pots of herbs and plants, and I had watched Sybel brew them up enough times to know what to do. I began lifting them up one by one, squinting to read their labels: barrel fever, black dog, dropsy, grippe, quincy, and winter fever. They had been arranged in alphabetical order, but the words were unfamiliar to me and I stumbled over their meaning. Standing on the tips of my toes, I moved my hand deeper, shifting between the pots to find what was hidden at the back. It was there that I felt my fingers touch the smooth glass of a jar. As I pulled it towards me, I recognised it at once.

'What are you hoping to find up there?' came the sound of Sybel's voice.

Guiltily, I withdrew my hand as she entered the room, but as always, she knew what I was doing.

'It's yours if you want it,' she said, but there was a hint of warning in her voice and my hand wavered.

'Why didn't you open it?' I asked.

She shook her head firmly. 'No. For there to be heart-break, first there must be love. It's not just the sadness it takes away; it's everything else that comes before.'

I returned to my room, leaving the jar untouched upon the shelf. Later, as I fell asleep, my mind drifted back to the jar buried deep in the bottom of Lemàn's drawer, and now I understood why it had never been opened. What is a world without memory? It is far worse for a heart to have never felt love, than it is for a heart to be broken. A broken thing is still beautiful.

Sybel and I didn't speak much during those days of the growing moon, not because I blamed her for anything – I didn't. I needed time for my bitterness to fly, then fall and finally float away, and I knew that eventually it would. I wanted to be ready when it was time to say goodbye.

It was almost dark when I reached the water and for a moment, I thought I had come too late. The moon was already high in the sky and the waves, like quick black cats lapped up the milky spill of its light. The world was

so full of murmurs and the quiet shushing of the sea. I
didn't notice her at first, swimming towards me, then I
felt her gaze and turned my head in her direction. Neither
one of us spoke, not for what seemed like a long time.
She disappeared under the water and I felt my shoulders
stiffen in a moment of panic. I didn't want her to leave
yet, there were words left to say. Then to my relief, she
reappeared again, much closer this time, and I could see
her face, pale as a church candle.

'I'm glad you came. I wasn't sure you would,' she said.

'I wanted to say goodbye,' I replied.

She swam right up the lagoon wall where I was standing
and pulled herself a little way out of the water. I could
see her hips were shining; the flesh I remembered was
now a pattern of thick iridescent scales glinting at me in
the moonlight. I crouched down, kneeling on the damp
stone, reaching out my hand to touch them.

'How?' I asked.

She smiled. 'The ancient Art of Meta.'

Making sure that my eyes weren't deceiving me, I
continued to brush my hand along the beginnings of her
tail; smoother than I thought they would be, perhaps
because of the coarseness of the skin that was there before.

'Sybel used ancient roots of unspoken herbs to transform
earth to water. The last few days I watched my legs fuse
together and my skin oil itself back into scales. Tonight,
all I had to do was stir in the salt and the moonlight.'

It was like a fairy tale. Beautiful and wicked all at once.

'I'm sorry I wasn't there when you said goodbye to your father,' she said sadly, 'but it is better that the person who helped you to say goodbye is still there afterwards to help you remember it.'

I nodded, lowering my eyes to conceal the emotion I felt, but I could never pull them away from her for long and I lifted them to meet her gaze again.

'I always told you the truth ... from the beginning you knew who I was,' she said.

'Yes, you did,' I conceded. 'I should have listened. I should have tried to understand you more,' I said.

'As I understood you,' she replied wisely.

'Yes, like that.' I paused.

She reached her arms out of the water and slowly began to unbutton my coat. 'It doesn't suit you,' she said, with a smile. I shrugged it from my shoulders and felt it slip down my arms until it fell silently behind me onto the grass.

'You're always hiding ... how exhausting it must be for you.'

Her eyes marvelled at my feathers one last time and I marvelled right back at her luminous scales, savouring every moment of the magic, and locking it in the drawer of memory.

'Know that you are beautiful,' she said, silently lowering herself back into the water.

It was the last thing she said, before silently floating away into the scar of moonlight. The enchantment had ended. Once, I thought I saw her turn back, but whether it was in doubt or just to admire the twinkling lights that had brought her here in the first place, I would never know. When I was finally ready to leave, I retrieved my coat from where it had fallen and, instead of fastening it back around my feathers, I threw it as far into the lagoon as I could, until it too was lost in the darkness, and washed far out to sea.

'Thank you,' I whispered.

I realised then that the woman I had been told to fear didn't live deep in the forest all alone, or at the bottom of the sea with her slick stone heart. The woman I had feared all this time was within me, and I had carried her everywhere, so heavy and dark. Now I found the courage to turn and face her. Quietly stepping forwards, I took her in my arms and that long-held chasing fear finally became the gift of self-acceptance.

The canals that night ran the colour of turquoise wishes. Everyone longed for freedom.

CHAPTER 41

There was a certain wisdom in saying goodbye. It helped me to understand so much more of myself and my place in the world. Losing Elver meant I had found myself, and was finally able to cast off the weight of my shadows and move unhindered through the city. Sybel had laughed and clapped her hands together when she first saw me leaving the house without the weight of one of her coats.

'Have you not noticed the people all around you?' she encouraged. 'The ravenous gypsy wheeling her barrow of filth; the nocturnal inhabitants of Vesper Square; the rat-catcher whose face has been half-eaten by disease; the Sky-Worshippers above us and the mermaids below; the Keeper of the Hours and the people whose hearts are so broken that they have to carry mist home in jars. Then, of course, there is me: a monster with a gift and a heart so full of love, but no one to give it to only a pack of flea-bitten dogs, and you.'

She lovingly squeezed my shoulder, and I realised just how much I meant to her. I should have known it from the moment she trusted me to look after her dogs. When you love something so much, giving it to someone else means everything. I smiled at the thought, knowing that I had so much to thank her for, most of all for not taking away my feathers. Now I loved how the sunlight warmed them, changing them from orange to gold; the way the rain washed them clean with scents from far away. She had helped to unwrap my gift and I had finally accepted what lay within.

'You see, here you are not so very different at all.'

It was this warmth that compelled me to write a letter to Lemàn and in it I revealed everything.

I told her about the wonder of the City of Murmurs; about Sybel and the dogs; about loving and losing and how my heart had anchored me here. I revealed that I no longer hid my feathers beneath my clothes, and how I was proud to have them. I laughed, imagining her hand flying to her mouth to hide the gasp of disbelief and then her delight as her eyes skipped over those words. What a remarkable letter! She would realise how much her little girl in the cellar had changed, and how she had stretched her wings. Lastly, I told her the most important thing of all – that I loved her.

I let my pen hover for the briefest of moments, before swiftly folding the paper and sealing it in an envelope. Tucked within it was a much smaller envelope addressed to Sorren. I still didn't understand everything of her story, but I understood enough to know there was nothing to forgive. My message to her was brief, but every word was infused with warmth and gratitude.

Leaving the house, I rushed down to where the boats waited for the stir of wind to release them. At the edge of the water something made me stop. It may have been the cry of a seabird, or the stab of my conscience, but whatever it was, it served as a reminder that my letter couldn't be sent – not yet anyway.

Hastening back to the house, I ripped open the envelope, unfolded the paper, and in a flurry of words, I continued writing the rest of the story. Lemàn longed for the truth and it was time to share it all with her. Later that day, I stood watching a boat depart until it was lost in the distance, knowing that it wouldn't be long before her eyes fell upon my words, and absorbed their meaning. It wouldn't bring my father back, but I hoped it would bring some sort of peace, especially after such a long time of wondering. If nothing else, at least I could give her the gift of his name; Eddero.

In amongst everything, there was still one person I wanted to see and so, instead of going home, I walked along further the water and waited for the lagoon boat. When it arrived, I slid along the wooden seat to the end where I could feel the gentle breeze in my feathers. I watched the sunlight glittering along the surface of the water and I sat and watched it dance. Along the salt line I could see a cluster of crushed shells, too fragile to bear the weight of the water.

Pushing the door open, he didn't see me at first and I took the opportunity to just stand and watch him. He was always so thought-filled and I could see his face was deep in concentration. His face was more unshaven than I had seen it before and there were dark shadows under his eyes. In his hand he held a pencil and I could hear the long loops of his ideas being etched on to the paper. He rubbed at the back of his neck, suggesting too many hours spent hunched over his work. Then he stretched back in his chair, taking only a moment to rest before continuing work. Suddenly, he looked up and saw me.

'Hello,' I mumbled, finally stumbling into the room.

He didn't respond and his face was impassive. I was so used to being able to read it that I was thrown off balance. Tentatively, I perched on the edge of on a chair without invitation, and I saw him raise his eyebrow in a gesture of disapproval. I did not have his permission to touch anything in this room and I rose to my feet at once, and retreated behind it as though it was my protectress. Still he didn't utter a single word. My eyes suddenly took in the room; it was littered with boxes, and half-packed crates scattered the floor; rolled-up parchment and stacks of knotted packages were propped high against the wall; a suitcase stood near the door. It was then that I noticed all of the feathers were gone.

'Are you leaving?' I asked, trying to make sense of what I was seeing.

When I turned my attention back to him, he was no longer watching me; he had returned once more to his writing – it was as though I was no longer there.

'Are you leaving?' I repeated hastily, taking a step forward.

The writing ceased, and I heard the quiet patter of his pencil as he dropped it onto the paper. Rising to his feet, he turned to face me and I wilted under the intensity of his stare.

'Why?' he asked.

'I—'

He shook his head, and pushed his chair back from the desk. Calmly moving across the room, he stopped to open the cabinet that was once so full of stuffed birds. I could see now that it was almost empty. My question seemed to have reminded him that there were still things left to pack. With his familiar tenderness, he lifted one of the few remaining birds from its stand and took it over to the table where he began wrapping it in brown paper. Everything was done with such careful precision.

'Are you here to say goodbye?' His tone was flat; he gave nothing away.

'Goodbye … . what? No!' I answered in a strangled little voice. I had come to say sorry, not goodbye. A terrible sickening feeling rose from my stomach, and I swallowed it back. I was not forgiven.

Leo sighed heavily. 'I will return to the north at the end of the month. From there I might join an expedition to the mountains in search of new discoveries.'

Might. The word held doubt, but his tone had the bitter chill of autumn: crisp and brittle and changing. 'There is no reason to stay.' His sentence felt more like a question, and I pounced on the hope that quivered there.

'Yes, there is,' I blurted.

Leo's head swivelled, and his eyes fixed on mine, waiting for something more.

'You're my—' I faltered. What was he? More than someone who shared my love of birds; someone who had devoted hours of his time patiently helping me discover who I really was; someone who was with me every step of the way as I searched for the father I never knew. He not only saw my difference, but he understood it better than anyone else could. He knew I was something other, but to him it didn't matter; he wanted me anyway. My heart was a puzzle and he was its solution. I had not prepared the words I wanted to say and I needed to find them fast. My heart stopped, then I took a deep breath.

'The mistake I made – it wasn't you.' My voice broke on the final word because it was that word that meant everything.

Nothing happened, and then all at once it did. He crossed the room and pulled me into his arms and the smell and familiarity of him was so overwhelming that I didn't think I would ever let go. I felt his breath on my neck and my feathers rose to meet it.

'I'm sorry,' I whispered. 'I'm so very sorry I didn't tell you.' He silenced me with his kiss, letting it fall on my lips like a drop of warm rain.

I knew then that I had come here for so much more than forgiveness.

CHAPTER 42

That summer, Leo invited me to my first opera. Even though Sybel had known how our story ended, she hadn't expected it to fill her with such happiness. She insisted that I wore her dress the colour of forget-me-nots; the one that had hung for so long unworn, from a hook behind the door. Something so beautiful shouldn't be shut up in a room, she insisted, as she helped to pull it over my head. I wasn't sure if she was talking about the dress or about me. Then taking the brush that Marianne had given to me, she swept it through my curls in long gentle strokes. Afterwards, I tried pinning up my hair using a dozen different clips, but it quickly escaped and I could feel it tickling against the back of my neck. With my glossy fiery feathers all aflutter, I opened the door and Leo stared back at me as though I was made of magic.

Later, walking through the twilight streets, the passion of the music still lingering, I suddenly felt compelled to stop at the entrance to the Street of Purring Cats.

'What is it?' asked Leo, wondering why I wasn't going any further.

Out of nowhere, a bird suddenly appeared, landing on my shoulder, as if it had been conjured there by a magician. Leo laughed in amazement, and it vanished into the sky. I bent down to pick up a feather it had left behind. Twirling it between my fingers, I tried to understand its message. It was just an ordinary street; like the countless others I had seen in this city.

'This way,' I said, wondering what I would find there.

Small shops huddled on either side of a narrow, crooked street. Even at this time, the warm smell of bread drifted from the first doorway. Opposite, the sound of a cobbler tapping his hammer rang out. We passed a toyshop, and I paused to admire its colourful puppets hanging in the window and the handmade wooden trains on the shelf beneath. I was reminded of home, and of the puppet I had destroyed in my childish temper. How young and silly I had been all those years ago.

'Look at those sweets!' exclaimed Leo. I turned to see the window of a real confectioner's lined with pyramids of sherbet and liquorice sticks and lollipops bigger than stirring spoons. Marzipan cubes and dusted slabs of jelly were enough to dazzle the eye and make the teeth chatter. A giggling congregation spilled through the door clutching their paper bags in glee. A little girl with wide worshipping eyes tugged on her mother's sleeve begging to be taken in to the sugar shrine. Her mother shook her head and hurried them away, the girl could do nothing but scowl in disappointment. We followed the curve of the street and I could see the low dwellings on the right suddenly fall away. There was one left, standing slightly apart from all the others. My heart stopped, and I knew at once this was what I was meant to find. It was small with a white front and a red-peaked roof from where a small square window gazed out across the sea to the sky. It was like the doll's house I never got to play with. The bird that had led us here was now watching us from the tiles; it looked like a tiny weathervane. Then it hopped into the rain gutter, and away.

I gasped, touching its walls. Shielding my eyes against the glass, I tried to peer through the grime to see what lay within. It was dark inside and empty as a shell.

'It's to rent,' said Leo, reading a sign on the door.

I stepped back to read the words and, although I didn't yet know why, I sensed that it was for me to find. Still twirling the feather between my fingertips, a curious idea suddenly flew into my mind, as bright and entertaining as a juggling ball.

'Do you want to rent a shop?' he asked in bewilderment. 'What on earth would you put in it?'

I smiled knowingly. 'Why, feathers of course!' I replied.

It happened so quickly. As soon as I told Sybel my plan, she announced that she knew not only the shop, but its owner, a gambling man with too many debts to pay. The following day, she had arranged a meeting where the negotiation was brief, and in my favour. By the end of the week, I was back outside the shop and this time I clutched the keys in my hand.

Upon opening the door, a conspiracy of dust leapt up from the floor and scurried its secrets into the furthest corners. The smell of sawdust made my nose twitch. Inside, it was just as I had imagined it would be. Large enough for a display counter at the front and the back was the perfect size for a workspace, where I could stitch and mend and gloss my feathers to my heart's content. Up a rickety ladder to the rafters, I found there was room enough for a bed, and the window was wide enough to welcome the morning sun. Its ledge would be a perfect place for the starlings to rest in the gathering dusk. Once all the windows were polished and the floor had been swept clean of dust, I could see how light-filled it would become. It reminded me of how I used to be: fearful and hidden and so full of secrecy.

'Wake up little shop,' I murmured, gently tapping the bell above the door and listening to the tinkle of its laugh float high into the air.

I filled the place with feathers from the university. Leo hadn't yet unpacked them from their crates and I arranged for them to be brought across the lagoon in a boat. After they arrived, I stored them carefully in glass cabinets and plucked them as I needed to. I washed each feather in hot soapy water, and pinned them up like bunting until they were dry. It was enough to begin with.

The plumassier had taught me her skills in the whorehouse. She had shown me about the art of willowing and how to lengthen the flues to create long and sweeping feathers, curled fancifully under the steam of a boiling pot. I remembered it well. There were enough feathers to last me for months and whenever one of my own moulted, I would save it alongside the rest. When the time came, I would seek out a boat sailing further east or back west, and order a shipment of the finest feathers to be brought back to me in an array of flamboyant colours and sizes. But there was one feather I would never touch. It lay under a glass lid, on a velvet green cushion, like a sunset sky over a little hill. Maybe one day I would send it back to Lemàn, but I wasn't sure what good it would do to stir her settled heart once more. For now, at least, I would keep it. It was my beginning and there was little bright or special left in the world with it gone.

Business was slow at first and I began to wonder if I had made a terrible mistake. Then I remembered the lady on the boat with her feather-filled hat worn with such pride, and how heartbroken and haunted she had become after it was lost in the storm. So, I held my nerve.

Sybel's tongue held attentive ears and soon ladies started to come through the door asking for a simple hat trimming, or a boa to be worn for a special dinner. As my skills improved and word spread further, I was asked to fashion corsets and stitch feathers to a selection of fine materials. I sculptured feather bouquets to be displayed at important events and even children brought their dolls' hats for me to decorate with cockades of tiny feathers. I was asked to create carnival masks and costumes to seduce a lover. Giggling girls would bound in and ask me to quickly curl a limp feather on their hat while they waited, before scampering off to be the envy of their friends or the object of a gentleman's affection. It kept me busy and for a while, at least, I was content.

One afternoon, I was returning to the shop with packages of new fabric and buttons for a cloak I had been commissioned to make. Upon reaching the door, I felt eyes skitter over me, like sun-drenched lizards, and I turned to see two women huddled together in gossip. They stared at me and I could see the cruelty in their smiles. I left the packages on the doorstep and approached them so unexpectedly that they stumbled back into the gutter. I looked from one to the other, waiting and watching as a mixture of alarm and guilt twisted their faces into masks of ugliness.

'Beautiful, aren't they?' I exclaimed.

They shuffled in shame and glanced nervously at each other. After that they lowered their heads to the ground, no longer knowing where to look.

'Would you like to touch them?' I teased, relishing the effect I was having.

Laughing I stepped back, and with mumbled apologies they scuttled away like rats; there was nothing to feast on here. Three girls had been watching the spectacle unfold with great fascination, and the tallest one stepped forward.

'Excuse me, could we have a go?'

'Have a go at what?' I asked frowning.

'Of your feathers,' she replied. The other two girls exploded into nervous giggles and she jabbed them hard with her elbow. 'She won't let us touch them if you keep laughing,' I heard her hiss.

Smiling, I knelt down on the ground and beckoned them over. They nudged each other, trying to decide who would go first.

'Are they soft?' one asked.

'Why don't you find out for yourself,' I encouraged, and so they did, right there in the middle of the street. Their eyes were wide with enchantment as they swept their hands through my feathers and I saw their little mouths fall open in gasps of delight.

'They are softer than rabbit fur!' announced one, in astonishment.

Their faces beamed. Then the smallest one rested her head on the top of my arm, closed her eyes and announced it was the fluffiest pillow she had ever felt. In that moment I was exactly where I needed to be. Smiling, I stood up to signal the end of the merriment, and the girls skipped away, happy at their discovery. Quickly I scooped up my packages and went inside. I was too distracted to notice the two familiar figures who had just appeared in the street.

In the back room I began to sort through the spools of thread and tangle of ribbons, deciding which feathers I would need. I suspected the woman who had requested the cloak was having an affair, and so I had selected only owl feathers. These were known for their secrecy: soft and barbed, to muffle the sound of movement. At night the city could drop cold and she needed to be kept warm and hushed as she flew through the streets in pursuit of what she most desired. As owl feathers were so short, I would have to knot the flues together to create long sweeping feathers. As I began to count out how many I would need, I heard the jingle of the bell, and knew someone had entered the shop.

'I won't be a moment,' I called, but before the last word had even left my mouth, I felt my feathers lift and quiver.

There was something familiar in the air, and for a moment, I tried desperately to remember what it was; something from so far away. Then it smoothed into place, like the last feather settling on a wing. The scent of a rainy day and lemons soaked in sunshine gave them away, and although I couldn't see into the front of the shop, I knew what would be waiting for me when I got there. I closed my eyes and the enormous rush of memory toppled me to the floor.

Professor Elms and Lemàn found me collapsed on top of a pile of cloth and crumpled feathers. Kneeling down, I felt their arms wrap around me, and, without saying a single word, we held onto one another for such a long time. Then I told them everything.

CHAPTER 43

From the beginning, Lemàn had told me they would not be staying for long. Their boat was leaving in a few days and they would be on it. It didn't matter when she left; days, weeks, months or even years from now … it would never be enough.

'We are leaving all the clocks behind,' she announced triumphantly, as though that could somehow stop time. When I asked her what they would do once they got there, she laughed and told me they would learn to make maps for lost lovers.

We spent our hours sitting by the water, filling in the long absence with touch and words and laughter. It was there that her questions finally found their long-awaited answers, and there was a lightness to her after that.

Professor Elms had been helping Leo bring crates of feathers from the tepidarium. I had them delivered every few months, brought over on merchant boats from distant Scatterings, some drifting so far away that they were at the very bottom of the world. I had learned that sometimes you had to search far and wide for something so special. Reading about them in books wasn't the same as seeing them with my own eyes, and opening each crate was always a delight. The feathers shone with colours I didn't even know existed; dipped in sunsets, brushed with honey and polished with the blue splendour of a summer's day. They were such a thing of beauty, I thought as I placed them into my tissue-lined drawers. Everyone wanted to be seen with them resplendent upon their backs, fanciful in their hats or wrapped around their necks to keep out the cold, begging that I made them as pretty as a bird.

This is how I liked us, Lemàn and me, sitting side by side, staring across the lagoon. I rested my head against her arm, and for a while I became a child again. Looking at the sky, I wondered if it was really meant for me, ever hopeful of what it might bring. My heart hadn't been broken – only dented – and not enough to let the water in, but always after a while, my eyes would fall to the sea. Lemàn recognised the sadness left behind, she knew it in only the way a mother could, and squeezed my hand in comfort.

'We both wanted the impossible,' she said, sadly smiling. 'The elemental love of air and water and the suffering it can bring.'

'She taught me so much,' I said wistfully. 'I imagine I
see her sometimes, out there in the water.'

'And Leo?'

His name made me smile. 'Just because I think about
her, doesn't mean I want him less.' I lifted my head from
her arm. 'You still think about Eddero, don't you? Even
though you have the professor now.'

Her face softened and I was reminded of the times we
would sit on the bench overlooking the sea. Always, her
mind travelled to a place called memory, and all those
years ago I didn't know the way. She was unreachable and
I was left behind. Now, though, it was different; I knew
longing and loss, and this time I could follow her there.

After a while she spoke again. 'All this time I have been
trying to catch a sunset and keep it in a jar. I should just
have enjoyed the moment and then let it go.'

'Like a bird in the sky.'

'Yes, just like that. No one should ever try to catch
something so beautiful.'

Keeping magic in the world was too difficult, and I knew
that neither my father nor Elver would ever come back.

'Do you remember when you used to sneak out of the
house each morning before the dew had dried on the
grass?'

'You knew about that?' I exclaimed in disbelief.

'Ha! Of course I knew … we all knew!' I could hear the
amusement in her voice. 'Those bolts on the door were
so rusty they rattled louder than the barrels that rolled in.'

'But if you knew … why didn't you stop me?' I asked.

She was thoughtful before she spoke again. 'Because I should have been the one opening the door for you.' She paused to watch Leo and Professor Elms wheel the crates up the street towards us. In front of them was Sybel; she had the strength of a bear and carried a crate effortlessly in her arms. 'Besides,' added Lemàn, 'there was always someone keeping you safe.'

'Do you love Professor Elms?' I asked. Her face had warmed at the sight of his approach.

She giggled and rolled her eyes, and I saw for the first time what she would have been like as a young girl. Her beauty then was so much clearer than the sky.

'He brings me much happiness.' She smiled at the thought of him. 'But love after loss is always that little bit more fragile – like a bird with a broken wing trying to fly again. There should be a word for that kind of love.'

'You both deserve to be happy,' I replied, realising that her smile seemed less crooked than before.

'We all do.'

She was a reminder of all I had left behind and I suddenly remembered so much I had almost forgotten. 'How is Sorren?'

Her answer came quickly. 'She left … not long after you did.'

'Left?' I was stunned, seized by an emotion I couldn't name. 'But where would she go?'

'In search of what she once gave away.'

'I—' but my question slipped away, like snow melting off a rooftop. Some things were a secret then and were still a secret now. A locket closed on a memory. It made me sad to think she would never read my letter, and that she would never know how much she meant to me.

'You have always been such an inquisitive soul, so curious about everything. So much about you has changed, but not that.'

'Then what?'

'You seem less afraid. Being here has opened you up and made you stronger.'

'Gutted me like a fish, you mean!'

'What is it with you and fish?' she exclaimed affectionately. 'All those months waiting for you to be born and I couldn't stomach anything else: bread, cheese, milk – none of it!'

I rested my head back against her arm and reminded her of the stories she used to tell me as a child. 'Tell me one more,' I said, closing my eyes.

'You always did believe in fairy tales,' she said laughing, then she began. After she had finished, she grew quiet and we sat listening to the murmurs of the city. 'Sometimes the end isn't where you think it is, and you have to travel further to discover the rest.'

Until that moment, I thought I was where I belonged, but her question opened a door I didn't even know was there and through it I heard Elver's voice; *You will find your way, I am sure of that. It is within you ... all you have to do is follow your instincts.*

Inside, I felt the tiny flutter of an idea slowly begin to spread its wings. Sybel had spoken of unity in the end, but perhaps there was something so far-reaching that even she hadn't been able to see it. But if Sybel couldn't sense it, then how could Lemàn?

'Perhaps you have the instincts of a bird,' I teased, feeling unsettled by her words.

'No, my little firecracker.' She laughed, batting away my words with her hand. 'I have the instincts of a mother.' Then she stroked her fingers through the long flames of my hair, and sighed. 'It is just as beautiful as I imagined it would be.'

This goodbye was no easier than the last one, and as I stood watching them leave with the sun, the scent of lemons lingered still and stung my heart.

In the silence of Leo sleeping, I sat in the window and waited for morning to come. A little before dawn, I lifted the latch and pushed it ajar. The familiar murmurs of the water came first, followed by the sleepy nocturnes of the slowly waking birds: an irresistible sorcery. The sounds filled the rafters and Leo began to stir. I left the window and sat beside him on the bed, stroking his hair until he finally opened his eyes. He smiled at finding me there.

'Do you remember the promise I made to you – the promise to always be truthful?' I asked into the soft dark.

So close, I could hear the steady tick-tock of his heart – my timepiece – against which I would measure all else.

He mumbled, not quite awake enough to make sense of what I was saying.

'There is somewhere I must go now, but one day I will come back to you.'

Wiping his face, still creased from sleep, he lifted himself up, hinged on both elbows. There was a question on his lips, but before he could ask it, I silenced him with a kiss and the promise of my return. My wings might spread out their tips to touch two different worlds, but my heart stayed in the middle.

Then I told him the ending to my story – the final chapter – my happily ever after.

EPILOGUE

Hours pass uncounted until the mist finally appears in the distance, as though summoned by my very longing for it. Had I not been sitting in my window, perhaps I would not even have noticed it, for it was nothing more than a little wisp of a promise kept. My boat is ready.

The sea is unbroken and still. I sail without a map, or coordinates to guide me, and I do not need the stars at night to help me navigate my way, but I am not lost. Elver was right: the way is within me; it has always been there, and now I am listening.

Reaching inside my pocket, my fingers clasp around the smooth shape of the watch Professor Elms had given to me. Like a heavy coin, I pull it out and turn it over in my hand. It catches in the light, and for the first time I notice the tiny swirl of letters engraved around the bottom: *Tempus fugit*. I smile at the simple truth. Then lifting my arm high in an arch behind my head, I throw the watch as far as I can into the twilight distance. It falls without a sound and I watch it sink into the starfish sea. I make my wish.

As before, the mist comes first, dampening my skin and leaving behind a silver sheen. Wands of warm pink light trapeze through the sky, casting their spell and I stand to greet them. The sun is reluctant to tuck itself in, and the light still lingers. Indefinite shapes begin to emerge: a green smudge of a forest and a flash and crash of a water-fall. The images I had seen wrapped within my father's wings are now so close, they are no longer just imagined. The mist slowly parts and dissolves and I can see the tremble of mountains and the stars that seem to hang, glittering from every tree. The Island of Mist exhales its long-held breath: damp and warm and alive with anticipation. I am expected and I am welcomed and there is such sweetness to it all.

Above me a swoop of birds appears, making a sparkling pattern in the sky. Like twirling pinwheels, they dip and dive and I feel the whoosh of their wings all around me. Suddenly, a rush of air shakes me loose and I am being lifted higher and higher, until there is nothing left beneath my feet, but mist. My feathers respond, unfurling them-selves one by one and stretching out further than I ever thought possible. I had never seen them so long and my laughter surprises the air. The birds split and scatter in a spray of musical light, and afterwards they fall and settle in the trees. I realise then that it is not stars amongst the leaves, but birds – hundreds of them – all bright and shining and filled with song. I had seen beauty in the sky before, but never until this moment had I been a part of it.

The world no longer stands. It flies – watchful, whisperful, wonderful – just like on the night I was born. With unhurried delight we mingle and soar, as the boat gently drifts further into the ever-widening sea. Everything else falls away – I am weightless, and boundless, and free. My feathers are aflame in the gleaming light of the slowly setting sun. The real enchantment has at last begun.

ACKNOWLEDGEMENTS

My thanks go to Ariella Feiner, who first saw a sparkle in the darkness and gave me a map to find it. You made this book so much better and I am fortunate that it fluttered onto your desk. Thank you also to Molly Jamieson for her support along the way.

To Katie Seaman, whose insight, expertise and wisdom made the sparkle shine even brighter. Thank you to you and the whole team at Ebury for giving me my happily ever after. Many thanks also to everyone at Cornerstone for such a warm welcome.

To my parents, who always knew I was a writer.

Gratitude to Jeannette, mentor and friend; to Dawn for always being there; to Becky with whom I shared the most magical childhood; to Louise and John for accompanying me on many of my little whims; to Mr G who helped to quieten the doubts; and to my PRU crew for filling the days with laughter – I wish I had found you earlier.

To the friends I grew up with who I see too little, but who mean so much.

To Poppy and Isobel, my constant companions, who are beside me as I write and as I dream.

As Leonard Cohen once wrote: 'Greece is a good place to look at the moon,' and I am lucky enough to spend my summers there with my head tilted towards the sun-warmed sky and my toes dipped into the deep blue sea. It is therefore thanks to my Greek family who welcome me back each time with open arms.

And finally, to Agapios, whose strength, kindness and patience make everything better.